BURIED SECRETS

ELIZABETH MEYETTE

BORIS PUBLISHING

PUBLISHED BY: Boris Publishing
BURIED SECRETS
Copyright © 2016 by Elizabeth Meyette
ISBN 10: 0-9960965-2-3
ISBN 13: 978-0-9960965-2-2
eISBN 10: 0-9960965-1-5
eISBN 13: 978-0-9960965-1-5

Cover Design by Meyette Photography
Interior format ©

Amazon 11.99

4-01-81

To Kristy, Matt, and Kate who bring joy to my life

CHAPTER ONE

Labor Day, Monday, September 2, 1968

Jesse Graham squinted through the windshield wipers at the rain-swept road ahead of her. In her twenty-eight years, she had never liked being out in a thunderstorm, and this one was a doozy.

"NASA plans to put a man on the moon next year, but nobody can invent windshield wipers that work in a downpour," she grumbled.

She hadn't meant to work until after sunset, but she'd obsessed with putting up creative bulletin boards and adding final touches to the course guides to be ready for the first day of school tomorrow. Though she had taught in Rochester for five years, no doubt her obsession stemmed from the fact that she was the newest faculty member at St. Bartholomew Academy for Girls.

Adjusting to the late-summer darkness was hard enough, but add this thunderstorm and visibility was nil. At least upstate New York didn't suffer through tornadoes or hurricanes. She gripped the wheel, concentrating on avoiding the deep ditch carved out along the shoulder.

A flash of lightning revealed a shape sprawled in the middle of the road ahead. She leaned forward, as if that would help her see if it was a deer someone hit and left to die. Another bolt of lightning illuminated the shape again, revealing blonde hair spread out on the wet pavement. In a moment of clarity—at least she could always count on that oddity in the midst of panic—she knew it was not a deer. Downshifting, she slammed on the brakes, her 1965 Volkswagen Beetle skidding sideways. She broke out in prickles of sweat as her car thudded against the form and halted.

"Oh my God! Oh my God! Oh my God!" she cried out.

She was pinned to her seat. Her legs shook, then her whole body. She fumbled for the door handle, unable to find it at first. Finally, she grasped it, threw open the door, and scrambled out onto the road. The sky strobed as a lightning bolt slammed into a nearby tree. Her nose stung with the acrid smell of sulfur. Her knees buckled, but she recovered, stumbling toward the immobile form. Slowing her pace, she neared the cloth-draped figure, afraid it might leap up and attack her. Afraid it might not move at all.

Have I just killed someone?

Trembling, she dropped to her knees beside the form. Bile rose in her throat at the sight of long, blonde hair streaming out from beneath the gray wool blanket that covered the shape. Pulling the blanket back, she gasped. A blonde wig was perched atop a dummy fashioned from burlap stuffed with hay. *What the...?* Slowly, she realized what she was looking at. She breathed with relief. But her relief was short-lived.

Son of a bitch. This prank could have sent someone flipping end over end. Storms weren't known to improve traction.

"Who the hell would pull a rotten trick like this?"

She looked around—was the perpetrator standing just off in the trees beside the road? Rain spattered against her hair. As she brushed the clinging ringlets from her eyes, she pulled up the hood of her nylon poncho. Heart pounding, she leaned back on her heels, inhaling deeply to still her trembling. Hot breath escaped through her flared nostrils. Grabbing the dummy, she wrapped the blanket around it and lugged it to the car.

"Marty needs to see this," she muttered. When Officer Marty D'Amato recently helped her solve the mystery surrounding Helen Cavanaugh's death, he risked his career so she could gain access to decades-old records for her investigation. They had become good friends; he would agree that whoever was involved in the prank needed to be held accountable for its potential danger.

"This is a cruel trick played by somebody with a warped sense of humor. There must be something illegal he can arrest the jerk for." She yanked the driver's seat forward, wrestling the form into the back seat of her car. Uncooperative legs splayed out. She stuffed them in and slammed the seat back in place. As she straightened to climb in behind the wheel, the hair on the back of her neck stood on end.

Someone was watching her.

Peering through the rain at the side of the road, she saw a faint glow through the leaves. Shimmering like a will-o'-the-wisp, it floated along before disappearing. She slapped the hood of the Beetle—not with the immediate anger she'd just felt upon discovering the road hazard, but with an ancient, pent-up rage, urgent and demanding. And sorrow. Overwhelmed with sorrow, she crumpled forward, resting her forehead on the roof of the car. She was weak with the intensity of these emotions—where were these feelings coming from? The turmoil within dissipated.

"What the hell?" Regaining her composure, she rubbed her arms trying to stem the chill bumps as she saw the light move through the trees again. She sensed a pull—an irresistible, illogical yearning to follow the light that was at once frightening and seductive. Should she follow?

The rain slackened. The thunder subsided. Off in the trees, she heard a drumbeat, slow and mournful.

"No," she whispered to the trees. "No. Not again."

She shook herself to break the spell and got in the car. "It was nothing," she said to her reflection in the rearview mirror, brushing unruly auburn curls from her eyes. "Nothing."

She froze at the mirror's reflection of the road. A dark shape moved along the shoulder some yards behind her. A flash of lightning illuminated a sleek black car that made a U-turn and sped away in the opposite direction. If the driver had not finally turned on its lights, she would have thought she'd imagined the car.

He was there the whole time.

Someone had watched as she discovered and moved the dummy. After starting the engine, she patted the dashboard of her VW bug. "Let's get out of here, Bert."

The rain picked up as she sped along Route 14 toward Seneca Corners. Checking the rearview mirror, she flinched at the sight of flashing red lights in her rearview mirror.

"Oh, crap," she murmured, pulling to the side of the road. It might cost her a speeding ticket, but at least she got some official attention. Shifting her Beetle into neutral, she opened the glove box, retrieved her registration and proof of insurance, and placed them on the seat beside her. When she rolled down the window, rain spattered her in the face. She ducked back in when a clap of thunder followed a blinding flash of lightning. A dark figure hunched in a rain poncho jogged up to her car. Even from this vantage point, she recognized him.

"License and registration, please!" The deep voice boomed through the rain.

She kept her hands on the steering wheel.

"License and registration, please!"

She tapped her fingers on the steering wheel as the police officer leaned toward her, his forearm against the top of the window frame.

"I could arrest you, you know." Officer Marty D'Amato's threat rumbled like the thunder reverberating above them.

Jesse held her hands out the window, wrists together. "Cuff me, officer."

"Geez, Jesse. Why are you speeding like a bat outta hell in this downpour?" He squinted into the rain pummeling his face. Holding his hand up to shade his eyes, he blinked at her. Drops danced off his poncho. He crouched when a bolt of lightning struck nearby and thunder obliterated her response.

With her thumb, Jesse indicated the back seat. Her friend's deep brown eyes bugged out at the sight of the "body."

"What the...? Who is that?"

"We haven't been formally introduced yet, Marty. Why don't we get out of this storm? You can follow me home, and we can meet her together."

He nodded, sending a stream of rain running off his poncho and down the inside of her window.

They drove the few miles past Seneca Corners to the small house Jesse had moved into three months earlier, the one the locals called the Cavanaugh House. Along with the house, Jesse had inherited a ghost and a decades-old mystery that Marty had helped her solve, putting the ghost to rest. Even though the house had been deserted and dilapidated, she had grown to love it and its symbolism of the new start she had made with her life. Every time she pulled into her yard, she smiled—even tonight.

Her attempts at renewal were evident as her car headlights swept across the house. The paint still peeled and the porch roof still sagged, but evidence of her tender, loving care showed in the freshly painted front door, the neat lawn she'd reclaimed, and the new shrubs she had planted. What couldn't be seen from the road was the work in progress on the plumbing and electrical systems.

She had no garage, so she pulled into the driveway as close to the porch as possible. Getting out, she flipped the seat forward and wrestled with the form. One of the dummy's legs lodged under the front seat; she tugged until it snapped free and sent her falling backward onto the wet grass. Rain pelted her and splotches of mud splattered her shorts.

"Damn!"

"You know, one of my fantasies is to watch two women mud wrestling, but this just isn't doing it for me, Jesse," Marty yelled to her over the downpour.

She glowered at him.

"Check the back seat to see if I left any body parts, Marty. Then help me get this thing into the house." The blanket was soaked now and exuded the musty odors of wool, burlap, and hay.

Marty checked the back of the Volkswagen, patting the floor beneath both front seats.

"All body parts present and accounted for," he said, helping her to her feet. His six-foot frame and muscular body dwarfed the dummy as he flung it over his shoulder, causing the wig to tumble to the ground. "What is this? Are you getting ready for Halloween two months early?"

She unlocked the front door, turned on the hall light, and held the door open so Marty could edge in with the dummy. Fresh paint and turpentine wafted to them from the living room.

"Smells like you've been working on the house," he said as he propped the dummy against the wall. Slipping his poncho over his head, he draped it on a hook by the door then smoothed his tousled, thick, black hair. He hefted the dummy once again, following her into the kitchen.

She flipped on the overhead light and turned to him.

"Lay her on the table."

"Okay, I'm not even going to respond to that remark." His dark eyes twinkled as he dropped the form on the table.

She frowned at him and opened her ancient refrigerator with its rounded top. The appliance had been in the house since the 1940s and sent up gurgles of protest whenever she opened the door. She would have to replace it soon. Grabbing two Genesee Beers, she held out one bottle to Marty.

He shook his head. "I'm on duty."

Replacing one, Jesse opened the other and took a swig. The cold liquid hit the back of her throat, chilling her. She savored the yeasty, malt flavor, sighing. It had been a long day with a bizarre ending. Setting her bottle on the counter, she ladled water out of a large pot on the oversized gas stove, poured it into the coffee carafe, pulled out some coffee, and put it on to brew. Marty looked at her, puzzled.

"What, you don't have running water in this mansion?"

She snickered as she grabbed the dishtowel, wiped her face, and began to towel-dry her hair. "Joe has one of his plumbers working on the ancient plumbing system." Even saying Joe's name caused a flush of pleasure. Despite her recent broken engagement and subsequent vow to be as independent as the popular women's liberation movement demanded, she could not deny her feelings for Joe Riley. In an attempt to hide her blush, she buried her face in the towel, pretending to dry it. She looked up to see Joe's life-long friend grinning at her.

"Joe, huh?"

"Yes, Joe. He thought the plumbing system was in its death throes. I think it dates back to the Roman aqueducts. My water has been shut off for a couple of days, so I steal reserves from St. Bart's. I also head over there in the pre-dawn hours to shower in the girls' locker room."

"Stealing from nuns and orphans? I should arrest you for grand theft." He jangled his handcuffs.

"They're not orphans, Marty. They are daughters of the wealthy."

"Like you, *bella*." He examined the wool blanket.

"Please, don't remind me."

The richest family in the region, the Wyndhams owned a vast estate and winery and had founded St. Bartholomew's Academy for Girls. In solving the mystery of the Cavanaugh House, she had discovered that she was the daughter of a Wyndham—the heir to the fortune. And she wanted no part of it. The two people closest to her, her mother, Eileen Graham, and her ex-fiancé, Robert Cronmiller, had been wealthy, beautiful, and cruel. Wealthy people had brought her nothing but heartache, and the farther she could distance herself from them, the better.

Her kitchen had faded yellow walls, a scuffed linoleum floor, and dated appliances. She smiled to herself. She much preferred this cozy, warm kitchen to the enormous, well-appointed Wyndham Manor with its mahogany staircase, Tiffany stained-glass windows, and marble floors.

She joined Marty as he began inspecting the dummy. Fashioned of burlap, it was secured with string at the feet and hands. Blackened cork or charcoal outlined a crudely drawn face. Marty had plopped the wig back on the form, but it was askew, trailing across the kitchen table in an eerie web. Grabbing the woolen blanket, Jesse examined it, starting at one edge.

"So are you going to tell me where you picked up your friend here?" he asked.

"She was lying in the middle of the road just outside St. Bart's property," Jesse said. "Hey! This blanket is from the school; it's stamped Property of St. Bartholomew Academy for Girls in this corner. The good sisters are probably afraid it might get lost when one of the girls sneaks out for a secret tryst with a boy from St. Andrew's."

"St. Andrew's is a seminary, Jesse."

"I rest my case, Officer D'Amato," she said, pouring a cup of coffee from the carafe and handing it to him. "Look, Marty, something is written across the burlap: 'Your next.' Aside from scaring me because it's grammatically incorrect, this scares me with its intent."

"It sure sounds like a threat—but for who? Whom? Now you've got me all nervous about my grammar, Miss English Teacher."

She chuckled, continuing her examination of the cloth. "This burlap is stamped with a brand. I can't quite make it out because it was cut up to make the limbs. It looks like a circle with a letter inside—an e or c, but I'm not sure."

Marty leaned over her shoulder. "It's a general, all-purpose feed sack. You can buy these anywhere."

"But who would think to use it for a prank like this? This is just weird." She squinted at the label, trying to discern more details.

"Looks like somebody's getting a jump on Halloween tricks. I'll bet a few of your St. Bart's girls know something about this. What they *don't* know about are charges of malicious mischief or worse if it had caused an accident."

"It did freak me out. I thought I'd hit a real body." That thump. The awkward angle. The hair. *It's not real, Jesse.* But there was a glowing light moving through the trees. And a car.

"As I drove away, I saw a car in my rearview mirror pull away from a spot farther down the road. Unless the driver was sleeping, he saw me." She drained her beer. "You know I don't like mysterious cars on the road at night."

"Yeah. The last time you went airborne, as I recall." He studied her as he sipped his coffee. "You gonna to be okay, Nancy Drew? Mysteries seem to follow you around."

She waved her hand at him, brushing away his concern. "Trust me, I don't want anything more to do with mysteries. When I started—*we* started—to investigate Helen Cavanaugh's death, it opened a Pandora's box. Little did I know I would put your job and my life in danger. You risked a lot for me, Marty. I hope you know how much I appreciate it."

"I was happy to help. You were like a terrier with a sock in its mouth. Nothing was going to stop you."

"Unraveling the secret of what happened here in the Cavanaugh House was mystery enough to last a lifetime. All

I want is a boring, ordinary life. Ordinary—just like me."

"You are anything but ordinary, *bella*." Marty smiled at her. His face turned serious. "Besides, you did unravel the mystery and brought a killer to justice."

"I could never have done it without you. Remember that night we broke into the archive room at the courthouse?"

"I'll never forget it. We had a close call there." He laughed, then looked away.

She touched his arm. "You could have lost your job. You did all of that for me. Thank you."

"Hey, *bella*, that's what friends do for friends. I've got to get back to work. You sure you're okay?" Marty drained his coffee cup and set it in the sink.

She nodded, straightening the dummy's wig. "Yeah. Harriet here is going to sleep on the couch tonight. I'll take her in to St. Bart's and see if Sister Therese wants to follow up with this since it's apparently connected to the school."

"Like I said, mysteries seem to follow you around." Marty rubbed the back of his neck. "Look, kiddo, I've gotta get back to my shift. Let me know if Harriet sits up and starts talking to you during the night."

Jesse grimaced. "Ugh, don't even say that. Too many weird things have happened to me already. Yeah, I've got to call it a night, too. School begins bright and early tomorrow. Earlier now that I have to sneak Harriet in before the girls finish breakfast and start heading over to the school building. I wonder what Sister Therese will make of this?"

"I'll escort Harriet to her bed." He lifted the dummy, carried it to the living room, and plopped it on the couch.

"Let me know what you find out. Looks like an end-of-summer prank to me." Marty wrangled his hat over his mop of hair as he headed down the hall. She followed and lifted his drenched poncho from the hook near the front door to hand to him.

"Thanks for your help, Marty."

"Sure, Jess. Anytime."

He pulled the poncho over his head and opened the door.

"Be safe out there," she said, patting his arm.

He turned and winked at her. "You be safe in here, Nancy Drew." He nodded toward the living room and laughed.

She locked the door behind him and returned to the living room where the form stretched across the couch, legs immodestly spread, arms extended in either direction.

"Why do I feel like I need to get you a blanket and pillow?" Jesse said to the figure. She turned off the lamp and headed back to the kitchen. "Good night. Oh, geez, I'm talking to a damn dummy."

She returned to the kitchen to clean up the coffee pot and turn off the lights. Walking back through the hallway, she glanced at the crude form on the couch and shivered. *That thing is creepy. Maybe I should have left it in the car.* She jumped at the sound of the doorbell.

"What did Marty forget?" she mumbled.

She opened the door to find a tall man leaning one arm against the doorjamb. Joe Riley. The glow of her porch light lit up his red hair, mussed by the wind. With his Irish good looks, he would have fit in with a Kennedy family football game on Hyannis Port. His slim body was muscular and toned from the physical demands of construction work. Though he owned his company and employed several crews, he always helped out when he was on site.

Tonight, his hazel eyes danced, his smile, roguish.

"Causing trouble again, Just Jesse?"

Her heart skipped at the sound of Joe's endearment for her—a name he'd christened her with on their first meeting three months earlier when she'd explained her name was not Jessica, just Jesse. Every time he said it, she smiled.

"I saw Seneca Corners' finest driving away from your

house." Rain spattered his red hair and the shoulders of his jacket.

"Joe, come in. You're getting soaked!" She laughed as he entered the hall. "Why are you out on a night like this?"

"I just finished my volunteer shift over at the VA hospital." He brushed raindrops from his hair. "So, why the cops? You're not in trouble, are you?"

"That was Marty. He was going to give me a speeding ticket until he met my new friend here." She swept her arm toward the living room.

Joe's stopped when he caught sight of the dummy. "What the hell…?"

"Meet Harriet. I almost killed her."

Joe walked over to the form and waved his hand in front of his nose. "Your friend is pretty ripe. Perhaps some lessons in hygiene are in order."

She wrinkled her nose. Harriet had become much more pungent as the rain soaked into her. "She must not have been lying in the road for long because she didn't smell this bad when I drove her home."

"Lying in the road?" Joe asked as he examined the charcoal-drawn face.

Jesse recounted what had happened, including the car that drove off, how Marty had pulled her over then followed her home. "He thinks it's an early Halloween prank, but I disagree."

She pointed to the stamp in the corner of the wool blanket.

"Oh ho. The plot thickens. The innocent young ladies at St. Bart's are involved in this…or the good sisters. Somehow I can't see your friend Sister Angelina and her colleagues in their nuns' habits dragging a dummy out into the road in the dark of night. So I'm betting on the young ladies."

"That's what I think, too. I'm going to bring Harriet into the principal's office in the morning. I'm sure it's innocent fun, but it could have caused an accident in this storm."

"The girls might have left the dummy in the road, but what about that car? Why would a car just sit there in the dark watching until you drove away? Jesse, you need to be careful."

At some level she knew Joe was right, but she didn't want mysteries to invade her life. She didn't want black sedans on a dark road again. She didn't want to be covertly watched and followed again. She wanted a logical, simple explanation. She brushed her hair back from her face, and with it any possibility this was more than a prank.

"There was probably a St. Bart's senior making out with a St. Andrew's senior in the black car, that's all." But she suspected that wasn't true either. No matter what reason she gave, her explanation sounded lame.

"Maybe, but why speed away if you hadn't seen them? Why not wait in the dark until you'd left? Doesn't sound like innocent necking."

"I never said the necking was innocent."

Joe shook his head, giving her a half smile.

"I came over to wish you a happy first day of school." He reached into his jacket pocket and extracted a box. "I hope you have a perfectly ordinary year, Miss Graham."

Jesse flushed; he always melted her heart with that crooked smile. Pulling off the ribbon, she unwrapped the box and opened it. She gasped as she lifted out a crystal apple. It caught the lamplight, casting prism refractions against the wall.

"Joe, it's beautiful," she whispered.

"I know you're a great teacher, and you should have an apple on your desk every day."

"Thank you." The lump in her throat blocked any further words. None were needed as he traced his finger along her jawline, tipped her face up, and brushed her lips with his. When he wrapped her in her arms, she felt his breath soft against her hair. Desire stirred within her, followed by disappointment when he released her.

He stepped back. In his eyes, dark with passion, Jesse recognized shared desire. But they had agreed to take things slowly. Like a garden growing—their shared joke. But there was a snake in the garden. While she hated to ruin this moment, she needed to ask the question.

"I told you about the Fall Soiree at Wyndham Manor. I hope you'll go with me."

Talk about throwing cold water on a fire. He stepped away.

"I've told you how I feel about that sort of gathering. I'm not comfortable hanging around with the rich and powerful. I've had to live surrounded by the entitlement of the Wyndhams –especially Al—my whole life. While I was in the mud and muck in Vietnam, his type was sitting at a desk in the Pentagon. Veterans I hire tell me how they were greeted with protesters throwing tomatoes at them when they came home—like any of *us* had a choice. While *they* either got a deferment or cushy state-side duty." He ran his hands through his hair, pacing. "Look, I'm not proud of my prejudice, believe me. But I can't stomach all the superficial small talk and social climbing that goes on at those things. I'm sure the people are nice, and I know the Wyndhams are very generous, but I really want no part of that family."

She couldn't breathe. Her chest felt like a boa constrictor was preparing her for lunch, squeezing tighter and tighter.

He must have realized what he'd said because he held her shoulders.

"I don't mean you—"

She couldn't speak; she nodded.

"Jesse, you know how I feel about you. I lo—"

She pressed her fingers to his lips. She couldn't bear to hear it. Not right now.

"Don't worry about it. I'm fine going on my own." She

forced a smile. "I get it. No problem."

"Are you sure?"

She nodded. A bit too vigorously. "I'm sure."

"I'll leave you to get a good night's sleep." He glanced at Harriet. "I think you're going to need it."

She walked Joe to the door. Before venturing out into the storm, he turned to her and brushed a lock of hair behind her ear. Kissing the tip of her nose, he winked then darted into the rain, sprinting to his truck. Jesse waved as he backed into the street.

Her stomach hurt. More than ever, she did not want to be a Wyndham. Not if it meant losing Joe. Yes, his words had hurt. How was she going to balance her relationship with him and her heritage? She had resisted falling in love with him, but she was finding it harder to deny her feelings. She was beginning to realize the peaceful life she longed for included Joe. But being a Wyndham might destroy that. She slumped against the doorframe.

As she closed the door, lightning struck a nearby tree.

"I don't know if it's more dangerous out there or in here," she said, eyeing the dummy. Catching sight of herself in the hall mirror, she was mortified. Her auburn hair was a mass of spiraling curls, and she had wiped off any trace of makeup with the kitchen towel.

"So much for a romantic encounter with Joe. Of course, we did have company." She glanced into the living room. "Good night, Harriet. Damn, I'm talking to that dummy again!"

As she climbed the stairs, she caught sight of the attic room door. Jesse wanted no more to do with ghosts.

She halted at the sound of soft chanting. She searched for the source of the sound, but all she heard was a rumble of thunder.

CHAPTER TWO

The dormitory was the first building along the curved drive of St. Bartholomew Academy for Girls—a Gothic Revival style building, with its ivy-surrounded, leaded-glass windows tucked into thick bluestone walls. Five stories high, the dormitory loomed above the academic building beside it where classes were held, and beyond that, the convent where the nuns lived. Farther out on the property sat the home economics building, the gymnasium, and the stables.

Jesse had made quick work of a shower in the gymnasium locker room, knowing she had to accomplish her mission before anyone else was around. Now she wrestled Harriet out of the back seat and threw the dummy over her shoulder. She had wrapped it in a bed sheet, so if anyone observed her, it would appear as if she was bringing in a display for her classroom. She hoped. Scanning the windows that faced the faculty parking lot, she saw no curious observers.

As she entered St. Bartholomew's academic building, she was reminded more of her college experience than of high school. The grand stone entrance with its carved cherubim and seraphim, hands clasped, eyes gazing upward, gave the impression she was entering heaven. Two large oak doors with massive brass escutcheons and doorknobs stood sentry at the top of five wide, stone steps. Jesse always expected the gatekeeper at Emerald City to poke his mustachioed head out if she knocked.

Relieved to find the main door unlocked, she heaved Harriet up on her shoulder and drew the door open. She inhaled scents that had mingled over generations: spicy wood polish, leather furniture, old books. She liked the smell of academia. Perhaps some learning occurred by osmosis, by simply breathing in the heady scent of knowledge. Her footsteps echoed as she neared the main office on the left. The top half of the wall was made of windows, the blinds still drawn. Beyond the main office, two massive staircases rose on either side of the hall, and just beyond them corridors ran to the east and west wings of the building. Straight ahead was the north wing where her classroom was located.

With the blinds drawn, she couldn't see who was in the main office, but the door was unlocked, so someone was inside. She entered. There was a tall counter designed to hold students at bay while visiting the office and a waist-high swinging door at the end of the counter that allowed staff to enter the inner sanctum. Students did not want to enter through that swinging door, for it surely meant a visit with Sister Therese. Though she had a reputation for warmth and fairness, the nun was also a strict disciplinarian. Jesse liked her and appreciated her organization and dedication to the students. The secretary wouldn't arrive until 7:30 a.m., so Jesse cleared the outer office area without being seen. With relief she saw a light on in Sister Therese's office. Lugging her burden through the swinging door, she approached the principal's open office door and knocked.

"Come in," the woman said, concentrating on a document she was reading. Her face was surrounded by the crisply starched white linen wimple that contrasted with her black veil and habit. What color was her hair? Was it cut short like Audrey Hepburn's in *The Nun's Story?*

After finishing the sentence, Sister Therese looked up

and gasped. Jesse hadn't realized strands of blond hair had escaped and were dangling out the end of the sheet.

"Is there something you need to tell me, Jesse?"

She dropped the bundle onto a chair, sitting in the one beside it.

"It was a dark and stormy night," she said unwrapping the figure. "When I left school last night, Harriet here was lying in the middle of the road about a quarter mile from the entrance to St. Bart's. I slammed on my brakes but slid into her and thought I'd killed someone."

"And why does this concern St. Bartholomew's?" Sister Therese asked.

Jesse pulled the bed sheet down, revealing the woolen blanket beneath it, pointing out the St. Bartholomew stamp on the corner of the blanket and the threatening words.

Sister Therese placed her elbows on the desk and steepled her fingers, pressing them against her lips. Eyeing the stamp, she nodded slightly. "I see."

Students were forbidden to leave campus without permission, and only seniors were allowed to have cars. Transporting this form from the campus to the road would have required a vehicle, or more than one student. And where could it have been assembled? The mere act of getting it out of wherever they put it together would have required secrecy on the part of any students who witnessed it. The deed would have been done under cover of darkness, probably while Jesse was working in her classroom. And why? Was it just a prank, or was something more sinister behind it? She knew the nun was working through all of these thoughts just as she had the previous night.

Arnie Newhart, the head custodian, popped his head in the door. "You wanted to see me, Sister? Oh, excuse me, Miss Graham, I didn't realize you were in here."

"Come in, Arnie. I wanted to discuss the setup for the student assembly tomorrow, but while you're here, you might want to see this. Miss Graham brought something in that she found out on the road last night."

Arnie caught sight of the dummy. He slowly approached it. His eyes widened when he saw the scrawled message, and he turned to the nun. A message seemed to pass between them. The muscles in his jaw twitched.

"Do students have cars on campus?" Jesse asked, even though she knew the answer.

Sister Therese turned to her. "Why do you ask?"

"Because as I was driving away, I saw a black car that had been parked along the shoulder of the road turn around and speed off." Jesse added, almost to herself, "Although that direction is away from the entrance to St. Bart's." She tapped her index finger against her lips. When she looked up their faces were as grave as if she had told them someone had just died.

Sister Therese sat up and cleared her throat. "Yes, some seniors own cars and have them here. Did you notice the model or possibly the license plate?"

"No. It was too far away, and the rain was coming down hard. If the driver hadn't eventually turned on his—or her—lights, I wouldn't have been certain I'd seen a car at all."

Sister Therese nodded, turning to Arnie.

"Would you be so kind as to store this somewhere until we can get to the bottom of it?" Her words were precise, crisp. As he reached to pick up the dummy, his hands were shaking. He again looked at Sister Therese, nodding slightly. Her gaze slid to Jesse and back to him with an almost imperceptible shake of her head. He shuffled out of the office, leaning against the doorjamb as if the dummy were made of solid concrete.

"Each girl is provided one of those blankets," Sister Therese said. "This time of year they are stored in the closets in the dormitory rooms until they're needed for the cooler weather. Girls are allowed to put a padlock on their closets to lock it if they wish. I think today would be a good day for a spot inspection. Perhaps right after breakfast, before classes begin."

"Yes, Sister," Jesse said, flooded with the memory of being in second grade at St. Cecilia's School. Did she just say that in a high, squeaky voice? These nuns had a definite effect on Catholic students of any age.

As she walked across the parking lot, Jesse realized she never told Sister Therese about the light she saw in the woods.

∞

Returning to her car to retrieve her briefcase and purse, Jesse watched girls who had already arrived at the academic building scampering back to their dormitory rooms in a flurry of gray plaid, the color of their uniforms. She grinned, remembering how she would draw a line with eyebrow pencil up the back of her legs to mimic the seams of the requisite uniform stockings she had to wear. Sister Dominic had caught her as she climbed the stairs and the nun noticed the disappearance of her nylon's "seam" just above the back of her knee. She had received two demerits. Nowadays, students didn't have to wrangle with girdles or garter belts because pantyhose had become all the rage. Girls were rolling up their skirts when they went off campus to imitate the newly popular mini-skirt. She laughed at the thought of how little things change—students were going to break the rules.

"Good luck, girls," Jesse whispered as she walked toward the academic building and her classroom.

The day Maggie, whose professed name was Sister Angelina, had shown her this classroom—room 36, her favorite number—it had echoed with emptiness. Now as she entered it, Jesse admired the bright posters hanging on the walls, books lining the shelves, and materials for student projects stacked on the counter. She smiled, happy with the transformation she had achieved in her room, anticipating energetic students and lively learning. Setting her briefcase on her desk, she reached into it and withdrew the crystal apple Joe had given her, placing it on her desk. It was going to be a new beginning; it was going to be a good year.

Life had taken a turn for the better. Moving to Seneca Corners was her escape from Rochester and the nightmare of a broken engagement. Because of musician Robert Cronmiller's fame, their breakup was magnified by newspaper reports and gossip columnists. They had been the darlings of the society pages, and Robert's concerts were always sold out. He was a gifted classical pianist, as handsome as Paul Newman but as faithful as Hugh Hefner. Jesse had been crushed by his infidelity, vowing to live independently, not requiring any man, never giving her heart away again.

She wanted autonomy, where the only person she had to answer to was herself. Not dependent on anyone who could pull the rug out from under her at a moment's notice. She wanted an uncomplicated life. With Robert, she'd lived in a social whirl—often an artificial one of air kisses and backstabbing. And Robert had been the worst backstabber of all. She wanted a life where what people said to her was true. Where people valued each other more than possessions or status. She wanted honesty and simplicity.

Maybe she'd read too much Thoreau.

So she moved to bucolic Seneca Corners. She snorted. *And hasn't life been peaceful since then?* Not at all. She met Joe, who had helped her through a dangerous and shocking time, but was it just gratitude that she felt for him? Was she ready to commit to a serious relationship? Was she willing to abandon her quest for autonomy? Everything they had experienced in the last three months had been colored by the danger and mystery surrounding her. It was vital their relationship not be based on her need for him or his need to protect her.

She shook her head. This was not the time to be thinking about such things. Students would be arriving any minute and she had to focus. Besides, she was anxious to hear what the fallout was from this morning's spot inspection.

Returning to the classroom door, her gaze swept the hallway with its marble floor and vaulted ceiling. Wyndham ancestors had built this school so their daughters could be properly educated without moving far from the family estate. If only she could shed the inheritance and all it entailed. But for the moment, she planned to keep her connection to the Wyndham family a secret for as long as possible.

Voices echoed from the main hallway, interrupting her thoughts. She took a deep breath, focusing on her plans for the day ahead. Waiting at the door, she prepared to greet her first-hour students and begin her first day at St. Bartholomew Academy for Girls.

By fifth hour, the walls of St. Bart's thrummed with discussion of the surprise inspection that morning and the inevitable rumors it birthed. Theories of a drug bust, hidden caches of alcohol, stolen merchandise, a counterfeit ring, even a supposition that someone was keeping a boy in her closet had floated to Jesse's ears as students speculated on the reason. Jesse stifled a chuckle as she greeted one of the girls who was confirming that rumor. Nobody mentioned a "body" or a prank, however. At the sound of the bell, two girls who had huddled outside the room hurried in, taking the last two seats.

"Good afternoon, ladies."

"Good afternoon, Miss Graham," they responded in unison. Jesse picked up on a voice whose sarcasm slowed it just a touch behind the rest. She willed her eyes not to look in its direction and give its owner any due. Glancing around the room, she was struck by how similar so many of her students looked. Long, straight hair with long, straight bangs a la Cher or British model Jean Shrimpton was the style these days. Hippies in Haight-Ashbury were wearing headbands or flowers in their hair, but not St. Bart students. She resisted the urge to pat down her own wildly curling hair; she could never pull off that style. Hers was more a Shirley Temple look. They might look alike to her now, but once she got to know her students, she would laugh at which ones she confused at the beginning of the year.

"Before we start with the usual logistics of the first day in a class, let's talk about how you're feeling about this morning's inspection."

Dead silence.

As a product of Catholic schools taught by the Sisters of St. Joseph, Jesse knew that referencing students' personal lives was seldom, if ever, broached. Unless, of course, it was trouble. The result was excellent academic achievement, but not always a sense of camaraderie with the teachers. She'd been fortunate to have a few teachers to whom she could relate on a friendlier level, but most had been all business. The faces staring back at her now each reacted differently with a variety of surprise, hope, and mistrust. She waited. She had found in her teaching career that not only was silence golden, it spurred people to talk.

One girl raised her hand.

"Name please?"

"Valerie Bauer," the brown-haired girl responded as she stood.

I have to get used to students standing when they respond. Her public school students never did this, although Jesse remembered that practice as a student at St. Cecilia's.

"Miss Graham, I think it was unfair. What were they looking for, anyway? They never even told us," Valerie said. Sounds of assent accompanied nods around the room. Sister Therese informed Jesse at lunch that one senior, Adrianna Rutherford, was missing her woolen blanket. The student had been brought to the office and questioned about it but said she had never received one when she was assigned her new dorm room. Sister Therese had let it pass and allowed Adrianna to return to class.

Another girl raised her hand.

"Name please?" Jesse asked.

"Eleanor McHenry," she said, pushing up her round John Lennon glasses as she rose from her seat. "I think it's a plot to keep us under control through the use of fear and intimidation. A surprise inspection on the first day of school sends the message, 'We will be watching you.' It's like Big Brother in George Orwell's *1984*." She sat back down.

"I think it was utter nonsense."

The comment slid across the room from a desk occupied by one of the last two girls who had entered.

Lounging back in her seat, arms folded across her chest, the girl smirked as she held Jesse's gaze. Perhaps this was who had uttered the sarcastic response earlier.

"Name please?"

The girl remained seated. "Adrianna Rutherford."

"Please stand while you are speaking, Adrianna."

The girl glared at Jesse. Finally, she rose.

"Anything to add, Adrianna?"

She shook her head and slumped back into her seat.

Valerie raised her hand.

"What do *you* think they were looking for, Miss Graham?" Valerie plucked at her skirt.

"Nothing." Adrianna Rutherford turned to scowl at Valerie. "They won't find *anything*, Valerie."

The girl who had entered at the bell with Adrianna raised

her hand. Jesse acknowledged her with a nod. The girl glanced at Adrianna.

"Name, please," Jesse reminded.

"Madeline Stewart." The girl hesitated, looked at Adrianna again, and finally stood. "I think they are overstepping their bounds. We have rights. Our parents pay a lot of money for us to attend St. Bartholomew." She flipped her blonde hair back over her shoulder.

Jesse was definitely going to confuse this girl with Adrianna Rutherford for a while. Both had long, straight blonde hair, both carried an air of arrogance and superiority. The girl sank into her seat, glancing to see who approved of her comment. Adrianna smiled at her, but others didn't look her way.

"Some parents do. Other students get a free ride." Adrianna's voice was sugar, but her eyes blazed into those of the student sitting in front of Valerie.

The slender girl hitched her breath. She resembled Valerie, with shoulder-length brown hair and a gentle face, but her face held sadness. Jesse saw her lower lip quiver. Adrianna noticed, too. She smirked again.

"Name please?"

The girl eased out of her seat and whispered something.

"I'm sorry. I couldn't hear you," Jesse said gently.

"Becky Newhart." Her voice was barely audible even in the quiet classroom.

"Are you all right, Becky?"

The girl tried to speak, but a soft squeak was all that came out.

Adrianna snickered. Jesse threw her a warning look and repeated her question.

The girl stood silent, looking down at her clasped hands.

Adrianna made a *tsking* sound. "How rude. What can you expect from someone who wasn't raised with the proper social skills?" she asked as she studied her bright pink fingernails. "You belong in the basement with your father."

A few girls snickered; Becky's face turned scarlet. Valerie patted her arm.

"That will be all, Adrianna," Jesse said.

The girl tossed back her hair, turning sideways in her seat.

"Becky, you may be seated."

Becky sank into her seat and buried her face in her hands.

Jesse decided to answer the last question and rein in the discussion. "Valerie, to answer your question, I suspect there are many reasons to have a spot inspection the first day of class. It could be a basic audit to ensure all of you had the necessary materials." Jesse knew her suggestion was a weak one, but most of the girls seemed to accept it. Adrianna and Madeline exchanged a look of skepticism.

"I do like your theory of Big Brother, Eleanor. I think we should explore it further later in the semester when we read *1984*. But for now, we'll concentrate on a different classic that poses many questions." She reached behind to her desk and swept the course guide up. "If you look at your course guide, you will see that the first work we are going to read is Shakespeare's *Hamlet*." The noise of shuffled papers and expectant whispers echoed throughout the room as the girls focused on their materials. Jesse puffed out a slow breath, relieved as the focus shifted from the mystery of the inspection to the mystery of Hamlet's father's death.

∞

As the girls hurried out of class at the end of the period, Jesse called out to Adrianna, "Please remain for a moment, Miss Rutherford." Adrianna rolled her eyes and approached the desk. Jesse waited for the others to leave before looking up at the girl.

"Your remark about Becky Newhart was uncalled for."

"But she is the daughter of our *custodian*, for Christ's sake."

"Do not swear, Adriana. It makes no difference who her father is; Becky Newhart has as much right to be here as you do."

"I beg to differ, Miss Graham. Some people deserve a life that is better than others. They work harder and donate more money and are smarter—"

Jesse had to still her temper. She cocked her head.

"I'm sorry that your world view is so skewed. I believe you have some difficult life lessons coming your way."

Adrianna sneered. "Just because you live in some little dump of a house, you stick up for the wretch. How did you get this teaching position, anyway, *Miss* Graham? Did your father work for the Wyndhams?"

"You've overstepped your bounds, Adrianna. You have just earned a detention."

"Which my father will have dismissed. He is the president of the school board, you know. And you work for him, Miss Graham."

"You now have three detentions, Miss Rutherford, and you will serve your first one after school today. I will see you at three o'clock. During that time, we will discuss how you treat other people."

"I doubt you'll see me at all."

Adrianna picked up her books and flounced out of the room.

Oh, to be seventeen again, living with all that drama.

∞

Sister Angelina poked her head into Jesse's classroom just as Adrianna was leaving from her first detention. Scowling, Adrianna brushed past the nun as she exited. Sister Angelina tried to keep a straight face.

"My, my, Miss Graham. Giving a detention on the first day of school? And to the daughter of the school board president? You do know how to make a strong first impression."

Jesse frowned at her. Maggie—Sister Angelina—had been her best friend since high school. She was still taken off-guard when she saw Maggie in her full habit; she looked like she was wearing an oversized baby bib. And, darn it all, she did look like Audrey Hepburn with her fair skin and large brown eyes that tilted at the corners, thick, black lashes, and beautifully shaped eyebrows. Maggie had entered the convent of the Sisters of St. Joseph right after graduating from high school, and though their lives had taken different paths, they were still best friends. When life had broken Jesse's heart along with the engagement, Maggie told her about the English teaching position at St. Bartholomew's. Eager for a new life, Jesse had jumped at the chance to move away from Rochester. And how convenient that the house she had inherited was just a few miles from the school, thus she was able to live close enough to commute to St. Bartholomew's.

"That girl needs a swift kick in the pants," Jesse growled. She explained the exchange that had occurred during class.

"Yes, Adrianna has been a pain the whole time she's been here, and she started in fifth grade. I suspect her father got tired of putting up with her nonsense and sent her to us," Maggie said.

"She is not going to talk to other students like that in my classroom, nor to me."

"Expect a visit or a call from Mr. Rutherford tonight. She must not have been able to reach him in time to get out of today's detention."

"Let him call. I'd be happy to talk to him about his daughter's arrogant attitude."

"The nut doesn't fall far from the tree, my friend." Maggie laughed.

"What's he going to do? Fire me?"

"He probably would. You're not a Sister of St. Joseph,

which is our only protection against him. You might be on shakier ground. Oh, except that you are the heir to the Wyndham fortune, so you own this place."

Jesse waved her friend's comment away. "Let's not talk about that, Maggie."

"You've got to come to terms with it, Jess. I know it's a whole new concept for you since you just found out a couple of weeks ago that a Wyndham was your father, but it's a fact."

"Let's just keep that quiet for as long as possible. Number one, I don't feel any claim to Wyndham Estate or its fortune. Number two, Ben and Bart Wyndham are doing just fine running the show. And number three, my cousin Al was all set to step into the role of Wyndham heir, and that's just fine with me."

"But the fact is, as the eldest Wyndham's daughter, you are now one of the richest, and probably most influential, people in the area. You are set for life," Maggie said.

Jesse brushed her hands through her hair.

"I just need time to sort through all that," she finally said. "There are so many consequences in this newfound title, not the least of which is Joe's negative reaction." She recounted her conversation with him the previous night.

"You two are going to have to work through this somehow. One consequence is that Mr. Rutherford can't fire you because the Wyndham family founded and own St. Bartholomew's Academy for Girls."

"Maybe I could fire Adrianna. Fire her ass right out of St. Bart's."

"No swearing in these hallowed halls, Miss Graham."

"Oh, shit. Sorry." Jesse grinned.

Maggie glared at her in mock disapproval.

"C'mon, Miss Graham. Let's get the soap."

Jesse twisted a lock of hair around her index finger as she waited for Sister Therese to return. Sitting in the principal's office apparently still made her nervous. She scanned the diplomas on the wall behind the desk, impressed with the advanced degrees from Catholic University and Notre Dame. Sister Therese was a real Renaissance woman. Of course, she had the requisite bachelor's degree from Nazareth College that all the sisters, including Maggie, had.

Glancing at the clock, she had only half an hour before she was to meet Maggie for a picnic—and a much needed beer. Dealing with Adrianna Rutherford was stressful enough, but she hadn't slept much the night before with Harriet in her living room and thunder crashing half the night. Finally, she heard Sister Therese's voice talking to Ruth, the school secretary, who was closing the blinds to the hall.

"Sorry to keep you waiting, Jesse." The nun collapsed into her chair. "I got a call from Mr. Rutherford today."

Jesse shifted in her seat. "I thought you might. But Adrianna…"

Sister Therese held up her hands, deflecting any excuse she might have been about to offer.

"Adrianna is challenging. I am sure whatever discipline you meted out was deserved, and I told Mr. Rutherford so. You may, however, receive a call from him this evening. He couldn't come by because he's out of town on business. He demanded your number, and I gave it to him. If he were in the area, he would have stormed over anyway. I suspect a call from Los Angeles will be easier."

Jesse relaxed into her chair. "Thank you, Sister Therese."

"You break the record for earliest detention ever given in the history of St. Bart's. Some nuns are in awe of you; some want to throttle you. Make your way carefully around here." Sister Therese grinned. "You're already a bit of a legend, you know."

Jesse sighed. "Just what I need. What did you discover

about Harriet today?"

The nun gave her a questioning look.

"You know, the dummy I brought in this morning. The surprise inspection."

"Oh, that." Sister Therese straightened some papers on her desk. "Apparently it was a prank. Nothing to worry about. Adrianna had a rough day—she was the only one missing a wool blanket. But she had a plausible excuse. We'll watch her for more mischief, but I think she'll settle down. So don't worry about it any longer. I doubt more will come of it."

"But what about the 'you're next' threat?"

Sister Therese shrugged it off. "Young girls' imaginations. Everything is dramatic and profound to them. You've taught long enough to know that. It's exponential when you herd them all together twenty-four hours a day."

"What about the fact that someone could have been injured—either the girls as they goofed around in the road in the dark or a motorist who tried to avoid it and ran off the road? And the driver who sat there and watched me?"

"It's nothing, Jesse. Let's just put this behind us." Sister Therese turned off her desk lamp, dismissing her.

Jesse's skin tingled. Something didn't feel right.

CHAPTER THREE

Standing atop a bluff on the edge of Seneca Lake, Jesse savored the breeze blowing across her face. The September sun was still warm, but the air held a hint of cooler autumn temperatures. She listened to the waves languidly lapping the shore below, their sleepy rhythm hypnotic. A perfect balm for her tense muscles at the end of a stressful day. The knot in her shoulders eased as if washed away by the tide. She heard Maggie behind her laying out items for their picnic, and her heart warmed with the peaceful beauty of the scene and gratitude for her dearest friend. Nature and friendship were the soothing solace she needed right now.

Maggie wore blue jeans and a madras button-down blouse instead of her habit. Short, black curls framed her face, now free of the veil and wimple she wore during the day. Kicking off her sandals, she joined Jesse in looking out at the lake.

"Isn't it beautiful?" the nun breathed. "God's creation."

"Or just nature taking her course."

"Jesse!"

"Sorry, Mags, I don't have the deep appreciation for God that you have. Let's just say I'm a big bang girl—take that how you will."

"Jesse, my virgin ears!"

"Well, I guess that's true in your case." Jesse snickered.

Laughing, Maggie slapped her arm.

Ripples sparkled like diamonds on the gently undulating water. Far off, a boat sliced across the lake, leaving a foamy white wake. Circling and calling, seagulls swooped and skimmed the water, looking for food, or they strutted along the shore. A colony of the birds sat at attention along a breakwater like medieval soldiers along a parapet.

Jesse took another deep breath, inhaling the scent of pine from the stand of trees nearby. The cool air flowed through her nostrils and hit her lungs, filling her with renewed energy. This was what she wanted. Peace, simplicity. "It's gorgeous. Isn't it amazing how water calms us?"

"You need some serenity in your life after all that's happened recently," Maggie said, giving her a sideways hug. "I hope your job at St. Bartholomew's will help you settle into a serene life. And who knows…you and Joe…"

Jesse glanced at her. "Don't start, Maggie. I don't know where things will go with Joe. My trust in men has been pretty low after Robert cheated on me."

"But Joe isn't Robert."

"That's for sure. And he has been really supportive through this whole episode with my house, and the murder…but I'm afraid our feelings for each other are based on the dangerous time we just went through. What will we be like now that life has settled down to normal, daily routine? Will the intensity of our feelings slacken off with no danger to heighten our emotions?" She scrubbed her hands through her hair. "I know I sound like I'm overthinking it, but I don't want to be hurt again, Mags."

"I get it, Jess. It just seemed like you were falling in love with Joe. It's obvious to me that he loves you."

"Mags…"

"Well, it is! I understand your caution, but you can't play with Joe's feelings, either."

"I would never do anything to hurt Joe."

"I know."

Jesse turned back to her, changing the subject. "You and Marty helped me so much, too."

Maggie looked away. Moving back to the picnic blanket, she smoothed it out with her toe. "Let's eat. I'm starving."

Maggie passed a sandwich and a beer to Jesse. Ripping open a bag of chips, she scattered them on a paper plate while Jesse opened a carton of French onion dip.

"Now tell me again what happened with this dummy. I was stunned when Sister Therese ordered a room check before classes started on the first day of school."

"My guess is that it was some kind of prank some students were involved in. Maybe an initiation ritual or something. The dummy was made out of hay and wrapped in a St. Bart's blanket. Maggie, I'm not kidding—it freaked me out. I thought I'd killed somebody. That blonde hair spreading out on the pavement...I still saw it in my sleep last night."

Maggie chewed slowly as she stared out at the lake. "But why? What were the girls trying to do? Or prove? And how did they get it to the road?"

"There was a black car there. I didn't notice it until it drove away. Maybe the students brought it in the car. And what about the message, 'You're next?' Who will be next? And for what? To be left in the road? If it were some kind of hazing, wouldn't they make the students being initiated do something, like be there when I hit the damn thing? I didn't see anybody...but I sensed somebody. And there was the light off in the woods."

"A flashlight?" Maggie suggested.

"Too soft. More like a glow. Almost iridescent." Jesse cast her memory back to the previous night. "It seemed to be moving deeper into the woods."

"Maybe the girls had a flashlight but were covering it with something to dull the beam," Maggie said.

Jesse nodded. "That's possible. It was awfully big for a flashlight, though."

"Or maybe it was a ghost."

Jesse glowered at her friend. "Ghost? Just what I need in my life is another ghost."

"But look at how Helen's ghost helped you solve the mystery."

"Yes, and now I get to work with the bitchy sister of the man I almost killed because *he* was trying to kill *me*."

"Sister Alphonse is a pain, that's for sure. Though I shouldn't speak ill of people." Maggie made the sign of the cross and raised her eyes to heaven.

"Oh, please, Sister Angelina. Spare me your saintly posing. Remember the slam books in sophomore year were *your* idea, oh virtuous one."

They laughed.

"We did get into trouble together, didn't we, Jess?"

"Yes, and that's why I was so shocked when you entered the convent. Do they let girls who make out on the dance floor take those vows of chastity?"

Maggie gasped and crossed her arms in mock indignation. "I never gave up my virtue and you know it. You, however, sealed your place in hell behind the home ec building, as I recall."

"I did. And let me tell you, I should have saved myself for a better first time. Wham-bam-thank-you-ma'am."

Maggie plugged her ears. "Please, Miss Graham! Keep your conversation pure."

"Oh, please. You wanted every detail. At the time we both thought it was so romantic. Hey, that's not why you entered the convent, is it? Because my first roll in the hay was so… underwhelming?"

Maggie laughed. "No. I felt I was called. I want to do God's work."

"I guess my phone was out of order. Nobody called. I don't think God's got my kind of work."

"You underestimate yourself, Jesse. You touch people's

lives with many of your gifts. Look how you brought a murderer to justice."

"So my gift of being as stubborn as a terrier with a bone is from God? I'm feeling holy already."

Maggie threw a potato chip at her. "You goofball. I'm serious. I think you were put in the world to help people. Yes, with your stubbornness but also your courage and your sense of fairness. And that's all the charity I can bear to bestow on you for one day. Have another beer."

"Mags, I have this feeling that there is more to this dummy thing than meets the eye. Sister Therese practically ordered me to leave it alone. She should know that will only make me dig deeper. If it were just a prank, why not bring in Adrianna and others who were involved and interrogate them? I remember what good interrogators the Sisters of St. Joseph could be."

"That's because you got in trouble so often," Maggie teased. "Jesse, your mind is still in overdrive after the secrecy behind Helen's murder. Everything isn't a conspiracy. Maybe Sister Therese is right. It was a prank. It's over. Let it go."

"Okay, I'll try, Mags. God knows I've got enough to do just teaching English."

"God knows everything, Jess. God is omniscient." Maggie folded her hands, a smile playing at her lips.

"Then God knows I need another beer."

Jesse fought to stay awake as she wrote the names of her students in her grade book. The first days of school were always exhausting as she adapted to a new routine, met so many new personalities, and awakened at 5:30 each morning. Dealing with Harriet and Adrianna today had provided even more of a challenge than a first day of school usually offered.

As she entered names for her fifth hour class, she pictured each student. One of her major goals in the first couple weeks of school was to know the students' names even when outside the context of her classroom where a seating chart helped. As always, a couple of girls resembled each other so much that she was apt to mix up names. Madeline Stewart and Adrianna Rutherford for example. Both were beautiful young women with blonde hair and big blue eyes. Each also had an air of superiority and knowledge beyond her years. The other two she struggled with were Valerie Bauer and Becky Newhart who were antithetical to the first pair. With brown hair and eyes and slender builds, Valerie and Becky seemed almost childlike. Eleanor McHenry, a.k.a. John Lennon glasses, was one girl who stood out as someone who marched to her own drummer. She was clearly the intellectual of the group; her observation about today's spot inspection was insightful and demonstrated thinking beyond the literal level.

Yawning, Jesse leaned back, stretched, and jumped when the phone rang. She went to the front hall and picked up the receiver.

"May I speak to Jesse Graham?" a man's voice demanded.

"This is she." *Here it comes.* She straightened her shoulders and spread her feet in a power stance.

"This is Howard Rutherford—Adrianna's father. My daughter tells me that you kept her after school today for detention and she has two more. Is that correct?"

"That is correct, Mr. Rutherford."

"Why in the Sam hill are you punishing my daughter when it was the other girl who directed disparaging remarks at Adrianna?"

Jesse almost laughed into the phone.

"I am afraid that is not what happened—"

"Are you calling my daughter a liar, Miss Graham?"

"Is that what you are calling me, Mr. Rutherford?"

Silence.

"Why you impertinent little... I don't know why you are even teaching at St. Bartholomew's. The good sisters are the teachers, and they instill moral values in the girls there."

"I'm sure none of them would have put up with Adrianna's hurtful remarks to the other girl today either."

She could hear his chair tumble over as he jumped out of it.

"What did you say to me? I'll have none of this from you, young lady! This is not the last you will hear from me!" He slammed down the phone.

"Thank you for calling, Mr. Rutherford. It's been a real pleasure speaking with you about your lovely daughter," she said into the dead line. Shaking her head, she replaced the receiver on the cradle and turned toward the kitchen. A knock on the front door stopped her.

She found Joe standing on the porch with a six-pack of Genesee Cream Ale tucked under his arm. His mouth curved up in a mischievous smile.

"I thought this would be better than 12 Horse Ale on a school night." His grin always caused a tiny flutter in her gut that spread deliciously throughout her body.

"You tease. You know I have to get schoolwork done tonight."

"C'mon, Just Jesse. It's only eight o'clock. You need a break."

He gave her a peck on the cheek as he breezed by heading toward the kitchen.

They sat at the kitchen table and popped the caps off their beers with a churchkey. The Beatles' newest hit, "Hey Jude," played softly on the radio. Gentle night breezes teased the window curtain over the kitchen sink.

Jesse took a sip, relishing the beer. "This is exactly what I needed after the phone call I just had," she admitted.

"Not someone breathing into the phone again, was it?"

She hugged herself. After the calls that preceded the attempt on her life, she had become reluctant to answer any phone calls, fearing she would hear only silence. Or measured breathing on the other end. Breathing that let her know that someone was watching her, could get to her. Even then, she hadn't realized the extreme danger she was in—but now that she did, the urge to roll into a ball in the corner was hard to control. She took a deep draw of her beer.

"No, thank God. This was an angry parent."

"Jesse, it was the first day of school."

"I know. I know. Now you sound like Maggie. Look, his daughter was so mean to another girl that I had to nip it in the bud." She explained the exchange between Adrianna and Becky. He listened intently, nodding.

"Joe, if anyone understands this, you do. Al Wyndham got quarterback instead of you because Ben bought all new football equipment for Seneca Corners High. You were more qualified, and you were a senior."

"I do hate that kind of entitlement," Joe agreed. "And Al was never blatantly mean or anything; it was just all of the perks he got because he was a Wyndham. If he had rubbed it in my face like that, I would have beaten him up."

"Precisely. And Becky Newhart can't exactly beat up Adrianna Rutherford, can she? Becky seems like a sweet girl, and her father, Arnie, is great. He's the head custodian. He helped me set up my room, even scrounging up some extra bookshelves for my classroom library. He lives in the converted carriage house right on the property, but Becky stays in the dorm with the other girls. I imagine that doesn't ease her isolation, because she isn't one of them. She didn't come to St. Bart's in fifth grade like most of them. Late-night talks after lights-out is when they share all the secrets and fling insults in the dark. Anyway, I wanted to stop Adrianna's verbal abuse, at least in my classroom. I have no doubt it continues other places."

"It sounds like Becky is going to need a champion, and you are it." Joe raised his beer in a toast.

This might be the time to broach another topic.

"So, Joe, have you decided whether or not you'll come with me this Friday night?"

He slumped in his chair. "Jesse, you know I hate all that dress-up, fancy gourmet, string trio kind of stuff."

"But I need support when Ben introduces me at the Fall Soiree. Parents and benefactors of St. Bartholomew's will be there...oh crap, that means Howard Rutherford will be there. Ugh. Now you have to go with me to hold me back from decking the man. Please, Joe." Jesse's gaze held his, conveying her plea.

"I just don't fit in with that crowd."

"Neither do I, Joe. At least if you were there, I would have company."

"But you've at least had exposure to the jet set with your... you know." Joe picked at the label on his beer bottle.

The wall clock ticked the minutes by as neither spoke.

"You mean with Robert." Her voice was flat. Life with her former fiancé had been a procession of social events, concerts, and a life of luxury. Finding him in bed with her friend had ended all that, propelling her on the journey to Cavanaugh House and teaching at St. Bartholomew's. What she had learned from that journey was that money didn't matter, but true friends and family did. And Joe. She had been fighting her feelings for him since the day he pulled his pickup into her driveway, his red hair tousled in the summer air, his hazel eyes lit with amusement at her quick exit from the mouse-infested house. Now he finished peeling off the label, rolled it into a ball, and tossed it over to the wastebasket.

"I'd better go so you can finish your schoolwork." He stood up.

She nodded, trying to stem her disappointment. She would have to face the soiree alone. But isn't that what she had been insisting on all along with Joe? Holding him at arm's length, sending the message of "Don't get too close; I can make it on my own"? She had to respect his boundaries, just as he respected hers. She took a deep breath.

"I get it, Joe. It's all right—'uptight, outta sight.'" She smiled, hoping levity helped her to look more sincere than she felt.

"Cool. 'Night, Jesse." He reached out and brushed his hand up and down her arm, sending warmth throughout her body. His nearness always unbalanced her, and his touch was electric. She battled the urge to capture his hand and pull him toward her.

"Goodnight, Joe. Thanks for the beer. Here, take the rest of the six-pack," she said, holding out the cardboard carrier with the four remaining bottles.

He held up his hands, declining them. "Save them for the next time I interrupt your homework." He smiled, leaned forward, and kissed her forehead. Turning, he left through the kitchen door.

Jesse stood there, savoring his brief touch and briefer kiss. Her journey was far from over. Being the heir to Wyndham Estate was going to cause difficulty if her relationship with Joe was to deepen. She hoped it would never come down to that choice.

CHAPTER FOUR

Adrianna Rutherford's head was down, and she was practically carving through the paper into the desk with her angry scribbling. This was her third and final detention. Somehow, Howard Rutherford had been unable to absolve his daughter from them. The girl's fury was tangible, her shoulders hunched over the desk, occasional deep sighs escaping through her nostrils. Jesse had a soft spot for Adriana because she recognized herself in the girl —especially with her own red-headed temper. Life was so hard at that age, what with raging hormones and "justified" anger at the world. But this was an opportunity to introduce a life lesson that Adrianna sorely needed.

"Adrianna, do you understand why you were given three detentions?"

The girl said nothing, merely scribbled harder.

"Adrianna, please put your pen down and look at me."

The girl kept scribbling.

"We could add a few more of these meetings if you like."

The girl slapped the pen on the desk, flopped back in her seat, and folded her arms across her chest. She glared; Jesse stared back until the girl's gaze flicked around the room and she shifted in her seat. Jesse kept her voice gentle.

"Do you get it, Adrianna? Do you understand why you can't treat people like that?"

Adrianna glared at her.

"Becky is the daughter of the custodian, for Christ's sake—"

"Don't swear, please."

"… and she belongs in the *carriage* house with him. She doesn't belong here. She should go to the public school like the rest of her kind."

Jesse cleared her throat, swallowing a reprimand. She tapped her pen on the desk a few times to give herself a moment to respond in a reasonable way.

"True, Becky is not wealthy like you, but that does not make her any less a person or any less deserving of attending St. Bartholomew's. Money doesn't make one person better than another, and you already know this, Adrianna. So what is it about Becky that bothers you? I don't think you are as snobbish as you would like people to believe."

Adrianna tossed her blonde hair and sniffed. Jesse noticed her eyes glistening, but the girl pulled herself up, straightening her shoulders.

"Well, you think wrong, Miss Graham. That is *exactly* what I believe."

If looks could kill, I'd be sprawled out in chalk dust on the floor. Jesse saw the pain in the girl's eyes. Was this a case of "hurting people hurt people"?

"I think *anyone* who can't afford to be at St. Bartholomew's for *any* reason should not be welcome here."

Jesse caught the meaning behind Adrianna's words. At some point the fact of her rightful place in the Wyndham family would become public knowledge, and Adrianna would have to eat those words. For now, she let it slide.

"You need to understand one thing and understand it clearly." Jesse's voice had lost its gentle tone. "In my classroom, you will not make disparaging remarks about *anyone*. If you do so, you will be spending a lot of time with me after school. Do I make myself clear?"

Adrianna lifted her chin, flaring her nostrils. "Perfectly clear, *Miss* Graham. May I leave now?"

Jesse glanced at the clock. "Yes, you may leave now, Adrianna."

Grabbing her books and papers, the girl stormed out of the room. Jesse was sure that if she had been able to, Adrianna would have farted on the way out.

❦

Jesse locked her classroom door, glad this day was over. Her feet ached. *Why don't I break in new shoes before I have to wear them all day?* Reaching the main hall, she collided with Sister Alphonse, who was striding down the east corridor, reading a paper.

"Watch where you're going!" the nun barked.

"Oh, excuse me. I didn't see you," Jesse said, even though it was clearly not her fault.

The women stood, looking at each other. Their last exchange had been a couple of weeks earlier outside the hospital room of Sister Alphonse's brother—right after Jesse had shot him in self-defense. Sister Alphonse narrowed her eyes, leaning toward her.

"I don't know what Sister Therese was thinking, hiring you." Venom twisted her voice. "You do nothing but meddle in other people's affairs, ruining lives. Now you can't even manage your own students."

Jesse leaned in, too. "I am managing my students very well, thank you, Sister Alphonse."

The nun sneered at her. "You don't belong here. I wish there were a way to make you disappear."

The threat was clear, and Jesse inched back a step.

"Yes, Miss Graham. I intend to see you dismissed any way I can."

She lifted her chin. "Your threat is empty. There is nothing you can do to get rid of me."

"Just because you're a Wyndham? You think that's going to protect you? Don't count on it."

"That sounds like an unchristian thing to say, Sister." Jesse stepped closer.

"Call it whatever you like. I know right from wrong, and sinners will always pay for their sins. So will you. You'd better be more alert."

"Is there a problem, Sister Alphonse?" Sister Therese stepped out of the office. "Why does Miss Graham need to be alert?"

Sister Alphonse's stare never left Jesse's. "She is so rude. She almost ran me down in the hall."

Sister Therese's gaze swept from one woman to the other. "I see you are still standing. Why don't you walk to the convent with me, Sister?"

Sister Alphonse glanced at the principal. "Of course." She glowered at Jesse. "There's nothing here I need."

The nuns left the building together, Sister Therese speaking in low tones. Sister Alphonse shook her head once, looking back at Jesse.

Jesse took a deep breath. Even though she believed the nun's threats were empty, stemming from her brother's incarceration, she was uneasy, sure the woman would try to make her life at St. Bart's miserable.

Sighing, she continued out the door and headed toward the serenity of her home.

Staff meetings were held after school every Thursday, on the first Thursday, they extended into a cocktail hour and dinner, a tradition Sister Therese had started. Every month place cards were shuffled to different tables, encouraging interaction among all staff. In addition to Jesse, the lay teachers included the business teacher and the gym teacher, who shared duties with Scott Stanton, the new equestrian coach.

Since horseback riding was a major part of life at St. Bart's, resulting in contributions from many parents and alumni, this program was essential to the school. She was relieved to see that Sister Alphonse was not at her table today, but she knew at some point they would be seated together. She was not looking forward to another encounter.

Glancing around the room, she saw Maggie talking with a group including Scott, whose broad shoulders and tall frame blocked the others. His stance looked military: straight posture, hands clasped loosely behind his back as if he stood "at ease." Jesse had not met him yet, but from the back she could see his solid build and short-cropped, chestnut-colored hair. He had not gone in for the "mop-top" Beatles look so many men were sporting these days. Of course, the sisters probably would not allow that anyway.

She studied the other groups gathered in conversation throughout the room, some still standing, some already having claimed their seats. The large room had an institutional feel with vertical blinds, eggshell walls, beige linoleum tile, and utilitarian furniture. Jesse felt a bit intimidated here, as if she were once again a student and not a faculty member. Being around the sisters could do that to her.

"Hello." The voice was deep and resonant.

She turned to look into piercing eyes the color of a summer sky. *No one has eyes that color.* She blinked. Aware that she was gaping, she snapped her mouth shut.

The man stuck out his hand. "Scott Stanton. And you're Jesse Graham, right?"

She shook his hand. *He would give Paul Newman some stiff competition.*

"Hi. Yes, I'm Jesse. Nice to meet you."

"I figured out who you were since you weren't dressed in black and white." He grinned, his white teeth dazzling against his tan skin.

She straightened her shoulders and looked around the

room as if gauging the number of people in black and white, but she knew it was because she had to break the spell of his gaze.

"What strong powers of perception, Mr. Stanton."

"You're not really going to call me that, are you?" He raised his eyebrows, grinning.

She laughed, trying to sound blasé, but it came out like a snort. *Oh, good first impression.* "No, of course not, *Scott.*" The way she said his name sounded like she was trying to pronounce Japanese. "Scott." *Why did you repeat yourself? You sound like a fool.* This was one of those times when she actually did wish the bland linoleum floor would open up and swallow her. But Scott seemed unfazed.

"I wish we were sitting together, but I'm afraid we're not—this time," he said, winking.

"Oh, yes. Oh, no. Oh, I see." Jesse flushed, unable to create a coherent sentence.

Maggie approached and smiled at her. "We're sitting together tonight, Jess."

She sent up a silent prayer of thanksgiving for Maggie's excellent timing.

"Groovy, where's our table, Mags?" *Did I really just say groovy?*

Maggie raised her eyebrows at Jesse. "It's nice to see you again, Scott. How is the equestrian club coming along?"

"Great, Sister Angelina. We're preparing for the St. Bartholomew Dressage Schooling Show next month. We've got some outstanding riders."

"That's one of the biggest events of the year here at St. Bart's. I'm looking forward to it. Dinner is about to be served; shall we take our seats?" Maggie asked.

She steered Jesse toward their table, whispering out the side of her mouth. "You are beet red."

"Stifle it, Mags. I know how I must look. What is with that guy?"

"He certainly had an effect on you, Miss Independent Woman."

Jesse scowled at her. Maggie crossed her eyes in answer. Lively conversation swirled around their table. They sat and were immediately caught up in tales of the first days of school. No mention was made of Adrianna's detention on day one, though Jesse sensed that topic in the air. Like most conversations in the past few months, they veered into discussing just how horrified they were at images of Martin Luther King crumpling on the balcony of the Lorraine Hotel. Jesse certainly felt a gut punch when she watched the clip. Some of these sisters had marched with Dr. King, supporting the Civil Rights Movement, a stand Jesse admired. And to have Robert Kennedy assassinated, too! If someone had an answer to stop the world from spinning out of control, it wasn't her.

She was glad when someone asked who'd seen *The Sound of Music.* Julie Andrew's performance was a much lighter conversation.

Not only did Jesse enjoy the conversation, but, tired of her own dinners of sandwiches and boxed macaroni and cheese, she thoroughly enjoyed this meal. She inhaled the scent of the roasted chicken, mashed potatoes, and fresh green beans. Her mouth watered when she caught the cinnamon and nutmeg aroma of apple pie. Savoring each bite, she let the sweet slices of apple rest on her tongue while her taste buds took full advantage of the spicy flavors. For a moment, with her eyes closed to focus on the tasty dessert, she listened to the conversation around her. The sisters at the table were delightful dinner companions, and Jesse was glad she had decided to join St. Bart's faculty.

As she was saying her good-byes, she sensed a presence hovering near her. Glancing in a wall mirror as she approached the door, she saw Sister Alphonse, the nun's face a thundercloud. The woman swooped into her path.

"You shouldn't be here," she spat, grabbing Jesse's arm. Her grip tightened. "You bring nothing but trouble."

Jesse was shaken by her vitriol. "I have every right to be here…"

The nun hissed, "You give one of our star pupils three detentions on the first day of school? You won't last long at St. Bartholomew's. You'll soon be…"

"Good night, Sister Alphonse."

The nun's mouth clamped shut at the sound of Scott's voice. Both she and Jesse turned to the coach towering over them, smiling.

Sister Alphonse coughed and straightened her wimple. "Good night, Mr. Stanton." She turned on her heel and strode away.

"I hope you had as wonderful a time as I did," he said to Jesse. He reached out to shake her hand. She took his, expecting to drop it in a casual handshake. Instead, he clasped her hand in both of his.

"Yes, I had a nice time." The warmth from his hands spread up her arm and through her body, tingling in her scalp.

"Are you okay, Jess?" Maggie was beside her. "You look flushed. She stopped, noticing their hands. Jesse pulled hers away.

"Yes…um…fine. Yes, I'm fine," Jesse lied.

CHAPTER FIVE

Jesse's yellow Volkswagen Beetle chugged up the oak-lined drive to Wyndham Estate. Although she had been here several times, the enormous manor still awed her. Turrets at the junctions of the four-story structure proclaimed the wealth—and ostentation—of the original owner. The first Albert Wyndham had made his fortune introducing Riesling grapes to upstate New York in the 1800s. His estate was vast—the largest in the region, and the manor attested to that affluence. Large leaded-glass windows imbedded in the red Medina limestone walls winked in the evening sunlight. Like green velvet, lawns swept up from the lake to the manor, topiaries and trees adorning the yard. As she neared the front entrance, she sighed at the sight of valets assisting the owners of Mercedes, Lincolns, and Cadillacs. She patted her Volkswagen's dashboard.

"Sorry, Bert. I'm going to put you through this humiliation again." She got in line behind a Black BMW, awaiting her turn. When the valet saw her, he tipped his hat.

"Good evening, Miss Graham."

She glanced at his nametag. She made it a point to address people by their names—especially if they were serving her.

"Good evening, Paul. Think you can handle this muscle machine?"

He laughed. "I'd be honored to try, Miss Graham."

She laughed as Paul hopped in her car and drove off with a wave. She turned, contemplating the broad front steps leading up to the huge carved oak door, stopping at the Tiffany window above it. She loved the fleur de lis motif that bordered the edge of the window, a design repeated in the hall windows within the house. Taking a deep breath, she climbed the steps.

I absolutely do not want to be here.

Being raised by Eileen Graham had afforded Jesse an extremely comfortable life with the best schools and all the proper training in etiquette and social graces. Eileen had not been a warm, nurturing mother; in fact, she was often cruel in her comments. She had provided all the comforts of a good life, but at the cost of little affirmation or affection. Because she had helped host many such gatherings for her "mother's" interior design business, Jesse was familiar with this kind of soiree. But that didn't mean she enjoyed them. She would much rather be in blue jeans, hanging out with her friends on her patio, drinking a beer and grilling hot dogs.

The butler opened the door and greeted her.

"Good evening, Miss Graham."

"Good evening, Gerald."

He reached to take her gold lamé wrap, but she shook her head and smiled at him.

"Thank you, I'm rather chilly this evening." *And I might want to make a quick exit.*

He bowed and led her toward the living room.

"I'm just going to powder my nose before I go in, Gerald."

"Very good, Miss Graham." He gestured toward the hall that ran alongside the massive mahogany staircase.

She detoured across the marble foyer and headed toward the back of the manor. Slipping into the powder room, she feigned checking her makeup and hair and applied an unnecessary coat of lipstick. Sighing, she smoothed the skirt of her empire-waist, emerald-green shantung dress, appreciating how it matched her eyes and complemented her red hair. She had styled her hair up in a French twist, hoping it would behave itself. Licking her fingers, she smoothed some coppery tendrils that had escaped, but it was futile. She would never wear the Cher look that was so in vogue.

She was not looking forward to this evening. Her uncle, Ben Wyndham, had persuaded her to come and help represent the family. But Jesse's discovery that she was part of the Wyndham family had come at a cost, both emotional and physical. Jesse had lived in danger for most of the time since moving to Seneca Corners three months earlier. Now, with that behind her, she looked forward to an ordinary life of teaching and enjoying the company of new friends. How she wished Joe were beside her, but she had made it clear when they met in June that she was independent and self-reliant.

Self-reliant. Right.

She didn't feel so confident now. Having no more stalling techniques up her sleeve, she again smoothed her skirt, pulled her wrap across her shoulders, and opened the door.

The bassa nova music of Sergio Mendez and Brasil '66 echoed against the marble floor as she entered the living room. Observing the crowd through the massive double door archway, she tried to see them through Joe's eyes. Nice people but used to living life on their terms. Now a member of this "in-crowd," she risked losing Joe and the possibility of exploring what life would be like with him, that simple life she longed for. How hard would it have been for him to be here for just a few hours? She pushed away an uncooperative wisp of hair and the prick of resentment that stuck in her gut. She straightened and put on a smile. Upon entering, she spotted her twin uncles, Benjamin and Bartholomew, just to her left, talking to a few people. Ben

excused himself from the group and approached her.
"Jesse, you look beautiful." He kissed her cheek. She
caught the scent of woodsy aftershave.

Her impression of Ben Wyndham had changed drasti-
cally since their first meeting. What she had interpreted as
arrogance was confidence and openness. His striking blue
eyes and wavy dark hair, graying at the temple, had stuck
her as cliché, but there was no denying how attractive his
strong, tan face was as evidenced by the sideways glances
many women were sending his way. The kindness he had
shown her as she discovered her heritage revealed a man
of power but compassion, wealth but generosity. With her
new awareness of his personality, she thought he looked
like Gregory Peck, perhaps with all of the attributes of
Atticus Finch. The one thing she didn't understand was his
immediate acceptance of her as the Wyndham heir, usurping the position from his son, Al. She glanced across the
room at her cousin. They had become fast friends, but now
his resentment of her was palpable. She caught his eye; he
turned away. Another person lost to her because of Wyndham wealth. She breathed deeply, gearing up to endure this
night.

"Nice party, Ben," she said.

"I can't wait to introduce you to St. Bartholomew's parents, benefactors, and school board. All those years we spent
searching for Bert's child, and one day you just wandered
into town." He squeezed her hand.

"I guess we have Maggie—Sister Angelina—to thank for
that."

"That's right. It was Sister Angelina who brought you to
us. In any case, I'm so glad you're here with us now, Jesse.
Let me introduce you to some people."

Taking her elbow, he steered her to the small group he
had just left. They stopped talking and opened the circle to include the two of them. These people could have

been transplanted from a party of the year at Robert's lush apartment. The same glitz and glitter, the same sense of refinement. She tried to quell the urge to run out of the room.

"Hello, Jesse. It's so good to see you again." Bart Wyndham kissed her cheek. The only way Jesse could tell Bart and Ben apart was because of Bart's closely cropped hair. As the official patron of St. Bartholomew Academy for Girls, Bart's presence at the soiree was obligatory.

"Hello, Bart. Are you up from New York City just for the party?" she asked.

"I'm mixing business with pleasure this trip." Turning to the tall man on his left, he said, "Trevor Underwood, may I present Jesse Graham?"

Jesse was glad she had heels on so she didn't have to crane her neck to look this man in the eye. He was at least six foot four. Smiling warmly, he offered his hand. His handshake was firm, his hands warm and smooth. His gray eyes perused her as if assessing an acquisition.

"How do you do, Miss Graham?"

Beaming, Bart patted the man on the back. "Trevor here is the CEO of Digson Energy Corporation. He's scoping out a possible building site for an energy complex in Geneva. We're competing with Syracuse and Ithaca."

"'Far above Cayuga's Waters,'" Jesse said.

Trevor nodded, leaning forward conspiratorially. Old Spice and breath mints preceded him. "Exactly. The water resources in the Finger Lakes area make it an ideal spot for a plant."

"So, are you building a dam? I don't know much about hydro-power," she said, leaning back slightly. This man seemed to epitomize all that she disliked about wealthy, powerful people. Nothing would stand in the way of his plans. He was the kind of person who wrested his success from the hands of fate and drove whatever forces blocked him to comply with his will. She shuddered inwardly.

"No, not hydro—nuclear. Trevor wants to build a nuclear power plant," Bart explained.

She got a chill. "Nuclear? Like an atomic bomb?" The images of Hiroshima after the United States bombed it just twenty-three years earlier still shook her.

Trevor laughed, tilting his head back as if it were a full-blown guffaw. Not an inch of his salt and pepper hair budged. "We'll obviously need to educate the public about the safety of nuclear energy. It's the wave of the future; it's cleaner than coal and cheaper than oil."

"And safer than...?" Jesse asked.

"Safer than you think, Miss Graham."

The woman standing beside him touched his arm and he turned to her. Was it her imagination, or had Jesse just been dismissed?

Bart was talking to another man in the group and didn't seem to notice. Instead, he introduced Jesse, and she made polite conversation until Ben steered her to another group, one of many they visited as they made the circuit of the room. Soft music served as a backdrop, smooth jazz, light classical, and Latin tunes intertwining with the rhythmic rise and fall of conversation. Laughter, punctuated with ice clinking in glasses, an occasional outburst of "You don't say," or "She didn't, really?" followed by hushed whispers. As they approached a group near the patio doors, the people parted to make room for them to join. Jesse heard one man say to another, "Isn't that right, Rutherford?"

Howard Rutherford.

Though she had steeled herself for this moment, she started at his name, spilling her wine on his sleeve.

He jumped, brushing at the vicuña wool. "What the devil...?" Scowling at her, he used a cocktail napkin to dab at the expensive fabric.

Ben assisted with his own napkin, motioning to a waiter

to help. "Sorry, Howard. I must have bumped Jesse's arm."

Howard brushed Ben's hand away. "No harm done, Ben." The glower he directed at Jesse belied his words.

Ben took her arm and brought her into the group. "May I introduce Jesse Graham?"

"Jesse Graham?" Crimson rose from above Howard's shirt collar to his chin, up his cheeks to his receding hairline. It was like watching a thermometer when someone had a serious fever. He leaned into her, trying to impose more height than he could claim. The aroma of pipe tobacco wafted about his head. "You're the teacher who has been harassing my daughter, Adrianna. You called her a liar and let other girls gang up on her in class. Ben, again I insist you fire this girl. She has no business teaching at St. Bartholomew's!"

Everyone in the room had stopped talking, intent on the scene.

"Howard, we've already discussed this…"

"No excuses, Ben. This girl must be let go."

She felt her face flame with embarrassment. Her ears were ringing; the man's insults seemed to echo, rolling around inside her head as if she were in a tunnel in an amusement park crazy house. Shaking, she felt everyone staring at them and wished she could magically disappear. She was glad she hadn't eaten before she came because the contents of her stomach would be all over the white wool carpeting at that moment.

"Stop, Howard." Ben's tone had taken on authority that would brook no opposition.

Howard Rutherford's face was as red as Jesse's but with rage, not embarrassment. His chest heaved in his effort to still his allegations.

The room was silent. Acknowledging the silence, Ben took Jesse's arm, turning her toward the larger group.

"Ladies and gentlemen, it's an exciting night for the Wyndham family. One of our members was lost to us for years, and we searched to no avail. Call it fate, karma, or luck, she has returned home. I'd like to introduce you all to Jesse Graham, the heiress of Wyndham estate. Please raise your glasses with me in a toast to my niece."

Oh my God. Can this night get any worse?

A brief, awkward silence followed Ben's words as people grappled with this revelation. Then one person applauded, gradually followed by others, and toasts of "welcome" and "hear, hear!" erupted throughout the room. In the midst of the crowd of stunned guests, she picked out Scott's impassive face.

To her left, Jesse noticed someone exit to the patio. Behind her, Howard Rutherford grumbled, "Well, I never…"

Seething, she pasted on a frozen smile as Ben led her through the crowd with brief introductions while steering her toward his office. Jesse felt like a wooden puppet, hinged arms and legs jerking as she walked, being manipulated by a puppeteer. No matter how she resisted, the force and fate of her heritage seemed to thwart any desire she had for her destiny. Resentment grew within her, its taste bitter.

After he ushered her inside, he closed the door to the noise and speculation. He poured two drinks from a crystal decanter, handing one to her before they sat in the taupe leather chairs in front of his desk.

"Sorry about that, Jesse. There was nowhere to go with Howard's outburst, and you were already the center of attention. I thought casting you in a better light while putting him in his place was the best way to handle it. Are you all right?"

She nodded, unable to speak. Still shaking, she took a healthy swig of the golden liquid, and the taste and aroma of Johnnie Walker Blue Label slid down her throat and wafted through her nose, hitting her empty stomach. Closing her eyes, she savored the drink, hoping to subdue her anger. She tried to control her voice.

"You didn't have to do that. Introduce me to everyone like that. Without any warning. And, anyway—why?" She gripped her elbows to still her trembling.

"Because you're the heir—the board needs to know that…"

"No! The board doesn't need to know it because it makes no difference!"

His voice began to rise with hers. "Yes, it does. You will be making decisions, running—"

"I'm not running anything—although I'd like to run away from here right now. I am teaching English. That's all I'm doing." She tossed back the rest of her scotch.

"We'll discuss this later. You had a tough moment out there with Howard." He sounded like he was speaking to a misbehaving child. "Rutherford is a real pain in the ass. He throws money everywhere and thinks it can buy him everything in life—and everybody. I'm sorry he attacked you like that."

She inhaled, tamping down her anger. She tried to capture the mellow feeling seeping through her with the scotch.

"It wasn't our first conversation." She briefly explained what had happened with Adrianna.

"Is she a senior already? My gosh, it seems like she was just a toddler last time I saw her. So sad that she lost her mother at such a young age." He freshened her drink.

"What happened?"

"Cancer. She died when Adrianna was about five years old. Howard has done his best, I'm sure, but a girl needs a mother."

For the second time that night, she thought about the woman who raised her. Cold and aloof, Eileen had given Jesse all the comforts and advantages possible, but never cuddling, never attention, never nurturing. How different her life would have been if her biological mother had raised her. Jesse empathized with Adrianna.

Ben sat forward, his eyes alight. "Why don't you move in here and live at Wyndham Manor, Jesse? Monica and I would love to have you here. And it would be a much shorter commute to St. Bart's for you."

"That's quite generous, Ben, but I have grown quite attached to the Cavanaugh House."

"I've heard rumors about Helen's ghost appearing to you."

"Not rumors, Ben. I did see her."

He patted her knee. "Think about it."

She gritted her teeth at his patronizing attitude but couldn't muster the energy to respond. Her anger seemed a separate entity sitting next to her on the couch.

He drained his glass. "Are you ready to face the 'madding crowd' now, Miss Graham?"

Rising, Jesse felt a little dizzy. "I guess so."

"You are a remarkable young woman. I'm so proud to have you in the family. But being the heiress to this fortune has its drawbacks."

"I haven't accepted the fact of my inheritance. I don't think anything needs to change. I will continue to go about my life, and you and Al will continue with yours here."

He chuckled, taking her hand. "The invitation to live here always remains. Things will change for you, Jesse. I hope for the better. Only for the better."

He hadn't heard a thing she'd said. He wanted things his way regardless of her wishes. Was trying to get her drunk part of the plan?

By the time she returned to the party, the guests had forgotten, or were too polite to mention, the scene between Howard Rutherford and her. Everyone was enjoying the lavish Wyndham hospitality. People were gathered in clusters in the living room or lounging on the patio, enjoying the mild September evening. Huddled in one corner, Trevor Underwood and Howard Rutherford were engaged in what appeared to be an intense, private conversation. Howard nodded his head several times, before Trevor strode out of the room. Had Howard just landed a sweet deal for a nuclear power plant in Geneva? What would his cut be?

Feeling lightheaded, she loaded a plate with cheese, crackers, and fruit. She wasn't hungry—especially after the bizarre events of the evening—but she recognized the need to counteract the effect of the Johnnie Walker Blue. She walked to the patio, seeking the person she knew had left during Ben's introduction of her. Ben's son, Albert, stood at the edge of the patio, looking out at the grounds. Just a year younger than Jesse, Al had been one of her first friends in this town even before they discovered they were cousins. They had enjoyed each other's company until Ben had ordained Jesse as the lost Wyndham heir. She didn't blame Al for snubbing her. He had been groomed to inherit the estate his whole life; now he was demoted to second place. Despite the fact that the seeds of Joe's disenchantment of Wyndham wealth was due to Al's seeming entitlement when they were in school together, she felt sorry for him.

He did not flash the ready smile she was hoping for as she neared.

"Hello, Jesse."

"Hi, Al."

"Quite the soiree for you." His scrutiny shifted from her to the people nearby.

"It's not for me, Al. It's for St. Bart's and the, you know, parents, benefactors…" Her voice drifted off as he scowled at her.

"Oh, no. It's to introduce the newly discovered heir of Wyndham Estate."

"Al, I have absolutely no desire to be that. *You* are the heir. *You* will inherit the estate, not me."

"I beg to differ with you. You are the rightful heir, and all of this is yours. So when are you moving in?"

"I'm not moving in. Al, you're being a jerk!" Her voice was rising, and the people around them turned to look. Jesse smiled at them, patting Al's arm until they resumed their conversations.

"Listen, bozo," she hissed through her teeth. "I have no interest in your inheritance, your estate, or your damn money. All I want is a simple, quiet life. Is that so much to ask? I move down here and what do I get? A haunted house and someone trying to kill me. I try to escape from a life with the ass who cheated on me and end up in a town where another guy wants to murder me. I'm not so enamored with men right now." She glanced across the room at Howard Rutherford. "Now you're going to tick me off with your 'poor me' crap. Well, guess what, buddy? You can take your damn estate and shove it."

∞

Jesse didn't care that she was crushing her emerald-green shantung into the dust as she slumped on her back porch steps, drinking a Genesee Cream Ale. The cold carbonation tickled its way down her throat while warm tears slid down her cheeks. The full moon had risen to just above the trees, a clear, creamy yellow against the blue-black sky. The luster made each blade of grass almost visible, except where shadows stretched across the lawn. A mild breeze blew across Jesse's face, playing with wisps of her hair that she futilely brushed back in place. She wiped at her tears, emotionally drained from the confrontations she'd had in the last few days, angry at her weakness right now, angry at how life had turned out.

"Damn!" she breathed. "Damn, damn, DAMN!" Each curse increased in volume, concluding with her hurling the beer bottle at the nearest tree. It shattered, spilling shards of glass into the hostas below.

"Bad night?"

She jumped at the sound of Joe's voice.

"I need another beer," she said.

"I don't think the landscaping could handle that."

He sat down beside her on the steps.

What might have been different tonight if Joe had been beside her? Howard Rutherford still would have exploded. Ben would still have made the grand introduction. Al would still resent her. But Joe would have been there. And that would have made a difference to her.

"It was awful, Joe." Her voice was barely audible in the stillness of the night. She felt as if she had collapsed inside herself, small and scared like *Alice Through the Looking Glass* with the trees towering over her, her clothing too large. She couldn't meet his eyes. Staring mutely at the ground, she remembered her first school dance, the feel of the smooth plaster as she pressed her hands against the wall, nervous that a boy would approach her. The shoes she'd insisted on wearing because they had heels had been just a little too big and slopped and clopped when she walked. Inside she felt thirteen years old again and vulnerable as hell.

Reaching over, he took her hand, still saying nothing. They sat like this for several minutes, and then she told him about the party. He stared out at the yard while she spoke, occasionally nodding, allowing her to reveal the events as she needed. When she finished with her last words to Al, he let her hand go and put his arm around her, drawing her to his side.

"Hell of a party, Just Jesse."

Yes. And all I wanted was you beside me.

"It's been a couple of tough months for you, that's for sure. You know, I've had my troubles with Al Wyndham, but I kind of feel sorry for him. The rug's been pulled out from under him."

She sat up and pulled away. "But I didn't do that—" she protested.

"I didn't say you did. It's not your fault, and deep down, I don't think Al blames you. But you're the easy target right now. I imagine there's all kinds of legal red tape that was established years ago to determine the proper Wyndham heir."

"And I suppose no other Wyndham became involved with a woman 'below his station,' so to speak. My mother was certainly not bred to be mistress of Wyndham Manor. My father sure botched things up for that family. But I don't want any part of it, Joe. Can't I just say, 'Thanks, but no thanks' and walk away? Can't their lawyers add a codicil or whatever it's called to let me opt out?"

"I suspect it's much more complicated than that, Jesse."

He brushed back a wisp of her hair and his fingers caressed her face.

"You look beautiful tonight."

Despite her wanting to be independent and autonomous, despite her disappointment in his refusal to attend Wyndham functions, she couldn't deny her attraction to him… and her deepening feelings. He leaned in and she closed her eyes, preparing to surrender to his kiss. She felt his lips press her forehead softly. Her eyes popped open in surprise—and disappointment. She regained her composure as he pulled away. His eyes twinkled in the moonlight, and she suspected he was aware of her reaction. His mouth hitched up in a teasing grin.

"You're going to be okay, Just Jesse."

"Are you going to chuck my chin now, Joe?"

"You drive me crazy with your contradictions. You know that, don't you?" His smile was full now, his eyes danced.

She chucked his chin. "Gotta keep you guessing, Joe."

He swept her in his arms and kissed her long and full. Releasing her, he stood and tipped an imaginary hat. "'Evenin' Miss Graham." He disappeared around the corner of the house before she could catch her breath.

CHAPTER SIX

October 1968

Saturday's gloom followed Jesse into St. Bartholomew's. Stillness surrounded her, amplifying the echo of her footfalls on the marble floor. Reaching her classroom, she hesitated before unlocking the door.

Must be the gloom getting to me. Get on with it, Graham. Time's a wastin'.

Even before she walked to her desk, she knew something was off. Her small, apple-shaped desk clock, a gift from her students when she left her teaching position in Rochester, was face down. Lifting it, she saw that the glass face was broken. She turned the clock over and over in her hands. It would be impossible to replace the apple-shaped glass. An item next to her chair caught her eye; her pearl-handled letter opener lay on the floor. Helen had left that in her desk at the Cavanaugh House, and Jesse had brought it in to use at school. Frowning, she picked it up and placed it in a drawer. Papers fanned across the edge of her desk. She straightened them, tapping the edges against the desk to align them. She was a bit dizzy at the sight of the disorder. This was intentional.

"Oh no," she cried, spotting the crystal apple Joe had given her perched on the edge of the desk. Another inch and it would have shattered on the floor. Laying the papers in a neat stack, she picked up the apple. A crack now ran along the top near the stem. She felt a tug at her heart, gripping the glass piece in her hand as if that would repair the crack. She cradled it to her chest as if that would magically reverse the damage.

Her intuition whispered, "Be careful," but she wanted this to be a simple mistake. Perhaps the custodian who cleaned her room was in a hurry and got clumsy. She'd talk to Arnie about it. As head of maintenance, he could get to the bottom of this. Surely it was just an accident. She resisted other possibilities. Adrianna would have no way to access her classroom, but Sister Alphonse…

Jesse finished straightening the mess, placing the crystal apple in her top drawer. She felt violated. Someone had been in here disturbing her property.

A sudden chill permeated the air. A breeze sent papers flying off the desk. Even though she knew they were closed, Jesse looked toward the windows, searching for the source of the cool air. Scanning the room, she saw nothing to cause the draft. She rose, walked to her classroom door, and stepped into the hall; the air was much warmer. Sensing someone watching her, she turned, but the room was empty.

"Hmm," she murmured. "Just a breeze from the air ducts, I guess." She spoke aloud, as if that would make it so.

But back in her room, she caught her breath as the air turned decidedly colder. She felt a draft rush by her, and the papers whirled then fell to the floor. She rubbed her arms against the chill, against the foreboding. The room returned to its normal temperature.

I've felt this before.

She heard a door close down the hall and listened to the approaching footsteps. What had just occurred had nothing to do with footsteps, yet she wanted to hide, to close and lock her door. No, to flee.

Maggie walked in.

Jesse hadn't realized that she'd been holding her breath. She exhaled. "Do you feel that, Maggie?"

Maggie looked around the room. "Feel what?"

"The icy cold?"

Maggie's gaze was almost as troubling as the temperature, but for the opposite reason. "Are you okay, Jess?"

"Yes. No. I don't know." At what point would she frighten her friend too much?

Maggie led her to her chair and eased her into it. "What's up?"

"Do you remember what we felt when Helen's ghost appeared at my house?"

Maggie nodded slowly.

"I just felt it. Here. In my classroom. But it was different, Mags. With Helen, there was a softness or gentleness…I don't know. This was…harsh. Threatening." She rubbed her arms.

Maggie sank into the student desk next to hers. "I want to say you're imagining things, but I felt Helen's presence at your house." She looked at the papers scattered on the floor. "And I know for certain you wouldn't throw student essays on the floor."

"Oh, some I might," Jesse said, bending to pick them up. Maggie helped her. As Jesse straightened and organized the essays, she couldn't hide the trembling in her hands. Finally, she laid the papers down. She rubbed her forehead and inhaled deeply. "I'm tired, Mags." She sighed, her voice ragged. "A quiet, peaceful life where I'm not recognized wherever I go, where no ghosts invade my life, and I lie around bored all weekend. Is that so much to ask?"

Maggie took her hand. "No, Jess. That's not too much to ask." She reached for one paper under the desk that they had missed. "But I don't think peace and quiet is in the plan for you right now."

⊙⊙

The late afternoon sun spilled through the classroom windows and reflected off the shiny green cutout letters Jesse had just put on her bulletin board. "To Be or Not to Be…" Her seniors had been reading *Hamlet,* and she was anxious to present a compelling discussion question for them based on Hamlet's soliloquy.

Outside, she saw Arnie Newhart talking to Howard Rutherford on the sidewalk just below her window. The stance of the men caught her attention. Though he was shorter than Arnie, Howard leaned into him, jabbing his finger into the custodian's chest.

"You are such a pain in the ass," she said aloud. She understood why Adrianna was so pushy and demanding—she'd learned from an expert. Jesse balled her fists; the idea that Howard Rutherford would treat Arnie with such disrespect because he was a custodian was maddening. But now Arnie was leaning over Howard. His face was getting redder as he spoke, and as his voice rose, Jesse could hear his some of his words.

"…danger. How could you tell him? No one was supposed to know! Especially you…"

He poked his finger into Howard Rutherford's chest, causing the man to step backward a few paces. Jesse watched in disbelief. The president of the school board held up his hands as if to deflect the heated words Arnie was firing at him.

Arnie lowered his voice, and all Jesse could discern was a fierce scolding. Finally, Howard bobbled his head in agreement, put his fedora on, turned on his heel, and hastened away. As Arnie watched the man's departure, his face transformed from an angry mask to a look of…despair? Fear?

Jesse shook her head in confusion. All was not what it

seemed at St. Bart's.

A short time later, Arnie showed up at her door.

"Hello, Miss Graham. You left a note in my mailbox about a problem in your classroom."

Jesse had to bite her tongue to keep from saying, *Yes, but I'd rather know about your conversation with Mr. Rutherford.* Instead, she nodded and explained the broken and misplaced items on her desk.

Arnie listened patiently. When she was finished, he assured her he would talk to the custodian assigned to clean her room. Even as she told him about the disarray, she regretted bringing it up at all. She recalled the looks he exchanged with Sister Therese when she brought the dummy in the first morning. What was that about? And what was his connection to Howard Rutherford? Whoever damaged the items on her desk was sending a message—a message designed to get rid of her. A message Howard Rutherford had verbalized. When she told him to forget it, he waved a hand and smiled.

"We'll get to the bottom of this, Miss Graham."

Perhaps you already know all about it.

∞

In the month she had been teaching at St. Bart's, Jesse had become accustomed to the noises of the old building, but the sound that interrupted her concentration this day was different. She paused, her red pen poised over a particularly bad essay on the characteristics of the tragedy. A faint sound of distant drumming slowed, then stopped. She listened for a minute but heard nothing else During a weekday, any noise would be masked by the bustling energy of the students, but when Jesse came in on Saturdays, the building was deathly quiet.

Sighing, she returned to the student paper on her desk. *This paper is a tragedy.* She jotted notes to the student as she read, gave a final comment at the end, and marked the grade at the top of the page. "Sometimes I think I spend more time on their essays than they…"

There it was again. The drumming and a haunting echo of chanting. She was drawn to it by an invisible energy she could not resist. a driving need to discover the source of the music. She rubbed her arms as if that would erase the goose bumps. Was this what a trance was like? Because there was nothing she could do to resist this pull—even though she suspected what she would find.

Rising from her desk, she walked out into the shadowy hall, instinctively looking both ways down the long corridor before stepping into it. Through the tall, leaded windows, the gray October sky peeked between the trees that lined the. building. In yesterday's sunshine, the leaves had been brilliant oranges, reds, and yellows; today they were dull, tossing in the autumn breeze and filtering out the dim daylight. The sudden hissing of a radiator made her jump. Her senses were keener, noises louder, the cold more biting. An irresistible urgency pulled her toward the sound. This sensation was familiar—she'd had it when Helen's ghost appeared to her in the attic—a captivating feeling that drew her against her will, despite her fear. And she'd never wanted to feel it again.

Reluctantly, she turned from her classroom and walked to the intersection of the main hall. The drumming grew louder, and yes, the chanting, too. The drumming was rhythmic but soft, a muted beat. *Bah-boom, Bah-boom, Bah-boom*…Creeping along the east wing hall, she strained to listen. Was it an SOS? No, that was three dots, three dashes, three dots. Whoever was drumming this out was not in distress. Was it a different signal of some kind? The chanting floated to her ears. The words were indistinguishable, only syllables that ebbed and flowed in an effortless rhythm, smooth against the solid drumming sounds.

She pressed her ear against each of the classroom doors, but none of the rooms seemed to contain the sounds. Once she reached the end of the wing, the sound was behind her. Puzzled, she retraced her steps and, again, listened at each door. The drumming echoed up from beneath the floor. That meant it was coming from the basement.

I hate basements.

Jesse paused by the door to the basement, pressing her ear against it. The sounds were hollow against the wood. She flipped through the keys on her key ring, trying various ones in the lock. None worked. Frustrated, she rattled the doorknob. The music ceased. She waited for a while, but no further sound issued from behind the door.

With the basement door locked, her urgency to find the source dissipated. She was relieved. Vague memories of having to stay in a dark, dank basement still haunted her: Eileen hushing her quiet sniffles and holding her tiny frame against her chest. Eileen never held her close, so Jesse knew it was to quiet her, not to comfort her. She could still hear the pounding of Eileen's heart as she pressed against her, but she'd no idea until recently why they would be hiding. Now that she knew the story of Eileen's whisking her away from Seneca Corners, she assumed that hiding place was part of the fleeing. In any case, she'd grown up with an aversion to basements, her blood pressure increasing any time she was below ground.

Her thoughts were interrupted by the drumming. She closed her eyes, mesmerized. Someone grabbed her shoulders and a flood of adrenaline shot through her. She screamed.

"Jesse, what the heck is wrong?" Maggie grabbed her arms as they lashed out.

"Oh, my God, Maggie! You scared the shit out of me!"

"No swearing allowed in the hallowed halls of St. Bartholomew's." Maggie waggled a finger in front of Jesse's face. She stopped. "What is it, Jesse?"

"Did you hear those sounds, Mags?"

"Sounds? In this creaky old building? Of course not." Maggie smiled.

"No, Mags. Not the usual creaks and coughs we hear. Someone beating a drum. And humming…no, chanting." They were silent for a few moments, heads cocked as they listened.

Silence.

Jesse exhaled. "I swear I heard it."

"You swear a lot," Maggie said.

"You know what I mean." Jesse scowled at her friend, still feeling unsettled.

"Listen, Jess, I have to grab a book from my classroom. Why don't you come over to the convent for supper?"

"No, I'm determined to get these papers graded so I can enjoy a relaxing Sunday tomorrow."

"C'mon, just stop over for supper. We'll eat at six o'clock—it's only quarter to four right now; that gives you more than two hours to finish up. I'll have a place set for you. If you get there early, you'll have time for a beer."

A delicious dinner with the Sisters of St. Joseph would be a delightful break from her own quick forays into the kitchen. "Okay. Maybe having a deadline will spur me on to a more ambitious reading of these tragic essays on tragedy. If beer is involved, the latter papers may all get As and I'll be done with them." She felt cheerier just accepting the invitation. "I'll see you around six."

"Or sooner. I'll have a cold one or two ready for you. See you later, Jess."

"Thanks, Mags."

Jesse returned to her desk, half listening to her friend's footsteps echo down the hall. Thank God someone else was in the building. Picking up the next essay, she read the first sentence. Her calm dissolved as she heard Maggie exit the building, the large oak door thudding shut behind her. Silence enveloped Jesse like a dusky cloak.

∞

The nuns around her chatted cheerfully while Jesse sipped her Genesee Beer. The incident in the school had put her in a somber mood. The sounds had been ethereal, haunting. She was struck by how the ordinariness of this room at the convent contradicted her disquiet. Lamps defeated the gloom of the day, and overstuffed sofas gathered around an Oriental rug. The beige walls were soothing almost to boredom, while the blonde end tables and coffee table held beverages and appetizers. She willed herself to relax.

"Jess, what do you think?" Maggie interrupted her thoughts.

"About what?" She pulled herself out of her reverie.

"About the new equestrian coach, Scott Stanton. All of us think he's quite dreamy."

Jesse gaped at the women surrounding her. "Dreamy? I didn't think nuns…that is, I never suspected that nuns would…" Her voice trailed off as the women laughed.

"We are human, Jesse, and we have eyes," Sister Catherine said. She had a sweet face and looked too young to have already taken her final vows.

"Yes, but to think about a man that way…" Jesse stammered. She felt her face heating up with embarrassment.

"We can look, but we can't touch," Sister Catherine said. The others laughed.

"So to your un-vow-taken eyes, Jesse, how does he look to you?" Sister Catherine's eyes twinkled with mischief.

Recalling the impact of their first meeting and picturing his broad-shouldered six foot two frame, she nodded absently. His brown hair was usually mussed just enough to look sexy, and his square jaw and crystal blue eyes gave him a screen idol appeal. In a way, he reminded her of her cheating former fiancé, so she found his looks off-putting. After finding Robert in bed with her good friend, incredibly handsome had become incredibly unappealing to her. Now Joe was not movie star handsome. He was ruggedly handsome, comforting handsome, her kind of handsome.

"Apparently our newest English teacher *has* noticed Mr. Stanton," Sister Catherine teased.

Jesse regained her composure. She had to play along and deflect. "Yes, he's pretty gorgeous. I imagine all the students are besotted with him."

"No doubt," Maggie said.

"And they feel safer with him around the premises," Sister Catherine added. She snapped her mouth shut, pulling in her lips.

"Why safer?" Jesse asked. How convenient the sister would mention that while Jesse was still skittish from the unnatural sounds.

The sisters glanced at each other in bemusement. Sister Catherine recovered. Leaning in closer, her eyes grew big.

"The legend," her voice dropped to a whisper.

"Catherine, it's just that—a legend," Maggie said.

But Sister Catherine would not be silenced.

"The legend of the Weeping Woman, the Seneca Indian who haunts our property." The nun glanced left to right. "Apparently, the Wyndham family ignored legends about this land when they purchased it to build St. Bartholomew's Academy back in the 1800s. During construction, a few unexplained accidents occurred, but the first Bartholomew Wyndham was undeterred. One worker was killed when the scaffolding he was standing on unexpectedly collapsed. Another was crushed when a huge log being carried by chains suspended from a wagon swayed out of control, slipped off the chains, and pinned him against the pilings—"

"Catherine, that is all myth and conjecture," one of the other women interrupted.

"Still, sightings continue to this day." Her wide-eyed gaze returned to Jesse. "People still report seeing ghostly figures on our property at night. And some see eerie lights in the woods."

Like a glowing light watching a dummy in the road?

"And some hear things..."

"Hear things? What kind of things?" Jesse broke in. She felt like a colony of ants had just invaded her skin.

"Oh, sounds like drums beating or some kind of singing—more like chanting."

Jesse took in a sharp breath as her eyes met Maggie's.

"Holy Jesus," she murmured.

"Amen!" said Sister Catherine.

CHAPTER SEVEN

"Joe, I know what I heard," Jesse said.

"Maybe one of the custodians was working in the basement and had a radio on."

"It was no kind of music I've heard on the radio. It gave me the willies." Jesse poured a little water into the simmering tomato sauce. Jim and Susan were joining them for dinner.

Joe chopped vegetables for the salad while Jesse added spices to the sauce.

"The legend of the Seneca ghost freaked me out. What Sister Catherine described sounded just like what I was hearing."

"Maybe the Weeping Woman is moving into the basement for the winter. Nights are starting to get cold outside," Joe said.

The humor in his eyes lessened her irritation, but she maintained a straight face. "Laugh if you like, Joe Riley, but I know how it felt listening to those sounds. And I trust my intuition."

He shrugged, smiling. "Your intuition was right on with Helen's ghost, that's for sure. So, what if St. Bart's is haunted? Are you going to quit your job?"

Jesse blinked. She raised her eyebrows. "I hadn't thought that far ahead. If there were a dangerous ghoul roaming St. Bart's and killing people, I would have heard about that by now. Everyone there seems hale and hearty, so I guess whatever, or whoever, is making these sounds is harmless." She shivered. "Somebody just walked over my grave."

"What?" Joe frowned at her.

"You know, when you feel a sudden chill, it means that someone just walked over your grave."

"But you're not dead, Jesse."

"I know. It means someone just walked over where your grave will be someday." She paused. "Come to think of it, that is a pretty weird saying, isn't it? Especially when what we're talking about is already so creepy." She shivered again.

Joe wrapped her in his arms. Jesse relished his warmth, but she remembered his words about involvement with the Wyndham family. And, like it or not, she was a Wyndham. Her head felt like Medusa with snakes of complications writhing around her.

"Are you cold, Just Jesse? Do you need some warming up?" He kissed the top of her head.

"Hello, you two—we're here!" Susan's voice rang out from the front hall.

Jesse jumped back and straightened her hair.

Joe waggled his eyebrows at her. "Hey, Mom, we're in here."

Susan and Jim entered the kitchen, and Susan took in the scene. She paused. "Are we early?"

"No, not at all." Jesse gave each of them a hug.

Joe took the pie from his mother, setting it on the counter while Jim placed the wine bottle on the table. She saw Jim wink at Susan. A romance appeared to be blossoming between them, much to her delight—her adoptive father and Joe's mother were made for each other—although Jim and Sue's bond did complicate her own relationship with Joe.

Hearing the sauce bubble over, Jesse returned to the stove. Overwhelmed with emotion, she stalled by adding spices and tasting the sauce before she turned around to join the lively conversation behind her. She heard the front door slam.

"I was driving by and I smelled pasta!" Marty's deep voice rang from the hall.

"Come on in," Jesse yelled back, grabbing an extra plate.

"Your timing is perfect, man," Joe said as he slid his chair over to make room for Marty.

"How's everybody doin'?" He shook hands with Jim and hugged Susan and Jesse. Patting Joe's shoulder, he plopped down beside him.

"Jesse's been telling me about the hauntings at St. Bart's," Joe said.

"They are legendary. Something to do with a Seneca woman protecting sacred burial grounds," Susan said. "Apparently apparitions have been seen on the campus for years."

Jim nodded. "This area is thick with ghost legends, and many are Iroquois tribal stories. We've studied some of them in my literature classes at Hobart."

Joe looked at Jesse, and she knew he was wondering if she would mention the sounds she had heard at St. Bart's yesterday. Her shoulders rose with a deep sigh. She'd jump in. When she had told them about her home being haunted, none of them had mocked her. They were open to paranormal experiences, and hers certainly convinced them of the reality of those kinds of occurrences.

"I heard some strange noises while I was working in my classroom. No one else was in the building—except when Maggie came in to pick something up, so she was there briefly—otherwise, I was alone. Anyway, first I heard a drum beat, rhythmic and repetitive. It was joined by chanting. I tried to locate the source, and it seemed to be coming from the basement. I don't have a key to that door, so I couldn't explore any farther. Later at dinner, Sister Catherine mentioned the hauntings and the legend."

"Hey, I told you before, my grandmother had 'the sight,' and I witnessed a 'visit' once." Marty's voice dropped. "My grandmother told me they came to her because she was sympathetic, maybe even empathic, to them. She said they choose special people who have the gift, and once they find you, other spirits will come, too." His eyes, usually filled with humor, darkened. "Like it or not, you may have the gift." He shifted in the chair. His voice lightened. "I believe in that stuff, but this sounds pretty ordinary. Maybe you're still affected by what happened here in your house. I'll look into it, *bella*."

"Thanks. I wonder why Maggie never mentioned the ghostly appearances at St. Bart's?"

"Maybe she thought you'd had enough ghosts in your life with Helen," Joe said.

Susan nodded. "That's true. Discovering you'd moved into a house that was haunted was pretty overwhelming. Since St. Bart's ghost is a legend and apparently no one currently residing there has seen a ghost, she probably never thought to mention it."

"Until now. Until I heard weird music. That would have been a good time."

"Ask her next time you're together. I don't think she was holding out on you or trying to hide anything," Joe said.

"You're right. Mags is my best friend. We've always been honest with each other." Jesse stirred the sauce. "Jim, do you know if the local library keeps archived newspapers, or would I need to drive to Albany? How about any local books or sources that would have more information about these Indian legends?"

"Yes, the Geneva library has public records, archived newspapers, books on local history. Maybe St. Bart's even has records you could study."

"Good ideas, thanks."

"I have some news," Joe said. "I've been approached by a man named Trevor Underwood about submitting a bid to Digson Energy Corporation. Apparently, they are investigating the possibility of building a power plant in Geneva. When he called, he said he's impressed with my company and thinks we'd work together well."

Everyone spoke at once, congratulating him. Everyone except Jesse. Trevor Underwood said they hadn't decided on Geneva as the site yet. Why would he ask Joe to submit a bid? Noticing Joe's frown, she rallied.

"That's great, Joe. I met Trevor Underwood at Wyndham Manor the night of the party with the board."

He sat back. "I see."

"He seemed nice. I'll bet it would be great to work with him," she said with more enthusiasm than she felt. She reached for his hand and squeezed it.

"Another reason to celebrate! Now, where is the corkscrew, Jesse? Time to crack open this Merlot." Jim laughed as she pointed to a drawer. He retrieved the corkscrew while Joe got out wineglasses. Jim poured a healthy serving into each glass and held his up.

"To a new chapter in Jesse's life. English teacher par excellence! And to a new ventre for Joe!"

"To Jesse and Joe," Susan said.

"*Salud!*" Marty said. clinking his glass against the others.

"To Just Jesse!" Joe winked at her and smiled.

Jesse warmed at her friends' caring. But underneath that serenity lurked disquiet and foreboding.

⌘

"Miss Graham, why does Hamlet hate his mother so much?" Valerie Bauer's brow creased with her question. She twirled a lock of her long, brown hair.

"What makes you think Hamlet hates his mother?" Jesse asked.

"He says mean things about her like, 'Frailty, thy name is woman,' and he thinks she was fooling around with Claudius before his father died—maybe she even helped kill him."

"He was lucky to have a mother." Becky Newhart's voice was soft. She seemed startled when everyone turned to look at her, as if she hadn't realized she'd spoken aloud. Her brown eyes glistened.

No one spoke. Jesse noticed Adrianna Rutherford stir in her seat, lowering her head so her blonde hair hid her face. Maybe it had something to do with Adrianna's losing her mother to cancer when she was only five years old.

Pushing a lock of brown hair behind one ear, Becky continued. "I don't think Gertrude helped kill the king. I think she doesn't know what else to do but marry Hamlet's uncle, Claudius. Sometimes in life you don't have many choices, so you do what seems best at the time. Mothers aren't cruel; they love their children." Her voice cracked.

"Don't be silly, Becky. Not all mothers love their children. Some are cruel, or at least somewhat cold," Eleanor McHenry said.

Like Eileen Graham. The woman had criticized Jesse for her looks, her career decision, and for her relationship with Robert. In fact, when Jesse broke off the engagement with him, Eileen said she wasn't surprised he cheated because "What could Robert possibly see in you anyway?" Judging by Becky's emotional condition, her experience of her mother had been the opposite.

"Mothers do the best they can," Valerie piped up. "Sometimes they may not give us everything we want, but they love us and want what's best for us."

Becky nodded, chewing her bottom lip.

Madeline Stewart lounged in her desk, examining her crimson fingernails. "Mothers can be a pain in the..." She glanced at Jesse and continued to examine her nails.

"Mothers can be a pain."

It wasn't just looks that had made Jesse mix up Madeline and Adrianna at the beginning of the year. Both had arrogant attitudes. But as she glanced now at Adrianna, the girl seemed subdued, inanimate as stone, her head still bent.

"Shakespeare seems to keep many issues ambiguous in *Hamlet*. How does he feel about his mother? Why doesn't he check behind the curtain before stabbing Polonius? Ghosts, murder, secrets…"

"I don't like secrets." Becky seemed to swallow the last word. Her gaze flicked to the other girls. Adrianna sat straight up as several other girls shifted in their seats.

The dummy in the road. What did these girls know about that?

"I mean in literature…secrets in literature. Shakespeare should just say what he means…" Becky stuttered.

Adrianna relaxed. Becky locked her eyes on her desk.

Jesse made note of the atmosphere of the room. Teenage girls came up with strange traditions in a public school where they were together for a few hours. She couldn't begin to imagine what might be happening with girls who lived together. Cliques, hazing, shifting friendships, popularity clubs. She remembered those practices all too clearly from her own high school years. Not to mention raging hormones. The dormitory must be quite a cesspool of cruelty at times. She brought the discussion back to schoolwork.

"Okay, ladies, for homework tonight I want you to write a paragraph explaining what you believe about Gertrude. Was she involved in the king's murder? Cite lines from the play to defend your position." The bell rang. "See you tomorrow."

Adrianna was up and out the door before anyone else. Jesse noticed that her eyes were rimmed with red.

∞

Arnie was wiping down tables in the lunchroom when Jesse found him. His brown-haired, brown-eyed Becky must resemble her mother since Arnie's hair was jet black, his eyes gray. Clean-shaven and well groomed, he looked more like a businessman than most custodians she had worked with over the years. Even his bearing was different—straight posture, alert intelligent eyes, and a quick wit. In the few conversations she'd had with him, he'd used puns and references that indicated a well-educated man. His work was meticulous but not particularly efficient. Sensing her eyes on him, he turned and smiled.

"How's St. Bart's star English teacher doing today?" he asked. "I have to tell you how much Becky enjoys your English class. She says you actually—how did she say it? Oh, you 'actually listen to us like we have a brain or something.' I guess she finds that unusual." He laughed. "I remember the nuns I had. They were extremely strict, expecting—no, demanding—strict obedience and academic excellence. Until I got to college, of course, when they all turned human—" He cut himself off and returned to wiping the table. "What can I do for you, Jesse?"

"A couple of things. First of all, I'm pleased to hear that Becky likes my class, because there is another student who makes it rather unpleasant for her in there."

He shook his head. "The Rutherford girl. Yes, we've discussed possible solutions as to how to handle that young lady. Becky needs to grow a thick skin, I'm afraid. People with that kind of arrogant attitude usually don't change. All Becky can do is let it roll off her back."

"That's a pretty tall order for a teenage girl."

"That's the only variable she can control in this equation."

Jesse tilted her head, nodding. *Interesting terminology, Arnie.*

"I'll do my best to eliminate derogatory remarks in my class. Becky is a sweet girl. She does seem rather fearful at times. I suppose it's because of Adrianna—who knows what kind of threats she makes when no teachers are around to scold her."

"All I can do is help her deal with cruel people. Thank you for being her advocate in your classroom, Miss Graham." He flashed her a smile. "You said there were a couple of things you wanted to ask me about."

"Yes. I wondered if I could get a key to the basement."

His movements stopped.

"Why would you want that?"

"Last Saturday when I was working in my classroom, I heard some strange noises coming from the basement. At least that's where they seemed to come from. I wanted to go down and investigate, but none of my keys fit the door."

"What kind of sounds? That old boiler will sing a different song every day." Now he was scrubbing the table vigorously.

"I've become pretty familiar with most of the boiler's songs," Jesse said, chuckling. "No, these sounds were a rhythmic beat accompanied by chanting."

His rag stopped in the middle of the table. He turned back to her, his serious eyes belying his smile. "Mice?"

Jesse raised her eyebrows at him.

He tapped his head as if a thought had just occurred to him. "Oh, you know a couple of the guys came in to clean out some old furniture down there in preparation for some electrical upgrades we're having done. I'll bet they had the radio on. Music seems to motivate them."

"Sure. If I'd had a key, I could have reassured myself that day instead of thinking this place is haunted."

Arnie studied her. "I don't have any extra basement keys available, Miss Graham. Besides, now you know what it was."

"Right. Thanks anyway, Arnie. I'd better get back to my classroom." She turned toward the door.

You are lying to me, and I have no idea why.

Jesse paused at the door to Maggie's classroom. A knot had formed in her stomach at the idea of confronting Maggie. She couldn't believe her friend had intentionally deceived her about St. Bart's being haunted—Maggie's honesty was one of her virtues that Jesse most admired. But Jesse needed to know why she never mentioned the legend.

Maggie was helping a student with an algebra problem on the chalkboard.

"Now I get it! Thank you, Sister Angelina!"

"Great, Sarah. That should get you through tonight's homework." Maggie beamed at the girl. Spotting Jesse at the door, she said, "Come in, Miss Graham. Sarah has just experienced an epiphany."

"Congratulations, Sarah. Nothing like a good epiphany," Jesse said as the girl flounced past her, grinning.

Jesse took a seat at the first student desk in the center row. She clasped her hands on the desk as the nuns had taught her.

"What's up, Jess?"

"Mags, why didn't you tell me that St. Bart's is haunted?"

Maggie sighed, sitting back in her chair. Finally, she spoke.

"Honestly, Jess, I never thought about it. Of course I'd heard of the legends when I first moved here, but I never saw or heard anything. I'd forgotten about it until Catherine mentioned it the other night. Remember how freaked out I was at your house that night Helen appeared? When you told me about the sounds you'd heard here at St. Bart's, I never connected it with a ghost. I don't think that way. I like logic and numbers and things that add up. I figured there was a logical explanation. Ghosts aren't logical." She rubbed her forehead. "Jess, I wasn't hiding anything or trying to deceive you, if that's what you think."

The knot in Jesse's stomach relaxed. "Thanks, Maggie. I needed to know. It makes sense now."

Maggie leaned forward, crossing her arms on her desk. "Do you think St. Bart's is haunted? I mean, there are rumors, but I've always thought they were just that—rumors. Surely, there is a logical explanation for what you heard."

Jesse shrugged. "I suppose so." She rose to leave.

"Are you coming to the St. Bartholomew Dressage Schooling Show this Saturday? It's our major autumn festival and includes an art fair. The girls compete in different events throughout the day," Maggie said.

"I don't know. I'm still working on the house. With winter coming, I need to install some insulation and figure out how to keep the wind from blowing through the windows."

"The weather is supposed to be beautiful, and it may be the last nice weekend of the year."

"You sweet talker. Yeah, it would be nice to interact with my students in a more casual setting than the classroom. Okay. I'll come."

"Plus you'll get to watch dreamy Scott Stanton ride a horse." Maggie laughed.

Jesse's eye widened. "I couldn't believe a *nun* said that the other night!"

"Nuns are human, too, Jess."

"Now I can imagine *you* saying that, Miss Sister Angelina. I've always thought you were too naughty to be a Sister of St. Joseph."

"Only when I'm with you, Miss Graham. Usually I'm quite virtuous." Maggie pressed her hands together as if praying and raised her eyes heavenward.

"Don't make me puke," Jesse scoffed.

With her foot, Maggie pushed the trashcan that sat beside her desk over to Jesse. "In the can, please."

Jesse laughed, waving as she left the room.

Hearing a knock on her classroom door, Jesse looked up

to see Becky Newhart standing there. She had been absent for several days, so add the weekend and Jesse hadn't seen her in almost a week. A furrow creased between her eyebrows, her mouth pulled down at the corners. Her uniform hung on her slight frame, the skirt puckered where a belt tightened it at the waist.

"Come in, Becky." Jesse set her pencil on the desk.

"Miss Graham, may I talk to you?"

"Of course."

Becky sat in the front desk. She fidgeted with her hands and avoided Jesse's eyes.

Jesse walked to the student desk across the aisle from the girl and sat in it. "What is it?"

When Becky raised her eyes, Jesse was shocked by how sunken they were. Her cheekbones stuck out, sharp and raw. Jesse stifled a gasp.

"Miss Graham, may I tell you something in confidence?"

"Of course, Are you all right?"

Becky nodded, focused on her fiddling hands. Her fingers were bone-like, the knuckles protruding. "Last night I heard something." She was silent for a while. "I hope you won't think I'm making this up…or that I'm crazy. But I heard girls saying that you had a ghost in your house…"

"Go on." Hopefully, her smile disguised her disquiet. The clock ticked off minutes as Jesse waited for her student to continue.

"I heard a woman singing, and I heard a drum."

Jesse's heartbeat quickened. "Where did you hear this?"

Becky shrugged one shoulder. "We were playing a game." She glanced at her. "It was after 'lights out' and all the others were asleep."

"Who was with you?"

Becky was silent. She shook her head.

"Okay. Where were you?"

"We had gone to the basement of the dormitory. It was

one of our challenges."

"Challenges?"

Becky pulled her lips in as if she'd said too much. "It's a game we play. If you want to be part of the club, you have to pass the challenges."

"A secret club?"

The girl nodded. "I don't like secrets," she whispered.

"So you were in the basement, and you heard the woman and the drum. Did the others hear it, too?"

"No, I was down there alone when I heard it. They brought me down to the basement, turned off the lights, and they all left. My challenge was to stay there all night. I had a flashlight and a blanket. That's all you can have; I had to swear I wouldn't turn on the lights. It was scary down there—all kinds of noises from the furnace and the water pipes. I hate basements."

"I'm with you," Jesse said. "How long were you down there?"

"I don't know. It seemed like hours. We went down around eleven thirty. The others stayed just long enough to do our chant and ritual." She twisted the fabric of her jacket as she spoke. "I wrapped up in my blanket and sat in an old broken chair. I think I fell asleep after a while, and the singing woke me up. The singing and the drum."

"Becky, could the other girls have snuck back down and played a trick on you?" She sat rigidly, hardly breathing. Part of her felt guilty that she questioned Becky's story, just as others had questioned her own. Part of her desperately wanted to confirm that she was not the only one who had heard these sounds.

"At first, that's what I thought. Actually, at first I thought I was dreaming. But when I knew I was awake, I took my flashlight to look for the other girls. I searched the whole basement—nobody else was there. I couldn't figure out where the music was coming from. It seemed to surround me. Everywhere I walked, I could hear it. It got so cold. I was too afraid to stay down there. I ran upstairs and woke Eleanor; she's really hard to wake up. She just mumbled something and fell back to sleep, so I climbed into my bed to warm up."

She looked down at her twisting fingers again. "They say I can't be in the club now. They say I've made all of this up so I didn't have to stay in the basement." Her eyes, so large in her thin face, searched Jesse's. "You believe me, don't you, Miss Graham? I really did hear the woman and the drum. I...I think it's a ghost. That's why I came to you."

"I believe you, Becky. Tell me about this club. What other challenges have you had to do?"

The girl sat quietly for a few moments. "I was sworn to secrecy."

"That was when you were a member, but they kicked you out, didn't they?"

"We swore a secret for life. We even became blood sisters, so our blood runs throughout each other's bodies."

Jesse hid a smile. Oh how she remembered the solemnity of girls' clubs. "If they know your blood runs through their bodies, how can they kick you out? Aren't you a part of them eternally?"

Becky nodded.

She waited.

"If I tell you, will you promise to keep it secret?"

"Becky, I'll be honest with you. I promise to keep it secret unless I see some danger to you or to the other girls. Is that fair?"

"All right. I'll tell you. St. Bartholomew's is haunted by a Seneca Indian woman. She stalks people at night and kills them in revenge for the white settlers who killed off the village that used to be on this property. She strangles them. She cuts out their heart and eats it. Blood runs down from her mouth, and she has a wicked grin. If you look at her, she hypnotizes you so that you can't move. That's when she kills you. Our club, the Sacred Circle, tries to appease her by offering our bravery through challenges. When we meet, we follow the same order: light the fire, though sometimes we have to use a flashlight if we're indoors, say the sacred words of the Circle vow, do a spirit dance. Whoever is due for a challenge takes the Sacred Circle pledge, and we lead her to the place of her challenge."

"Did one of your challenges involve a straw dummy with a blonde wig?" Jesse asked.

"Yes," she whispered. "How did you know? We thought the Weeping Woman took it as an offering."

"No, I took it after I almost ran it over. That was a rather dangerous challenge, don't you think? Leaving a dummy in the middle of the road to cause an accident—or frighten a driver out of her wits?"

Becky frowned at her. "We didn't leave it in the road. We left it in the sacred spot."

"How did it end up in the road?"

She shrugged her shoulders.

"So now you're excommunicated from the Sacred Circle, right?"

"Right."

"So you won't have to worry about any more challenges or needing to spend the night in the basement."

She nodded.

"Is that a bad thing?" Jesse smiled.

The hint of a grin played at Becky's lips. "I guess not." She turned serious. "But they are my friends, as least Eleanor and Valerie are. Valerie is my best friend—like a sister because we look so much alike. Adrianna didn't want me in the club in the first place. I don't know why she hates me."

"I don't think she hates you. I think she's just trying to figure out where she fits in the world."

"I don't know what that means, but if she doesn't hate me,

she sure doesn't want me around. She's the one who came up with my challenge. And she's the one who kicked me out of the Sacred Circle."

"Maybe if you let things settle for a while, they'll let you back in. In the meantime, I'm worried about you, Becky. You look anxious and tired. Is there anything else you want to tell me?"

Becky interlaced her fingers so tightly they turned white.

"Nothing. I guess it's all the weird things that have been happening lately."

"Maybe being out of the circle will calm things down," Jesse suggested.

"Maybe."

"Do any of the nuns know about this club?"

"No! They would dissolve it instantly. Once, when we were talking about ghosts in Sister Alphonse's class, she yelled at us and made us all bless ourselves with holy water. She said she didn't have enough for all of us to drink it, but she hoped the blessing would be enough. But there is a ghost, Miss Graham. People have seen it out in the woods."

"Who has seen it?"

"We have."

Jesse gaped at her.

"You have seen this Weeping Woman?"

"Not up close. We've seen a ghostly light back in the woods. It moves through the trees and disappears."

Yep, their stories continued to align. She patted her student's hand. "You going to be okay?"

Becky gave her a slight smile and nodded.

"You know you can come talk to me any time, right?"

She nodded again. "Thanks, Miss Graham. I feel a little better."

"I'm glad. I'll see you tomorrow."

Feeling strangely unsettled, Jesse watched the girl walk out of the classroom. Becky was hearing the same manifestations. Perhaps they had both seen the ghost. Marty explained why the ghost might choose her. But why had this ghost chosen Becky?

And who had placed the dummy in the road?

CHAPTER EIGHT

The Rolling Stones' "Jumpin' Jack Flash" blared from the jukebox as Jesse and Joe sat in a booth, enjoying the Friday night fish fry at Tony's Diner. Soon all the tables would be pushed to the walls to make room for dancing. In the corner one guy was practicing the Mashed Potato, much to his date's dismay. As usual, it was packed, and friends wandered over to say hello. Jesse was still learning names in Seneca Corners, but many faces were familiar. This had been the site of her first date with Joe, although she still refused to refer to it as such. Maggie teased her about how she defined their date simply as a "sitting-across-from-someone-and-eating" event. But Jesse knew the impact of words, and referring to something as a date took it to a different level.

"Would you like to come out to St. Bart's with me for the dressage schooling show tomorrow? I hear it's a whole fall festival," Jesse said.

Joe cocked his head. "Are you asking me out on a date?"

Could he read her mind? Or was he stalling, looking for a reason to say no? After all, he would be on Wyndham property. *Just keep it light.*

"No. I just asked if you would like to be out at St. Bart's at the same time I am and perhaps we could arrive in the same vehicle."

He winced. "I don't know. You come on a little too strong

for me. I'm not used to you aggressive women's libber types."

Laughing, she rolled her eyes. "Would you like to come along or not?"

He picked at the label on his beer bottle, his silence loud in her ears.

"Never mind. Forget I asked. I guess it will always be like this, even though this isn't a fancy Wyndham social gathering. Geez, it's just a sporting event at my school." She flopped against the booth, crossing her arms.

"I'll come with you."

"Never mind."

He reached for her hand. "I want to come with you."

God, why was this so hard? How could they resolve this barrier?

"Yes, I will go with you tomorrow." He smiled at her.

Her anger subsided, but she was cautious. While she was pleased he would join her, she knew this wasn't the last time a Wyndham event would come between them. She needed to let it go for now.

"I could show you my classroom...and maybe we could listen for any unusual sounds."

"You mean like a student who smuggled in a boy and..."

"No! I mean sounds like drumming or chanting."

Joe scanned the room before he finally spoke.

"You're not going to let this go, are you?"

"Joe, I know what I heard, and what's more important, I know what I *felt*. There's something weird there. Besides, one of my students reported hearing the same sounds in the basement. Don't ask why she was in the basement. I'm sworn to secrecy."

Her eyes held his as he apparently assessed the situation.

"Actually, I'll be hanging around St. Bart's quite a bit now."

Jesse eyed him. "And why is that?"

"I've just been awarded the contract to repair the abandoned east wing of the dormitory. Apparently it was condemned back in the 1940s and hasn't been used since. With the increase in enrollment over the last few years, Sister Therese wants to reclaim it, so Bart Wyndham put it out for bids. I won." He beamed. "I went through it with the building inspector last week, and we determined it sound, provided some structural work was done and electrical and plumbing were updated."

"Between that work and the contract for Digson Energy Company, you will be one busy guy."

He frowned. "I haven't heard any more from Trevor Underwood. He said he'd get back to me by last week. It's almost as if..." He shrugged. "I don't know. It's just strange."

"Maybe he hasn't settled on the location yet," she said.

"What do you mean—location?"

"Where he plans to build the nuclear plant. As I recall, he was looking at Ithaca, Syracuse, and Geneva."

She recognized this expression. Though he was looking at her, his mind was sorting through this information. He grunted. "News to me. Underwood never said other sites were under consideration." He scratched his jawline, shaking his head. "I don't know. It's strange," he repeated. "What I do know is that I will be on St. Bart's campus for the next several weeks, so I will be working right alongside you...a building away and in the basement level."

Gasping, Jesse leaned forward and grabbed his hands. She whispered excitedly, "Joe, you can get me into the basement!"

"No, Just Jesse. I'll have access to the dormitory building, not the academic building."

She slapped the table.

"There has got to be a way..."

"Tomorrow, we'll go to campus and listen for ghosts, okay?"

"It's a start. Thanks, Joe."

∞

People strolled through the stable area and milled around the white tents that housed artists and vendors of all sorts. The dressage schooling show at St. Bartholomew's was the occasion of the year. She and Joe ambled through the rows of tents looking at leather goods, woodcarvings, jewelry, and paintings. While Joe stopped to talk to a woodworker, Jesse strolled to the next tent to examine some woven table runners, hoping to buy a couple of artisan pieces for her home. She picked up one end of a runner in muted earth tones and pulled gently. It resisted.

"You have excellent taste. Miss Graham, isn't it?"

Jesse looked up into Trevor Underwood's smiling face.

"Yes. Hello, Mr. Underwood."

"I see we're both eyeing the same fabric." He held up his end of the same table runner.

Jesse let her corner drop. "Great minds think alike."

"You know, Miss Graham…"

"Please, call me Jesse."

"You know, Jesse, the night we met at Ben's, I got the distinct impression that you disapprove of my proposed nuclear power plant."

"I guess I don't know enough about nuclear power…you know, besides Hiroshima and Nagasaki."

Trevor covered his almost imperceptible wince with a smile.

"I know it seems terrifying, but harnessing that power properly can bring energy to many people at lower cost. I hope you'll attend one of the educational meetings about the company so you'll feel more comfortable, perhaps even come to embrace this new technology."

"Perhaps."

"We'll be holding town hall meetings in all three cities

we are considering."

"So you haven't decided on the location yet? Are you requesting bids in each town?"

"No, it's too early for that. First, we'll settle on the location; after that, we'll open it for bids."

Jesse glanced at Joe standing in the next tent. Something didn't add up.

"In any event, I hope you'll take part in the meetings regardless of which town is selected. I'd like to see you there." Trevor smiled at her. Picking up the woven table runner they had been looking at, he gave it to her. "I defer to you, Jesse." He bowed slightly and moved on.

She put the fabric back on the table and watched Trevor Underwood weave through the stalls, not pausing to look at anything else, not stopping to talk to Joe.

"Hello, Jesse."

She turned to face Scott Stanton's chest. Raising her gaze to his, she was struck by how the blue of the sky intensified the blue of his eyes. He looked dashing in his riding outfit. *Dashing, Graham, really?* His black riding coat emphasized his already broad shoulders. White breeches tucked into tall, black leather riding boots accentuated his long, muscled legs. She tried not to stare, but she could not ignore the effect his appearance had on her. She controlled her voice.

"Hi, Scott. Are the girls ready for competition today?"

His laugh was deep and warm. "I think girls are always ready for competition."

"And what does *that* mean?" She folded her arms and tapped her foot. Who would have thought Scott could be a male chauvinist pig? The media might call the women's lib movement too aggressive, but it often took that tack to change society, so she couldn't afford to let any comment with a potential to offend go unchallenged.

He held up his hands, palms toward her. "No, no, no. I didn't mean that in a bad way. I—"

"You might as well give up right now. You're not going to win this one." Joe's voice came from behind her. He stuck out his hand. "Hi. I'm Joe."

Scott glanced at Jesse's bare left hand. "Oh, I didn't realize… Hi, Joe, I'm Scott. Scott Stanton. I'm the equestrian coach here."

Joe looked him up and down and chuckled. "I sure hope so." He put his hand on the small of Jesse's back.

She shifted away from his touch. She felt like a trophy. If he wasn't willing to support her when she needed him, he shouldn't claim her now.

"Sorry, I didn't know you were standing there, Joe. Scott, this is my *friend,* Joe Riley."

Had she emphasized the word "friend"? She hadn't meant to, but from the look in Joe's eyes and the hint of a grin on Scott's face, she knew she had.

"I'd better get back to the team. The competition begins in just half an hour. Nice to meet you, Joe." The men shook hands. Scott turned and left.

Silence fell between them. Finally, Joe said, "So, that's your equestrian coach."

She stared at a nearby tent, unable to look him in the eye. Her insides felt like a mixer on the bread dough setting— rumbling around and pulling in different directions. What was it about Scott that threw her off balance? Why did she distance from Joe like that? God, she was a mess.

"He's not *my* equestrian coach, Joe. He's St. Bart's equestrian coach." Her voice was sharp.

"You sure seemed happy to have him around."

Turning, they walked along the outside perimeter of the tents.

"Look, Jesse, I get it. You need your freedom. You say you aren't ready for a relationship. That's okay; I accept where you're at." He stopped and took her by the arm, turning her to face him. "But you obviously aren't done looking. You know how I feel about you. I was hooked the day I saw you bolt from your mouse-infested house, and there's nothing I can do about that. You need to decide whether you don't want a relationship or you don't want a relationship with *me*.

She jolted as if she'd been slapped. Looking into his hazel eyes, she felt a mixture of remorse for hurting him with her words and warmth for this man who had supported her, believed in her.

"Joe, I didn't mean to hurt you…"

"I guess you had to clarify things—for all of us."

"Jesse, there you are!" Ben Wyndham strode up to them, waving hello.

She took a breath, trying to gather herself.

"Hi, Ben. You know Joe Riley, don't you?"

"Yes, of course. Joe has done work for me out at the estate, and now I hear you've won the contract to update St. Bart's dormitory." Ben shook his hand but immediately turned to Jesse.

Joe put his hands in his pockets.

"Jesse, I hope you will help me give out ribbons today at the closing ceremony. Since you are the—"

"Sure." She could have bit her tongue. While she didn't want to hand out ribbons, she did not want to hear about being the heir again…ever. Out of the corner of her eye, she saw Joe back off a little more. *Geez, can this day get any worse?* She had a thought. "But isn't Al here? He could help you."

"Al was here for a while, but he left." Ben shrugged. "He's been distant lately. Not sure why."

Oh, yes, you are.

She sighed. "I'm not all that comfortable doing things like that, Ben."

He patted her shoulder. "You'd better get comfortable. After all, you—"

"Yeah, I know." She stole a glance at Joe. He was staring out at the arena.

∞

Though Joe sat beside her as they watched the girls compete in the third level event, he kept space between them, not holding her hand as usual. Jesse tried to ignore the sick feeling in her gut, knowing she had hurt him, and instead tried to concentrate on Adrianna as she walked her horse from the entrance to the center of the arena. The girl saluted the judge in front of her, then began her test. She was impressed by the girl's posture in the saddle, seamlessly riding through each phase. As much as Adrianna was a pain in the classroom, she was skilled in handling a horse. Jesse applauded heartily when she finished.

She held her breath as Becky entered the arena next, following the same routine as Adrianna. Where had Becky learned to ride so skillfully? A janitor's daughter would have little opportunity to compete in a sport that was so expensive. She was either an extremely quick learner, or she had been training for years to be able to compete in the third level.

Stealing a glance at Joe, she saw that he stared straight ahead, but she knew he was paying little attention to the event. Leaning against him, she whispered, "Want to go ghost hunting?"

He shifted away a bit, then nodded in assent.

Rain-laden clouds formed a backdrop behind the academic building. In less than an hour, all of the festival-goers would be sprinting for shelter. Jesse loved October when the sun etched bright red and gold leaves against a clear blue sky, with stormy slate-gray clouds looming in the distance. *Kind of a metaphor for life.*

As they walked, she reached over and took Joe's hand and squeezed it. He didn't respond but studied the ground as they walked.

"I'm sorry that your feelings are hurt, Joe. But this is something we need to work out."

He was silent for a few moments. He stopped and turned toward her, dropping her hand.

"You've made it clear that you're not ready for a relationship. I get that. But apparently you're ready to keep all options open. I guess I hadn't figured on that."

"Joe. I..."

She ran her hands through her thick curls.

He looked away. "Scott is good looking, I guess. I don't know what women want. Anyway, if you want to see where things will go with him, I've got no hold on you." He brushed his hands through his hair. "But I can't hang around and watch it, Jesse. That would hurt too much."

"I know," she whispered as he walked away.

CHAPTER NINE

By the time she joined Ben to present awards, clouds hovered ominously above them threatening a downpour that would cause a mass exit. She glanced toward the cars that choked the circular drive, leaving little room for escape. If needed, the ambulance poised at the dressage area could squeeze through in the event of an emergency, but that was about all.

Jesse shifted from foot to foot, hating every minute of standing in front of a large audience. She was fine in front of a classroom of students, sharing her passion for literature and writing, but this was more like a performance. Feeling the gaze of so many people on her, she kept her eyes down.

Ben, however, seemed to love this sort of thing. He spoke easily to the crowd, praising the students for their abilities and their conduct. He waxed eloquent on the joy of competition and respect and how this day represented the best of both. She just wanted to return to her seat. Finally, he began the presentations. Ben shook the students' hands and presented the ribbons; she gave each her score sheet. When Adrianna came up, she smiled sweetly at Ben, cooing, "Thank you, Mr. Wyndham." She made no eye contact with Jesse and snatched the score sheet, saying nothing.

Occasional drops of rain spit on the crowd, but in good spirits, the spectators stayed in their seats for the ceremony.

In the distance, thunder rumbled, heralding the oncoming storm. Casting an eye to the west, Ben sped up the proceedings. A fine drizzle began, and he good-naturedly opened an umbrella to keep the ribbons and score sheets dry.

Becky Newhart stepped forward just as thunder resounded close by. Ben smiled at the girl warmly as he shook her hand. Jesse spotted Arnie in the stands, grinning broadly. As she handed Becky her sheet, a loud report echoed. Jesse felt something sting her temple. Another shot rang out. Grabbing Becky, she dropped to the dirt, shielding the girl.

Chaos ensued as people lunged to the ground, jumped from the bleachers, or ran screaming from their seats, bumping into each other. A woman running in high heels slipped and fell. Her husband lifted her into his arms and ran toward their car with their daughter. Jesse heard the mother cry out, "My God! What's happening?" Others were scrambling to hide beneath the bleachers. It looked like a Keystone Kops movie she had once seen.

As if on cue, the rain teemed. Jesse cowered as bits of mud spit up from the ground, landing on her face. Becky whimpered beside her, and she patted her back, whispering, "Stay down."

Her blood pulsed through her body, throbbing at her temples. What should she do? Stay down covering Becky? But they were so exposed. The nearest place to hide was the stands, and that would require sprinting out in the open. She didn't know if Becky was hurt—hell, she didn't know if *she* was hurt. Staying low where they were seemed like the best option, but it didn't make her body shake any less. Her vision, though, was clear.

Men were racing toward their vehicles, but a pursuit by car would be impossible with the congested driveway. Looking up, she saw Scott spring to his horse and gallop toward the woods. The sound of a motorcycle roared off in the distance amid the cries of fear, and a bike with a helmeted rider dressed in black burst out of the woods and swerved onto the driveway, snaking between the cars. Scott was in pursuit, but his horse could not catch up with the motorcycle as he chased it down the drive.

Ben shouted orders to the men who had immediately surrounded him at the sound of the gunshot. He ordered some of them to Jesse's side, while the others hustled him toward the buildings.

Arnie was helping Becky to sit up. His gaze darted around the arena as he pulled his daughter to his chest and rocked her. Stroking her hair, he kept repeating, "No, no, no. Not again," as his haunted eyes searched for the sniper. Becky was ashen, trembling with shock. She didn't speak.

Jesse felt hands helping her sit up, and Joe's voice was soft in her ear. Joe was here? She thought he'd left.

"Jesse, are you all right? Jesse? Jesse?"

Warm arms cradled her, and she felt his hands brush back her hair. The intensity of his feelings exposed on his face stunned her. Scared her.

"Yes, I'm fine, Joe." Blood stained his fingers on the hand that had just brushed back her hair. Shaking, she reached up and touched her temple. Wet warmth trickled down it; pulling her hand back, she saw that it was bloody, too.

Sister Catherine crouched beside her, and she could have sworn she saw the nun tuck a pistol into the pocket of her habit. "Are you all right, Jesse? Where were you hit?" Though she was still in shock, Jesse noted how expertly the nun checked her.

"I'm fine. Is Becky okay?" She saw Arnie's jaw twitching, rage smoldering in his eyes.

As if waking from a trance, he turned and looked at her, jolted out of his thoughts.

"My God, Miss Graham. Are you all right?" He reached over to her, grasping her hand. "Thank you. Thank you for" — his voice caught— "protecting my daughter."

Jesse nodded, exhausted. She leaned back against Joe, who stroked her hair. The ambulance driver appeared with a first aid kit. Sister Catherine waved him off and began dabbing alcohol on the wound.

"Ow!" She pulled away.

The nun was relentless, swiping vigorously as Jesse protested.

"Sit still, Jesse. It's only a flesh wound, but we need to sterilize it."

Scott returned and dismounted. He sped to Arnie's side, speaking softly while he quickly checked Becky for injuries. Satisfied, he moved to kneel beside Jesse. She saw him look at Sister Catherine, imperceptibly shaking his head. The nun nodded slightly, and all the while Arnie watched the exchange. Jesse had a queasy feeling her wound was a secondary concern. Something more was behind this shooting.

Leaning forward, Scott took Jesse's hand. "How are you feeling?" His voice was tender, but his tone changed as he took control of the scene. At his look, two of the maintenance men hastened over.

"Find the bullet. Figure out the trajectory," he directed the first. To the other, he said, "Search the woods. See what you can find." Both men nodded and hurried off.

He turned to Jesse. "We need to get you inside."

Lifting her from Joe's arms, he carried her toward the convent.

"I'm fine. Put me down. I can walk."

Over Scott's shoulder, she watched Joe walk toward his truck.

Jesse lay propped on pillows on the couch in the convent's parlor. Maggie sat on the floor beside her, holding her hand, studying her face.

"Mags, I'm all right, honestly."

"I know." Maggie's voice quavered.

She squeezed her hand. "I want to thank you for inviting me to the bucolic world of Seneca Corners," she teased. "My life has never been so peaceful."

"I am so sorry that I ever mentioned this job to you! Look at what has happened to you since you arrived..." Her voice broke.

"Sssh. I was only teasing. Honestly, I'm glad I came here because I found so many answers to questions about who I am. I found Jim, I met Susan, and..."

"And Joe," Maggie finished.

"I hurt him today. When I introduced him to..." She stopped when Maggie shook her head slightly.

"How's the patient doing?" Scott came around the couch to perch on the coffee table next to Maggie. His eyes held Jesse's for a moment before he examined the dressing Sister Catherine had applied.

Sister Therese joined them. "I think it best for you to stay with us tonight, Jesse."

"No, I feel fine." As she sat up, her head throbbed, stars dancing before her. She eased back on the pillows, covering her eyes.

"I rest my case. Here, take this for the pain."

Sister Therese gave her a pill and a glass of water. Just rising up to drink launched the pounding in Jesse's head again.

"Lie here for a while and when you're ready, Sister Angelina will help you to your room."

"No need to wait. I'll take her up," Scott said.

"That is highly irregular, Mr. Stanton," the nun said.

"Forgive me, Sister, but so is being shot at. Besides, we have some things to discuss before I leave."

A look passed between them; Jesse was too tired to determine whether it was a power struggle, but she again sensed an underlying secrecy at St. Bart's.

Scott lifted her into his arms. "Sister Angelina, would you show me her room?"

Overcome by dizziness, Jesse breathed deeply to combat nausea. Puking all over Scott would be the perfect ending to a perfect day. She closed her eyes to stem the trembling, resting her head on his shoulder. By the time Scott placed her on the bed, she was almost unconscious. One thought troubled her as she dozed off.

Why hadn't the police arrived yet?

CHAPTER TEN

After listening to her unrelenting begging, Sister Therese finally had agreed to let Jesse go home in the morning if she promised to rest. Clouds smudged the sunrise as Maggie drove her home. With the promise to return and check on her later, Maggie went back to St. Bart's for Mass. Giving into self-pity, Jesse ate a quart of Neapolitan ice cream for lunch, leaving the container on the coffee table. The Sunday newspaper fanned out around her on the couch, sports section and want ads drifting to the floor.

Puffy, red eyes stared back at her when she looked in the mirror over the hall table. Her hair was a mass of uncontrolled curls pinned back on one side where the bandage Sister Catherine had applied was starting to curl away from her skin. She stood here for the third time today, wanting to call Joe and not wanting to call. What could she say? *Sorry I carved your heart out and trampled on it yesterday. Want to come over for a beer and comfort me? I need you but only on my terms.*

She jumped when the phone rang. Heart pounding, she lifted the receiver, hoping for his voice—and dreading it.

"Jesse, how are you feeling?" Concern was evident in Sister Therese's voice.

"Fine. I'm fine, thanks."

"I wanted you to know that Becky Newhart is doing fine, too. As is Arnie."

"That's great. I've been worried about her—"

"No need. She's fine." Sister Therese interrupted. "You were brave out there yesterday, Jesse. Mr. Stan…um…that is, the grounds were searched and there was no sign of the gunman. It was a thorough search. I wanted to reassure you," Sister Therese explained.

Why are you telling me this? What are you not saying?

"What did the police say? How is the investigation going?" she asked.

Silence.

"Sister Therese? Are you there?"

"Yes, sorry. Someone knocked on my door," the nun said. "The investigation will continue, of course. Nothing for you to worry about. The authorities have been notified."

The doorbell rang.

"Now someone is at my door. Can you excuse me for a minute, Sister Therese?"

"Certainly. I was just calling to check on you and let you know that Becky is fine. Will you be up to teaching tomorrow?"

Ah, the real reason for the call.

"Yes, I'm resting today, so I'm sure I'll be fine tomorrow," Jesse replied as the doorbell rang again. She leaned forward toward the table, anxious to end this call, anxious to replace the receiver in its cradle, anxious to see who was at the door.

"Fine. I'll see you in the morning. Good-bye, Jesse."

"Good-bye." *So glad to know that we're all so damn fine.*

She hung up the phone and rushed to the door. Her emotions battled each other: hope that it might be Joe, dread that it might be Joe. But Maggie stood there with a steaming pizza box in her hands.

"C'mon, Jesse. This thing is hot, hot, hot!" She hurried into the living room and eyed the mess as she shoved the newspaper and ice cream carton aside to make room for the pizza. "I see you're having a day."

Jesse looked around and shrugged. "It's better than the day I had yesterday."

Maggie placed her hands on Jesse's shoulders. "You look rough, sweetie."

"Thanks."

"Are you in pain? Do you need to see a doctor? I can't believe they didn't take you to the hospital to have you checked out after what happened." Maggie studied her bandaged head.

"My head is fine, Mags." *Oh, geez, fine again.* "Sister Catherine must have some medical training; she knew exactly what to check for and how to clean and dress my wound. And I think I saw…" She stared into space. *Did the nun actually have a pistol, or did the excitement of the moment put ideas in her head?*

"Saw what, Jess?"

"Never mind. Things were so chaotic. I was probably in shock or something. How long has Sister Catherine been at St. Bart's?"

"She joined our community last spring. She had been teaching upstate, and we needed a biology teacher."

Jesse puffed out a huge sigh as she sat on the sofa. "So did Marty come to take the report after I fell asleep?"

Maggie stared at her, a frown playing across her face. She shook her head.

"No. The police never came yesterday…"

"That's weird. Shouldn't a report be filed? Sister Therese just said there's an investigation."

Maggie pursed her lips. "I should think so. Maybe they'll be by later."

"Have you seen Becky today?"

"Yes, she and Arnie were at Mass this morning. She looked…fragile; Arnie looked worried. I think she'll be all right now, surrounded by friends."

Jesse snorted. "Yeah, as long as Adrianna doesn't get her claws into her. Something's odd about this whole incident."

"Here goes your overactive imagination again." Maggie opened the pizza box. "Have a slice of pepperoni and extra cheese pizza. It's your favorite."

"I'm not hungry."

"I know yesterday was traumatic for you, but you have to eat something besides ice cream."

"This will sound strange and morbidly dramatic, but getting shot is not what's spoiling my appetite."

"What is?"

"I hurt Joe yesterday."

"Here, eat while you tell me about it." Maggie pulled out a slice of pizza, stretching the cheese and plopping it on top of the slice. Putting it on a napkin, she handed it to Jesse.

"I don't know if I can eat anything today."

"You polished off a quart of Sealtest with no problem," Maggie said. "You need to keep up your strength so you can tell me all about what happened with Joe."

So between bites she related the encounter emphasizing how she introduced Joe to Scott. It felt good to just let it all out to the friend who never judged her, freeing to be honest about her confusion.

Maggie listened without interrupting, nodding and murmuring sympathetic "awws" at times. When Jesse finished, Maggie hugged her. "Your day was worse than I thought. I thought you just got shot."

Jesse smiled through her tears. "You always know the right thing to say, Mags. I don't know what to do. I never wanted to hurt Joe. I care for him, I really do, but…"

"I know. You don't have a mean bone in your body. You haven't had time to put your breakup with Robert behind you, what with everything that's happened since you moved here. Give yourself a break. If you two are meant to be together, you will be."

Jesse nodded. "I guess."

The doorbell rang. The women looked at each other.

"What will I say if it's Joe?" Jesse whispered.

"You'll know what to say, Jess. Trust your instincts," Maggie whispered back at her.

The bell sounded again.

"I'll get it," Maggie said, rising from the couch.

Jesse listened to the voices in the hall.

"Marty!" Maggie's went up an octave. "Hey, how are you? Come on in, we're just having pizza."

"Hi, Maggie. Gosh, I didn't know you were here."

Jesse glanced out the window at the convent's car.

Yes, you did, Marty.

They entered together, both smiling.

"Hey, Jesse—what happened to you?" Marty asked.

"A slight accident. I got shot yesterday."

Marty tossed his hat on the chair and sat beside her. "*You* were the person who got shot? I was off duty yesterday. I didn't even hear about the incident until this morning."

Jesse and Maggie proceeded to tell him about the shooting, each providing details the other didn't know. Marty's brows furrowed with concern.

Finally, Jesse stopped. "Wait, Marty, didn't you read the report on this incident?"

He shook his head. "No. I'm kinda confused about it. During our briefing this morning, the sheriff said it was being handled 'quietly.' That usually means someone big doesn't want a lot of publicity. I figured Ben Wyndham didn't want bad press for the school."

Jesse stared at the floor. "Something's weird about all this. You know what's strange? No one asked me the usual question: 'Who would want to shoot you?'"

Marty nodded. "That's SOP. One of the first questions to be asked. So who would want to shoot you? Sister Alphonse? Did you give a student an F?"

She shook her head, recalling Arnie's face and his whispered words: "*No, no, no. Not again!*"

"I don't think I was the target," she murmured.

Maggie frowned. "Who was?"

"Becky Newhart."

"But why?" Maggie asked.

"Good question. Maybe I can talk to her tomorrow."

"I'll see what I can dig up about any 'unofficial' investigation," Marty said.

"Thanks, Marty. That would be great."

"You look tired, Jess. We should probably let you get some rest." Maggie gathered up the half-empty pizza box, ice cream carton, and scattered newspapers to take them to the kitchen.

Jesse sank into the cushions, exhausted. "Thanks, Mags."

Marty stood to leave. "You take care, *bella*. Sounds like someone has a serious issue with St. Bartholomew's."

Maggie returned and gave Jesse a hug. "See you tomorrow."

"Yeah." She yawned.

Marty gave her a peck on the cheek. "Call if you need anything."

They left together, and through the window, Jesse saw them talking on the front lawn. Marty gestured toward town and Maggie nodded. They got in their cars and drove away.

Drained, she staggered up the stairs to her room, stopping at the top. She glanced at the attic room door, remembering Helen's ghost shimmering beside the armoire.

"I wish you were here to help me with the strange occurrences at St. Bart's," Jesse whispered toward the door.

Climbing into bed, she couldn't shake Joe's face at the festival the previous day. She felt like she was keeping her feelings for Joe in a pressure cooker that was bubbling on the stove. But she was so afraid of being hurt again. The image of Scott Stanton in his riding outfit came to mind; she squeezed her eyes shut to block the image. "Crap. I'm hopeless." She punched the pillow a few times and flopped onto her side. Like a movie, events of the previous day floated through her mind as she drifted off to sleep.

CHAPTER ELEVEN

Rain slashed sideways, pelting Jesse as she sprinted toward the school. Hunkering beneath her umbrella, she tried to protect the papers jutting out the side pocket of her briefcase. The slick steps to the building slowed her progress until she finally reached the massive oak door to pull it open. As she hurried toward her classroom, she collided with someone at the intersection of the main hall. Her bag slipped off her arm, and papers slid across the floor wet with her footprints.

"Oh, crap!" she blurted.

"Sorry, Jesse. Let me help." Scott's deep baritone caught her by surprise.

"Oh—Scott. No, that's okay. I can get this." She'd been too upset to look at whom she'd plowed into. She was relieved it wasn't Sister Alphonse again.

She bent forward to retrieve the papers just as he did, and they bumped heads, the impact near the spot where the bullet had grazed her temple two days earlier.

"Ow!" Jesse straightened, holding her forehead.

"Sorry. Geez, I'm making a great impression this morning."

He gently rubbed her forehead and brushed back a lock of her hair, exposing the smaller bandage that replaced Sister Catherine's. Jesse tingled at his touch. He moved toward her; she stepped back. He laughed.

"My mother always says I'm hard-headed. I guess this is proof. You're going to have a lump there." His gaze moved from her forehead and captured her eyes. More grayish blue today, his eyes riveted her in place.

Holy crap.

Breaking the spell, he bent down and gathered the scattered papers, handing them to her. His hand briefly brushed hers. She shook her head in an attempt to regain her composure.

"Are you all right? I smacked you hard there."

"No, I'm fine. I mean, yes, I'm fine." *Pull it together, Graham.* "What are you doing here?" Her voice was sharp. *Oh that sounded nice. Why not accuse him of being an axe murderer?*

He broke into a dazzling smile.

Jesus help me.

"I was looking for you. Here, let me help you to your classroom." He took her briefcase and umbrella and made a sweeping motion with his arm. "After you, Miss Graham."

When she flipped on the lights to her classroom, the familiar buzzing sound of the fluorescent fixtures welcomed them into the room. Walking to her desk, Jesse gasped. Her large desk calendar had been torn to shreds and scattered about. It looked like the aftermath of a kindergartner's temper tantrum. Who would do such a thing?

"What happened?" His voice was close.

Arms crossed, she paced back and forth in front of the desk.

"I think someone is playing a nasty trick. This is the second time things on my desk have been destroyed. At first, I tried to chalk it up to a clumsy maintenance guy, but this is deliberate. Whoever did this wanted to make sure I know I'm not welcome." Sister Alphonse could easily access her classroom whenever she wished.

Scott set down her bag on a front student desk, then knelt to pick up shreds of the calendar. Jesse joined him. They scooped up the pieces and dumped them in the trashcan.

"Why would anyone do this to you?"

Sitting back on her heels, she crossed her arms. How much could she trust him? She thought back to Sister Alphonse's attack on her after the staff dinner. He had not just randomly appeared but showed up to calm the nun down. Maybe he would understand.

"I think you overheard Sister Alphonse when she insulted me at the convent. She doesn't like me—in fact, she hates me. She has made some threatening remarks, and I could see her pulling something like this."

"I've met all the nuns; they seem nice, even Sister Alphonse. And they're women of God; I mean, c'mon, that's a pretty harsh accusation."

She picked up the last tiny bits of paper and dusted her hands off over the trashcan. Standing, she picked up her briefcase, pulling out the sodden essays. She didn't know how to answer him; her words had made her look cruel. Obviously, he didn't believe her. Turning to him, she avoided his eyes.

"Thanks for your help, Scott. I need to get ready for my first-hour class."

"Look, I didn't mean to say you're lying. I just meant it seems so strange."

"Sure. I get it," She concentrated on laying out the damp papers.

He touched her shoulder. "Hey." He turned her toward him. His eyes burrowed into hers. She looked away, afraid he would see the effect he had on her.

"In answer to your question from a while ago, I came here looking for you. I wanted to make sure you were okay… and invite you to go riding with me."

She glanced up at him. "Riding?"

"You know, horseback riding." He laughed. He seemed aware of his own charm and sex appeal; he was comfortable, sure of himself, and fascinating.

Jesse shuffled the damp papers. She'd been with his type before, and look where it had gotten her.

"I don't know, Scott. I'm pretty busy."

"You work hard, Jesse. I can see it just looking around your classroom." His hand swept across in an arc, indicating the room full of student projects and bulletin boards alive with student work. His gaze returned to her as he placed his hands on her shoulders. "Come riding with me. You need a break. I'll show you the grounds. Just for an afternoon, then you can get back to work."

She wavered between disliking this man and wanting him. What could an afternoon ride hurt? How would Joe feel about it?

Taking silence for consent, Scott beamed at her. "Great. I'll meet you at the stables on Saturday at one o'clock." He squeezed her shoulders.

Two of Jesse's first-hour students walked in the room and giggled.

Lordy. She hadn't agreed with this plan; he just assumed she wanted to join him on this ride. Now, with students in the room, she couldn't exactly debate him. He had a way of forcing his wishes on her.

"I'll see you Saturday, Miss Graham." He winked at her.

The girls walked to their desks, whispering behind their hands, glancing at Jesse.

Oh great. She rubbed the knot on her forehead.

Scott Stanton led two horses from the stables. One was a spirited chestnut Thoroughbred measuring about sixteen hands. On Scott's other side, a graceful gray Arabian mare pranced out; its arched neck and high tail gave it a regal look. Jesse winced. She hadn't ridden a horse since freshman year of college ten years earlier. She prayed she wouldn't break her neck.

"Jesse, I'd like you to meet Misty," Scott nodded toward the Arabian, "and Jack." The Thoroughbred tossed its head as if in acknowledgement.

Jesse approached the horses. "How do you do, Misty?" she asked, stroking the mare's forehead. The horse nuzzled her arm in return.

"Looks like you've already made a friend." He moved to help her mount, but she swung into the saddle herself. Chuckling, Scott swung up on Jack's back, the leather squeaking in a soft, easy sound. "Let's explore the grounds, shall we?" He clicked to the horses and both moved off toward the trees.

He followed a path that led into the woods. Sunlight filtered through the russet and golden leaves as birdsong floated from the trees. Pine needles muted the hoofbeats as they trotted along. Jesse followed Scott since the path was too narrow to ride side by side. The woods were thick, and though she tried, Jesse could not see far into them. After a while, they came to a bluff above Seneca Lake. Scott reined Jack in, and Misty dutifully stopped beside them.

Dismounting, Scott tethered his horse to a nearby tree branch and turned to help Jesse down. She had already alit. He grinned at her.

"You like to do things for yourself, I see," he said.

"I do." She said as she tethered her horse.

"There's a path along the bluff that we can take." He nodded toward the ridge.

Jesse hesitated looking along the path he indicated. Why should she trust him in this deserted area? Yet her gut told her he was no threat. He might be egotistical, but he wasn't dangerous. At least not in the conventional sense.

They walked in silence for a while. Though Jesse enjoyed his company, being with him lacked the ease she felt with Joe. She pressed her lips together; they hadn't spoken since she had introduced him to Scott. Stealing a glance at the man beside her, she had to admit he was gorgeous. She pressed her lips together again. *And you're not ready for a relationship, remember?*

"So how do you like teaching at St. Bart's?" he finally asked.

"I like it here. Sister Therese has been especially accommodating, She's been under a lot of pressure this week after the shooting at the dressage event. Somehow she's calmed parents' fears about the safety of their daughters. I haven't heard anything about the outcome—did they find the sniper? Sister told me last week there was an ongoing investigation."

He shrugged. "If that's what Sister said, I'm sure it's true. So what else do you like about teaching here?"

She noticed how quickly he changed the subject.

"I like the curriculum, and I'm excited about teaching the girls."

Scott looked out at the lake. "Yeah, the girls."

"That was a rather cryptic remark, Mr. Stanton."

"Some of these girls are really nice, you know? But some of them are pretty spoiled."

"I've found that out already. I had an incident with Adrianna Rutherford on day one."

"Ouch. Her daddy's a bigwig. One of the biggest. How did that turn out?"

She pursed her lips. "Oh great. He yelled at me and wanted me fired." She frowned at him. "Actually, you were there when it happened."

Scott stopped. "But he didn't get his way like he usually does when he throws his weight around." He'd sidestepped her comment. "I know you're a Wyndham and all of this," he spread his arms, "belongs to you."

"Not to me. To the Wyndhams."

"But you *are* a Wyndham. In fact, the heir. But I don't

think you need the Wyndham name to save you. I think you know how to get out of difficult situations on your own."

"What do you mean?"

Scott stooped to retie his shoe…which wasn't untied.

"What do you mean?" she repeated.

He straightened, glancing at her. "Just that you seem very resourceful…"

"No. You have a specific event in mind. What do you know about me being in difficult situations?"

"If you were in danger, say. Or if you were being threatened or suspected of…something…"

"Example."

"Say, something happened and you were there, and say it looked suspicious…"

Jesse grabbed his arm to get his full attention. He didn't meet her eyes.

"You already know this, don't you?" she asked.

He glanced at her. "Know what?"

She pulled his arm, forcing him to look at her.

"You know all about me. Why the game, Scott?" she demanded.

He grimaced, glancing at the lake again.

"Yeah, I know about you. I guess I wanted you to tell me so that…

"Oh, you wanted to hear it from the horse's mouth? Pun intended." Her voice was low with displeasure. "I don't like games, Scott. I'm an up-front kind of person. Let's head back."

"Wait. What I meant is that I wanted *you* to know you told me. So you wouldn't think I was spying on you."

"Why would I think that?"

"Look, I like you. I like talking to you and being with you. I wanted to find out about you in the normal way— not secondhand, like gossip."

She turned and walked back toward the horses.

"Jesse, wait." Scott hurried after her. He took her arm, swinging her to face him.

"Look, I was a jerk to play that game. I promise from now on to be absolutely truthful. Cross my heart." He made an X across his chest.

She studied him, trying to gauge his sincerity. Finally, she had enough. If this was about truth, she'd give him truth.

"Okay, so we'll be honest. I don't trust men who think their good looks will give them a pass on honesty. Somebody always ends up hurt, and it's never them."

She continued down the trail.

Catching up to her, he said, "Jesse, listen."

She folded her arms and tapped her foot.

"Sister Therese told me about your background. Everything that happened with Helen Cavanaugh's murder, Eileen's murder, and you questioned as the suspect—the whole deal. I pretended not to know because I believed it was yours to tell however you liked. I wanted to hear *your* story about you, not somebody else's version. That's the truth."

His blue eyes bored into hers, seemingly begging her to believe him. She softened. Why would he lie to her? Surely, he couldn't look her in the eye like this and lie at the same time.

"Fine. Okay, fine," she relented, and his shoulders relaxed.

He raised his right hand. "I promise—no more dishonesty."

She shrugged. "Okay. I believe you."

"Come on; let's ride farther on," Scott said, heading back toward the horses.

She mounted her horse and followed him along the trail, his comment about Sister Therese echoing in her ears. Why was the principal revealing her background to Scott? Wasn't there some ethical rule that ensured the privacy of faculty members? Although, since most were nuns, maybe they didn't enjoy the protection she did. Maybe Sister Therese wasn't used to dealing with lay teachers who had more personal rights and freedoms. Maybe she needed to be more guarded around Sister Therese.

Riding alongside the ridge, they followed the lakeshore for a couple of miles, doubling back toward the campus. If Jesse had her bearings right, they had only seen a small portion of the property. She nudged her horse toward a trail that led into the woods.

"Let's ride through the trees. The leaves are so pretty."

"No, it's better to continue back along the lake," Scott said.

But there was something pulling her toward the woods, something insistent. "Couldn't we just ride back in there a little way?"

Scott tugged on his horse's reins, directing Jack back along the shoreline. "We'll go back this way." His voice held a command more than a suggestion. She filed his reluctance in her "things to ponder later" folder.

She pricked up her ears, certain that she heard a distant drumming.

"Scott, listen."

He reined in his horse and stopped.

"Did you hear that?"

He looked at her, puzzled. "What?"

Jesse shook her head. "Nothing."

They continued on. She heard it again, coming from the direction she'd wanted to ride. Scott didn't look back. She checked over her shoulder but saw nothing unusual. The sound faded as they rode away. All was quiet save for the chattering of a squirrel.

Their horses lolled along the path, Misty following Jack at a leisurely pace. Jesse was lost in thought when Scott halted.

"I didn't mean to sound like a drill sergeant back there, but there's a lot of marshy land in that area. I wouldn't want the horses to have a misstep or anything." He flashed a dazzling smile.

Not going to work, Scott. I know there's more to this than you are telling me. So much for honesty. She smiled back with as much charm as she could muster, considering she was being lied to. "That's cool, Scott."

They returned to the stables in silence except for an occasional comment on the beautiful scenery. She couldn't wait to be finished. Scott was just like Robert. Beautiful and deceitful all at the same time. Part of her was terribly disappointed; part of her was incredibly relieved.

Arriving at the stables, she quickly dismounted before Scott could offer any help. She led Misty into her stall and began to remove her saddle.

"Here, let me help you with that," Scott said, his breath brushing her hair.

"I can get it," she protested.

"Did I offend you?" Scott's eyebrows furrowed.

"You promised to be honest with me, and I think you were lying to me again—about the marshy property. Sorry, I just can't stand deceit." She yanked the saddle off the horse and removed the blanket beneath it. Pushing past him, she slung the saddle over the railing of Misty's stall.

"Why do you think I'm lying about that? Have you been in that area of the property?" His voice was curt and defensive.

"No," she admitted.

"Then why call me a liar?"

"I get a feeling in my gut things don't ring true. I wanted to see that part of the woods. Why not just show me and not go in where it's marshy?"

"Ride with me again. Soon. I will show you whatever part of the property you want to see. We'll ride all over the place, okay?" His voice was sincere, so why did she doubt him? She was projecting Robert's infidelity on him just because he was good-looking.

She lifted one corner of her mouth in a half smile. "All right. I'll go riding with you again."

"Great! You can ride lead; I'll follow so you'll know I'm not leading you astray. No pun intended."

They laughed.

"I'm sorry I was so harsh, Scott. I'm still working through some stuff from…from before."

"I'll help you get over it." He moved toward her, reaching for her shoulders. His height blocked the sun streaming in the open door, his shadow falling over her. She felt caged in. Gentle neighing and the soft sounds of horses shifting in their stalls hovered in the space between them. His eyes were mesmerizing; she had to force herself to look away.

"Thanks for the ride. I'll see you around." She backed away.

"We'll ride again soon. Very soon." Scott smiled and turned to finish grooming the horses.

∞

After school on Monday, Maggie stopped in the classroom to visit.

"So how was the riding lesson with Scott?"

Jesse made a face at her. "It wasn't a riding lesson. It was a…just a ride."

Maggie tilted her head. "And?"

"Sister Catherine is right; he is dreamy. But it was weird." She didn't leave anything out, including their disagreement, as she recounted the afternoon for Maggie. She shrugged her shoulders. "Why, Mags? Why? First I like being around him, then I can't stand him. I am so confused."

"I'm certainly no expert, but I can see why you would be confused. You seem to be attracted to Joe—more than attracted. And you two are so good together."

"I know. I like being with Joe, but it irritated me when he came up to claim me in front of Scott."

"Is that what he did? 'Claim' you?"

She shrugged. "Okay, maybe 'claimed' is too strong. But that's kind of how it felt to me. Oh, God, I'm so confused."

"You can't have it both ways. You need to give Joe some slack, too. Don't treat him like a yo-yo."

"But I've made it clear that I'm not ready for a relationship."

"Then you'd better be ready to set him free. You can't hang on to him while you're out seeing if Mr. Dreamy is right for you. You say you don't want dishonesty, so you'd better start being honest with yourself."

"That's pretty harsh, Mags."

"What do you want, platitudes or honesty? We've known each other too long for you to expect me to sugarcoat things. You need to shit or get off the pot."

Sister Alphonse passed the door at that moment. The nun stopped, stomped into the room, and pushed her face into Jesse's.

"Now you have a decent nun using language fit for a sailor! Your presence here is not only disruptive and unprofessional; it is infecting our sisters!" Her face was red with rage. "Sister Angelina, you'd best see Father Stephen for confession this evening. Why, I can't believe such profanity from a Sister of St. Joseph!" The nun turned back to Jesse, shaking a finger in her face. "You need to leave here. The sooner the better." She leaned in toward her. "And I don't care how that is accomplished! You corrupt everything around you," she hissed. Turning on her heel, she swept out of the room.

"That was the perfect ending to an uncomfortable conversation," Jesse said as she dropped her head in her hands.

Maggie patted her back. "Don't listen to Sister Sunshine.

She always has something mean to say to someone. I didn't intend to be mean or hurtful, Jess. You know how much I care about you, and I don't want to see you hurt."

"Or Joe," Jesse said through her hands.

"Or Joe," Maggie said in a soft voice.

CHAPTER TWELVE

Jesse tossed her purse and briefcase into the back seat of her VW. She glanced at the dormitory as she passed; it looked peaceful with golden light shining from the windows. She chuckled, imagining the drama that actually unfolded in those rooms. Guiding her Beetle along the curved drive, she reached the road and turned right, looking forward to a hot bubble bath and a cold beer. Taillights of a dark car were visible farther up the road, but they sped away. Directly ahead, she saw a bundle lying in the road.

"What the hell? Not again."

Tempted to accelerate and run over this dummy, she let reason prevail and slowed down, stopping right in front of it. Illuminated by the headlights, the rumpled bundle cast an eerie shadow across the road. Once again, strands of hair fanned out against the pavement and a wool blanket wrapped the rest of the figure tightly.

"Okay, enough of this nonsense," Jesse said, kneeling to lift the dummy into her car. She stopped. A small hand lay white against the black pavement. Her heart thudded as her mind grappled to make sense of the scene. Trembling, she folded back a corner of the blanket and gasped.

Valerie Bauer.

"Oh my God, no!" Jesse screamed. "Valerie! Valerie, do you hear me?"

The girl did not move.

Jesse touched her face; it was cool in the damp night, but not cold. Was the girl still alive?

"Valerie, honey, wake up!"

She stirred.

Jesse slid her arms under the girl but stopped. Hadn't she read that moving someone who had been injured could cause more harm. *Oh my God, what should I do?* She couldn't leave the girl here—someone else might run over her. She had to get to a phone. She scanned the area, even though it was a rather futile gesture. No one would be around at this hour. Glancing into the woods, she froze; a soft glow moved through the trees. She had to get Valerie out of here. Now. She had no choice. Forcing down panic, she again started to lift the girl. Headlights appeared from around a bend in the road.

"Oh, thank God!"

She walked to the middle of the road, waving her arms. Was it the same car that had been in front of her a few minutes ago? If so, why hadn't they seen Valerie? This could be the person who had injured Valerie, coming back to finish the job. There was nothing Jesse could do now. She had already been spotted.

The car—actually a truck—slowed and stopped a few feet from where Valerie lay. Out jumped Scott Stanton.

"Jesse? What's up? Are you out of gas? Do you need... Holy shit! What happened?"

"Scott! Thank God you're here!" Trembling, she knelt beside Valerie and stroked her hair. "I don't know what to do. I'm afraid if I move her, I could injure her more."

Scott drew back the wool blanket and expertly examined Valerie's limbs and neck for breaks before gently carrying her to his truck. Jesse opened the passenger door, and Scott placed the girl on the seat. She moaned softly and slumped against the doorframe. Jesse propped her up and gently closed the door, allowing the frame to support her.

"I'll take her. Will you be all right to drive?" Scott asked as he slid behind the wheel. He pulled away.

"Yes. I'll follow you to Geneva General," Jesse called after him.

Still shaking, she climbed into her Bug and turned the key in the ignition. What the hell was happening? Too many strange occurrences lately, and now a student's life was in danger.

Pull yourself together, Graham. You need to get to the hospital.

The taillights of Scott's Chevy were disappearing; he was driving too fast. Straightening her shoulders, Jesse shook her head to clear it while she put the car in first gear. By the time she drove up the road, his truck was nowhere in sight.

"Bert, it's going to be a long night."

Jesse cupped her hand over her nose and mouth as familiar smells of alcohol, antiseptic, and humanity at its neediest invaded her nostrils. She hated hospitals, and recently she'd found herself in them more than she liked. She hurried to the registration desk.

"May I help you?" asked the nurse.

"A young girl was just brought in by my friend. Her name is Valerie Bauer."

The woman checked the charts.

"I don't see anyone registered by that name."

"Perhaps he didn't know her name. My friend. Who brought her in." Jesse sensed the woman's disbelief. She jangled her car keys—Valerie needed help and time was passing. She wanted to shake the woman. She steadied her voice. "The girl was wrapped in a blanket. The man was handsome, extremely handsome…"

The woman's eyes narrowed as she studied Jesse. She gestured to the waiting room where a couple hovered over their toddler.

"It's been an extraordinarily quiet night, miss. If a man had arrived with a girl wrapped in a blanket, I would have noticed."

Jesse glanced toward the hall where the examining rooms were. "Maybe he rushed by you. Maybe you were on the phone or in the bathroom." She panicked and dashed toward the hallway.

"You can't go down there, miss. Miss! Stop!" The nurse's voice trailed behind her.

"Valerie? Valerie? Where are you, honey?" She swept into a room where a doctor was listening to a man's heartbeat. The startled men gaped at her. She ran to the next room, where a woman was hooked up to an EKG machine. Her eyes bugged out at the sight of Jesse.

"Oh, sorry. Hope I didn't make things worse for you," she said, ducking back out of the room.

By now the nurse and a security guard were running toward her. Jesse halted. The guard grabbed her arm and thrust her against the wall.

"What the hell do you think you're doing, lady?" he growled.

"Please, help me. One of my students was injured. My friend—a guy I know—brought her to the hospital, but she's not here." Jesse's voice was rising with her panic.

"Settle down, lady. No man brought any student here tonight. You can't just wander around here, busting in on people. I could have you arrested for disorderly conduct."

"Please, you've got to believe me. Is there another hospital close by? Or a clinic?"

"There's a VA hospital over in Canandaigua," he said.

"That wouldn't make sense. Geneva is much closer. Surely he would have arrived before I did—he was speeding. Oh my God, what if he got in an accident on the way here? But I would have seen it…"

Jesse couldn't still her shaking. The woman led her into a room and eased her into a chair. She slipped out of the room as the guard entered.

"Let me get this straight. You witnessed an accident, didn't call the police, and the victim disappeared?" The security guard pushed his hat back on his head and rubbed his forehead.

"I don't know if it was an accident. She was lying in the road when I drove up. I don't know how she got there. Scott came along, and he put her in his truck to bring her here. At least, I thought this is where he was taking her."

"So some guy you know abducted this girl?"

Jesse took a deep breath, fighting down panic. "I don't know what happened."

The nurse returned with a cup of coffee and wrapped Jesse's unsteady hands around it. "Drink this, honey. It will help."

Jesse sipped the dark liquid, grateful for its warmth coating her throat. She nodded her thanks. Her head throbbed as she tried to make sense of this. Scott should have been here by now. Valerie needed medical care. Where were they?

A thought stuck her. "Could he have taken her to the front entrance? Maybe they're in the wrong part of the hospital." She grasped at the wisp of hope, but hope crumbled at the nurse's sympathetic look.

"Honey, they would have brought them here by now. Listen, is there someone I can call to come get you?"

She shook her head. "No. I'm fine." She set the cup on the metal table beside her and stood. "Do you have something I can write on?"

The woman reached for a prescription pad on the counter. Jesse quickly wrote down her name and phone number.

"Please. If they show up—call me." Her voice shook.

"Sure, honey. I'll call you right away." The woman glanced at the guard.

Jesse left the bright lights of the emergency room and stepped out into the darkness. Where were Scott and Valerie? Was Valerie all right? She climbed into her car and started the engine. The ER parking lot was empty save for three cars.

Probably the couple with the sick baby, the sick guy, and the woman whose heart monitor will show a spike where I burst into her room.

She pulled out onto the road and glanced in her rearview mirror. A dark sedan pulled out from the shadow of a large tree and turned its lights on, slowly exiting the parking lot. Jesse's skin prickled. It reminded her of the car that had chased her and forced her off the road three months earlier. That had been Helen's murderer, who was now in jail. This was déjà vu. Should she report this to Marty or whoever was on duty tonight? Geneva Hospital wasn't exactly in his jurisdiction, but police were police, right? Plus, pulling into a police station might scare this guy off.

As she'd guessed, when she pulled into the Seneca Corners police station, the black sedan did a U-turn and sped off down the road. Jesse let out a sigh, realizing she'd been holding her breath for a while. She took the steps two at a time and burst into the building. It was eerily quiet compared to the last time she'd been here. No phones were jangling, no bustle of movement or buzz of conversation. Just one cop sitting in the spotlight of a desk lamp, filling out a report. His eyebrows shot up when she entered.

"Is Marty D'Amato on duty tonight?"

"No." He was a rookie, it appeared, by his youthful looks and new uniform. That's probably why he pulled this shift. He stood to address her. "Can I help you, ma'am?"

"I'm looking for my student…that is, a girl."

He pursed his mouth to the side. He probably got all the crackpots at night.

She struggled to gather her thoughts. Deep breath.

Explain clearly.

"I found my student unconscious on the road. Another teacher took her to the hospital for treatment, but he didn't. That is, they weren't at the hospital when I arrived."

"Do you want to file a missing person report?"

"No. I just don't know where he took her."

"He? Do you think she was abducted?"

"No! I just can't find her." Her limbs began to shake. Every minute wasted could mean serious consequences for Valerie. How could she make this cop understand when *she* didn't even understand what was going on?

"Unless you want to file a report, ma'am, there's nothing I can do for you." He spread his hands out, indicating his powerlessness.

"Oh, my God, this is a nightmare." She slumped into a chair.

He sat and pulled out a form. "If you want to file a report, I can send out an APB on this guy. What kind of car was he driving?"

Car. She remembered the car.

"A car followed me from the hospital."

"What was the license plate and make?"

She felt like she would burst. She scrubbed her head.

"I don't know. I was driving. It was dark."

He squinted at her. "So you don't want to file a missing person report on a student you've lost, and you want me to find a mysterious car that you can't describe?"

She shot up. "Never mind. Obviously you can't help me." She strode to the door, slamming it behind her.

She swiped hot tears off her cheeks. Frustration rumbled in her stomach as she clenched the steering wheel. The only choice she had was to return to St. Bartholomew's on the chance Valerie had been treated elsewhere and Scott had brought her back to the school.

When she turned off Route 5 & 20, Jesse searched for signs of the black sedan. Seeing nothing unusual, she exhaled, shrugged, and rolled her shoulders trying to relax. Perhaps it had been an innocent occurrence after all. Her fingers were pasted to the steering wheel. She uncurled them one by one, stretching them out to regain circulation.

She drove south until she reached the driveway into St. Bartholomew's. Pulling up to the convent door, she ran up the steps, rang the bell, and waited. On her first visit, the "Pange Lingua" chiming amused her. Tonight, it seemed to mock her terror. No one answered. She tried the bell again, but still no one appeared. Grabbing the door handle, she wiggled it frantically, but the door was locked.

"Please," she whispered, "please answer the door."

She tried the bell one more time. Shoulders slumped, she returned to her car. She hit the steering wheel in frustration. *Damn!* Her only choice was to drive home and call Maggie. Facing the convent, she peered into the property. Far off behind the dormitory a soft glow emanated from the woods.

∞

Racing through the front door, Jesse didn't bother to turn on the hall light. By the soft glow of the nightlight on the hall table, she dialed the phone number to the convent.

"Come on, somebody pick up the phone." Jesse paced as far as the phone cord would let her in the dimly lit room. "C'mon—answer!" The ringing echoed back to her as she counted nine; at last a sleepy voice spoke.

"Hello?"

"This is Jesse Graham. To whom am I speaking?"

The voice grew cold. "What do you mean calling here at this late hour? Decent people are in bed asleep at this time."

She recognized the nasally voice. "I'm sorry to disturb

you, Sister Alphonse, but this is urgent. Earlier this evening I found Valerie Bauer unconscious and lying in the road. Is she with you?

"What are you babbling about? You're not making any sense."

Jesse took a deep breath. "As I was leaving St. Bart's this evening, I found Valerie Bauer lying in the road, unconscious. Scott Stanton drove up and helped me with her. He put her in his truck, and I thought he was taking her to the hospital, but they weren't there when I arrived." Her voice rose in desperation. "I don't know where Valerie is…"

"Stop this nonsense. Are you hallucinating? I know all you young people are taking drugs like LSD. Lord knows what will happen to our country."

A click, and the line went dead. Hearing an engine, she peeked out the front window. The dark sedan was edging down her road with just its parking lights on. Her stomach flipped. So it hadn't been an innocent occurrence. He had been following her. Her fingers trembled so, she couldn't work the lock for a moment. She fought the urge to run upstairs, run anywhere away from here. Moving away from the dim light, she leaned back against the window and peered out. She held her breath as the car crept forward. It slowed and stopped in front of her house for a moment, then quietly eased back down the road. Reaching the main road, the driver turned on the headlights and sped east on the highway.

She slid to the floor, blowing out her breath. She tried to calm her pounding heart, and wiped the sweat from her forehead. Images from the night bounced around like popcorn in her brain, all of the voices a cacophony in her mind. Who was in that car? And most important, where was Valerie?

Closing her eyes, the image of Valerie lying on the road was emblazoned across her vision. She concentrated on what had happened, trying to sort fact from conjecture, because she was making a lot of guesses tonight. Exhausted, she dozed off, her last thought the sound of Becky Newhart saying, "I don't like secrets."

CHAPTER THIRTEEN

Jesse grimaced as she threw her purse over her shoulder. Her body ached from spending the night on her front hall floor. She'd wanted to be near the phone in case someone called with news of Valerie. Though she had slept, her dreams were more like nightmares inhabited by discordant voices and angry faces…and a dark sedan. A sliver of light glowed along the horizon heralding the sunrise as she hurried in to the academic building. As she had hoped, the light was on in Sister Therese's office. She paused at the door. How to start this conversation? Would Sister Therese already have knowledge of last night's events? She knocked.

"Enter."

The nun was poring over a ledger and finished writing her entry before looking up.

"Good gracious, Jesse. Are you all right?"

She collapsed into the chair across from the nun.

"Sister Therese, last night I found—"

"I know. Valerie Bauer. Mr. Stanton explained everything to me. Thank God you came upon her before anyone ran over the child."

Jesse's mind buzzed. "You already know about this?"

"Yes, Mr. Stanton brought her to me. She awoke in his truck and seemed fine, so he brought her back here. Apparently, some girls were experimenting with drugs, and things got out of hand. Mr. Bauer arrived early this morning to take his daughter home to recuperate. We will have a surprise inspection in about fifteen minutes to search for drugs in the students' rooms."

This wasn't making sense.

"I called the convent last night. Sister Alphonse didn't mention anything about this."

Sister Therese smiled. "Sister Alphonse is one of our earliest retirers. She's usually in bed before the supper dishes are done."

If that were so, why didn't someone else answer the phone? Where was everyone else? Her eyebrows narrowed as her brain worked through the nun's explanation.

As if reading her mind, Sister Therese said, "The rest of us were in the chapel for evening prayer." She rose. "I must see to the inspection. Will you be all right to teach today, Jesse?"

She was startled out of her reverie. "What? Oh, yes. I'll be fine." She rose to leave. "Thank you for your time, Sister Therese." She sensed the woman's eyes burning through her as she left the office.

Jesse felt an undercurrent of tension as her students took their final test on *Hamlet*, and she surreptitiously watched each girl as she worked. Adrianna and Eleanor peeked at one another a few times. Jesse would normally cough or walk over to them to prevent cheating, but they weren't mouthing answers. They were exchanging furtive glances that seemed to have nothing to do with the test. Besides, they would probably get the highest scores anyway. Those two always did. No, their glances were nervous and, she guessed, related to the previous night's events. Since the test required the whole hour, the girls could not talk to one another.

Too bad. Gossip would be flying around these walls, and maybe I could learn something about what happened to Valerie.

Five minutes before the bell, Adrianna sauntered up and dropped her test face down in the bin. Her eyes slid up to meet Jesse's; she smirked and returned to her seat. She laid her head on her desk, her blonde hair fanning out around her, reminding Jesse of the night she found the dummy. Becky was the next to turn in her test. Her eyes were pleading, frightened. She had to remain silent, but she cast her eyes down to her test and back to Jesse. Yes, something was scrawled on the back of the test. Taking it from the girl, Jesse tucked it face down under Adrianna's and winked at Becky. The girl nodded imperceptibly and returned to her seat.

"Two minutes left, ladies," Jesse announced.

Several girls gasped; some of them would be hard-pressed to finish. Eleanor approached the desk intentionally keeping her back to the class. She caught Jesse's gaze and refused to blink, widening and narrowing her eyes like Shere Khan. Clearly, Eleanor had something to say. Changing her mind, or remembering the silence-during-a-test rule, she placed her test face down and walked back to her seat. She flopped down and stared out the window.

The bell rang, and frenzied girls squealed, running up to hand in their tests. When they had all left, Jesse dug to the bottom of the pile and pulled out Becky's. Scribbled across the blank last page was "I don't like secrets."

"Jim, none of this makes any sense at all." Jesse placed the stewpot on the table in front of her adoptive father.

He was the only person she could turn to with this information. Marty had already risked enough helping her solve Helen's murder, and Joe—asking Joe for help seemed heartless given where things stood right now. She hadn't seen Maggie and wasn't even sure her friend could help.

"What time did you discover the girl?" Jim asked.

"I left school around nine o'clock. It was dark, and when I first saw Valerie, I thought she was another dummy. My God, Jim, I actually thought about running her over because it ticked me off so much. What if I had?" Her gulp was audible. She shook her head, trying to erase that image.

Jim patted her hand. "But you didn't, Jesse. What else happened? Tell me everything, even if it seems unimportant."

"Valerie was unconscious. She was wrapped in a St. Bartholomew's wool blanket like the dummy had been. I didn't know what to do!" She spread her hands out. "I couldn't just leave her there, but I didn't want to injure her more. Just as I was about to try to carry her to my car, Scott Stanton arrived in his truck."

"What direction did he come from?" Jim asked.

"The same as me—from St. Bart's."

"Okay, what else?"

"He examined her, almost like a doctor would. He checked along her arm and leg bones and checked her neck and spine carefully. He lifted her into his truck and said he'd take her to the hospital."

"Did he say that? Did he say, 'I'll take her to the hospital'?"

"No…he never said 'to the hospital.' He just said, 'I'll take her.' Oh my God, Jim. Where did he take her? I followed his truck—at least the direction he took—but I never caught up to him."

"Could he have turned off somewhere? Or turned around and headed back to St. Bartholomew's?"

The road she had driven that night was a secondary one leading to Route 14. He could have easily reached Route 14 before she caught up with him. Or did he turn off well before that? Was there a back entrance to St. Bart's that she didn't know about?

"He must have turned off somewhere. I would have seen

him pass me if he'd backtracked. At least I think I would have noticed—I was pretty freaked out. Wouldn't he have honked to let me know as he passed me?"

Jim shrugged. "Whatever he did, he didn't let you know about it. Take me back driving on the road. Did you notice any other cars around? Anything unusual along the shoulder?"

"There was another car. I saw taillights about a quarter of a mile ahead of me just before I saw Valerie in the road."

"Taillights? Heading in the same direction you were? Wouldn't they have noticed Valerie?"

Jesse nodded. "That thought struck me, but I was so concerned about her, I forgot about it until now. They would've had to pass Valerie, but how without running over her?" Her eyes grew wide. "Jim, they must have left her there. Left her in the road, unconscious. She could have been killed." Pounding the table, she stood. As she paced the room, she waved her arms and shouted, "She could have been killed! And if I hadn't had the presence of mind to stop, I could have killed her."

When she passed his chair, Jim caught her hand and stopped her.

"But you didn't. And apparently she is all right, safe at home." He pulled her back into her seat, patting her hand. "What else? Any other details you can remember?"

"As I was trying to decide what to do about Valerie, I glanced up and saw a light moving through the woods. It was just as I was about to lift her. That's when I saw the glow of...something. It wasn't a strong light like a flashlight. More like a lantern."

"Didn't Scott's truck arrive at that moment? Could it have been his headlights reflecting off something?" Jim asked.

"No, he was coming from behind me; this light was off to the right."

"A house?"

"No, it's just woods there. Actually, it's still St. Bart's property. I've never walked the whole acreage. It probably has nothing to do with what happened to Valerie, but, you know, it's the second time I've seen a glow of light on the property."

"What next? Scott came and took Valerie…" Jim encouraged her.

"Yes, and I followed him—at least, I thought I followed him—to Geneva General Hospital."

Jim ran a hand across his chin. She offered him more stew, but he waved her off.

"Oh, and there was a car."

Jim raised one eyebrow. "On the road where this happened?"

"No. At the hospital. As I was leaving the parking lot, a dark sedan—black, I think—I hadn't even noticed pulled out behind me and followed me until I pulled into the police station. And it came back later, right after Sister Alphonse hung up on me. With only its parking lights on, it crawled down the road, stopped in front of my house, and drove away."

He frowned. "How do you feel about that?"

"I can't deny that it brings back scary memories of being forced off the road or of someone trying to break into my house to kill me." She shook her head. "But if they wanted to do that, why drive away? In fact, how do they even know who I am and where I live? This is pretty spooky, Jim."

"You know you're welcome to come stay at my house if you like."

She set her jaw and pursed her lips. "If a ghost couldn't drive me away, this phantom driver won't either."

He chuckled. "I thought not. So Sister Therese said Scott simply returned to St. Bartholomew's with the girl?"

"Yeah. Pretty much. None of it makes sense. Something is fishy."

"And it might be best if you left it all alone. I'm sure the sisters have only the best intentions for their students."

She rose from the table and went into the living room where she'd left her briefcase. Returning, she pulled out a paper and handed it to him. It was Becky's *Hamlet* test. He read the back page aloud. "I hate secrets."

"That's the second time she's said that. Once aloud in class, where she was hushed by some other students, and now on her test."

"It sounds like the girls are doing what students do— create secretive clubs, send coded messages, include and exclude members. Typical teenage shenanigans."

Jesse shook her head. "I get a more desperate sense from her. It's not something I can put my finger on—it's a gut reaction. This girl is troubled."

"Do you think she knows what led up to Valerie's being left in the road?"

"Mmm. Yeah, I do. And I think she's scared."

The doorbell interrupted their discussion.

Jesse flinched when she opened the door.

"Scott?" Her voice stuck in her throat and she cleared it. "What are you doing here?"

"Hi, Jesse. I just wanted to see how you were doing after last night's little escapade."

"Little escapade? You're kidding, right?" She balled her fists.

A "little escapade" when Valerie could have been killed? Why was Scott really here? And how did he find her address? His eyes studied her as she chewed on her lip, fighting back an expletive. A minute passed before she composed herself. She heard Jim come up behind her.

"Is everything okay, Jesse?"

The two men scrutinized each other, and she felt a surge of pride in Jim's stance of defense against the muscular coach. She smiled to herself. If it ever came down to it, Scott could eat Jim alive.

"Yes, Jim, everything is fine. I'd like you to meet Scott Stanton, the equestrian coach I was telling you about."

Jim raised one eyebrow. "I see."

Scott extended his hand. "How do you do, sir?" Next, he'd salute at the rate this was going.

Maybe now she could get some answers about last night. "Come in. We were just having dinner. Won't you join us?"

"I'd hate to interrupt..."

Jim swept his hand back in welcome. "No interruption. Jesse made enough stew for a small army, and I think she expects me to finish it all. Come help me out."

Scott scanned each room as he walked to the kitchen, as if he were counting the windows and doors. Or doing a perimeter check. Setting another place at the table, she spooned a healthy portion of stew on his plate. His eyes were warm when he smiled at her, and his half grin gave him an impish look. She quickly looked away, catching Jim's fleeting smile.

"Beer, wine, water, or coffee?" Her voice sounded rougher than she intended. She caught Jim stifling another smile; she narrowed her eyes at him. Scott didn't seem to notice.

"A beer would be great. Thanks!"

She set the bottle in front of him with a thud. "Glass?"

He frowned slightly. "No. I'm good."

I'll bet you are. Where the hell did that come from? Crap. Jesse took her seat. *Settle down, woman. He didn't do anything wrong...I don't think.*

"Jesse tells me you helped her out last night." Jim smiled at Scott.

"Yes. Guess I arrived at a good time. That's why I came by today. I wanted to explain what happened." Keeping his gaze on it, he turned his beer bottle in circles while he spoke. "I was heading toward the hospital when Valerie woke up. She was confused and a little scared, but not injured or sick. She's afraid of hospitals and wanted to go back to St. Bart's. I told her she needed to be checked out, but she started bawling and wouldn't stop. Based on the volume of her complaints, I figured she was fine. I pulled down a side road to turn around, which must have been when you passed us. I felt bad when Sister Therese told me how upset you were." He looked up at her.

His story matched Sister Therese's. Exactly. And that made her uneasy.

"Thanks for filling me in, Scott. I spent a pretty restless night wondering where Valerie was and if she were all right. I called the convent, but Sister Alphonse didn't know anything about the incident."

"Oh, we took her to the infirmary. No one else in the convent would have known."

"Just you and Sister Therese." Jesse didn't pose it as a question. "A phone call would have been nice."

Scott shifted in his chair. "Yeah. Sorry, Jesse. I didn't have your number." His eyes sparkled at her. "Maybe we should rectify that right now."

She wanted to explode.

"Let me get this straight, mister. I thought one of my students was badly injured or possibly dead last night, and you came here to get my phone number?" Her voice rang around the room.

"No. I just meant that since it came up in conversation... why not just...man, I'm messing up." Hanging his head, he mumbled, "I'm sorry. I really screwed up. And I seem to keep doing it."

She caught Jim's eye. He shrugged. Her ire abated at Scott's forlorn face. It wasn't his fault Valerie was hurt. He had tried to do the right thing and made decisions as events unfolded. Jesse wouldn't want to be faced with a screaming teenage girl in a car. And being a male faculty member, he had even more to consider in this situation.

"Things have just been so weird lately that I'm on edge."

A thought struck her. "Wait a minute, how did you find my house?"

His face reddened. "Sister Therese gave me your address. I told her I wanted to let you know what happened last night."

"So she gave you my address and not my phone number? Wouldn't it have been easier to just call me and tell me over the phone?"

Jim cleared his throat. "I hate to interrupt, but I told Susan I'd stop by to help her with a leaky sink. She said Joe has been so busy preparing for this new project..."

Jesse's face warmed at the mention of Joe's name; she shifted and brushed imaginary crumbs from her lap. Scott caught her expression and winced.

"Is that your friend Joe I met at the dressage competition?"

She wanted to melt into the floor. She glanced at Jim, then back at Scott.

"Yes, that Joe."

Jim rose. "All right, I'll be going. Sorry to leave you with the cleanup, Jess, but I promised Susan I'd be there by seven."

"I'll help," Scott said.

Jesse's heart sank when Jim caught her eye as he left the room. Why did she feel like this? She wasn't Joe's girl. Hearing Jim close the front door, she turned to Scott.

"No, you don't have to help. I can clean this up lickety-split." *Where the hell did that word come from? I'm losing it.*

"Lickety-split, huh? Haven't heard that since I was a kid." His grin was captivating. He crossed to the sink. "I'll wash since I don't know where things belong." He ran the faucet and plugged the sink.

"No, Scott. I'm sure you have better things to do." Once again, he ignored what she said.

His hands were swishing the water to increase the suds, and she reached in to stop him. She brushed up against his arm and froze. His face was just inches away. She didn't look up at him but backed away and wiped her hands on the dishtowel.

"Let me help. I haven't started off on the right foot tonight; let me redeem myself." His voice, soft and low, washed over her. She nodded. He turned, took the towel from her, and wiped his hands on it. "The truth is, I didn't ask for your phone number because I wanted to see you. You were pretty shaken up last night, and I wanted to see for myself that you are all right. Things happened so fast that it was too late to call you anyway. With a full day of instruction, I couldn't get away until tonight. You've been on my mind all day."

She nodded again. Seldom was she at a loss for words, but his nearness was magnetic; she felt pulled into him. She could feel him moving toward her even before he took a step. He placed a hand on her shoulder and with his other tilted her chin to look up at him. She stood, vulnerable, her mind screaming "No!" and her body saying, "Let's see where this is going."

"I haven't stopped thinking about you since we met at the first faculty meeting." He bent his head and his lips brushed hers. Soft lips pressing gently. She resisted, but he pulled her closer. His kiss became more demanding.

She jerked away. "Scott, no, I can't do this." She moved to the other side of the kitchen table, placing her hand on her heart to stem the pounding. Why did she feel so disloyal?

"Is there someone else? You made it pretty clear that you and Joe were just friends."

That confirmed it. If Scott had heard it that way, Joe certainly had.

"Yes. No. Joe and I…" How to explain to someone else what you didn't understand yourself? "I don't want to get involved with *anyone* right now, Scott. I'm still healing from a breakup—I was engaged." She did not want to rehash the

Robert story again. How could she heal if she kept ripping off the scar?

He nodded. "I get it. So Joe is your transition relationship."

She wanted to slap him. "Joe is *not* my transition relationship! How dare you suggest such a thing!" She quaked, her guilt deepening.

He studied her. "Sorry. Geez, I'm *really* screwing up tonight."

"You certainly are. Maybe you'd better just leave before you say anything else."

"You know, Jesse, I watched you with Valerie last night. I watched how broken up and scared you were, and it only confirmed what I already suspected—you're a deeply sensitive and loving person. I was attracted to you when I first met you because you are so beautiful, but last night I think I fell in love with you because of your compassion. Now I see how right I was—you love deeply. It's good that you're protecting your heart, because it's vulnerable. I'll leave because I don't want to hurt you any more with my thoughtless comments. But, trust me, *you* won't leave *me*."

He walked out of the kitchen, and she heard the front door close. She stood frozen in place.

"Shit."

∞

The next evening, Maggie curled up on Jesse's sofa, cupping her wineglass in her hands.

"Holy Mary, that is so romantic," she sighed.

"Maggie, I need you to tell me what a jerk he is, not that he's some Rhett Butler."

"Oh, sorry. Scott's a jerk. Stay away from him."

"Oh, very effective, Sister Angelina. Honestly, I don't know what to do. Do you think Scott is right? That I'm using Joe as a 'transitional relationship'? I warned Joe that I wasn't ready to be involved, but when he's around, I feel all mushy inside. Oh, God, I sound like one of my students."

"Love can do that to a person."

"I didn't say 'love.' I said 'mushy.'"

Maggie sipped her wine. "So you 'mushy' Joe, but you don't love him, right?"

"Give me a break, Mags." Jesse slumped back against the cushion. "Yeah, I guess so. I don't know how else to describe it. It's just that...he helped me so much when I was in danger that I can't judge how I'd feel in a normal relationship."

"Think about life without Joe. Like, if he totally disappeared from your life—joined a traveling circus or something."

"A traveling circus—now that's an imminent threat. But you're right; I'd hate it if I never saw Joe again." Jesse stared into the crimson wine in her glass, shaken by the truth of her statement. She jumped when the doorbell rang. Looking at Maggie, she put down her wineglass but didn't move.

Maggie raised her eyebrows. "So are you going to answer that, or leave the person standing in the cold night?"

"What if it's Joe? What if it's Scott? Geez," Jesse hissed, running her fingers through her hair.

Maggie imitated her hiss. "Why don't you find out by answering the door?"

Jesse nodded and rose, straightening her hair. She wished she had some makeup on.

Stop!

The doorbell rang again, and someone pounded on it.

"Hey, *bella*, I know you're in there! This is a raid!"

Jesse jolted with relief at the sound of Marty's voice. She flung open the door.

"Hi, Marty! C'mon in!"

"What? Did you need time to stash the drug paraphernalia?" Laughing, he walked into the living room and stopped in his tracks. "Oh, you and the sister dropping a little acid?

Hi, Maggie." Jesse noticed his face flush.

"Beer or wine, officer? I'm afraid we've depleted our supply of LSD."

"Beer for me. Thanks." He sat beside Maggie on the couch. "So what's up with you two troublemakers tonight?"

"We're discussing choices people have to make in their lives." Maggie smiled but stopped speaking after Jesse gave her a look.

Marty became interested in the pattern of the carpet. "Yeah, sometimes there is no choice."

Maggie studied her wineglass.

Jesse cleared her throat and handed Marty a Genesee Beer. She felt like she should go upstairs and clean the bathroom or something. Instead, she shifted the conversation to the strange goings-on at St. Bart's.

"Maggie, were you there when Scott brought Valerie back to the school?"

Maggie shook her head. "No. I was asleep—you know I go to bed early, Jess. Actually, most of us do right after Vespers because we are up at five for Morning Prayer"

Marty looked from one to the other. "What happened?"

Jesse poured more wine into Maggie's glass and then her own. "I stopped by the precinct, but you weren't on duty. The guy on duty wasn't very helpful. It was just like the night of the dummy, only this time it wasn't a dummy in the road. I found one of my students unconscious instead." She related the story, reliving the fear she had faced that night. "It's all so strange, Marty. There's more to this than people are saying. Valerie was unconscious. I can't believe she simply woke up and said, 'Take me back to school, please,' or even more that she had enough strength to throw a fit like Scott said she did."

"Surely, you don't think that Sister Therese lied to you?" Maggie raised one eyebrow.

"I don't know. Suddenly Valerie is whisked off home by

her father? How convenient."

Maggie sat straight up. "But Sister Therese wouldn't lie."

"Settle down, Mags. I'm not accusing Sister Therese of sinning. I just think it's strange. And the students know something about this, too. My seniors were unusually nervous in class during their test yesterday."

"Maybe they were just nervous about the test," Maggie said.

"Yeah, I'm sure that was part of it, but there was more to it." She told them about Becky's scribbled message.

"Your instincts are usually spot-on, Jess. I'll keep my ears open around the convent to see if anyone knows anything."

"Jim suggested it might have to do with typical teenage stuff like clubs, cliques, and cruel girls. He could be right. Maybe it was some kind of initiation ritual."

Marty nodded. "That could explain the dummy and the threat written on the blanket."

"'You're next' might have been meant for Valerie,'" Jesse agreed. "They may be playing with fire. I was so ticked off, I thought about running over what I thought was another dummy." She covered her face with her hands.

"But you didn't, and Valerie is all right now." Maggie's voice was soothing.

Jesse looked up. "Is she? I sure wish I had seen her myself so I could be certain."

"Why would Scott or Sister Therese make that up? And if she were not all right, surely Scott would have taken her to Geneva General. I suspect she'll be back to school in a few days, and you'll see for yourself."

"Maggie's right. If she weren't okay, they would have taken her to the hospital. You worry too much, *bella*." Marty winked at her.

"I guess you're right." She shifted in her seat, unconvinced.

"Hey, I did some investigating of my own into strange

occurrences at St. Bart's—besides panty raids. Oh, sorry, Maggie." Marty's face flushed scarlet.

"Did anything strike you?" Jesse asked, trying to help Marty save face.

"Sure did. The file—the one I never saw—wasn't handled according to normal procedure. Instead of being assigned to an officer, the sheriff took it himself. In fact, what's even stranger is, when I asked him about it, I was told to let it go because it belongs to the Special Investigations Unit."

"But it was some guy in the woods shooting at us. Why is that special? Sounds like some run-of-the-mill weirdo going off the deep end."

Marty shook his head. "As usual, Nancy Drew, you've stumbled into something *un*usual. All I know is I was told 'hands off.' I even spotted the file on the chief's desk, and it was stamped 'Secret.' I've never seen that before—it was kinda cool."

"Fits right in with all the other weird stuff happening there, including unexplained lights in the woods at night."

"That might be the easy part to explain. As I was looking into the archives for anything related to St. Bart's, I came across some spooky stuff."

Jesse's ears perked up.

"Some of the incidents go way back to the 1800s, even before the construction of St. Bart's. Apparently the Seneca in this area held their burial mounds as sacred and promised revenge if they were disturbed. Some of the sites were excavated, and some of the people doing the digging had encounters with ghosts. There were suspicious deaths connected to the excavations, and people traced them back to settlers reneging on their promise to keep the burial grounds intact. One man was strangled, another drowned under suspicious circumstances. St. Bart's happens to be built in that area. There have been sightings of a Seneca woman on the grounds of St. Bart's, sometimes singing and beating a drum."

Jesse looked at Maggie.

"What? You already knew all of this, didn't you?" Marty said.

"I've heard the woman."

He whistled. "They won't leave you alone, will they? The ghosts. Just like my grandmother, once they find someone with 'the sight,' they all start to hang out with you."

Jesse covered her face with her hands again. "Great," she mumbled through her fingers.

Maggie sat forward and patted her knee. She glanced at Marty, frowning. "But Helen's ghost was mild and loving. This ghost sounds dangerous. Jess, you need to be careful."

Jesse nodded at her friend. "Maybe I won't work in my classroom on weekends any more."

CHAPTER FOURTEEN

Jesse worried about Becky Newhart. Though the girl was shy and quiet, she usually took part in class discussions and chatted with other students—in the past, Valerie—before class. But lately, Becky had grown quiet and pensive. Her physical appearance was changing, too. Becky didn't wear makeup, even the modest amount allowed at St. Bart's, so the shadows beneath her eyes were not caused by smudged mascara. Her cheekbones seemed sharper, her face gaunter. With the bulky uniform jackets the girls wore, Jesse couldn't see her arms, but at the base of her throat, her collarbone protruded like two sharp knobs.

Giving the homework assignment just as the bell rang, Jesse added, "Becky, could I please see you for a moment?"

The girl looked up in surprise. "Yes, Miss Graham."

When the others had left, Jesse motioned for her to sit in the student desk directly in front of her own. After closing her classroom door, she took the student desk across from the girl.

"Are you ill?" Jesse asked, her voice soft.

Becky shook her head.

"Have you heard the chanting again? And the drum?"

Although she shook her head again, the girl's bottom lip quivered. Jesse handed her a tissue from the box sitting on the corner of her desk.

"I'm good at keeping secrets, Becky," she said.

The girl's voice was barely a whisper. "I hate secrets."

Jesse waited while Becky stared at her hands folded in her lap. Finally, she looked up.

"Sometimes things move in my room."

Jesse dug her fingernails into her palms, resisting the urge to shudder.

"Once, I put my history book on my dresser before dinner, and when I came back to my room, it was on my bed."

"Who is your roommate?"

"Eleanor McHenry."

"Do you think she might have moved it?"

She shook her head. "I asked her. She said she hadn't touched it."

"Could someone else have come into your room?"

She shrugged. "I suppose so, but everyone was at dinner." Her voice dropped to a whisper. "There was the bead necklace."

"Tell me about that." Jesse smiled at her.

"Last week I found a small bead necklace out by the—outside. I looped it over the post of my bed. The next day, it was on my closet floor. Eleanor said she didn't move it. I placed it back on the post, and when we got back from class, it was on my closet floor again."

Jesse listened in silence.

"Sometimes I wake up in the night and the room is icy cold. It makes me shiver, even though I'm under my blanket."

Jesse's heart lurched.

"Have you seen or heard anything unusual at these times? When it gets so cold?"

"No. I can't sleep well. I wake up so tired."

"I can see why, Becky. Have you told anyone else about this?"

"Just Eleanor. She thinks I'm crazy. She says my mind is

conjuring things up because of the…"

Jesse waited. Becky looked back down at her hands.

"Because of what?"

"Nothing. She just thinks I'm crazy." Becky stood up. "May I have a pass to my sixth hour class?"

Jesse wrote the pass for her. Walking her to the door, she said, "If you ever need to talk some more, just stop by, Becky."

The girl nodded and elbowed her way through the freshmen waiting at the door.

Jesse inhaled the crisp autumn air. The girls' volleyball game had been a squeaker, but they had defeated St. Matthew's Catholic High School to proceed to the final round in the regional tournament. Her breath puffed out in misty wisps, as if trying to join the clouds scudding across the almost-full moon. She hurried to her Beetle, unlocked it, and threw her purse into the back seat. She had left her briefcase at school since it was already past nine and she didn't feel like grading papers when she got home. It was a bubble bath night, and she couldn't wait to be surrounded by hot water and candlelight. As she climbed into her car, she caught a glimpse of a figure running toward the woods. The clouds moved, bathing the grounds in bright moonlight. Seeing the short hair and glasses, she was sure it was Becky's roommate, Eleanor McHenry.

"Now what is she up to?" Jesse mused aloud.

Climbing out of the car, she eased the door closed and followed the girl. Once Eleanor reached the edge of the woods, she slowed to a walk. It was obvious that she knew where she was going. After moving into the trees, she flicked on a flashlight, keeping the beam focused on the ground. Jesse knew instantly that the light she had seen in the woods was not from a flashlight. The beam was too bright, too focused. What she had seen was more of a glow. She glanced around—might she encounter the source of that glow tonight? Nothing. The woods beyond the flashlight beam were murky.

Jesse walked quickly but carefully so as not to snap any twigs beneath her feet. Although it was doubtful Eleanor would even notice, she was so intent on her mission. Fortunately, the moon was bright enough for Jesse to make out the path, but in some places it went uphill or was rocky, so she had to keep one eye on the ground while still tracking the girl. Jesse stumbled, swore quietly, and grabbed a sturdy tree branch to regain her balance. Still Eleanor did not turn around.

Finally, the girl slowed and looked back. Jesse ducked behind a tree. Turning off the path, Eleanor strode through the underbrush along an invisible trail. The trees thickened here, and it was more difficult to remain silent as she walked. Dropping behind, she followed from a distance, her eyes on the beam of the flashlight. It stopped, then disappeared.

Jesse kept her eyes focused on the place where the light was last visible as she crept through the underbrush toward it. *I'm going to end up with a whopping case of poison ivy.* But she continued on until she came to a clearing in which stood a small wooden cabin. Staying at the edge of the trees, she studied the structure. Square windows sat on either side of the rustic door. A paltry wisp of smoke rose from a narrow chimney, and a lean-to holding a scattering of logs was propped against the right side of the cabin. Covering the windows was a thin, torn material—perhaps a paper bag or butcher paper—illuminated by a soft, amber light.

Like a whisper across the night, she heard it. The same drumming and chanting that she had heard in her classroom. Her heart pounded. Creeping up to one of the windows, she peeked into the interior through a rip in the paper.

She gasped. Sitting on the floor in a semi-circle around the fireplace were Eleanor, Adrianna, Madeline, and three other girls who were not her students. Lying beside them was a figure wrapped in a wool blanket, the girl's long, brown hair spread out on the rough wood floor.

Adrianna tapped the drum as the girls chanted. Madeline threw a handful of powder into the fire; it flamed, shooting embers up the chimney. Finishing their chant, Adrianna stood and held her arms out, eyes closed as if in a trance.

"Oh, Weeping Woman, protect us from your wrath. Forgive us our trespasses on the sacred land of your ancestors. We offer you sacrifices to appease you. Keep us safe, Oh Great Woman." She sat down.

Their chanting resumed as the girls swayed with the rhythm of the drum.

Jesse felt a sharp sting in her neck, and the scene before her swayed. Everything went black.

Fuzzy light wavered before her eyes. Jesse felt like she was moving, but something was solid against her back. She squeezed her eyes shut to block the shifting images, but the floating feeling continued. Slowly opening her eyes, she peered at the swimming scene and recognized the interior of her car. Moonlight streamed through the windows, illuminating the dashboard.

How the hell did I end up here?

The swaying feeling subsided, but her head was throbbing. She rubbed her eyes. The girls—were they all right? There was no way she could retrace her steps without Eleanor's guidance. Where was Becky? Should she call Sister Therese and report what she had seen? Glancing at the clock, she was shocked to see it was almost two o'clock in the morning. *What happened to me?* She looked back at the woods as if to find an answer, pressing her fingertips against her temples to try to stem the pounding.

Looking toward the dormitory, she saw a light on in one of the rooms. Adrianna and Madeline were leaning out their window, smoking cigarettes. They were too engaged in conversation to notice her. She watched until they stubbed their cigarettes out on the brick beside the window and ducked back into their room.

Apparently the girls got back safely.

Joe's truck was parked in her driveway when Jesse reached home. Pulling in, she veered onto to the grass so as not to block him in. She assumed he wouldn't be spending the night, though she would have liked to linger on that prospect a bit. He was bundled in his jacket, dozing on her porch chair.

This night just gets crazier and crazier.

He stirred when she closed the car door. Sitting up, he rubbed his eyes, stretched, and yawned. She rubbed her throbbing temples and took a deep breath.

"Joe? Is everything all right?" Still a little dizzy from whatever had knocked her out, she tried to steady herself as she walked up to the porch.

"Hey, Jesse." He yawned again.

"Come on in. You must be freezing."

He followed her in. "I stopped by to tell you about something I found today."

She led him into the living room and sat on the couch. He moved to sit beside her, hesitated, and sat in the chair instead. She felt like the kid who didn't get the pony for Christmas.

"I was working in the east wing of the dormitory at St. Bart's today, and I came across something strange."

The living room clock chimed the half hour. He glanced at it and did a double take. Two-thirty.

"Where have you been?" He raised his hands, shaking his head. "No, it's none of my business."

She gave a wry smile. "I was at school, Joe."

"I see." He looked away. "Listen, sorry I bothered you."

"I was at a volleyball game."

"Must have been a hell of a game—lots of overtime." He stood to leave.

He thought she was with Scott. *Oh, my God*. What could she say that would convince him? The hammering behind her eyes threatened to make her scream. She wanted to scream anyway. Scream, "I was not with Scott. Why can't things be the way they were with us? Don't you know that I…"

Stop.

"Joe, I have to tell you what happened." The pounding in her head was a jackhammer now.

He paused.

"You know, Jesse, I don't think I want to hear the details." He walked out the door.

The clang of the school bell between each class had been like a spike driven into Jesse's skull all day. Aspirin had done nothing to ease the throbbing in her head, which had morphed into a constant, dull ache—except when the bell rang. Then it was a piercing stab. Whatever drug had knocked her out the previous night resulted in monstrous aftereffects.

Her freshmen filed out the door, and she settled in for what she hoped might be a productive prep period. She held her head, trying to still the hammer hitting the anvil inside, but to no avail. Picking up her textbook, she flipped to the page she sought. Despite her pounding head, she was determined to forge on. She was excited about planning a new literary unit on Edgar Allen Poe. Perfect for the gloomy late October weather.

Hearing a knock at the door, she looked up. Scott stood there, no doubt awaiting authorization.

"Hi," she said. The memory of his kiss and her rejection floated between them like a sour note in a choir. *How do you start a conversation after that?*

"Hello."

She waited to see what he would say.

They stared at each other.

"Permission to enter?" he asked.

"Permission granted." She rolled her eyes, but even that hurt her head. She composed her face.

He saluted and came into the room.

"How are you today?"

Jesse peered at him. "Fine. Why do you ask?"

"I was just, you know, making conversation. 'How are you' is a pretty common opening. I guess I could comment on the weather." He stuck his hands in his pockets, strolling around, examining the room. He whistled. "Your classroom is much cooler than what I remember from my school years." He paused in front of a bulletin board covered with student poetry. "This is great. They must feel pretty good when you put their work up like this."

"My favorite way to decorate a room is with student work." *What was this visit about?*

"You love what you do, don't you?"

She nodded.

"Look, I guess I came on too strong when I was at your house."

"Yes. You did."

He shrugged. "I'm sorry. I'd like for things to be okay between us, you know? So we can be around each other without feeling uncomfortable."

He tried to sit in the front student desk, but his height and frame didn't fit. He winced and sat on the desk.

"Sitting on the desk is not permitted in my classroom," she teased.

He smirked as he looked around. "It seems my choices are the floor or your lap. Crap! I didn't mean that the way it sounded. I only meant that was the other choice, not that I wanted to sit on your lap…Shit." He rubbed his hands across his face.

He was usually so sure of himself, but when he slipped up, he turned into an eighth grade boy: awkward and uncomfortable. He didn't seem to be aware of that, which made it even more charming. Damn, she didn't need him to be charming. "Swearing is not allowed in my class, either. So, given a choice of those two places, I'll allow you to sit on the desk."

They laughed.

"Miss Graham?" Adrianna stood at the door, glaring at Scott, fire in her eyes.

"Yes, Adrianna? Did you forget something?"

The girl clenched her jaw as she approached Jesse's desk; her eyes never left Scott. She tossed a paper into the IN bin, ignoring Jesse. "I forgot to turn in my in-class response."

"Then it isn't an in-class response any more, is it?" Jesse asked.

Adrianna's eyes slid away from Scott. "Do you mean I can't get credit for my work? I just forgot to turn it into your stupid bin."

"Unacceptable tone with me, Adrianna. Did you want to spend some more quality time with me after school?"

"Would you please accept my paper late, Miss Graham?" Adrianna's voice was sweet and mocking, her glare, venom.

"I'll accept your late paper with the usual condition. Ten percent off."

"Thank you." The words, laden with sarcasm, slid out of her mouth. Her eyes were again fixed on Scott.

"And we'll discuss this later. Good day, Adrianna."

"Good day, *Miss* Graham." She walked out the door swaying her hips.

"She's a piece of work," Jesse said. She noticed the heightened color in Scott's cheeks. *Good God, does he have a thing for young girls?*

He looked at her intently. "It's not easy being a male instructor at an all-girl school. I'm always glad when there's another teacher around." He glanced at the door. "Some of them get pretty bold."

"Nothing Adrianna might do would surprise me. I feel sorry for her in a way. I think she's just begging for attention."

"That's for sure."

"So why the visit today?" she asked.

His eyes traced the border across the top of the chalkboard. "The faculty has been invited to the annual Harvest Party at Wyndham manor. I figured you would be there, since you're a Wyndham and all, and I wondered if you would allow me to escort you for the evening. I promise I will behave like a perfect gentleman." He avoided her eyes, and she sensed he was bracing for a rejection.

She ought to ask Joe first. *Why? He hates these events.* Plus, last night's encounter left little doubt how he felt about her. Nonetheless, it seemed like she was cheating on him to say yes to Scott.

"Let me think about it, Scott."

His eyebrows shot up. "Really? You'll think about it?"

"Yes. You see…it's complicated."

"Joe?"

"Yes, Joe, but other things, too. Let me sleep on your offer."

"I'd love it if you would sleep on my offer…crap, that didn't sound right. I mean, you know what I mean," he stammered.

Jesse warmed at his fumbling attempt to clarify himself.

"I know. Thanks for the invitation, but I'll have to let you know."

"Great. I'll talk to you tomorrow." He rose, bumping into another desk, straightened it and made his way out of the classroom.

Jesse watched him leave. He was indeed a fine looking man, and his apparent discomfort and desire to make things right with her made him even more attractive. And she sensed trouble brewing about that.

☾☽

Jesse walked the grounds of St. Bartholomew, looking for Joe's work crew. Spotting men gathered around the foundation of the east wing of the dormitory, she headed that way. The sun broke from behind a large, gray cloud, and Joe's red hair lit up like a beacon. He was holding a blueprint while giving his men instructions. Glancing up, he saw her approach and wound up his spiel. The men dispersed.

"Hi, Joe." She tried to sound upbeat, but after their conversation last night, she had to circumvent a lot of pain to do so.

"Hey, Jesse. What's up?"

"Do you have a minute?"

Joe looked over at his crew regrouping nearby. "I'll be back in a few minutes," he called to them.

Jesse's heart sank. Obviously, he was in no mood for deep conversation. They walked along the path that led toward the stables.

"Joe, about last night…"

He turned to her. "You've made your need for 'space' abundantly clear, Jesse. What you do with your life is your own business."

"I wasn't with Scott. That's what you think, isn't it? At least admit it!"

He avoided her eyes.

"Yes, all right? That's what I think."

"I was knocked unconscious. I came to in my car. I don't know what happened. I don't know who did that to me."

"What do you mean, you came to in your car? Where were you?" His eyes narrowed.

"I followed one of my students into the woods. I spotted her as I was leaving the volleyball game. Some weird stuff has been happening to Becky, and I think it's connected to a ritual of some kind that a few of the girls are involved in. Anyway, I followed Eleanor to a cabin and saw the girls chanting around a fire inside. There was a girl wrapped in a blanket just like that dummy, just like Valerie in the road. I think it was Becky. The next thing I knew, it was two a.m. and I was tucked into the seat of my car."

"That's quite a story, Jesse."

"Do you think I'd make up something like that?" She touched his arm. "Please, Joe. You've got to believe me."

One side of his mouth turned up in a half grin. "It's too bizarre to be made up. I believe you. You're right—there's pretty weird stuff going on." He looked at her closely. "You need to be careful, Jess. No more going into strange places alone at night."

"Since you don't want me to go into strange places alone at night, would you consider—"

She was cut off by Scott's greeting from the stable. Startled, she hadn't realized they'd walked this far.

"Hi, Jesse. Oh, hi there, Joe."

The two men shook hands.

"So, Jesse, can I pick you up for the harvest dance this weekend?" Scott asked.

Her heart dropped to her feet. This was the invitation she had just been ready to offer to Joe. If he would even consider attending a function at Wyndham Manor. She turned to him; his eyes were flat and cold.

"No, Scott. That is…"

Joe backed away from her. "I need to get back to my crew." He turned on his heel and walked back down the path. She watched him leave. Well, that couldn't have gone any worse. A hollow spot lodged in her chest, nestling there, reminding her of how much she missed him.

"Ooops. Did I say something wrong? Geez, I'm sorry, Jesse. I thought you were thinking about going to the dance with me."

He knew damn well what he'd done. But it was Joe she was worried about. He was normally so easy-going, but lately he'd become different—judgmental and short-tempered. All she could surmise was that Scott threatened him. There was plenty to be threatened by. Yes, Scott sent her blood pressure up when he was around. Animal magnetism they called it. Hard to ignore even if you've been hurt by someone who also had it. But Joe had something special, too, something that went deeper than just physical chemistry. When she was with him, the world seemed like a better place, and she felt like a better person.

But Joe had jumped to conclusions about her, practically accusing her of being with Scott the previous night. He hadn't even given her a chance to explain. Besides, she knew he wouldn't go to the harvest dance with her. Hadn't he refused to go to the soiree Ben Wyndham had thrown for the faculty and board? He had said he wasn't comfortable in that setting. She kicked at a stone, frustrated. Joe wasn't being fair, nor was he being supportive.

She turned to Scott.

"Yes, I'll go to the harvest dance with you, but I will meet you there."

"I can pick you up," he protested.

"Those are my terms. I'll go with you if we meet there." She folded her arms.

"Okay. I'll meet you there. I'm glad you agreed. Being with you will make the night extra special."

She was tongue-tied for a moment, pulled in by his charm. "Fine," was all she could muster.

She had negotiated a date based on setting her own terms. How romantic.

CHAPTER FIFTEEN

Tugging her auburn hair into braids, Jesse scowled into the mirror. Her agreement to meet Scott at the harvest dance rather than have him pick her up had seemed like a fair compromise. But why did she feel the need to compromise? Joe would have refused her invitation to attend, so it was fine to go with Scott. Tying green ribbons at the end of each braid, she sighed, trying to clear the confusion tumbling within.

She checked her outfit in the full-length mirror of the armoire in her study. Since it was a barn dance, she had selected a pale green blouse with a darker green patterned bandana around her neck. Her blue jeans fit snugly around her waist and hips and flared out into the new bellbottom style hiding most of her cowboy boots. Finally, she donned Helen's leather jacket with its fringe along the sleeves and yoke. The cream-colored leather complemented the green of her blouse and scarf. Satisfied with the results, she took a deep breath, leaning closer to the mirror.

"This is going to be fun, Graham. You're going to have a *great* time," she insisted to her reflection.

When she arrived at the front of the elegant Wyndham manor house, valets were directing traffic toward the stables. Bert bumped along on the grass until reaching the large barn. Lit with lanterns and Christmas lights, the barn was a festive backdrop for the partygoers filing inside. A valet motioned for her to stop at the door.

"I do this to you all the time, don't I, Bert?" She patted the dashboard. "Go have a gas with the Mercedes. Oooh. No pun intended."

The interior of the barn had been transformed into a Hollywood set for the musical *Oklahoma*. Lanterns flickered on tables and serving bars. Hundreds of white Christmas lights draped along the rafters and posts, twisting through bales of hay stacked in various configurations. Tables were scattered throughout the barn in clusters, some tall for standing, some for sitting. The glowing scene mesmerized her.

Perched on a stage erected at the back of the barn, six musicians performed a lively Virginia reel. The fiddler and banjo player were engaged in a spirited competition, each taking his turn with a solo. Dancers lined up, men facing women, forming an aisle. They clapped to the music as a couple met in the center to prance down the middle.

"Hey, Jesse!"

Turning, she saw Scott waving as he approached her. His good looks rivaled Clint Eastwood's in his recent movie *The Good, the Bad, and the Ugly*. He wore a pale blue shirt with navy piping, jeans on slim hips, and cowboy boots polished to an ebony sheen. Brown hair tumbled over his forehead, teasing his crystal-blue eyes. She pasted on a smile, trying not to reveal the effect he had on her.

"You look great! Do you know that your scarf matches your eyes?" he asked.

"Thanks, Scott. You look like a rootin' tootin' cowboy yourself."

He took her hand. "I think we can still get in on this reel." Pulling her along, he placed her at one end of the line and joined the other side. Her body pulsed to the beat of the music—she loved to dance. Clapping, she laughed as someone nudged her into the middle so she could do-si-do with Scott. The song ended, and he put his arm around her shoulder, laughing.

"How about a drink after that workout?" he asked.

She nodded, a bit out of breath.

After getting two beers, Scott chose a table in a corner farthest from the music.

"I'm glad you came with me tonight, Jesse."

"This is a great party, that's for sure."

A waiter came along with tray full of hors d'oeuvres. Scott stacked deviled eggs, cocktail wieners, and skewers of grilled vegetables on a couple of plates, grabbing some utensils and napkins.

Jesse laughed. "You must have worked up an appetite during that Virginia reel."

"I did. Hey, you're a great dancer!" He grinned at her.

"Lessons. I know 'em all." She laughed.

He grabbed her hand and pulled her to the dance floor for a square dance. They took their corners and bowed. She laughed—she actually almost giggled as she released all her worries, even if just for a few hours. How long had it been since she'd felt lighthearted like this? She would embrace it, enjoy it, if only temporarily.

Turning, she was startled when her next partner was her cousin, Al Wyndham. She had seen him with his girl-friend, Barbara, on the other side of the room earlier, but he seemed to be avoiding her. His raised eyebrows indicated that he was equally surprised. She smiled at him, but he merely gave her a cursory nod. Finishing the steps, they continued on to other partners. At the end of the dance, Al took Barbara's hand, leading her to the opposite side of the room from their table. Scott slid his arm around Jesse's waist for a slow dance. It took her a moment to recover from Al's obvious snub, so she kept her head down to hide her sadness. Her forehead lightly rested against Scott's chest, and misinterpreting it, he pulled her in closer. She straightened, maintaining the space between them.

He chuckled, bending his head toward hers. "You are a puzzle."

"Keeping you on your toes, am I?" She forced a smile.

"As long as I'm not on *your* toes, that's the important thing," he said, swinging her into a small dip.

She had to admit that he was pleasant to be with. What would it have been like if Joe had come with her instead? Would he have moped in the corner and refused to dance?

Returning to their table, Scott held her chair as she sat down.

"I'll rustle up some ale to quench our thirst." He tipped his hat and walked off.

"May I join you?"

Trevor Underwood stood at the table holding two beers.

"Of course." She searched the room for Scott. He was in a long line at the bar.

Setting a beer in front of her, Trevor sat in the opposite chair. He raised his glass in a toast. She had no choice but to tap her glass against his.

"Are you enjoying the evening, Miss Graham?"

"Jesse, please."

He nodded.

"Yes, I'm having a great time. And you?"

"Indeed, I am."

"How long will you be in the area, Mr. Underwood? Are you staying in Geneva or one of the other towns in contention?"

"Please, call me Trevor."

She nodded.

"Ben Wyndham—your uncle—has been kind enough to offer me a place to stay. I will be here until we finalize the decision for the location of our power plant. Once that's accomplished, our engineers and designers will arrive to lay out exact plans. After that, the construction will begin."

"The final decision hasn't been made?" Yet, he offered the

job to Joe. "I'd heard differently."

Trevor scanned the room. He smiled at her. "Ah, yes. Well, let's say we haven't *announced* our final decision." Leaning toward her, he winked at her conspiratorially.

Her deceit meter sent a jab to her gut, but she hoped what he was saying was true. Joe would certainly be glad to get started; the Digson project will be quite a boon for his business. "Yes, I know you've met a friend of mine—a *very good* friend—about bidding the job."

"Oh? Who is that?"

"Joe Riley."

But Trevor's attention now was on someone behind her. She didn't have to turn around to know it was Scott, and that he'd heard her emphasis.

Crap.

Trevor stood, holding out his hand. "Hello. I'm Trevor Underwood. You must be Joe Riley."

What? He hadn't even met with Joe in person to talk about the contracted work?

Scott did not offer his hand right away. "I know who you are." His voice was level. Finally, he extended his hand. "Scott Stanton."

Trevor's eyebrows creased, but he quickly recovered. "Oh! Nice to meet you, Scott."

"Trevor is the CEO of Digson Energy Company. He's assessing the best place to locate their new nuclear power plant," Jesse said. She had never seen this side of Scott before; he was cold, almost rude, to Trevor. Not that she particularly cared for the man. Like Howard Rutherford, he lived in the land of power and wealth. Just the way he hovered too close and leaned in too far signaled a need to be in control.

Scott nodded. "So I've heard."

"News travels fast in a small town." Trevor reached for his beer, surrendering his chair to Scott. "Enjoy the evening."

He raised his glass and sauntered away.

Scott stared daggers at him as he walked away, then sat down. His blue eyes were darker than usual, his lips a thin line. His demeanor transformed as he smiled at her. Almost like a chameleon.

"So what are your favorite works to teach?" he asked.

"*To Kill a Mockingbird,* of course. Shakespeare. And I love ancient works like *The Odyessy.*

"'Sing in me, Muse, and through me, tell the story of that man skilled in all ways of contending...'"

She raised her eyebrows. "Impressive, Mr. Stanton."

He grinned. "I've traveled Odysseus's route."

"What?" she exclaimed. "That's my dream. When did you do that?"

"When I was in the navy. I was stationed in Crete at Souda Bay. The Mediterranean is absolutely beautiful. I had the opportunity to sail the route while I was there. Fortunately, I did not meet up with Circe, nor were my men transformed into swine."

She laughed.

"Seriously," he continued. "Odysseus is one of my favorite literary characters. Larger than life, committed to his mission, and stronger than any other man. No one could string his bow. And there's his devoted wife, Penelope, who waited for him all those years, never unfaithful, always believing he'd return..." His voice trailed off.

Jesse felt a twinge of guilt. Apparently loyalty was not her strong suit. She raised her eyes to see Scott watching her.

"C'mon. No more talk about work or mythology." He pulled her up from the chair and on to the dance floor. They joined in another lively reel, and gradually, she let the music and dancing dispel her guilt. They chatted and danced for the next hour until dinner was served.

Waiters circled the crowd, carrying plates loaded with barbecued pork, beans, butternut squash, and roasted potatoes.

"Oh my gosh! I wouldn't have eaten so many appetizers if I had known this was coming," she wailed.

"Don't worry. We'll dance it off." Scott dug into his meal with gusto.

Reluctant to overeat, Jesse sampled the pork and moaned. The tangy barbequed meat was tender and juicy.

"Holy smoke! This is unbelievably good," she said.

She dug into the salty roasted potatoes and sweetened butternut squash spiced with cinnamon and nutmeg. It would take plenty of dancing tonight to work this off.

As guests were dining, Ben Wyndham climbed up the hay bales to the microphone.

"Are you enjoying yourselves?" he shouted.

Hoots and hollers answered his question.

"There's plenty more food, so don't be shy." Clapping and "bravos!" rang out. "How about a hand for Andy and His Band of Rowdies?" More applause and whistles. At a nearby table the band members stood, waving their hats in appreciation. "We here at Wyndham Manor are truly blessed, and it seems fitting at harvest time to celebrate all the good things in our lives." He looked directly at Jesse. "This year especially we have much to be grateful for." He raised his glass to her.

She felt many eyes on her, and her face grew hot. She smiled and looked down at her plate. She did not want to meet Al's eyes.

Ben continued, "Enjoy your evening, and thanks to all of you for coming out tonight."

A burst of applause echoed through the rafters, and the musicians resumed their places on the bales of hay. After tuning their instruments, they jumped into another lively dance. They played continuously through the night, finally announcing the last dance at midnight.

Scott took Jesse's hand and led her to the dance floor. Pulling her to him, he held her close as they swayed to the music. At this moment, in Scott's arms, she yielded to the romance of the twinkling lights, the steel guitar, and the feel of his body against hers. Her defenses were down; she just wanted a little TLC. They moved together, Scott rubbing her back as they danced. Her face rested against his chest, and she closed her eyes, surrendering. He pressed a kiss against the top of her head, and while her mind said, "Pull away," her body remained. She was drowsy and floating and content. The last strains of the music reached its crescendo, and they stopped swaying, still in each other's arms.

"Thanks for a beautiful evening, Jesse."

"Thank you, Joe—I mean Scott!" She pulled away, mortified. "I'm so sorry."

He snorted, stepping back. "Obviously you have some feelings for the man if he's who you're thinking of while dancing with me."

Jesse felt her face flame. "No…I mean, I wasn't thinking of Joe while I was dancing with you. His name just jumped out of my mouth."

Scott held her jacket for her. She was happy to have a reason to turn away from him. Shrugging into it, she kept her head bowed, waiting for the color to disappear from her face. They joined the partygoers spilling out of the barn and walked to her car in silence. She was grateful for the cool night against her blazing cheeks, hoping it would return them to their natural color.

Reaching her car, Scott turned her to face him. "Look, I had a great time tonight. You're interesting and exciting, but I don't want to step in where I don't belong. If you and Joe Riley are together, I get it. I respect that."

How could she explain her confusion to Scott? She had to try. He had been nothing but kind to her. Kind and helpful at a time when she desperately needed help. And maybe explaining it to *him* would clarify for *her*. Lord knows she was confused.

"Joe and I aren't 'together' in the sense you mean. I mean,

we're friends, maybe more than friends. I don't know."
She threw her arms out in frustration. "I'm trying to sort
through all my feelings, Scott."

"So you and Joe aren't a couple?" he asked.

"Noooo. Not really." *Not yet.* "I don't have a definitive
answer for you right at this moment."

Jesse brushed her hand across her eyes as she spoke, so
she didn't see Scott move toward her. She was in his arms,
his lips pressing urgently against hers. Adrenaline electrified
her with the passion of his kiss. She wanted to pull away;
she wanted to stay. She didn't stop him.

As he released her, Scott's gaze bored into hers.

"Then my goal is to make you forget Joe Riley."

CHAPTER SIXTEEN

Arnie pushed a mop into Jesse's classroom, whistling a tune. He jumped when she popped up from behind a desk in the back row.

"Oh! Hi, Miss Graham. I didn't see you in here. I can come back when you're finished."

"Actually, you are just in time. I spilled glitter on the floor back here, and I don't have a broom in my broom closet." Should she mention her concerns about his daughter? But she had promised to keep Becky's conversation in confidence.

He chuckled. "Yours is not a broom closet; it's a coat closet. And I guess a boot closet, a purse closet, and a briefcase closet. Not to mention treats you buy for your students." He winked at her.

She laughed. "You're so astute."

"Let me sweep this up now; I can return to finish later."

"Thanks. And please stay and take your time. You won't bother me."

"Thanks, Miss Graham. I appreciate it."

"Arnie, please call me Jesse. Don't be so formal—I'm not a formal kind of gal."

"I don't know. The sisters prefer to adhere to formal—and rather old-fashioned—standards around here."

"I'm not a sister. Number one, I never wanted to be, and

number two, they wouldn't have me. So let's make a deal. If a nun is around, you can be formal. No nun, informal—just my first name."

"Okay, just Jesse it is."

Hearing Joe's nickname for her was like being hit with a bucket of ice water.

"Everything okay?"

"Yes. Great." She shuffled some papers on her desk.

After Arnie finished sweeping the floor, he left, returning shortly with a pail and rag to wash the desktops. His movements were efficient and precise, with no sign of slacking off or doing a mediocre job.

He didn't strike her as a man whose career would end at head custodian. The way he carried himself, his polished way of speaking, even his physical build, didn't fit the stereotype of a janitor.

"Arnie?"

He looked at her, eyebrows raised.

"How long have you worked at St. Bart's?"

"Almost a year."

"Have you always been a custodian?"

He scrubbed at an unseen spot on the desk.

"More or less."

"Were you head custodian at the last place, too?"

He stopped and rubbed his chin.

"I guess you could say I was."

He was clearly uncomfortable, so she stopped asking questions.

"I think we're in for a cold snap this weekend," she offered.

His shoulders relaxed, and he began washing the desk with an easy motion again.

"Yes, death, taxes, and winter, there is no denying those. Sometimes, no matter how hard we fight it, unpleasant things occur in life. See you, Miss…that is, Jesse." He smiled and left the classroom.

Had she been insensitive, or did Arnie, too, keep secrets?

The deep circles under Sister Therese's eyes indicated a lack of sleep. Her mouth curved down in sadness. Her call had awakened Jesse at five thirty this morning, asking her to come in by six thirty, before anyone else was about. She was definitely about to hear bad news.

"Jesse, I am sorry to tell you that Valerie Bauer died last night."

She dropped back in her seat. Lightheaded, she grasped the arms of the chair to steady herself. "What? But you said she was fine. Her father came and took her home. How could she be dead?" Jesse cried.

"Apparently her injuries were worse than we thought. There was some internal bleeding…"

"Internal bleeding? What actually happened to her? I thought the girls were taking drugs."

"I was mistaken." Sister Therese sat back in her chair. "I apologize for withholding the truth from you. A group of girls has been participating in some peculiar activities. Not satanic—we'd never allow something like that to occur— but based on Seneca Indian myth. Legend has it that our property sits on sacred burial ground. The ghost of a Seneca woman walks the land at night, seeking revenge for the desecration of the sacred ground." She sighed. "I think it's a lot of superstitious gossip and folklore. The girls have been meeting at a cabin in the forest trying to appease this spirit—it's nothing new. Generations of St. Bartholomew's girls have practiced similar rituals, even meeting in the same place. But these students have carried the rituals too far. We've been keeping an eye on them, but they are sneakier than past groups. Nothing like this has ever happened before."

"So you know about the cabin," Jesse said.

Sister Therese narrowed her eyes. "*You* know about the cabin?"

Jesse related the events of the night she followed Eleanor. When she got to the part about being knocked out somehow, the nun's raised eyebrows confirmed that she didn't know about everything occurring at St. Bart's.

"Are you all right?"

"Yes, just a pounding headache the next day. It's better now." She rubbed her temple.

"Valerie's death is a shock and a tragedy. The other night these girls had left campus and were out doing heaven knows what. I suspected drugs were involved, but we found nothing during our search the next morning. All of the girls have denied knowing anything about Valerie's being left in the road, but if you actually saw some of them in the cabin, we can begin a thorough investigation. You're sure who the girls were?"

"I knew three of them—maybe four. Eleanor McHenry, whom I followed to the cabin, Madeline Stewart, and Adrianna Rutherford. The others were already there. Sister, there was a girl wrapped in a blanket. I think it was Becky Newhart, but I can't be sure."

The nun couldn't hide her sudden intake of breath. "Becky? Are you certain?"

"No, I couldn't see her face. Her size was right, and long, brown hair was visible. I wanted to go in and stop the ritual—that's when I got knocked out. The girls' hijinks don't explain what happened to me. Unless another girl came out to join them, found me spying, and conveniently had something to knock me out. Or someone else followed us into the woods. I don't remember being hit, and I had no lumps on my head that would have resulted from a blow. Plus, they would have had to carry me back to my car."

Sister Therese folded her hands on the desk. "Jesse, there are some things occurring at St. Bart's that I am not able to reveal to you. I know you are curious, but I must ask you to leave things alone that seem unusual or odd. It's for your own good."

Jesse's stared at her. Sister Therese's words were more than a request. They felt like a threat.

The silence was interrupted only by sniffles and muffled sobs in the auditorium following Sister Therese's announcement of Valerie Bauer's death.

Jesse positioned herself to be able to see her students who had been in the cabin. There was no artifice in their reactions; they genuinely appeared to be stunned by the news. With mouths agape, they stared at each other, eyes wide with fear. For a moment, they angled away from each other, squirming to avoid eye contact. Finally, one by one, they inclined their heads together in a huddle, their whispers frantic.

Sister Therese had allowed the girls to absorb the news and comfort each other, but now she spoke from the lectern on the left of the stage.

"Valerie was a kind and cheerful girl, and St. Bartholomew's will be a little less bright without her smile. Father Steve is now going to lead us in prayer for the repose of Valerie's soul and for all of the faithful departed. When he is finished, please take out your rosaries. Sister Roberta and Sister Thaddeus will be in the counseling office throughout the day for any of you wishing to speak with them."

Father Steve stepped to the lectern.

"In the name of the Father, and of the Son, and of the Holy Ghost…" He crossed himself, and the student body, as one, did the same.

The day seemed interminable. Sister Therese had decided

on a shortened class schedule, but still, each hour Jesse listened to her students cry and relate stories about Valerie, soaking up their grief herself until she thought she would collapse. Rumors were flying about the Weeping Woman's taking revenge on St. Bartholomew's and its students. Her fifth hour was especially hard. These were Valerie's closest friends. Becky looked especially fragile, her skin translucent, her eyes haunted.

Rubbing her own dry eyes, Jesse swallowed the lump in her throat. All day she'd held herself together for her students. Now her sorrow threatened to erupt. As she locked her classroom door, Sister Alphonse approached.

God help me. Not now.

"Miss Graham…" The nun's voice held no harshness. Her eyes were rimmed with red, her hands trembled.

"Miss Graham." The woman straightened, no doubt mustering her strength. "Mr. Stanton told me about the care you took with Valerie Bauer the night you found her. If you hadn't tended to her, she might have died there in the road—alone." A tear escaped. "You called the convent that night, and I ignored your plea for help. I can never forgive myself for that. Perhaps if I had listened to you…"

Jesse wiped at her own eyes. "Sister Alphonse—"

"No, let me finish. Perhaps I could have helped, but instead I accused you of terrible things. I've been unfair, and my anger and, yes, hatred, have not served either of us well. Nor Valerie." Her voice caught. "I apologize, Miss Graham. I apologize for everything. And I ask your forgiveness."

Jesse took the nun's hand in hers. "Let's start fresh—for Valerie."

Sister Alphonse nodded, a faint smile at her lips. She squeezed Jesse's hand.

"For Valerie."

Ignoring the butterflies fluttering in her stomach, Jesse rang Susan Riley's doorbell. She hoped Joe was home, and she hoped he wasn't. If he was home, maybe they could finally talk and sort things out between them. Maybe then the grief that stabbed through her whole being would soften a bit. But if he rejected her again…what then? Would she be able to bear that along with the sorrow over Valerie's death? She needed him—bare, raw need. His rejection could destroy her tonight. If he wasn't home, she wouldn't have to face his potential anger.

She turned to hurry away. Too late. The door opened, bathing her in golden light.

"Come in, Jesse. How nice to see you!" Susan gave her a hug. She didn't say whether or not Joe was in. "I just made a pot of tea."

She led Jesse to the kitchen. No sign of Joe. Was she relieved or disappointed? She was too shattered to know.

"How are you?" Susan's glance confirmed what she suspected: she looked like hell.

"Not so good today." She slumped into a chair.

Susan sat across from her, covering Jesse's hand with her own. "What is it?"

Jesse told her about Valerie.

"I'm so sorry, Jesse."

Jesse nodded. She had no words as she dabbed at tears streaming down her face.

Susan bustled around the kitchen, getting out another cup and saucer, pouring tea, and grabbing the cookie jar. Watching her vitality made Jesse even more tired. Susan crouched beside her, putting an arm around her shoulder. Jesse crumpled against her friend, sobbing.

"It's okay. There are no students here you have to be strong for. Go ahead and cry, honey."

Susan's permission opened gates of sorrow Jesse hadn't known were within her. Finally, she was able to speak.

Gasping between snuffles, she explained her role in the events that had led up to Valerie's death.

"Valerie was one of the sweetest students I've ever had." She wiped her eyes. "I can't believe she's gone. I could have saved her if I'd gotten her to the hospital. Maybe she died because of me."

"Honey, you did all that you could. You aren't to blame for any of this."

"Why didn't Scott take her to the hospital? Why did he take her back to St. Bart's?"

"He probably thought she was okay. It's not his fault either, Jess. He did what he thought was right, too."

Jesse sniffled. Susan brought over a box of tissues.

"Have you eaten dinner?"

She shook her head.

"Lunch?"

Jesse hunched her shoulders.

"Oh, my dear girl, you must eat something."

Susan rose, pulling out food and pans. The noise comforted Jesse as she sat in her fog. The next thing she knew, a grilled cheese sandwich and cup of tomato soup sat in front of her. She blinked through her tears, realizing how hungry she was.

"Tell me about Valerie." Susan's eyes were soft.

Between bites, Jesse talked about the girl and her other students, ending with the occurrence at the cabin in the woods.

"So you think this little coven, or whatever it is, might have something to do with Valerie's death?"

"Valerie was wrapped in a St. Bart's blanket just like the dummy was. The girls seemed to be performing some kind of ritual to appease the Weeping Woman. Typical school girl stuff, nothing dangerous...I thought."

"Except that someone knocked you out and carried you away. Why? So you couldn't find the cabin again? So you wouldn't tell on the girls? So you would think it was all a dream? Or something more sinister?"

"All the questions I have asked myself. And I have no answers." Jesse glanced at the door to the living room.

"Joe's out tonight," Susan said.

"Oh." Jesse tried to sound casual and squelched the questions "where" and "with whom?"

"Are you feeling any better?"

Jesse felt restored and pampered. "Yes, thank you. I didn't even realize I was headed over here. I think I needed your TLC."

Susan gave her a hug. "Perhaps."

Jesse attempted a smile.

"I'll tell Joe you stopped by." Susan patted her hand.

She had just climbed out of a steamy bubble bath and donned her flannel pajamas when the doorbell rang. With the towel wrapped around her hair, she plodded downstairs.

"Joe."

"Hey. Nice outfit."

She looked down to make sure her pajamas were buttoned straight as the towel unwound and dangled in her face. After pushing it back in place and tucking it in, she opened the door wider, letting in the crisp air. "Come on in."

"If it's too late, I can come back another day."

"So Susan told you I stopped by?"

He raised his eyebrows. "You stopped by? No, I haven't been home." He looked at the floor. "Did Mom tell you where I was?"

"No. It's none of my business, Joe." Her heart hurt. He'd been out with someone else. "Hey, sit down. Do you want a beer? I could sure use one."

"Sure."

He followed her to the kitchen. "So, how do you get that

thing to stay on your head like that?"

She reached up; she'd already forgotten about the towel. "It's a woman's secret handed down from generation to generation." She handed him a beer. They looked at each other in silence.

"How are you doing, Jesse?" He didn't say "Just Jesse" as he usually did in that soft tone.

"It's been a rough day."

"More ghostly sounds?" he asked.

"One of my students died, Joe. Valerie Bauer." Her voice broke.

He stared at her, eyes wide.

"What? How?"

"It's all so confusing to me. I never saw her after Scott put her in his truck."

He bristled at the mention of Scott's name. "What do you mean 'put her in his truck?' Do you think he…?"

"No, nothing like that."

Joe didn't know about her finding Valerie in the road and all that had ensued. How had they grown so distant? He had been so much a part of her life until recently. *You have only yourself to blame, Graham.* For the second time that night, she quickly explained the bizarre sequence of events that led up to Valerie's death, reliving her terror and guilt. By the time she finished, she was shaking.

He reached up, unrolled the towel, and tossed it on the table. Running his hands through her hair, he seemed to study each strand.

Jesse thought she would burst with the urge to melt into his arms. She steeled herself against the desire, focusing on the story.

"Something is fishy. Scott claims that she awoke and demanded to be taken back to St. Bart's. I saw her condition; how did she bounce back so suddenly? You know, it would make more sense to me if she had died that night rather than that she recuperated on the spot. If you had seen her…"

Joe pulled her to him, holding her while she cried. She buried her head in his shoulder, allowing all of her pent up sorrow to flow. She felt safe. She felt loved. Her sobs subsided to sniffles and gasps. Finally, she took a deep breath, steadier now.

"This has been a shitty day."

"I imagine it has been." Taking her hand, he led her back to the living room. She curled up on one end of the sofa. Joe covered her with an afghan and sat at the other end.

"So did your ESP tell you I was a wreck and needed a hug? Is that why you stopped by?" Jesse asked. She wanted to add "and who were you with?" but caught herself.

"I wanted to tell you about something I found while we were working on the dormitory the other day. Jesse, I think there are two tunnels down there."

"Tunnels?"

"Yeah. We were reinforcing the interior foundation. When we repaired a crack, we found that a door had been covered over. It has to be an entrance to an underground tunnel. Another interesting thing: Sister Therese has instructed me to avoid one area of the academic basement."

"That's where I heard the drum and chanting."

He nodded. "I thought it was strange, considering the buildings are the same age and any problems we encounter in the dormitory will be duplicated in the school."

She brushed her fingers through her damp hair. "I think some of the good sisters are hiding something."

"I agree," he said. "The direction of this tunnel seems to lead to the school building. It's on the north side of the dormitory. I wonder if, at one time, the tunnels were used to distribute supplies from one building to the other. Or maybe the nuns used the tunnels to sneak over to the dorms for surprise bed checks." He laughed.

"It's interesting that Sister Therese restricted you from the school basement. Perhaps there's more down there than my chanting ghost."

"Here's the kicker. Curiosity got the better of me, and I circled the foundation of the academic building on the premise of checking for consistency in appearance. Jess, that whole basement has been retrofitted. The structure is sound, though it may have been repaired in places. What's interesting are the electrical cables leading from there. New shrubs were planted fairly recently to conceal this upgrade, and whatever it's running is pretty advanced technology."

"That doesn't make sense. Why would the Sisters of St. Joseph need advanced technology capability?"

"Good question. I couldn't hang around to explore because your friend Scott came along."

Jesse cringed. She didn't have the energy for that conversation tonight. As if sensing this, Joe took her hand.

"I'm sorry about your student, Jesse." His gentle voice brought a lump to her throat. She was once again wrapped in all the sorrow that had enveloped her throughout the day. She could only nod.

"It's getting late. I'd better get going." He stood.

Rising, she took his hand. "It was nice of you to come by and fill me in on what you found." She paused. "And for letting me...you know...cry on your shoulder." She felt so small, so vulnerable in that moment. "Thanks, Joe."

He stepped toward her but stopped. His eyes were soft, but she saw that pain lingered there, too. He squeezed her hand. "Good night, Jesse."

"Good-bye, Joe."

CHAPTER SEVENTEEN

As if the dreary autumn weather weren't enough to dampen the spirits of everyone at St. Bartholomew's, an atmosphere of despair cloaked the campus with the shock of Valerie's death. Sister Therese was busy with public relations as parents became distraught at the rumors they were hearing, many of them withdrawing their daughters for the remainder of the term. Jesse had difficulty concentrating; her usual enthusiasm for lesson planning had vanished. In her classroom, students wept openly in the days following the memorial service. Jesse allowed open discussion of their feelings, which they were so desperate to share, but she suspected other classes were business as usual.

She decided to start today with a ten-minute free journal writing. She put a prompt on the board but told the girls they did not have to write to it. They could write whatever they wished. There was just one caveat.

"Remember, I will be reading what you write. You will not be graded on your response, but you will be given credit for writing for ten minutes. For most of you, that will be about a full page. That doesn't mean that you should write in large letters, however."

Her comment elicited a few giggles, but they were short and quickly replaced by the grief-filled silence.

At the end of the hour, the girls stacked their journals on

her desk until one was one too many, and they all slid to the floor. Three girls stooped to pick them up and restack them in two shorter, stable piles.

"Thank you, ladies," Jesse said.

"You're welcome, Miss Graham," they replied in unison.

Sometimes the uniformity at St. Bart's unsettled her.

As she read through the journals, she was surprised to see that many girls responded predictably to her prompt about the most important characteristic of friendship. They did segue into feelings they had about Valerie, but some did not. While she scanned multiple comments of "being there for each other" and "telling all your deepest secrets," a separate piece of paper slipped out from between two notebooks. This note was printed in block letters that made it impossible to identify the writer:

"I know why Valerie died. It's my fault. Others are in danger."

Jesse sat back in her chair, staring at the message.

"That must be an absorbing essay." Maggie's voice made her jump. "Sorry. I didn't mean to frighten you."

Jesse pressed her hand to her heart to counteract the jolt. "Take a look at this." She handed her the paper.

Maggie read it, pursing her lips. "Do you think this is a prank?"

"I don't know. The events of that night are so bizarre. Valerie's death is still not real to me. I saw her unconscious, but she didn't look like she was dying. She just looked like she was sleeping. Mags, what else could I have done to help her?"

"First of all, you need to let go of any guilt you feel. None of what happened to Valerie was your fault. In fact, you were the only hope she had to be rescued. Once Scott put her in his truck, there was nothing more you could do. You went to the hospital. It's not as if you just walked away from her. Secondly, you need to stop taking on the grief of your students. It's great that you let them write about it, but maybe you don't have to read all of their sorrow."

Jesse eyed the stack of notebooks. "Someone has to hear them. Many of them have parents who are too far away to come get them or visit." She sighed. "I don't know, Mags. Sometimes I think too much wealth can destroy as much as it can help."

Maggie shook her head. "Most people get the biblical quote wrong. It's not 'Money is the root of all evil.' It's, 'The *love* of money is the root of all evil.' You've got to stop equating wealth with evil. Yes, Eileen was wealthy and a bitch, and Robert was wealthy and a cad, but not everyone who is wealthy has sin lurking in his soul. Look at all the good Ben Wyndham does—he's a generous philanthropist."

Jesse shrugged. "I know. I know. I've just been hurt by people who put wealth and the power it can buy them before everything else. And sometimes it gets in the way of relationships."

"You mean Joe and his aversion to the Wyndham fortune."

She shrugged again. "I don't even know where that's going. I'm pretty confused."

"Give it time. You've only known him, what, four months? Let it grow if it's meant to."

"Like a garden. Yeah. The thing is, Joe has made it clear that he wants nothing to do with the Wyndham family, and I, through no fault of my own, am a major player in the Wyndham family. Ben keeps pushing it on me. If I buy into this Wyndham heir situation, I might lose Joe forever. Hell, the way I've been treating him lately, I may have already lost him." She shook her head. "Anyway, back to this secret message. I can't determine whose writing it is; she disguised it."

They studied the paper.

"What do you think she means, 'Others are in danger'?" Maggie mused.

"A few of the girls have formed some kind of secret club. That's what was behind the dummy in the road. Do you think that was practice for what happened to Valerie? And that it will happen again?"

Maggie shook her head. "I just don't know. So many questions. But I do know this. These girls are playing with fire."

CHAPTER EIGHTEEN

November 1968

The knocking and groaning of the boiler once again serenaded Jesse as she graded papers on a dreary Saturday afternoon. Even though she had sworn off coming in alone on Saturdays, she'd left some tests in her classroom. Once she retrieved them, it was simpler to grade them here rather than lug them home and back again. A soft patter of rain against the windows signaled the beginning of a soggy evening. She had hoped to be finished grading the tests by four thirty so she'd be home in time to start the chicken. The people she had come to love like family were coming over for dinner, and she needed the comfort of their presence right now.

Sighing, she wrote a grade at the top of a quiz form, added in the essay grade, stapled the papers together, and placed them on the stack that was at last higher than the to-be-graded stack.

The noise hit her ears like an oncoming storm.

Bah-boom. Bah-boom. Bah-boom. Bah-boom. A haunting chant followed, joining the steady beat, raising goose bumps on her skin.

This was definitely not a radio. Someone—or something—was in the building with her. She rose from her desk. grabbing her key ring even though she knew there was no basement key on it. Tiptoeing down the shadowy hall, she reached the main corridor, stopped, and cocked her head. Again the sounds came from the east wing basement. Gloomy light filtered in from the windows, barely illuminating the hall. She automatically turned toward the east wing, but something caught her eye to the west.

Lying at the foot of the stairs, her body twisted like a broken toy, was Sister Catherine.

Jesse's scream rang around the hall and stairwells of the main corridor, echoing off the stone walls and leaded glass windows. She collapsed to her knees, shaking.

"Oh my God!" She pressed her fists into her eyes as if trying to deny what she had seen. "Dear God, let her still be alive." Half crawling, half walking, she scrambled to the nun and touched her face. Her eyes stared at the ceiling. Scarlet blood trickled from her mouth, pooling on her starched white wimple. Jesse rocked over the nun's body.

"No. No. NO!"

Dear, sweet Jesus. Perhaps Sister Catherine hadn't simply fallen. The scrape along her face could have been caused by a fall, but Jesse recognized the signs of her mottled skin and bulging eyes. Petechia. She had seen it in death before; it signaled strangulation. As she looked away, her eyes fell on the nun's wimple. A fingerprint smudged the crisp, white linen. A thought struck her like lightning: Sister Catherine's body was still warm. *Oh my God, what if whoever did this is still here?* She trembled. Her gaze darted into the corners shrouded in shadows, then up the staircase that disappeared into blackness. Someone could be watching her at that moment. Grabbing her keys, she sprinted to the main office. With shaking hands, she tried to find the right key but dropped the key ring. She heard a door bang down the hall.

"Please God. Please let me find the right key."

Fumbling, she tried several in the lock, scratching the metal around it. Finally, one slid in and turned. She threw the door open, slammed it behind her, and realized the door was still unlocked. Easing it open a crack, she peered out into the hall. Seeing no one, she opened the door just enough to insert the key and turn the lock. Shutting it, she leaned her back against it and slid to the floor, her heart hammering. The wall to her left was lined with windows on the top half, and the blinds were not drawn. Anyone in that hall could see her in the office. Not daring to look through the windows, she crept along the counter to the swinging half-door at the end and pushed through it to where the office staff worked. Reaching up, she pulled the secretary's phone down, stretching the cord as far as it would reach, inching under the desk. Her mind went blank. What was the phone number for the convent? She couldn't remember.

The memory of sitting in Eileen's bedroom, her mother's body draped across the bed, flashed before her. How could this be happening again?

"Think, Graham. Think," she hissed.

She tapped her head. Should she call the convent? Should she call the police? She was too frightened to think logically. What if she called the convent, and Sister Therese came over, only to be in danger herself? Questions reverberated as Jesse realized the danger she was in. She couldn't stay in this office forever. Trancelike, her fingers automatically dialed the number she always used when calling Maggie.

"St. Bartholomew's Convent, Sister Mary Judith speaking."

Jesse couldn't speak.

"Hello?"

"It's Jesse Graham," she whispered.

"I'm sorry, I can't hear you. Would you please speak louder?"

"Sister, it's Jesse Graham. Please, I need help."

"Jesse? Is that you? We must have a bad connection. Let me go get Sister Angelina for you."

She heard the nun set the phone down.

"NO! Please, come back. Please."

Jesse forced the groan back into her throat. *Please, please, please, someone help me.*

"Hey, Jess. What's up?"

Jesse jumped at the loud, clear tones of Maggie's voice. She pulled the base of the phone into her lap, cupping her hand around the mouthpiece.

"Shh. Maggie, shh."

"Jesse, where are you?"

"Maggie, I'm in the school. In the main office," she hissed.

"I can hardly hear you. Are you all right?"

"No! Maggie, Sister Catherine is dead. I think somebody killed her."

Silence.

"Maggie, can you hear me?"

"Where are you?" Maggie's voice was tight with panic.

"In the main office."

"I'll be right there."

"NO! Don't come over here. Whoever did this is still in the building. I heard a door slam."

Jesse heard the doorknob wiggle. Her voice was hoarse. "He's trying to get into the office, Maggie. Call the police."

The line went dead.

Jesse slid further into the knee space, pulling the chair in toward her. She heard the door rattle again, and a metallic sound from the lock. Someone was trying to break in; someone knew she was in here. She bent her head against her knees and prayed. She heard a *click*, and the door swung in. Stealthy footsteps sounded along the length of the counter, pausing at the swinging door. It creaked as it opened. She had never noticed that creaking noise before, but at that moment it sounded like a sonic boom. She heard the person skulking toward the desk. She held her breath.

The ring of the phone in her lap was a high voltage jolt. The intruder halted. Jesse covered her ears at the jangling, insistent sound. Covered by the ringing, the person crept forward, inching closer to the desk. She peered out between the legs of the chair she cowered behind, catching a glimpse of the toe of brown work boots.

He's going to kill me just like he killed Sister Catherine. Why did I come in to school today? My God, all the sisters—the girls—are in danger. I'm going to ram this chair into him, and then—

Boisterous voices sounded on the sidewalk just outside the office window. The intruder quickly retraced his steps, exiting the door just moments before voices filled the office.

"Jesse? Jesse, where are you?"

Maggie's voice had never sounded so wonderful.

"Here! I'm back here." Jesse untangled her limbs and crawled out from under the desk. "Did you see him? He just ran out of here! We can catch him if we hurry!"

The nuns looked at her, bemused.

"We didn't see anyone. There was no one here, Jesse." Maggie helped her out from under the desk.

"You must have seen him! He was in here while you were coming in. I can't believe you missed him."

The nuns looked at each other; all answered her at the same time.

"What's going on?" Arnie's voice shouted above the din. Everyone froze.

"Arnie?" Jesse said in disbelief. Surely it couldn't have been him in here. Yet, here he was, right on the spot. He had a master key. And he was wearing brown work boots. Were they the same? She couldn't tell.

"Arnie, did you see anyone in the halls?"

He shook his head.

"Jesse, what you said about Sister Catherine. There must

have been a bad connection. You didn't really say…" Maggie's voice trailed off.

She nodded. She led the nuns and Arnie to the west staircase where Sister Catherine's twisted form lay. Crying out, the nuns ran to her, surrounding her body.

"No. This just can't be!" Maggie cried.

"Did you call the police, Maggie?"

"No, I thought I must have heard you wrong. This can't be true. It just can't be." Maggie sobbed. Jesse knelt beside her friend, taking her into her arms while she cried.

"I'll go call the police," said one nun.

"I'll come with you," said another.

"Me, too."

Jesse stayed with Maggie and the other nun. And Arnie.

"How can this be? Did you see who it was, Jesse?" Maggie's plea ripped her heart out. "When he was in the office, did you see who it was?"

Jesse shook her head, glancing at Arnie.

"Didn't you see or hear anything?" Maggie's eyes pleaded with her.

"Yes, Mags. I heard the drum and the chanting."

Detective Harold Stone's voice echoed across the hallway as he spoke to the forensics experts who were examining the crime scene. Sister Catherine's body had been covered. Jesse stared at the spot. This wasn't how Sister Catherine was supposed to end up. She was full of fun and energy, teasing about Scott, winking at innuendoes.

Maggie and the other nuns huddled in Sister Therese's office, reciting the rosary in hushed tones.

"Hail Mary, full of grace…" Their voices blended in a kind of chant that was soothing, but Jesse had no desire to join them. Her faith had been tested enough with the revelation of Helen's murder, and now evil had once again barged in on her life.

If you're there, God, I'm not feeling it.

Harold Stone entered, looking around the office. He was the epitome of a hard-boiled detective with his trench coat and fedora. Glancing in at the nuns, Stone tipped his hat in apology for his interruption.

"You're Miss Graham?" he asked Jesse.

"Yes, sir."

"You're the one who found the sister?"

"Yes, sir."

"Hmm…"

Jesse shifted. What did that mean?

"Why were you in the building, Miss Graham?"

"I'm an English teacher." She presumed that was explanation enough, but obviously Detective Stone had no idea about the workload of an English teacher and misinterpreted her response as sarcasm.

"And I'm a detective, Miss Graham, so d'you wanna answer the question now?"

"I was here, in my classroom, because I had tests I needed to grade and I didn't want to carry them all home. So I came in today to work…in my classroom." She fumbled for words.

He stared at her in silence. Finally, he spoke.

"And where is this classroom?"

She pointed toward the north corridor.

"Why don't you show me?"

"Of course."

One of Detective Stone's shoes squeaked as he walked, echoing on the marble floor as they made their way to her room. Jesse clung to the sound as they passed the site of Sister Catherine's death. Squeak…step…squeak…step… squeak… She was reminded of the killer in *Wait Until Dark*. She shuddered.

Upon entering her classroom, Stone studied the layout as

if he were going to redecorate. Pulling the door forward, he glanced behind it, searching into the corner. Jesse suspected he could see everything in one sweep of the room. Crossing to her desk, he pawed through the papers, mixing the graded ones with the ungraded. She bit her tongue. He opened the drawers, groping through pencils, markers, and paper clips.

"So you were working here?"

"Yes."

"But you weren't finished grading papers?"

"No."

"Did you see or hear anyone else in the building?"

How should she answer that? *Yes, I heard the Weeping Woman chanting and beating a drum in the basement.*

"No. It was quiet today."

"Where's the restroom?"

"Oh. It's…actually, I don't know where the men's room is. I guess it might be over by the main entrance."

"Is that where the ladies room is?"

"I don't know if there is a ladies room there, but wouldn't you prefer…"

"Which bathroom do you use, Miss Graham?"

This guy was creepy. Was he going to use the same bathroom she did? "Why, I use the staff bathroom just down the hall. You're welcome to use it since no one else will be in there, but you'll need my key."

"So if you needed to use the restroom, you would use the one down the hall, right? Not the one by the main office?"

"Yes, of course."

"So if you weren't done with your grading and ready to leave the building, and you didn't need the bathroom by the main office, what were you doing down that hall?"

Jesse went cold with shock. How could she explain that she was going to try to check out the basement where she had been told explicitly not to go? She couldn't speak.

"How well did you know Sister Catherine?"

Her insides turned to jelly.

"I just came on staff over the summer. I met her at a faculty meeting. I've gotten to know her a little over the last couple of months."

Detective Stone stared at her. What did he know about her involvement in the investigation into Helen's murder? Did he know she had been brought in for questioning in Eileen's death? If so, would he find it strangely coincidental that she was also alone at the scene of Sister Catherine's? Did being a suspect in Eileen's murder automatically make her one here, too?

"How did you get along?"

"Are you suggesting—" Her temper rose at his insinuation.

"Let's look at the facts." His voice was flat. "You said you were alone in the building. You had no reason to be in the main hallway. And the good sister is dead. How would you explain that, Miss Graham?"

Maggie entered. "Are you all right, Jesse?"

Shaking with rage and fear, Jesse turned to her friend.

"Jess, what is it?"

"Detective Stone here thinks I killed Sister Catherine."

Maggie's mouth dropped. "You can't be serious. Jesse would never hurt someone," she said to Detective Stone. "How can you think that?"

"Actually, he has good reason, Mags. I was the only other person in the building."

Detective Stone's calculating gaze narrowed.

Maggie approached the man. "Please, Detective Stone. I swear on my life that Jesse could never do something like this. I've known her since high school. No one knows her better than I do."

"I have to cover all bases, Sister. Miss Graham is right— she is the most likely suspect. You're not planning on leaving town for a vacation or anything, are you, Miss Graham?"

"No. We're in the middle of a marking period." *Graham, only a teacher would say something stupid like that when she is the number one suspect in a murder case.*

A hint of a smile played at his mouth, but he coughed into his hand, frowning. "That's good. I can trust that between your promise and Sister's vouching for you that you'll be around if I need to talk to you again."

"Yes, of course."

He tipped his hat. "Good day, Sister. Miss Graham." He exited the room.

Jesse slid into a nearby desk. "What, Maggie? Do I have 'please suspect me of murder' written across my forehead? This is déjà vu—just like with Detective Holden when Eileen was killed."

"They just have to question people who were at the crime scene, Jess."

"And I seem to be the only one present because, again, the murderer has slipped away."

Maggie's eyes darted around the room. "That means the murderer is still around here somewhere."

"Damn, Mags. I hadn't thought of that."

"Come with me, Jesse. Lock up your room, and we'll go check in with Sister Therese."

Sister Therese was talking to the nuns in her office when they arrived. Jesse hung back in the main office area. She caught a flash of movement by the front door. Scott came rushing through, hair messier than usual, his face flushed. He strode over to the spot where Sister Catherine lay, dropping to one knee. Detective Stone hurried to him and grabbed his shoulder. Scott shrugged him off, rising. He towered over the man, leaning into him as he spoke.

"Be careful, Scott, or you'll end up in the pokey with me," Jesse whispered as she watched the exchange. But Detective Stone backed away. Scott spoke to one guy on the forensic team who couldn't be older than a college student. The guy scribbled notes like an undergrad, too. Scott waved Stone toward the woods, and the detective nodded—practically bowed—and headed out.

"It gets curiouser and curiouser," Jesse whispered.

The sweet, smoky scent of incense wafted in the air as Jesse sat beside Maggie in the chapel. Hushed voices surrounded her as nuns gathered for Sister Catherine's funeral. She stared ahead at the crucifix above the altar, her limbs leaden, ears unable to focus on any one sound.

Okay, Jesus, where is your mercy in this? How can you let a nun be murdered?

Her faith had been precarious at best recently. Sister Catherine's death threatened to destroy it altogether. The police had picked up an itinerate man who had been sleeping in his car just off the school's property. They had found a St. Bartholomew's wool blanket in his car and arrested him on suspicion in Sister Catherine's death. But how many of those blankets had wandered off campus?

The organ had been playing softly as people gathered, but now the crescendo signaled mourners to rise. Jesse faced the aisle as Father Steve followed the casket into the chapel. Encircled by voices singing "Amazing Grace," she remained silent. Closing her eyes, she focused on Maggie's sweet soprano voice, wishing she could believe as her friend did.

Scott was one of the pallbearers. Dark circles smudged his eyes, and his usually cheerful face was somber and drawn. His blue eyes didn't cast their usual glow, but were shaded with sorrow. Carefully combed hair replaced the mussed look he normally wore. He looked as though he carried more than the weight of Sister Catherine's coffin.

He moved slowly to the first pew after setting the casket

at the front of the altar. Scott and Sister Catherine were both new to the faculty like she was. He couldn't have gotten to know the nun that closely already. Before she could ponder this puzzle of his grief any further, Father Steve began.

"In the name of the Father, and of the Son, and of the Holy Ghost…"

"Amen," the congregation answered in unison.

Jesse went through the motions of the Mass, but inside she was hollow. Life had been too bleak recently. She closed her eyes.

Please, God. Send me peace.

CHAPTER NINETEEN

Becky Newhart stood on a chair stapling students' work to the bulletin board. She'd often offered to help in Jesse's classroom, but since Valerie's death she had appeared at the door every day. Most of her conversation centered on school, but occasionally she would veer off on more personal topics like favorite music or movie stars. Recently, she'd been quieter, and Jesse suspected, while the shock of Valerie's death still held, the reality was settling in for the girl. Keeping busy was healing. Jesse understood that and enjoyed her company.

The girl sighed as she read one of the assignments, a description of a person. "I like writing character sketches, Miss Graham," she said.

"Why is that?" Jesse was half listening while she sorted through her files on Edgar Allan Poe. Becky was quite a talker when it was just the two of them.

"Because you can write about a person and tell all the things you love about her. Like my mother. I wrote a character sketch about my mother."

Instinctively, Jesse stopped what she was doing. Becky's voice had changed; it was almost like a child's. The girl continued stapling, unaware of the difference Jesse had noticed. Jesse kept still.

"I could write all about how beautiful she was. She had long, brown hair, and at night when she finished brushing mine, she would let me brush hers. 'One hundred strokes a day!' she used to say. Sometimes we would dress alike. Not exactly alike, but if she was wearing a blue shirt she'd say, 'Hey, sweetie, you want to wear a blue shirt, too?'" Becky's voice was getting higher and tighter as she spoke. "And she was a good cook. Her favorite meal to make was Thanksgiving dinner because she said she always put a little extra love into it. On my birthday she would cook whatever I wanted for supper—even if I wanted pancakes. And at night when we said our prayers together..."

Becky crumpled into the chair, weeping. Jesse ran to her, wrapping the girl in her arms while she wept against her shoulder.

"I'm not supposed to talk about my mother." Her voice was tiny, muffled by Jesse's sweater.

"It's okay, Becky. It's okay."

"Dad says it's..." She shook with crying.

"I won't say anything, honey. It'll be our secret."

Becky nodded, sitting up.

"That will be the only secret I'll ever like. Now my best friend Valerie is gone, too. And it's my fault." Her face twisted with guilt.

What did that mean? What did Becky know about the circumstances of Valerie's death? Or at least what had happened the night she'd found Valerie lying in the road. Jesse took Becky's shoulders. "Do you know what happened to Valerie?"

Becky shook her head. "We left her in the cabin. She was taking the Ultimate Challenge of the Brave, which meant she had to stay there—alone—all night." She wiped her eyes.

"So you don't know how she ended up in the road? Or how the dummy ended up in the road?"

Becky looked down, her face turning red. "You know about the practice body?"

"Yes, I almost ran over it. It scared the...heck out of me.

Why did you put that in the road?"

Becky's gaze met hers. "We never put the dummy in the road. We left it in the cabin. We never knew what happened to it. We thought the Weeping Woman took it." Her face changed. "Is that why there was an inspection the first day of school?"

Jesse nodded.

"Ohhh."

"Did you write that note to me? Why did you say Valerie's death is your fault, Becky?"

The girl nodded, starting to shake. "Because it was supposed to be my turn for the Ultimate Challenge that night, before I got kicked out of the club. And I think—"

She hugged herself and lowered her eyes.

"What do you think?"

"I can't tell you. It's a secret."

☙❧

Jesse poked her head into the principal's office. "You wanted to see me, Sister Therese?"

"Yes. Come in and close the door, Jesse."

Jesse sat across from the woman, noticing how drawn and weary her face was. She suspected the gloom—and fear—that had settled firmly around St. Bartholomew's was taking its toll. Even more students had been taken out of school after Sister Catherine's death.

"How are you doing, Sister?" Where did this protective feeling come from? She had come to love these dedicated women—even Sister Alphonse.

"Oh, I am hanging in there, as they say. My heart breaks over these senseless deaths. I feel I should have done more. We must protect the girls, Jesse. That is our first priority. The police will be patrolling our grounds along with..." She stopped. Straightening the already aligned papers on her desk, she cleared her throat. "Frantic parents are calling or coming to remove their daughters from St. Bartholomew's. I can't blame them—I would probably do the same."

Jesse nodded.

Sister Therese sat forward, folding her hands on the desk. "Maggie tells me that your house is undergoing considerable renovation."

"Yes, that's true." Strange change in subject.

"In fact, you've had no running water recently, and heat may be an issue for a few days in the near future."

"I finally have running water, but they will be updating the wiring and heating systems soon." Great. She was about to be reprimanded for stealing water or taking showers on campus. Marty was right—it was stealing.

"It seems you have a need and I have a need." Sister Therese leaned her elbow on the desk and rested her chin on her hand.

Jesse raised an eyebrow.

"With Sister Catherine's passing, we are short staffed in the dormitory. We will rectify that with some staff shifting, but I want to be sure we are fully staffed until whoever"— she cleared her throat—"whoever killed Sister Catherine is brought to justice."

"Didn't the police make an arrest?"

Sister straightened the papers again. "Yes. But he has not been convicted. The investigation is ongoing. We need to protect the girls. Would you consider moving into the dormitory for a couple of weeks? It would help us out tremendously, and it would make things more convenient for you. I'm sure trudging out to the gym every morning has been inconvenient for you."

"You know about that?"

Sister Therese flashed an inscrutable smile.

"Of course we would increase your pay for the extra duty, although I may dock you for the water consumption of earlier weeks." Her face held a spark of amusement for a moment.

Jesse felt her cheeks grow hot. "I was going to go to confession..." She felt like a child caught with her hand in the cookie jar.

"While that's good for the soul, I think a more fitting penance would be to spend evenings with the students."

They laughed.

"Of course. I would be happy to take on dormitory duty for a while," Jesse said.

"Good. Thank you." Sister Therese opened a drawer and took out a key. "It's easier to give you a master key rather than adding your already burdened key ring."

Jesse's heart beat a little faster. Would the master key unlock the door to the basement? Did she want it to? Her hand shook a bit as she took the key and stared at it.

Sister Therese caught her gaze. "Is the weight of this responsibility giving you second thoughts? I know the girls can be troublesome at times, and we are all especially on guard right now, but I'm not throwing you into the lion's den." She smiled, but grief still showed in her eyes.

"No, no. It's fine. I was just thinking about...uh, what I will need to bring over during this stay." Jesse stumbled through the words, the image of the basement door distracting her.

"I appreciate your flexibility. Of course we are all in shock and are grieving over the deaths of Sister Catherine and Valerie, but it is my duty to ensure St. Bartholomew's continues to function for the students. It's so difficult to focus on practical logistics when my heart is so sad." The nun's eyes were misty, and Jesse realized what an enormous toll running the academy exacted from her.

"I'll do whatever I can to help," she said. "How is the investigation going?

Sister Therese looked at her blankly.

"You know, the investigation into Sister Catherine's death?"

"It's under control," the nun said.

Sister Therese wiped at her eyes, resuming her business-like posture.

"I appreciate your help with staffing the dormitory. I don't think I've told you that I hear many positive comments about your classes, although you got off to a rocky start with the Rutherford girl. She is a handful. You handled the situation appropriately."

"I assume you got a call from Howard Rutherford when that happened."

"Yes, I did." A small smile played at the nun's mouth, and Jesse realized that not only had the principal gone to bat for her, she had enjoyed it. "Some people have a warped sense of what is important in life. I always ask, 'Does this further the Kingdom?' Unfortunately, some people think of the Kingdom with a small k, as if it's their own. I am speaking in general, of course."

Jesse smiled. "Of course."

"And confidentially."

"Of course."

The women smiled at each other as Jesse rose to leave, the master key gripped tightly in her fist.

Page turns echoed in the empty library as Jesse researched the legend of the Weeping Woman. Documented in several regional history books dating back to 1733, the legend had it that a young Seneca woman had lost her baby to disease brought by colonists. Because she, too, was ill, as were many tribal members, white settlers buried her infant quickly and not according to Seneca tradition. The tribe, almost obliterated by the disease, had been forced to move from their village. The woman returned, searching for the grave of her child to bury him properly, but she was killed by a settler before she could do so. She was buried quickly, again with no regard for tribal custom; consequently, she and her child would never journey to the land of departed souls. Now her ghost wandered the area, searching for her child's grave.

No wonder the chanting sounded so doleful. Just reading this made her heart hurt.

Lists of sightings, several confirmed by reliable sources, seemed to agree on the details. The ghostly image of a Seneca Indian woman wearing a tunic over a skirt and leggings had been seen in the area of St. Bartholomew's. Almost every account agreed that the woman's hair was cut short, not long or braided. This would confirm that she would have been in mourning.

Ah, here's what she was looking for. "Many accounts relate that the appearance of the ghost was accompanied by chanting and often the beating of a drum." Jesse sat back, whistling softly. Feeling a cool breeze, she pulled her sweater tighter. The library was deserted. Sister Rita had left a few dim lights on for Jesse with a request that she lock the door securely behind her when she left. Rubbing her arms to warm up, she gazed around the airy room. Book-laden stacks stood along both sides of a main aisle. Down the middle marched rows of study tables with green-shaded accountant lamps on the center of each. Hers was the only lamp lit, casting eerie shadows into the recesses nearby.

Chanting drifted to her, a mournful sound rising and falling on the gloomy darkness. Jesse broke out in a sweat even though the library was chilly. Her encounters with Helen's ghost had possessed an emotional element; despite her fear, she always had experienced warmth and love. But this was a hollow feeling, like a murky November day. Was she taking on the emotions of the Seneca woman? Fearfully, she scanned the room. In the far corner, a glimmer of light hovered, a human form, barely visible.

Trembling, Jesse rose from her seat. If ghosts had common characteristics, this apparition had a message. As she neared the figure, it swept forward, a force of icy cold that took her breath away. Knocked backward, she hit her head on the corner of a table and collapsed. Her entire being quivered with rage. Everything went black.

Jesse slowly became aware of her surroundings. Lying beneath the corner of the table, she could see the manufacturer's sticker on the underside, pulsing and swaying. She closed her eyes until the dizziness passed. Her head ached. Reaching back, she touched the stinging spot, feeling something wet. Checking her hand, she saw blood. When she tried to stand, dizziness swept over her. She settled for merely sitting up. The room was dark save for the light from her table lamp and a small exit light near the door.

No way was she searching this room; even hidden she wasn't safe. She'd have to at least peek out to check the path to the door. If she ran fast, could she make it without battling that fury again? And she wasn't stopping to lock the door—sorry, Sister Rita. She slowly leaned forward, ready to jerk back at the slightest movement. No glowing light; no shimmering figure. Clutching the edge of the table, she eased up to stand, wobbling a bit. After closing the books she'd been reading and hastily stacking them, she gathered her purse and briefcase and hurried toward the library door. Still woozy, she grabbed the edge of a bookshelf to steady herself. After a moment, more grounded, she continued out the door, securing it behind her after all, per Sister Rita's instructions.

Cold air stung the wound on the back of her head as she walked across the grounds to the dormitory. But while it made the wound smart, the brisk air also steadied her, her steps becoming more sure. Letting herself into the dormitory, she climbed the stairs to her room. All was quiet except the comforting rumble of the boiler. Throwing her purse and briefcase on the bed, she went into the bathroom to check the damage. Using her compact and the bathroom mirror, she examined the back of her head. Blood had matted her hair and dripped down her neck, staining her blouse. She snapped the compact closed, still trying to comprehend what had happened. She had been blown over by a wind, by the force of the apparition in the library.

The Weeping Woman.

Why do ghosts follow me around?

She became aware of a presence in her room. She eased the door back and stopped. A figure in white stood by her bed.

Becky.

"Oh my God, Becky. You scared the… heck out of me," Jesse caught herself. "What's wrong?"

Becky's eyes were round with fear. "There's someone… something in my room." She pointed at Jesse. "What happened to you, Miss Graham?"

Jesse tried to hide her stained blouse, but it was too late. The girl's nightgown quivered with her shaking, but her fear wasn't just from the sight of blood.

"What is it, Becky? What happened?"

The girl's voice floated like a feather across to her. "There's something in my roo…roo…room." The words huddled around a stifled sob.

"Isn't Eleanor in there with you?"

"Yes, but she's sound asleep. And the thing doesn't seem to bother with her."

"The thing?"

"I don't know how to explain it. Please come with me." Her terrified eyes pleaded with Jesse.

Jesse lightly touched the sore spot on the back of her head. All she wanted was to get out of this blouse and wash the blood out of her hair.

"C'mon, Becky. Let's go check it out."

The corridors were silent but for the padding of Becky's bare feet and the echo of Jesse's shoes. The air chilled as they neared Becky's door. All of Jesse's senses sharpened, as if she could see the air and smell each doorframe as they passed. Details etched themselves into her brain—the yellow tack holding a note to a door, an abandoned navy-blue sock left on the marble windowsill for its owner to claim. Minutiae vied for attention in her effort to avoid what she knew she would find.

They entered the icy room. A small lamp stood on the bedside table. The light shining from the top of its shade cast a shadow on the ceiling—a round glow surrounded by wavering, feathery fingers. Jesse studied it closer—ah, a boa-like fringe trimming the lampshade caused the eerie effect. Despite the cold, Eleanor was fast asleep in her bed, the blankets snugged up to her nose. Becky stood at the door, fear burning in her eyes.

"I don't see anything," Jesse whispered.

"Shh. Wait." Becky's eyes darted around; she clutched her arms around her waist.

Jesse scanned the room. Except for painting the walls, the girls were allowed to decorate however they wished. The contrast between these two girls' halves of the room was extreme. Each had a beanbag chair at the end of her bed. Becky's was hot pink, Eleanor's, black. While Becky's side of the room had stuffed animals, a pink bedspread, and a Beatles poster, Eleanor's bedspread was decorated with geometric black and white patterns. A print of an Andy Warhol soup can poster hung above the bed. Yet Jesse noticed a copy of *Forever Amber* on Eleanor's desk. She chuckled. *You are secretly a romantic, Miss McHenry.*

She froze.

Becky's lamp flickered and the picture below it slid across the table before dropping to the floor, cracking the glass. Eleanor mumbled, then rolled over, facing the wall.

Becky's mouth was open in an "O," but no sound came out. Jesse wrapped her arms around the trembling girl. They waited together until, slowly, the cold air dissipated and the room grew warmer.

"I think it's okay now, Becky."

"How do you know?" The girl surveyed the room, her eyes hollow with dread.

"Trust me. I know."

Jesse led her to the bed and pulled back the covers. Lying on the sheet was a black feather. Becky gasped. "Is it the Weeping Woman?" Her voice was barely a whisper.

Jesse picked up the feather. It smelled faintly of a wood fire.

"Perhaps. I don't know."

Becky climbed into bed, pulling the covers up to her chin.

"I'm going to stay here with you. I'll sleep in your bean-bag chair," Jesse said.

Becky looked relieved. "Thank you, Miss Graham."

Jesse scrunched around in the beanbag, trying to get comfortable. Her head throbbed; her hair was matted to her scalp. She was beginning to smell less than fresh and longed for a hot bath. Finding an afghan folded at the foot of Becky's bed, she covered herself as best she could.

"You won't leave during the night, will you?" Becky's voice still sounded small.

"No, I won't leave during the night."

She heard Becky toss and turn for a bit, until finally her soft even breathing signaled deep sleep. When Jesse closed her eyes, the image of the figure in the library came to her. The memory of its fierce attack made her eyes pop open. Everything looked peaceful in the darkened room. She burrowed back into the chair and eventually dozed in a fitful sleep.

"Miss Graham?"

Jesse opened one eye to see Eleanor's eyes, magnified by her glasses, staring into her face. The girl kneeled close to the beanbag chair.

"Good morning, Eleanor."

"Why are you here?" An edge of accusation mingled with the curiosity in her voice.

Jesse eased into a sitting position against her protesting muscles. She rubbed her neck and stretched her arms.

"Eewww. You're all bloody!" Eleanor cried.

"Shh. You'll wake Becky," she whispered.

Eleanor backed up and stepped on the broken picture frame on the floor.

"What the...?"

What should she say? Relating the occurrences of the previous night would cause panic to sweep like a wildfire through the school. How could Jesse explain the broken frame, and worse, her own condition? Time to weigh the sin of lying against the virtue of truth accompanied by absolute panic.

"Uh, Becky had a nightmare last night, and she came to get me. I walked her back to the room and she was so upset, I stayed here." She kept her voice low.

"You really expect me to believe that story?"

The blood was trickier to explain. She'd have to try harder.

"I fell against the bed and hit my head."

Eleanor peered at her.

"Listen, Eleanor. I can't go into it right now. I'm going back to my room for a shower. I need you to keep this to yourself, okay?"

The girl looked at her skeptically. "This is weird. Freaky, y'know?"

"I know, but please. Just let me sort through something. It's important. Can I count on you?"

Eleanor sat back on her heels. "Yeah, I guess. But I'm not too good at keeping secrets."

Becky's voice echoed in Jesse's head. *"I don't like secrets."*

"Yeah, me neither." Jesse sighed.

The rejuvenating effect of a hot shower and clean clothes helped. Her first stop would be Sister Therese's office to brief her on the previous night's events. Then on to study Edgar Allan Poe. How fitting that today's lesson was on "The Fall of the House of Usher." She would have to watch Becky closely.

Leaning into the northeast wind, she hurried along the sidewalk from the dormitory to the academic building. As she walked past the secretary's desk, she avoided looking at the place where she had crouched to hide from Sister Catherine's killer. Her knees wobbled as she passed, fear threatening to suck her breath away. Being that close to danger—to death—kept the terror at the edge of her mind, ready to fill her at a moment's notice. She knocked on the principal's door.

"Enter," Sister Therese called out.

Jesse edged the door open. "Do you have a minute?"

"That's about all I have. What is it?" The nun indicated the chair facing her desk.

Where to begin?

"You need to be aware of two incidents that occurred last night."

Sister Therese raised her eyebrows, waiting for Jesse to continue.

Better to start with Becky's encounter before mentioning the library. She'd gauge the nun's reaction before she committed to exposing her injury.

"Something unusual happened in Becky Newhart's room."

"Oh?" The nun sat forward, leaning her crossed arms on the desk.

Sister Therese's face was impassive as she listened to Jesse's version of the eerie events. When she finished, the woman tapped her fingers on the desk.

"Is there any way something else could have caused the picture frame to fall? Was the table wiggled or bumped?"

"No." Jesse shifted in her chair; Sister Therese didn't believe her. Becky needed protection and support, not doubt and suspicion. Granted, convincing a Catholic nun about a vengeful spirit would take some doing, but right now Becky's health and safety were at stake. Sister Therese had to be on board with this so they could protect the girl. "You might want to ask Becky to recall the events. Perhaps she can add something I've missed."

"Have you spoken to the girl this morning?"

Jesse's temper rose. "Do you mean in order to corroborate our stories? No, I have not. The only student I've seen so far this morning is Becky's roommate, Eleanor McHenry. I told her nothing of the strange happenings. In fact, I lied about why I stayed." Jesse's fists were balled in her lap. She perched on the edge of her chair.

"There was talk of a ghost in your house, Miss Graham."

Jesse caught the formal address.

"We don't believe in ghosts here. We stay away from the dark practices."

Jesse stood and leaned over the desk toward the woman. "You'd better start believing, Sister, because you have a ghost residing at St. Bartholomew's."

She strode out of the office, slamming the door behind her.

Becky's worried expression as she entered the classroom eased when Jesse gave her a small wave from the back of the room. The girl's eyes were red and puffy with dark half-moons beneath them. Her shoulders slumped, giving her a caved-in appearance, as if all her strength had been knocked out of her. Sitting at her desk, Becky rested her head in her hands. Adrianna Rutherford bumped her as she passed.

"Good afternoon, girls." Jesse said as she walked to the front of the room.

"Good afternoon, Miss Graham." Their voices in unison; most of them sounded pleasant except Adrianna, who always dragged her sarcasm-laced greeting out a beat behind the others.

"Today we are going to read Poe's tale, 'The Fall of the House of Usher.' It's one of his best-known works, and it's really scary." She hunched, forward making claws of her hands and cackling. All of the girls laughed—except Becky.

Writing the page number on the board, she listened to the girls opening their textbooks behind her. She knew this would be a tough lesson for Becky, but the story was required content in the curriculum. She had planned to have the girls take turns reading aloud, and Becky's turn was scheduled for late in the story when the plot was at its scariest. She turned back to the class.

"Becky, would you please start us off?" Jesse kept her voice light, a smile on her face.

The students bent their heads to their books, but Becky kept looking at her. Jesse winked. Becky nodded and read.

"During the whole of a dull, dark, and soundless day in the autumn of the year…" Her voice was low and shaky.

"I can't hear you," Adrianna called out in a sing-song voice.

Jesse frowned at her.

"Well, I can't—nobody can," the girl said.

"Becky, please speak louder," Jesse urged.

Becky shifted her shoulders and held her book higher. "When the clouds hung oppressively low in the heavens…"

Adrianna glanced at Madeline, stifling a laugh. Becky's obvious suffering did nothing to stem their cruelty. She shook her head slightly at the girls, who slumped in their seats, still smirking. *Remember, they're only in their teens.*

At the end of class Becky approached Jesse's desk.

"What am I going to do, Miss Graham? What if that... thing comes back tonight? I'm so scared." The girl's ashen face was a mask of fear.

"Becky, have you told your father about this?"

The girl's eyes widened and she trembled. "No. I don't want him to know."

"Why not? He needs to know—he'll want to help."

"No! Please, Miss Graham, promise me you won't tell him."

"I thought you didn't like secrets." Jesse kept her voice soft so it sounded like a question, not an accusation.

Becky dropped her eyes. "Sometimes secrets are necessary. To keep you safe."

Jesse cocked her head. It was bad enough the other girls were ostracizing her, but now a vengeful ghost was haunting her. Why Becky? There had to be more underneath all of this. Becky had seemed nervous and vulnerable from the first day she met her.

"Perhaps you could stay in the cottage with your father. Would you feel safer there?"

Becky shook her head.

"Has Sister Therese spoken to you today?"

Becky nodded. "Yes. She called me to her office during first hour. She said you had talked to her about what happened last night."

"How did that go?"

Becky shrugged. "I told her what happened, but I don't think she believed me. Maybe it wasn't that she didn't believe me, but that she didn't want to believe what I was saying was possible."

"How do you feel about talking to her?"

"Okay, I guess. I don't know." Becky played with the pencils in the holder on Jesse's desk. "Was it my fault, Miss Graham? Did I make that ghost or whatever it is come to St. Bartholomew's?"

"Heavens no, Becky! That ghost has been here for decades. Maybe centuries. What makes you say that?"

"Sister Therese said that nothing like this has ever happened here before. I think what she meant was, 'before you came here, Becky.' She didn't actually say it, but it was like those words were hanging in the air between us, you know what I mean?"

"I know exactly what you mean." Jesse rubbed her eyes. "Did Sister Therese say what might happen? Did she give you any advice or help?"

Becky dug into her brown corduroy drawstring bag, fishing out a small glass bottle with a black screw-on cap. "She gave me this holy water to sprinkle around my room."

"Really?" Jesse rubbed the back of her neck. "Okay. Would you like me to help you sprinkle that? Maybe we could say a few Hail Marys and an Our Father."

Becky's face broke into a smile. "Yes! Thank you, Miss Graham."

"You're welcome. Anything else?"

"Eleanor is looking at me funny. She seems to know something happened, but not exactly what."

"I had a talk with Eleanor when she woke me this morning. She obviously knows something weird happened since I was sleeping in your room in my bloodstained shirt. I told her you had a nightmare and came and got me, and that I fell and bumped my head, thus the blood."

"She didn't buy it, did she?" Becky gave a half smile.

"No."

"Eleanor's the smartest girl in our class. She probably already has it all figured out."

Jesse gave a small laugh. "I doubt that, but I'm sure she suspects something more than my thinly veiled story."

"I don't think she'll like the holy water idea. She's kind of…different, you know? Not, I don't know, serious about religion."

"Eleanor is bright, and sometimes bright people need to question everything. Maybe we can sprinkle the holy water while she's at study group."

"That would be perfect. See you later."

Becky's gait was much lighter than when she'd entered at the beginning of the hour. She had been comforted by the idea of the holy water.

Jesse didn't share her faith in it.

CHAPTER TWENTY

Jesse was happy to be in her own house again even if it was just for the weekend. Switching on the lamp, she dropped the mail on the hall table as she passed it on her way to the kitchen. Despite her aversion to basements, she headed downstairs to check how work was progressing on her house. Flipping on the light, she fought the sick feeling that always overtook her there.

Forcing herself to move beyond the brown stain still on the floor from where she shot Helen's murderer in self-defense three months ago, she passed beneath the single light bulb in the ceiling toward the electrical box. Wires stuck out from a new metal box attached to the wall. Satisfied, she examined the pipes running along the joists. Half of them were shining, new copper, but a few were still the faded, galvanized iron. She noticed a new sewer pipe running down the back wall. Smiling, she returned to the kitchen and ran the water in the sink. At first, rusty water sputtered out, spewing against the white porcelain. After a couple of minutes, clear, sparkling water gushed from the tap.

Thank you, God. Geez, why do I keep talking to you if you're not really there? I guess Joe did this, not you, God. The thought of Joe hurt her heart, she missed him so.

She went to the hall and dialed the phone.

"Joe is, um, out this evening," Susan said after they talked briefly.

"Oh, okay. I'm home for the weekend, and I just wanted to thank him for all the work his crew has done on my house." Joe was out with someone. The pit in her stomach felt like a lead ball.

"I'll tell him you called." Susan's voice was light. Yep, she was trying to make this easier.

"Great. Thanks, Susan. Good night."

"Good night, Jesse."

Standing with the phone at her ear, she stared into the mirror above the hall table.

"You can't have it both ways, Graham. You've made it clear that you don't want to commit to him, and he is not going to wait around."

When she put the phone back on its cradle, the click sounded final.

∞

The yard was buried in late autumn leaves, and Jesse was buried in essays. But raking leaves, grading papers, and housework had been her refuge all weekend. She hadn't heard from Joe, and she needed to keep herself occupied. Putting away the last clean dish, she headed upstairs to pack for another week's stay at St. Bartholomew's dormitory. She'd checked on Becky a couple of times; there had been no other unusual events in Becky's bedroom, nor had she heard any chanting or drums. In fact, it all seemed rather surreal now.

After locking the house, she got into her car, patting the dashboard, her usual affectionate sign of appreciation for her Bug.

"Let's head back to school, Bert."

As she eased out of the driveway, she looked back at her house. When she'd moved in five months earlier, she'd been afraid. Embarrassed. She was running away from heartbreak and rejection. As if running could make her strong. But since she'd moved into the Cavanaugh House, she'd had to face *real* danger, *real* threats. Why had she thought losing Robert was life-shattering? Facing her worst fears, standing with someone who also was in danger—that was being strong. Wresting her fate from what happened to her and making it what she decided she wanted—that was being strong. Facing a ghost and allowing it to work through her even though people thought she was nuts—that was being strong. And, yes, balancing the reality of who she was against what she longed for—that was being strong. Accepting that, for some reason, she was a ghost magnet—scary but also strong. She smiled.

Damn, you're amazing, Graham. She had only lived there for five months, but how that house had changed her. Now she seemed to be a ghost magnet.

Jesse sat at her desk, recording grades in her grade book. Hearing a cough, she looked up to see Joe watching her from the doorway. His hands grasped either side of the frame, holding him back from entering. She caught a tender look in his eyes before he masked it.

"Hey." He still didn't enter. Instead, he looked around her classroom.

"Hey," she said, clasping her hands to tamp the joy surging within her. "Are you going to come in or talk to me from the hall?"

He sauntered in and sat on top of the student desk in front of her. She thought about teasing him the way she had Scott, but it didn't feel right using the same joke with both.

"Your classroom looks nice."

"Thanks."

This felt all wrong. Joe should be teasing her; she should be retorting. There should be an ease between them like there used to be.

"Mom said you called the other night."

"Yeah, I did. I've been staying here in the dormitory to help with the girls, but I spent the weekend at the house, and I checked out all the work your guys have done. I wanted to say thank you." She paused. "And maybe see if you wanted to come over to have a beer. And, you know, inspect the work."

"I don't need to inspect their work. They know what they're doing." His tone was level.

No, Joe, you're supposed to make some bawdy comment about inspecting my work. This isn't how it's supposed to be between us.

"I didn't mean to imply—" She broke off.

"Sorry. I didn't mean that the way it sounded. My guys are great. I do stop by occasionally to check out their jobs, and I had been there that afternoon. I'm glad you're satisfied."

She nodded, unable to speak.

"I came by to tell you what I found in the basement of the dormitory."

She perked up.

"There is a second tunnel down there, just as I suspected. The first one I found seems to head in the direction of the school. And here's the clincher—it's been used recently. There are signs that there is another one on the adjoining wall, which would lead to... I don't know, the woods, I guess. Maybe all the way to Seneca Lake."

Jesse rested her chin in her hand. First of all, why were there tunnels built? Second, who among the staff with keys to the basement would use the tunnels for questionable purposes?

"Don't you get it, Jesse? That could be your 'ghost.' A couple of the girls using the tunnel to access the school basement and scare the crap out of people."

"Did you follow it all the way to the school basement?"

she asked.

"Sure did. The doors are mammoth and heavy, but I'm sure if a few girls got together, they could manage to open them. But the tunnels are in bad shape. If your girls are running around in them, they're in danger. The walls are crumbling, and the support beams are rotting."

"Wow. That would solve the mystery of the noisy basement. But what about what happened in Becky's room, and to me in the library?"

"What do you mean?"

"That's right—you don't know." Perhaps this was why she felt so out of control lately. She used to share everything with him. Joe had been her anchor. His calm reassurance and logical interpretation of things steadied her impetuous, overactive imagination. She related the incident in the library, touching the back of her head where the healing gash was still a bit tender. Finally, she explained what had happened in Becky's room.

He whistled softly. "You sure bring on the ghosts. And you're going to be staying here for the week?"

His look of concern warmed her. She nodded. He rubbed his chin before saying, "I'll be on campus during the day if you need me."

"Thanks, Joe." She desperately wanted him to stay. How could she keep him talking? "Hey, when do you start work on the Digson power plant project?"

His jaw twitched. "There is no project."

"What?"

"I paid to have schematics drawn up after he accepted my bid, I even began to order supplies, but I was informed that Trevor Underwood had changed his mind. He also refused to reimburse me for my investment, so I got the shaft."

"Geez, that stinks."

"I don't know what his game is. I guess he changed his mind about location. Not sure why he waited so long to do that. He never even apologized—hell, he never even told me directly. One of his lackeys called to tell me."

Jesse's stomach ached.

He stood to leave, so she rose from her desk, walking with him toward the door.

"Thanks for filling me in on the second tunnel."

"No problem, Jesse."

She waited to hear him say it. But he said Jesse. Just Jesse.

∞

Moonlight streamed through the windows of the silent corridor as Jesse made her rounds for bed check. As usual, Adrianna and Madeline still had their light on and were talking. When she knocked and entered, their conversation halted. Adrianna raised her chin, looking down her nose at her. Jesse detected the faint smell of cigarette smoke and noticed the curtain stuck in the window sash.

"Lights out, ladies. Please don't set the place on fire."

Madeline sniffed as she slipped under her covers. Adrianna just glared at her.

Jesse closed the door and smiled. But her smile faded when the air got colder as she neared Becky and Eleanor's room. *Uh-oh.* She felt the frigid air escaping from beneath the door, the cold coiling around her toes. Gripping the knob, she turned it, easing the door open. An icy blast of air slammed into her, sucking away her breath. Gasping, she stumbled into the room. Becky cowered into the corner of her bed with her pillow clasped in front of her, eyes wide with terror. All the pictures on the walls were crooked, and her Beatles poster was ripped down the middle from top to bottom. Books had tumbled from the shelves and lay scattered in heaps. Once again the picture that had been on her bedside table had crashed to the floor. Eleanor was fast asleep in the midst of this chaos.

Jesse searched the room for any sign of the apparition,

but saw nothing. The air warmed again, and she knew the ghost was gone. Running to Becky, she wrapped the freezing girl in her arms. Easing the girl's trembling form up from the bed, Jesse grabbed her robe off the hook and took her into the hall. With an arm across her shoulder, Jesse led her back to the supervisor's hall. There, she checked the phone numbers listed on an index card taped to the wall above the table, picked up the phone, and dialed Sister Therese's room. As Mother Superior, she was the only one with a phone in her room.

It rang only once before she heard the woman's sleepy voice.

"Sister Therese? This is Jesse. You need to come over here at once."

She wanted to add, "Seeing is believing," but she bit her tongue.

⌒⌒

The nun's face went white when she saw the destruction in Becky's room. Jesse crossed her arms, vindicated, until the nun ushered them out into the hall.

"Becky, you must be honest with me. Did you create the havoc in there?" Sister Therese frowned at the girl, her voice low.

"How can you even suggest that? She was terrified when I arrived. Besides, I felt the icy air, and I know what that means."

Sister Therese leveled a look at her. "You seem to bring that myth with you, don't you?"

Jesse leaned toward the woman, hands on her hips. "Myth? I have several people who can confirm Helen's ghost, including Maggie." Her words stabbed the air. "And may I remind you that Helen helped bring her murderer to justice?"

Sister Therese folded her arms across her chest. "Ah, yes,

Sister Alphonse's brother is in jail because of you."

Jesse recognized the wisp of a threat curling up from that remark. She straightened, taking a step closer to the nun.

"He is in jail because of what *he* did, not because of what I did. Let's get that straight." She couldn't believe she was talking to a nun like this, but she wouldn't back down.

Sister Therese nodded her head once in acknowledgement. "Let's attend to this evening's events, shall we? There are cases of demonic possession that have manifested similar occurrences. Perhaps what we need is an exorcism. I can speak to Father Steve."

Jesse took a step back and put her arm around Becky's shoulder. "This has nothing to do with demonic possession. What happened in that room was not of Becky's doing. We need to help this ghost find peace. That will stop all of these strange happenings. Believe me, I know. Who is an expert on the history of St. Bartholomew's? We need to know what's happened here in the past."

The nun raised one eyebrow. "I suggest you talk to your family. The Wyndhams have all the archives concerning St. Bartholomew's."

"Thank you. Now, what shall we do about Becky and Eleanor staying in this room?"

The nun opened her mouth to speak, but closed it. After a few heartbeats, she murmured, "Rooms are at a premium in the dormitory because we have so many students. I believe there is a room available in the supervisor's hallway, but I must clear it with the other nuns who stay there."

"You don't have to clear it with anyone, and you know it. Becky needs to stay there tonight."

"Fine. What about the McHenry girl?"

Jesse looked in at the slumbering Eleanor.

"She'll be fine for tonight. I think our ghost has a con-nection to Becky."

"I don't like all this talk about the supernatural," Sister

Therese mumbled.

"You may not like it, but you'll have to deal with it. First, we need to discover who this ghost is and why it's showing up."

"Of course. I'm still of the opinion that we need an exorcism. I'll leave you to take Becky to her new room. Good night."

Sister Therese turned and strode down the corridor to the stairwell.

Jesse squeezed Becky's shoulders. "C'mon. Let's get some sleep."

Once she had Becky settled in the room two doors down, Jesse lay awake reviewing the conversation she'd just had with Sister Therese. If she had been just Jesse, English teacher, her ass would have been fired on the spot. But she was Jesse Graham, heir to the Wyndham fortune, and therefore owner of St. Bart's. She'd always had a prejudice against the sway wealthy people held, but maybe it was time to reconsider.

CHAPTER TWENTY-ONE

Jesse edged Bert up the winding drive to Wyndham Manor. She was tired after a full day of teaching, the dreariness of the late November afternoon adding to her fatigue. The only thing that energized her was the possibility of discovering the history of St. Bart's property—and its ghost.

"I don't think this will ever feel like home to me, Bert," she said. Pulling up to the front entrance, she parked her VW at an angle then climbed the steps to the massive front door. Gerald greeted her, taking her coat and scarf.

"Mr. Wyndham is awaiting you in his study, Miss Graham." Leading her across the marble floor, he indicated a door to the left. Knocking softly, he opened it.

"Miss Graham to see you, sir."

"Yes, bring her in." Ben Wyndham stood, moving around his desk to greet her.

"Jesse, it's so good to see you." He planted a kiss on her cheek.

"Hi, Ben. It's nice to be here." It wasn't a lie. She was glad because she hoped to find answers in the family archives.

"Your phone call was intriguing. So you want to explore the history of the Wyndhams?"

Now *that* was a lie. Jesse was not interested so much in the history of the family as she was in the history of the property.

"I can't tell you how pleased I am that you're coming around to the idea of your role as the Wyndham heir. Of course, you may have free rein of the library whenever you wish." He poured her a glass of Riesling and reached for his own on his desk. He saluted her and took a sip. "The archives go all the way back to the 1800s, when my ancestor first founded the estate in 1840."

"Are there records before that time?" she asked.

"Oh, I think we have records of previous property owners dating back to the 1700s." He cocked his head. "Why would you want those?"

She took a quick sip of her wine. "Oh, you know, I like to be thorough."

"I admire your enthusiasm." He drained his glass. "Let me give you a tour of the library."

Walking across the hall, Ben asked her how the faculty and students were doing after the tragedies that had struck St. Bartholomew's. Though he had visited the school after each incident, it had been during the day while she was teaching. How she wanted to tell him about the Weeping Woman just to see his reaction. But Ben seemed like a pragmatic man, not one to believe in the supernatural, so she kept quiet. He swept open the library door.

She sucked in her breath. *Holy crap!*

This room, surely the size of a football field, was lined to the ceiling with books on every wall. An enormous Oriental rug patterned with blazing reds, oranges, and gold gathered a deep brown leather couch and chair before a fireplace. Other leather chairs sat comfortably by windows or tucked in nooks with reading lamps beside them. Jesse clasped her hands, grinning. She slowly rotated full circle, taking in the shelves tucked just below the crown molding and covering the walls to just above the mahogany wainscoting.

"Impressive, isn't it?" His pride was not offensive; it was

obvious he loved this collection.

"Indeed it is," she said. "Thank you for allowing me to use it."

"Jesse, it is yours after all. Yours to use whenever you wish."

She bit back her reply. She did not want to antagonize Ben right now. For once, she was going to take advantage of her station as Wyndham heir.

"Let me show you where the earliest archives are." He slid a mobile ladder to the west wall and climbed to the top. "They were relegated to the top of the stacks because so few of us look at them. I can have them brought down for you."

But the idea of climbing that ladder brought out the child in Jesse. She couldn't wait. "No, that won't be necessary. I'd actually enjoy scanning the titles up there."

After he climbed down, he opened a secretary drawer, pulling out white cotton gloves. "Some of the volumes are fragile, so I'd ask you to wear these while you work." He checked his watch. "I have a meeting, so I'll leave you to it. You know, it would be much more convenient for you if you lived here. You'd have instant access to the library. Sister Therese tells me that you've been staying at the dormitory while your house is being renovated. Wouldn't you be more comfortable here?"

"You're generous, Ben, but I'm fine at the dormitory. Actually, I'm helping Sister Therese out because they were shorthanded for staffing after—"

"I don't think the Wyndham heir should be staffing the dormitory." His voice was stern.

Surprised at his harshness, she said nothing at first. Finally, she couldn't take the pressure from her screaming conscience.

"Ben, we need to have a conversation about this."

"About what, Jesse?"

"About my status in the family."

"No need. You are the heir. That's final. And you should be living here where you belong."

"But..."

Gerald appeared at the door. "Your appointment has arrived, sir." Trevor Underwood entered the room. Gerald sniffed, exiting.

"Hello, Ben. Oh, hello, Jesse. How nice to see you again."

"Hello, Trevor," Ben said. She did not hear the welcome tone she had received.

Trevor's wide smile never faded as he walked toward them. He glanced around the room, whistling as he sized up the collection. "Quite extraordinary, Ben. You must have the world at your fingertips here."

"Yes, well, shall we go to my office?"

Trevor's path had led him to tower beside Jesse. A little too close for her comfort. He smiled down at her. "Are you here to take advantage of this library today?"

She moved to a nearby table, placing her purse and satchel on it. "Yes. I am interested in the history of Wyndham Manor."

"Oh, of course. You would be."

No one spoke. Jesse was surprised at Ben's reticence—he was usually so gregarious.

Trying to ease the awkwardness in the room, she asked, "How is your search for a site for the new plant coming along?"

Ben's jaw twitched. Trevor shifted, moving away from her.

"We're closing in on our decision, make no mistake."

What mistake did he think she might make? Believing what he'd told her at the barn dance?

Moving toward the door, Ben finally spoke.

"We'd best leave Jesse to her research." He looked back at her. "Perhaps knowing more about the Wyndham history will convince you to move in here and take your rightful place. Please give it some consideration. Come, Trevor, we'll meet in my office."

She fumed at his remark. She hadn't asked to be the heir to this fortune and had no intention of dancing to the Wyndham tune. Ben held no strings to manipulate her; why was he so insistent? In reality, she was usurping his son's position, so it would make more sense if he resented her. So why did he insist on parading her out as the heir at every opportunity?

Finally, her hunger to start researching legends and ghost stories made her dismiss any questions about Ben.

For a moment, she stood transfixed. All of this knowledge at her fingertips, as Trevor had said. An English teacher's dream. Tucking the gloves into her waistband, she climbed the ladder to the spot Ben had indicated. This seemed to be where the earliest volumes were housed, some of them so old their bindings were paper and board. Books with calfskin covers also ran along this section of shelving. She balanced against the ladder, slipping on the gloves. Running her finger along the spines, she checked the dates and pulled out the earliest to carry over to a table near the window. Opening the satchel she'd brought, she took out a yellow legal pad and a couple of pens, laying them on the table. She carefully opened the yellowed, fragile pages, and studied them.

The earliest records described a Seneca Indian village called Ga-nun-da-saga, or Kanandesaga, where Geneva now stood. It was the capital for the Council of Six Nations, the Iroquois, and the site of their most sacred burial ground. Surrounded by an earthen wall, the village had contained longhouses constructed of bark and timber. Her earlier research had indicated the Seneca tribes located their burial grounds near the village, so the proximity of St. Bartholomew's to Geneva made it possible that the grounds were a part of that village or a smaller one nearby. The remains of their ancestors were sacred to the Seneca. To them, gravesites were the holiest places on earth.

She eventually found a passage about the Phelps and Gorham purchase of that land. The white men swore that the sacred mound would never be disturbed, and Seneca Indians often visited the site to ensure its preservation. Later excavation found the remains of Indians, their heads toward the east, buried with earthly goods like pipes, copper pots, and bead necklaces to allow their spirits to join their ancestors.

Bead necklaces. Becky had found a small bead necklace. Jesse's arms pricked with goose bumps.

"Hello, Jesse."

She jumped. Al Wyndham stood at the door.

"Hello, Al. It's good to see you," she said.

"Father told me you were here." Glancing at her then at the book, he approached the table.

"Sit down, Al. I'd like to talk to you."

"Is that an order from the Wyndham heir?" His voice was sharp.

"Al, please. Sit down."

He slumped into the chair across from her, and she leaned forward, her voice almost a whisper.

"Listen, I don't want this any more than you do. As far as I'm concerned, all of this is yours to own and manage. Al, I'm not interested in the Wyndham fortune."

His eyes narrowed as he looked at her. "You're serious."

She threw her arms out in exasperation. "Yes! I'm serious!"

His shoulders relaxed as he sat back. "There is little we can do. The inheritance provision was initiated by Great-great-great-grandfather Albert Wyndham. It clearly states that the property belongs to the eldest child of the eldest child."

"But can't I refuse it?"

He ran his fingers through his thick, dark hair. "I don't know. It would take a mountain of paperwork and a herd of lawyers."

"That doesn't sound pleasant." She rested her chin on her

hand.

"What are you thinking? I can see the wheels turning in those green eyes."

"Actually, Al, I can't believe I'm thinking this myself. But I have an idea."

Becky rushed into Jesse's classroom, gasping with excitement.

"I'm back in the club, Miss Graham!" She bent over, trying to catch her breath.

Jesse pursed her lips. "Is that a good thing, Becky?"

"Oh, it's groovy! Even Adrianna is being nice to me."

Jesse's hand stopped above the pen she was reaching for.

"Why do you think that is so?"

Becky straightened, brushing back her hair. "I don't know, but it sure makes it easier on me around here. Maybe with all that's happened, she realizes that she needs to be kinder."

Jesse nodded. "I see. You'll be careful, right? I mean with the challenges and all."

Becky paused and looked out the window. She looked back at Jesse.

"Yes. Gotta go. Just wanted you to know." She hurried toward the door and turned back. "And, thanks, Miss Graham." She smiled for the first time in weeks.

Jesse resisted the urge to caution her, instead simply saying, "You're welcome, Becky."

Jesse turned the master key over and over in her hand. In a way, she was abusing Sister Therese's trust in her; on the other hand, the noises from the basement could be the key to the occurrences in Becky's bedroom. The Weeping Woman had somehow zeroed in on Becky, and Jesse worried about her safety—and mental health. Something about

Becky's mother's death was a dangerous secret; she could certainly relate to that.

The school was silent on this Saturday afternoon. Maggie had told her that the nuns were participating in a day of reflection, so none of them would be coming into their classrooms today. Finished with preparations for that week's lessons, Jesse was about to head home. As she walked by the east wing corridor, the locked basement door beckoned her like a siren. She could not resist. The key burned in her hand, but she hesitated, not sure why. Was she afraid? Yes. But her need to find answers was stronger than her fear. Setting down her briefcase and purse, she inserted the key and turned it. A soft click indicated success. Her heart revved. Would the Weeping Woman be waiting to strangle her?

Summoning her courage, she flipped on the light and descended the wooden stairs, her nose twitching, irritated by the musty air. At the bottom of the stairs, she hit the next light, illuminating a large room lined with shelves of used paint cans, tools, filters, and other items normally found in a basement. To her right, a door opened into the huge boiler room, and the usual noises it emitted were magnified. Straight ahead was a tool bench with a vise attached to it, tools hanging neatly above it on a pegboard. Safety glasses perched on top of the bench, reflecting the beam from the fluorescent light that hung above it.

Corridors ran below the wings of the school. She would explore those momentarily.

Jesse circled around behind the stairs, searching for a drum…or a ghost. Her heart thumped, as if trying to slow her down or make her reconsider. Nothing looked unusual. To her best calculations, the wall to her left faced north, but she couldn't find any door that might open to a tunnel. The only possibility was that a passage might lurk behind the large metal cabinet that commanded the center of the wall.

Pressing the side of her face against the cement, she tried to peer behind the cabinet, but it was snugged tightly against the wall. She couldn't even tuck a hand between the two in order to feel for the seam of a door. She felt something on her face and reached up to wipe it.

"Ewww, ewww, ewww," she whispered as she brushed a spider and part of its web to the floor. She kept wiping her hands and dancing around, trying to shake off the willies. "I hate basements," she hissed. "Just don't let any mice jump out at me now or I'm done for."

She halted, hearing a noise from the other side of the wall. Not drumming or chanting, more like the static of a television station when it went off the air at night. She listened again, not willing to press her ear against the wall lest the spider had a family lying in wait. There it was. Static. Then a mechanical voice. She studied the wall, touching it warily. There was no indication of a doorway to the other side. She eyed the distance of the wall from the stairway; it was much closer than the exterior wall on the first floor was to the staircase. There was a room on the other side, but how to get to it?

She ran her hands along the wall gingerly, feeling for any seams that would indicate a secret door.

Nothing.

This isn't a Nancy Drew novel, Graham. The Secret of the Door in the Basement. She chuckled at herself. But the sounds were louder at this end of the wall she was examining, although still muffled and low. The wall was at the northeast corner of the building; the corner nearest the path to the stables. Perhaps if she had a look at the exterior of the building in that corner, she could determine what this was all about. She returned to the stairs.

The drier air of the main hallway was a relief, and Jesse had to admit she was glad to be out of the basement. She locked the door behind her and hurried to the front entrance of

St. Bart's. The yard was deserted. She circled the building, heading to the corner she wanted to examine. No one was back there either. She walked a little distance from the school, scanning the foundation. At this corner, the basement windows looked newer, darkened by shades. Above the windows, thick cables ran along the juncture of the foundation and the building's Medina limestone. Following their path to the corner, she noted the cables disappeared into the ground. She rounded the corner to the back of the building to find a repeat of the wires.

Walking up to the building, she bent over, running her hands along the thick cables. Surely, this was more power than any school building needed. She leaned in, looking for identifying marks or numbers, when a hand grasped her shoulder and yanked her around. Her heart stopped.

CHAPTER TWENTY-TWO

Arnie stood scowling before her. He had also been around the day Sister Catherine was killed, had appeared just as quickly that day. She fought down the fear surging through her body.

"Come with me," he ordered, grabbing her arm.

"No!" She pulled away from his grasp.

"Your curiosity has gotten you into something deeper than you imagined. You want answers? Come with me."

He turned on his heel and headed toward the school's service entrance. She stood rooted in place, undecided whether to run or to follow. But he wasn't forcing her when he could have grabbed her arm, dragged her, or drugged her.

She followed him into the building.

He had opened his office door and switched on the overhead light, the fluorescent glow lending a yellow tinge to his face, dark shadows haunting his eyes. She remained by the open door.

"What's this about, Arnie? Schools don't need wiring like that—it's like the CIA or something."

"You're right. It is like the CIA in a way. Have a seat." Arnie scrubbed his hands over his face and through his hair as he sat. He no longer appeared threatening but rather troubled, even frightened. Sitting forward, he rested his arms on his knees, clasping his hands together.

"Up until two years ago I worked as a design engineer. I was working on plans for a nuclear power plant on the Hudson River forty miles north of New York City. One night when I was reviewing the plans, I cross-referenced the site with a geological survey and found that the soil compaction was not suitable for a structure of that size or the weight it would require. I took the information to my supervisor. He later assured me that this problem had been investigated and a solution had been implemented. Something kept gnawing at me, so I did some further digging. I found contracts for land improvement but never found invoices for the completed work. I began walking around the site, examining the foundation of the structure, and already I could see stress fractures in one of the buildings. I again called it to the attention of my supervisor, who effectively told me to forget it"—he raised his hands to mime quotation marks—"'for my own good.' I knew it was a threat, and I was pretty shaken up."

He paused, again scrubbing his hands over his face. As if blocking an unpleasant image, he closed his eyes for a moment. He looked at her. "I talked to my wife about it; she was my sounding board." His voice thickened, slowing with dread. "The next day, we switched cars because mine was due for an oil change and she had errands to run, so she offered to take it in for me."

He was silent. Growls emanated from the boiler in the basement just below them. The clock ticks marking the time stood out against the stillness, growing louder against her eardrums with each *click* until her nose and her teeth and the back of her eyeballs threatened to explode.

"She ran a stoplight and was hit broadside by a semi." He inhaled, making a croaking sound. "My comfort is that she died instantly, but I can't image her panic when the brakes didn't work. At first they said she was at fault for running the red light. That devastated Becky and me. But we knew she was a careful driver. Finally, the investigation showed that someone had poked a small hole in the brake lines—just enough that the car could be driven for a while before the brakes failed." He snorted. "The irony is, the truck driver worked for the transportation department of my company. He wasn't charged—it was ruled an accident. He disappeared after that."

He stared at the floor. "That night I got a phone call saying that it should have been me. That if I continued talking about the power plant problems, my daughter would be next." He wiped his hand across his eyes. "Becky doesn't know about that threat, but she knows we're in danger. I contacted the FBI, and they immediately put us in the protection of U.S. Marshals. My friend Bartholomew Wyndham suggested St. Bart's Academy. The marshals were reluctant to place us in the same state, but the Wyndham men can be quite persuasive. Bartholomew set it up, and Ben welcomed us, promising to take every precaution for our safety. It seemed the perfect place to hide. Until now. We've been recognized and word has gotten out as to our whereabouts. I think Valerie Bauer was mistaken for Becky. Becky was the target, and..." He dropped his head in his hands again.

He breathed deeply, fighting to regain control. They sat in silence for a few moments. Jesse's head was spinning. She didn't want to burden him further, but this revelation explained so much.

"Arnie, you need to talk to Becky about what's been happening in her room."

He snapped his head up. "What? What has happened?"

Jesse took a deep breath and prepared for a reaction similar to Sister Therese's.

"There is a ghost or a spirit of some kind that seems to be focused on Becky."

He scrunched his eyebrows together. "A ghost?"

"I know it sounds irrational, but I've had a similar experience, although mine was less…intense than Becky's."

He looked at her skeptically, as if somehow that would distance him from what she was saying.

"Please, just listen to me and try to keep an open mind." She related the encounters in Becky's room as well as her own experience in the library. Arnie listened carefully, his gaze riveted on hers. She finished by detailing her conversation with Sister Therese, describing the nun's disbelief—even anger.

"I think this ghost—she's called the Weeping Woman—was causing the disturbances in my classroom, too."

When she finished, he took a deep breath and scratched the back of his neck. "I've never heard of anything so strange."

"Talk to Becky about it. She doesn't want to tell you, and I couldn't understand why at first. Now I realize she's trying to protect you. I think she knows more about what happened to your wife than you think."

The man looked defeated. Jesse's heart went out to him. He was desperately trying to save his daughter from human danger, and now he was faced with the supernatural. She watched him grapple with this new threat, no doubt so deep in thought he was unaware of his surroundings. Finally, he nodded.

"Follow me." Rising from his chair, he grabbed the mammoth key ring from his desk.

The narrow staircase seemed to close in on her as they descended to the basement. What if his story was a lie? What if he made it all up to lure her down here? His brown work boots clopped down the steps until he reached the bottom and flipped on a light. Arnie had to duck his head in the narrow hall to avoid the pipes and ducts that ran along the low basement ceiling. The musty odors of subterranean cement mixed with damp pipes made her sneeze. Turning down another corridor, he reached a door at the end and faced her.

"What I'm about to show you *must* remain a secret. Please promise me this."

She nodded. On the one hand, whatever was on the other side couldn't be as bad as her fear of the unknown. On the other…well, ignorance was, indeed, bliss.

Unlocking the large metal door, he swung it open and noise and movement accosted Jesse. How the hell could she be just on the other side of the door yet not hear any of this racket? Her mouth hung open as she scanned the room crammed with television screens, desks, maps, and radios. Two men wearing earphones crouched before a video screen and consulted maps lying on their desks. One of the men turned.

Scott Stanton.

"You know U.S. Marshal Stanton." Arnie's eyes lit up with humor.

"Hey, Jesse." Scott's smile was slow.

She felt like Alice in Wonderland again as she murmured, "'Six impossible things before breakfast.'"

Scott stood and approached her. "Sorry I had to keep so many secrets from you. I know how you value honesty." His eyes twinkled as his grin widened.

She was afraid to move lest the floor start to melt or the room rocket off into space.

Taking her arm, Scott led her to the chair he had just vacated. Video monitors surrounded her, and her ears were barraged with telephone conversations. She could be on the set of *Mission Impossible*.

"I suppose 'the Secretary will disavow any knowledge of my actions,'" she said.

Leaning against the desk, Scott smiled. "Of course. Therefore, it would be wise to take no actions." He knelt beside her, looking into her eyes. "Seriously, Jesse, this must remain secret. Sister Therese is the only nun who knows about it. You must not reveal this to Sister Angelina… or to Joe."

No worries there; she and Joe were barely speaking. But to keep this from Maggie? That would be difficult. And there was the matter of Sister Catherine, carrying a pistol and later lying dead on the marble floor.

"Sister Catherine…"

Scott's eyes clouded as he nodded. "Yes, she was a U.S. Marshal, too. In fact, she'd been my partner for three years. Her real name was Catherine Arndt, and she was also working undercover. She died protecting Becky…and possibly you."

What do I have to do with any of this? But Becky, yes, she was in peril—from both the corporal and the spiritual worlds.

Valerie!

"What happened to Valerie? Where did you take her?"

"Most of what I told you was true. Valerie did wake up and start screaming. Whatever they gave her was hallucinogenic. There's a government clinic in Syracuse that we work with, so I took her there. They specialize in hallucinogenic overdoses. Less public." He stood and began to pace, rubbing the back of his neck. "We thought the counteracting medication would do the trick, but she was still tripping when her father picked her up. She died from the overdose in the hospital near their home."

"So even if you'd brought her to Geneva General…"

"She wouldn't have made it. Probably not even through the night there."

"This is about what you were just explaining to me, isn't it?" she asked Arnie.

He nodded.

"Becky is in grave danger." Scott continued. "And because you've become her confidant, you may be now, too. We think whoever broke into the school and killed Catherine was looking for you. They haven't had much luck getting to Becky because of our surveillance."

"If you have all of this surveillance equipment, how could you miss Valerie's abduction?"

Scott stuffed his hands in his pockets.

"This secret club they've got...we monitored it as long as Becky was involved. Once she stopped going out to the cabin, we stopped going, too."

Jesse's eyes widened. "So you're the one who knocked me out and carried me back to my car that night."

Scott shrugged, grinning at her sheepishly. "Had to do it. You were in the way. If the henchmen were going to take action, you couldn't be collateral damage."

"Collateral damage? That's pretty cold."

"I know you had a wicked headache the next day, but it was better than a bullet to the brain. I'm not kidding here, Jesse. These men are killers. It's imperative that you keep this buried. No one can know about our operation or about Arnie's real identity. You must conceal this."

Arnie's voice was soft. "My daughter's life depends on it, Jesse."

In the greenish reflection of a video monitor, his eyes relayed fear. They begged her. She nodded.

"My lips are sealed," she whispered.

CHAPTER TWENTY-THREE

"Miss Graham, come quick!"

Eleanor's voice startled Jesse, causing her to drop the book she was reading while propped up in bed. She slapped her hand on her chest to still her heart.

"What is it, Eleanor?"

"It's Becky. Something's wrong with her. Come quick!"

Once again, Jesse followed Eleanor, this time down the dormitory staircase to the basement. Five girls huddled together at the gaping door opened to the tunnel Joe had told her about, the tunnel that ran east toward the woods and possibly to Seneca Lake. Jesse noted that Adrianna and Madeline were among the five girls. They stepped away from the opening as soon as she arrived.

"Where is Becky?" Jesse asked.

The girls pointed. Down the tunnel, Jesse spotted a dim beam of light. She started after her.

"Wait! Mr. Riley warned us not to go into the tunnel. He said it's dangerous and could collapse," Eleanor cried.

"I can't leave Becky in there. Why in heaven's name did she go in?"

The girls looked at each other. Apparently in that glance they managed to vote Eleanor president of the club because she was the one to speak up.

"She said she heard the Weeping Woman calling to her.

She said she had to pay for what happened to Valerie, and since the cabin is off-limits now, this is her Ultimate Challenge of the Brave."

"Shit," Jesse muttered.

The girls looked at each other with wide eyes. Adrianna smiled.

"Okay, listen. I'm going in there. If anything happens—you know the tunnel collapses or something—get Sister Therese immediately. Do you understand?"

The girls nodded as one. Even Adrianna. Eleanor handed Jesse a flashlight.

Jesse resisted the urge to hold onto the timbers that lined the walls. The dank air clung to her skin as she walked along the packed earthen floor. Cobwebs as thick as curtains hung suspended from the ceiling. Using her flashlight, she swept away those not disturbed by Becky's passing through. Easing down the passageway, she called Becky's name.

No answer. She quickened her step.

Jogging along, she caught sight of Becky up ahead. The girl's pace was steady, her arms stretched out as if balancing herself. Though Jesse called to her, she did not turn around. As Jesse neared her, she heard the chanting and the drum. *Bah-boom. Bah-boom. Bah-boom.* Chanting echoed off the walls, reverberating in waves of sorrowful notes. Catching up with Becky, Jesse grabbed the girl's shoulder and turned her around. Her eyes stared ahead, empty and glazed.

"Becky. Becky!"

Jesse shook her gently. The girl continued to stare straight ahead. Jesse slapped her. Becky recoiled and reached for her cheek. Her eyes came alive.

"Ouch! Miss Graham. Why did you do that?" She looked around. "Where am I?" At the Weeping Woman's grief-stricken chant, her eyes grew wide with fear.

"C'mon, Becky. Now!" Jesse grabbed the girl's hand, pulling her toward the entrance.

Becky dug in her feet. "No. I need to do this, Miss Graham. I need to atone for Valerie's death. It should have been me."

The chanting grew louder. The air grew icy.

"Valerie's death has nothing to do with the Weeping Woman. It has to do with your mother's death."

She froze. "You know about that?"

"Yes. Your father told me everything."

"But that was our secret. I was never to tell anyone about it." Her eyes clouded.

"He told me so I could help protect you."

Icy wind gusted down the tunnel and a faint glow appeared, growing as it neared them.

"The people who killed your mother also killed Valerie. Trying to appease the Weeping Woman will not help. We need to keep you safe from her and from the killers. Come with me now."

Becky stood still, her gaze transfixed on the form closing in on them, and she seemed not to hear Jesse. Timbers shifted from the force of the wind.

Jesse raised her voice above the gust. "We have to get out of here!"

With a rush of adrenaline, she grabbed the girl around the waist, lifting her off the ground. Becky was ice-cold, her limbs stiff. Jesse attempted to carry her as the Weeping Woman bore down on them. But the girl was too heavy. Jesse lowered her to the ground, pulling her, her feet dragging along the dirt floor. Dust and stones swirled up like miniature tornadoes, biting into her legs and bare feet.

"Eleanor! Adrianna! Come and help me!"

She heard no response. Reaching down for her last bit of strength, she lugged Becky down the tunnel. She could feel the fresh air as she neared the entrance.

"Eleanor, Adri—"

Someone's arms reached around to help with Becky. Eleanor. They dragged the girl out of the tunnel and into the bright fluorescent light of the basement. The girls slammed the tunnel door shut. Adrianna pulled a crate over from the wall and they lowered Becky onto it.

"Thank you, Eleanor," Jesse gasped.

"I saw it, Miss Graham," Eleanor whispered.

Jesse nodded.

Becky stirred. "What happened?"

"You were with the ghost in the tunnel." Eleanor's voice was low.

The other girls stared at them.

"I saw her. I saw the Weeping Woman," Eleanor told them.

The girls huddled closer together.

"Let's get Becky into a warm bed," Jesse said.

"Are you going to tell Sister Therese about this?" Eleanor asked.

Considering how Sister Therese had reacted to Becky's previous encounters, that would probably not be helpful. But Arnie needed to know. Although he was skeptical about the ghost haunting Becky, that danger was real—and increasing. And Scott needed to know that the girl needed protection from more than just the human threat on her life. Oh, how she would love to talk to Joe about this—he had experienced Helen's presence and would know Jesse wasn't crazy. Lord, this was all crashing in on her. "I won't tell Sister Therese if you girls promise to stay away from the tunnels."

A chorus of "we promise," and "yes, Miss Graham," was the answer.

"Cross your hearts," Jesse said.

They dutifully crossed their hearts.

"Good. Now let's all get some sleep."

"Miss Graham, you've got to come right now!"

Startled by Adrianna's voice, Jesse dropped the stapler,

hearing it clatter to the floor. She grabbed the edge of the chalkboard to steady herself as she stood on top of the stool. School had been out for two hours, and the girls were supposed to be in the cafeteria for supper.

"What is it, Adrianna?"

"It's Becky. She's gone into the tunnel again. She was saying crazy things about the Weeping Woman calling to her." Her eyes were wide as she gestured toward the hall.

Jesse clambered off the stool. "The tunnel to the school building?"

Adrianna shook her head. "No! The other tunnel. The one she went into the other night. She was in a trance, mumbling something about the ghost. Hurry, Miss Graham!"

Jesse grabbed her key ring from the desk and followed Adrianna out the door. With a sudden thought, she returned to her desk, snatching a flashlight out of the bottom drawer.

At the dormitory, Jesse turned to Adrianna. "Go to the convent and get Sister Therese. Tell her about Becky. You've got to make her believe this is dangerous, do you understand?"

Adrianna nodded, but her curled lip and aloofness were a sudden change at that moment. Jesse didn't have time to diagnose the girl's mood swings. Someone had to rescue Becky, and she certainly couldn't send a student to do it, even if that student did radiate enough disdain to stop a ghost.

∞

Despite Joe's warnings, the desire to see the basement tunnel again had consumed her, lured her even. Now Becky was down there in danger from the Weeping Woman.

Jesse heard the clatter of pots and pans, dishes, and glassware coming from the cafeteria. Not a soul was in the hall. She scrambled down the stairs, hurrying to the tunnel door.

Evidence of Joe's handiwork showed on the door: it boasted a chain secured with a padlock on the latch, but now the door gaped open. Becky must have used the crowbar on the floor to break it. Unlike the last time, no girls huddled near the entrance. All was silent.

"Becky? Can you hear me?"

Her voice reverberated against the walls. A timber creaked. Jesse stepped into the blackness of the tunnel and clicked on the flashlight. She took shallow breaths, trying not to inhale the musty air. As she moved forward, she felt the clinging wisp of a thick cobweb on her face. She scrubbed it away, ignoring any spider that might have lit on her.

"It's all right. It's me, Miss Graham." Her voice echoed into the darkness.

Stillness lay ahead. She crept along the tunnel, Joe's words echoing in her brain: "*But the tunnels are in bad shape. If your girls are running around in them, they're in danger. The walls are crumbling, and the support beams are rotting.*"

She headed deeper into the blackness. Behind her, a deafening *bang!* shook the walls, and the small bit of light from the basement behind her disappeared. She hurried back, sweeping the flashlight toward the entry. The door had slammed shut. Bits of dust and small chunks of wood hailed down on her. She pushed against the door, but it wouldn't budge. She heard the latch slip back into place. She fought the dread rising in her heart, tasting the bile in her throat. She pounded on the door.

"Adrianna. Open the door."

Nothing.

Stop it, Graham. You've got to get to Becky. Adrianna knows we're here. It will be okay.

Aiming the beam of the flashlight down the tunnel, she started along the uneven dirt floor. Stumbling, she grabbed for the wall but grasped a vertical timber instead. Losing her balance, she tried to regain it, but the timber slid along the wall, bringing her down with it. A sickening thud ricocheted off the walls as the timber crashed to the floor behind her. Like enormous dominos, another timber beside her followed, eerie in its graceful descent, then another.

Jesse tried to stand and sprint ahead, but the timbers were falling too fast. Dust clouded up, making it impossible to see. She ducked down and covered her head with her arms while timber, rocks, and dust beat her to the ground.

Jesse cowered beneath the rubble. She eased her arms down from over her head, cautious with each movement lest she disturb the timbers and cause another collapse. Rubbing her eyes, she coughed and spit out a mouthful of dust, but it was so thick that with every breath she took, she inhaled more fine powder. Overcome by a coughing fit, she pressed her shirt to her nose. Her flashlight lay just out of reach. The beam was thick with white motes floating down to rest on the fallen planks.

She eased away a board that had fallen against her back and propped up on her elbows to maneuver out from underneath the debris. Careful not to disturb the rubble around her, she slid a loose board off her legs. She wiggled her toes to see if they still worked. *Thank God!* Shattered bricks and stone surrounded her; it was a miracle none had struck her on the head. Stretching her limbs to test for breaks, she was relieved that everything was in working order. Warmth spread above her right eye. Touching her forehead, she felt a trickle of blood.

She retrieved her flashlight and swept it around to inspect the damage. Just the area by the door had collapsed; six feet away, the tunnel was still intact. Timbers crisscrossed above her head making it impossible to stand, so, crouching, she crawled over the broken boards toward the undamaged part of the tunnel. She inched her way along, trying not to disturb the precariously balanced beams. A few more feet and she would be able to stand.

Overwhelmed by the dust, she stumbled against a plank that shifted and, in slow motion, slid down the wall, initiating another small collapse. Squatting, she dropped the flashlight and covered her head with her arms as, again, rubble tumbled around her, raising yet more dust. This time, pulling up her shirt didn't stem the coughing. She was suffocating; the choking threatened to render her unconscious.

Settle down, Graham. You'll be okay in a minute. Just relax.

She tentatively inhaled. Her breathing evened out as the dust settled. The glow of her flashlight filtered through the powder from just below a nearby board. Gingerly leaning toward it, she shifted the board and felt a sting. *Damn!* She slipped the torch out and focused it on her left hand where blood oozed from the palm. Shining the light on the board, she saw a rusty nail sticking up. Great. Guess whose tetanus shot wasn't up to date.

Crawling forward, Jesse finally reached the undamaged part of the tunnel. She stood and stretched, grateful for the clearer air as she progressed. A sudden gust of icy air—air that was not so welcome. The Weeping Woman. Jesse hunkered against the wall as the cold intensified. She flicked off the flashlight, not that it made any sense. From her experience, a ghost didn't need a light to see. She pressed against the wall, trying to make herself as small as possible, knowing that didn't matter to a ghost either.

She had to get to Becky, but how?

A haunting chant emanated from down the tunnel, accompanied by a steady drumbeat. The song wrenched Jesse's heart. Just as she had sensed emotion from Helen's apparition, she could feel this woman's longing and grief. The slow, rhythmic sound echoed a dying heartbeat, each *boom* a farewell. The chant wailed along the walls, a scavenger bird's call, hollow against the black sky. *That poor woman.*

Her heart was torn from her. Jesse wept. She held her stomach, trying to stem the hollow emptiness that overwhelmed her. But wrapped around the sorrow, white rage tore at her insides. This woman mourned for the soul of her child and longed for revenge on those who had robbed her child of his afterlife. Jesse quaked with the opposing emotions that controlled her body and mind. Like an avalanche, the rage overtook the sorrow, and Jesse was aware that she was the surrogate target. Howling replaced the chanting. When she found Becky, the girl might be badly injured…or worse.

A deafening roar preceded the force that was a tornado barreling down the tunnel. Jesse covered her ears. Timbers creaked and groaned, shifting again as the intensity of the ghost's fury raced along the passageway. She knelt and protected her head, bracing herself for the impact. The apparition's glow was blinding in the dark tunnel, whirling and rebounding off the walls. Curled in a fetal position, she snugged against the wall and squeezed her eyes shut. She had never expected to die like this, but the agony of this woman's loss beat within her, making death almost desirable. How could anyone survive this black hole of grief?

The movement of the air from the force of the ghost made the timbers slide again. She had only a few moments left. She sat up, spreading her arms wide.

"I hear you," she cried. "Your sorrow carves into my heart. I know what needs to be done. I will find your child. I will bury him properly so he can live with his ancestors."

The whirling quieted.

"I promise." Her words were barely a whisper. But the woman's fury eased. The glow diminished until a single shaft of light stood before her. Jesse could make out the figure of a woman dressed in a deerskin dress and leggings, her hair cut short.

"I promise."

The figure flickered. Jesse saw tears shimmering on the

woman's cheeks. She nodded. Jesse nodded back. The apparition faded, and the air warmed.

Jesse collapsed against the tunnel and rested her elbows on her knees, holding her head in her hands. *How am I ever going to find her child?* She lifted her head. *How the hell am I ever going to get out of here?*

How much time had passed since the door slammed? Her breathing was beginning to quicken—no, she would not give in to the creeping aversion to being underground now. Her situation was too dire to waste the energy. And Becky was in danger. She closed her eyes.

Becky was not down here. She had never been down here. Adrianna had lied.

At the sounds of skittering feet, her skin crawled. Of course, it might not be mice... *Oh, Lord, help me.* She took a deep breath and continued on.

Finally, her flashlight lit up a huge oak door at the end of the tunnel. Large, cast iron hinges lined the right side of the door, with a large, brass escutcheon framing a keyhole on the left. Grasping the oversized doorknob, she tried to turn it. All it yielded was a screech. Using both hands, she tried again. It didn't budge. She ran her flashlight beam along the seams of the door, looking for any sign of weakness, but it was solidly sealed. She kicked it.

"Ow!" Her voice echoed down the tunnel, churning up more skittering noises. "That was smart, Graham."

She searched the door again. At the base of the door, the damp ground had rotted the wood at the bottom. But it wasn't damaged enough that she could break through it. Crap. She would have to retrace her steps and try to dig herself out at the other end of the tunnel. But where had this tunnel led her? She had walked too far for it to be the tunnel to the academic building. The damp ground suggested she was near the lake, and the time it had taken her to walk here would be about right. But why would St.

Bart's have this system of tunnels?

She trudged on. Her legs were becoming wobbly. Her stomach growled. She would have to dig out fast to make it in time for supper. When she heard a rustling noise just behind her, she quickened her steps. Finally, up ahead, she saw the edge of the pile of rubble. She ran the flashlight beam along it—it would be impossible for her to dig herself out. The pile of timber was at least three feet deep. Even if she moved it, chances were it could cause another collapse. Best-case scenario, if she had the strength and her flashlight batteries lasted, in two hours she could drag away enough timber to reach the door. The locked door.

"That's your only choice, Graham." Her echoing voice mocked her.

Perching the flashlight on a fallen timber, she began pulling boards, broken bricks, and pieces of stone away from the area nearest the entrance. She had to work methodically so she did not disturb the structure any more and cause another collapse. Careful not to injure herself on another nail, she propped the boards along the wall and placed the stones to the side. The work was tedious, and after a while her back and legs ached enough to convince her to rest. Stepping back, she surveyed her progress. The entrance was still blocked by twice as much debris as she had removed.

"You can't give up, Jesse Graham. This is your only way out."

She swallowed the lump in her throat.

"Stop it! You don't have time for self-pity."

She began to dig again with gusto, but her enthusiasm waned with her energy. The air in the tunnel was rank at best, so she had difficulty breathing. She sat to rest for another moment, until she caught herself dozing off. She stood and resumed her work. Stone and brick scraped her hands, and the boards left slivers in her fingers, but she worked on until she collapsed.

Sitting with her back against the wall of the tunnel, knees drawn up, she was too numb to cry. How could it end like this? She clasped her hands around her knees, lowering her forehead to them. She was going to die in this tunnel. A moan escaped her lips. She was so close to the answers she had been seeking.

"Damn! Life is not fair!" Her voice echoed back eerily along the tunnel.

She tried to stand, but her knees buckled. The light of the flashlight was dimming; should she shut if off to save the batteries until she had the strength to resume digging? She did so, the darkness enveloping her. There was not even a flicker of light; her eyes were wide open to velvet blackness. She heard scurrying paws down the tunnel and shuddered. Wiping her eyes, she bent her head and prayed.

"Lord, I know I haven't been good like Maggie." She gulped. "But I've done my best. Please protect Becky from the rage of this ghost. I tried to help, and maybe you'll take that into consideration when you decide what to do with me. But most of all, forgive me for how I've treated Joe." She stifled a moan. "I do love him, Lord, and now he'll never know that. I wish I'd told him. I wish I'd had a chance for a life with him. Not the peaceful life I thought I wanted. A rich life where you take what comes along and deal with it, and learn from it. Keep him safe, Lord. Find him someone who will love him as he deserves to be loved. Forgive me for all the screw-ups in my life."

Weak from hunger and dank air, she slumped to lie on the floor, closing her eyes. From down the tunnel came the sound of chanting and a gentle drum beat. Struggling to keep her eyes open, she peered in the direction of the music. A warm glow emanated from the spot and grew as it neared her. The Weeping Woman stood before her, tapping on the animal skin that covered her drum. Her plaintive song echoed on the walls and enveloped Jesse. It was her

death song. She was so tired that she welcomed the sorrowful melody and surrendered to the darkness.

CHAPTER TWENTY-FOUR

Jesse stirred, roused by rhythmic tapping. The drum was no longer soothing; it was harsh and metallic. She listened for the chanting that had comforted her as she lay dying. She heard a voice but not the wistful melody of the Weeping Woman. Rousing, she tried to make sense of her surroundings, but all was black. She blinked and widened her eyes to ensure she was actually awake, when a pinpoint of light stabbed the darkness. She heard the sounds again—it wasn't the ghost at all. Those were human voices calling her name.

Yes, I'm here. I'm here! Her mind screamed the words, but her voice would not work.

Struggling to sit, she slipped back twice before she was able to stay vertical. She opened her mouth, but it was dry and full of dust. Choking out a syllable scorched her throat. She tried again.

"I'm here!" Her voice was soft and thready. She knew they wouldn't hear it over the noise they were making.

The hole in the debris grew an inch. Her heart leapt. She could hear them. She inhaled the stream of fresh air that blew in through the tiny hole.

"Jesse, are you in there?"

Joe.

She croaked. "Yes, I'm here!" It was barely a whisper. She tried to cup her hands around her mouth like a cheerleader's bullhorn, but she couldn't lift her arms.

She heard Scott. "If we keep digging like this, the whole thing will collapse. I think we need to wait until the rescue team gets here."

No, please. Don't wait. Please.

"We can't wait," Joe answered. "She's been in there for hours. Who knows if she's even…?"

More tapping and digging.

"Jesse, are you there?" Joe's voice sounded frantic.

She faded in and out of consciousness. Unable to support her weight any longer, she slid to a prone position on the dirt. Enough light seeped in to allow her to see what was around her. She heard scratching and moved her head slightly toward it. Perched on a board was a rat, its red eyes gleaming in the tiny shaft of light. The board was jammed three feet above the floor.

Oh, no. Please, God, no.

The rat ran from one end of the board to the other, looking for a way to get down. Darting along the board in one direction then the other, it stopped and stared at her, its nose twitching. It stretched up and sniffed the air, wiggling its whiskers. Making a decision, it ran back to one end of the board, jumped to a pile of stones, and scooted down to the floor. It scurried along the ground, nearing her. She stretched her hand out, searching the floor. Finding the flashlight, she grasped it as the rodent edged its way toward her. She barely had the strength to hold on to the flashlight, let alone lift it.

You have a choice, Graham. Him or you.

The rat stopped to sniff the air again, as if it weren't sure what to do about this intruder. The incessant tapping and digging halted for a moment just as the rat ran at her. With all her strength, she raised her arm and struck the rat with the flashlight, emitting a grunt of pain as she did so.

"Did you hear that? Jesse? Jesse? We're coming for you,"

Joe's voice boomed.

She felt her eyes roll back as she fainted.

∞

Loud voices and bright lights alarmed Jesse. She tried to open her eyes but wanted only to sleep. Dust that had clogged her nose and throat was replaced with a stream of fresh air that teased her senses. Someone was near her, speaking softly, trying to wake her.

Let me sleep. I'm so tired.

She faded out of consciousness again, grateful for the empty bliss. Rousing, she thought she was floating on a cloud, but the cloud was hard and hurt her back. Now she squeezed her eyes tighter against a bright light, shivering from the cold. More voices faded in and out. Once again she floated. *Welcome, darkness.*

∞

Clicking and beeping stirred Jesse from the strange dreams that invaded her sleep. She struggled to open her eyes, but her lids were leaden. Voices murmured nearby, and she heard soft footsteps and the sound of a chair scraping across a floor. Her head throbbed. She tried to move her hand to rub it, but was immobile. Warmth from another hand covered hers. Dozing, she had only one thought: *Don't let go.*

Instinctively, she knew she'd fallen back to sleep, but the same noises woke her once again. Slowly, she opened her eyes. Images swayed in a blur as she tried to focus on the scene before her. The window shifted and melted like Salvador Dali's clocks. A figure wavered as he leaned nearer. Scott. Closing her eyes, she inhaled deeply against a wave of nausea. The warm hand still held hers, but it was on the opposite side of the bed. Carefully, she turned her head in that direction, expecting to see Maggie.

His smile could not conceal the worry in his eyes.

"Joe," she croaked. Her heart swelled.

He broke into a grin.

"Hey, Just Jesse."

A laugh bubbled up mixed with a sob. Unrecognizable sounds emanated from her throat, which made her laugh and then cry. She vomited all over her blanket and Joe's hand.

Scott jumped back. "Geez!"

Joe never flinched.

A nurse hurried to her and began to clean up the mess while she repeatedly tried to apologize, which came out as a series of grunts and honks. Joe never let her hand go until the nurse finally ordered him into the bathroom for a thorough scrubbing. He winked at Jesse. When he returned from the bathroom, the nurse hustled both men out of the room while she remade the bed. Each efficient, crisp movement sent shards of pain through Jesse's body. She took a deep breath when it was over.

The door opened and Joe returned, brandishing a bedpan in front of his face. He peeked around it, causing a tingling in Jesse that had nothing to do with her injuries. Laughing, he sat beside her again, taking her hand.

"Feel better?" His voice was tender.

She nodded. "Sorry." Her rasp was at least recognizable now. "Joe…"

He pressed a finger against her lips. "Just rest for now."

"*Agh.*" She grimaced at the cracked sound and tried again. "I have so much to say…"

"We have lots of time, Just Jesse."

"I thought I was dying."

He swallowed then nodded.

"I wanted to tell you…" She gasped with the effort.

He stroked her hair.

"I missed you, Joe." She felt hot tears stream down her face.

He wiped them dry.

"I missed you, Just Jesse."

She drifted off into a deep sleep.

The soft glow of a fixture over the sink bathed Jesse's hospital room in golden light. Through the window, the night sky was deep purple silk. She shifted in her bed, her gaze, halting at the sight of Maggie curled up in the one comfortable chair available. Her friend had wadded up a towel for a pillow and covered herself with a spare sheet.

As if sensing Jesse's movements, Maggie stirred and sat up, rubbing her eyes. Stretching and yawning, she smiled.

"How are you feeling, Jess?"

"*Grack.*"

"Oh? Is that some Middle English term unknown to the common man?" Maggie teased as moved to the closer chair.

Jesse tried to make a smart retort, but only another grunt came out.

Maggie held the straw in the water glass so Jesse could drink. She slurped down half the glass.

"I said 'Great.'"

Maggie laughed. "No, you didn't. You said '*Grack.*'"

"You're cruel, Sister An-*grack*-ina." She grimaced as her voice cracked again.

"Take it easy, Jess. You don't need to talk yet." Maggie took her hand.

Jesse closed her eyes for a moment. "Thanks for coming, Mags."

"Wouldn't want to be anywhere else. I was so worried about you. We all were. When you didn't show up for dinner, I got scared. When I couldn't find you in your room or anywhere on campus, I panicked. I called Joe, and he told me about the tunnel. I figured you had gone down there. Sister Therese called Scott and Arnie, who found the entrance destroyed. I don't know how Joe got there so fast; I think Marty gave him a police escort. Anyway, they dug for what seemed like forever before they got to you. By then the rescue team had arrived, but Joe was the first to get in to where you were. They managed to enlarge the hole enough to get a stretcher in there to bring you out. The minute everyone was out, the whole thing collapsed again."

She listened carefully, the burden of what might have happened to Joe, to any of her rescuers, weighing heavily on her. But she'd thought Becky was down there, lured by the Weeping Woman, and she had to help her. Could anyone understand that?

Maggie seemed to read her mind.

"Jesse, you need to let go of the guilt. You had no idea that tunnel would collapse. If anyone else had been in there, they would all have done the same thing to rescue that person, too."

She nodded, but her gut still ached with the awareness.

"I thought Becky was in the tunnel.".

"Whatever made you think that?" Maggie's eyes grew large.

"Adrianna Rutherford."

Sighing, Maggie closed her eyes and slid back against her chair. "Oh, dear…"

"I threw up on Joe." Why did she say that? It had nothing to do with what Maggie had just told her.

"What?"

"He was sitting beside me and I threw up. He didn't complain. He even came back after he cleaned up."

Maggie looked at her as if she'd lost her mind.

"I love him, Mags."

Maggie's look softened. She understood.

"I know you do, Graham." She smiled.

"I told him I missed him, Mags."

"It's about damn time."

"Get the soap and wash out your mouth, Sister Angelina." Jesse's voice faded as she drifted off to sleep.

∞

The first few days in the hospital were a blur for Jesse in her drug-induced state. She was beginning to understand how close to death she had been. Black and blue splotches painted her body, bruises from the impact of fallen rocks and timbers. The miracle was that the only serious injuries she suffered were a concussion and a puncture from the rusty nail. The wound was serious since the rust and dirt had lingered so long and entered her blood stream, causing septicemia. She was receiving a heavy dose of antibiotics to combat the blood poisoning, but she was still extremely weak.

As she became more cognizant, she tried to work out how to honor her pledge to the Weeping Woman. She had promised to find the child and bury him properly, but how could she do that? All of St. Bart's property had been Seneca territory. The village the woman had lived in must be near the site of the school. Girls had shown her collections of beads and arrowheads they found on the grounds. Becky even had that necklace she found intact.

That necklace. Too small to fit around Becky's neck, but the perfect size for an infant. Jesse's eyes flew open. Becky had discovered the site and didn't know it—that's why the Weeping Woman kept appearing to her.

Where had Becky said she found the necklace? Jesse racked her brain. She had never said. The cabin in the woods! It had to have been there. Jesse threw the covers back, moaning when a stabbing pain jabbed through her eyes. The IV needle stung as it pulled at her skin. She curled up on her side, facing the wall.

"Going somewhere, *bella*?" Marty's teasing barely hid his concern. "Let me cover your butt before you catch pneumonia." He gently pulled the covers over her. "Are you okay?"

She moaned as she rolled onto her back. "Thanks, Marty. Sorry I mooned you."

"My pleasure. Looked like you were trying to escape."

Jesse lay with her eyes closed, waiting for the pain to subside. Opening one eye, she peeked at him. "Did you really see my butt?"

"Naw. But I tried." He held out the Styrofoam cup of water, and she took a hefty sip through the straw.

"Oooh, maybe I shouldn't have drunk that so fast." She rubbed her abdomen, trying to stem the nausea.

"Don't tell me you're not hungry. Mom sent over some of her rigatoni for you."

Her stomach flipped over. She smiled ruefully at the Tupperware container he placed on her tray. "Maybe in a little while. Tell your mom thank you for me."

"So you need help getting to the john? I can call a nurse," he added quickly.

"No, I'm still hooked up to an autoflush," She grimaced. "Wow, you know a lot more about me than you did before you walked through that door." She laughed then held her head.

"It's okay. We've been through a lot together. So what's the hurry? Why are you trying to get out of bed?" He pulled the chair close to her and sat.

"I think I know why the Weeping Woman is focusing on Becky. Becky found an infant's necklace, and I'm betting it belonged to the woman's child. I suspect she found it near the cabin I told you about. If we can search that area, we may be able to discover the baby's grave. It's probably been disturbed already, so the remains may even be above ground. That would totally be against Seneca burial tradition. If her child isn't buried properly, he will not be able to live with the ancestors."

"So where were you going? To sneak out of the hospital in that fashionable gown? And I thought I was the only one who got to see your butt."

"I don't know what I was thinking. I just wanted to go find the site. I can hardly stand lying in this hospital bed doing nothing. I'm worried about Becky. What if the Weeping Woman swoops down on her again and no one is there with her?"

"Maggie's with her every night, just like you asked her to be."

"Did I hear my name taken in vain?" Maggie called from the door.

Marty stood so quickly, the chair tumbled backward. "Hey, Maggie," he crooned. The change in his voice made Jesse do a double take.

Maggie smiled at him so tenderly, Jesse thought she should get up and leave the room.

"Hey, Jess, how are you feeling today?" Maggie leaned over the bed rail and kissed her forehead. "No fever. That's a good sign." She unwrapped the cellophane from the bouquet she carried, half filled the aluminum water pitcher, and stuck the flowers in it. After assembling the alstroemeria, daisies, and roses, she placed the arrangement on the tray where Jesse could enjoy it.

Marty never took his eyes off her.

"Jesse just had a breakthrough," he said, setting the chair upright and holding it for Maggie. She smiled at him again.

How did I miss this?

"Maggie, remember that bead necklace I told you about? The one Becky found? I think it belongs to the Weeping Woman's baby; that's why she haunts Becky. If we can find out exactly where Becky found it, maybe we can find the child's remains and bury him properly."

"That's a bit of a stretch, don't you think?" Maggie said.

"What else do we have to go on?" Jesse asked. "We've

got to do something. Becky can't take much more, and the woman needs peace. Just like Helen did."

"When they finally spring you from this joint, I'll help you look around that cabin. It'll be like old times—like when we almost got caught in the Archive Room." Marty laughed.

"Only this time we'll be out in the cold, haunted forest with the wrath of the Weeping Woman after us," Jesse said.

He rubbed his chin. "Oh, yeah. I hadn't thought of that." He scratched his ear for a moment. "Doesn't matter, kid. I'm with ya' anyway."

"You two are impossible. It's like dealing with a couple of kids," Maggie said.

"But at least we're cute kids." Marty winked at her.

She blushed and lightly hit his arm. "Kids nonetheless. But first things first. Jesse, you have to recuperate, and that requires rest. You look pretty tired."

"Yeah, I'm pretty sleepy." She fought to keep her eyes open.

"It's the drugs. Get 'em while you can. Otherwise, I'd have to arrest you," Marty said.

Jesse yawned. Maggie pulled the sheets up around her shoulders.

"You scared the dickens out of me."

Jesse smiled at her. "The dickens? You potty mouth."

As she dozed off, she heard Marty say to Maggie, "Can I buy you a cup of bad hospital coffee?"

Jesse woke in the stillness, the hospital corridor quiet. The hushed calm indicated the hour was late, but she wasn't sure of the time. She became aware of warmth enveloping one of her hands. Turning her head, her gaze met Joe's.

"Hey there." His voice washed over her like a warm shower.

"Hey there yourself. What time is it?"

"Almost midnight." Leaning forward, he brushed a curl away from her eyes with his free hand.

"Were you on a date?" Somewhere in her fog-filled brain, she cringed at her words. But the way she was floating at that moment made her feel like she could say whatever she damn well pleased.

"No, I wasn't out on a date." Joe's voice was low.

"But you were, weren't you? That night? The night you came to my house."

"Yes. And yet, for some reason, I needed to stop and see you."

"I wasn't with Scott that night."

"I know."

"How long have you been here?"

"I don't know. Long enough to know that you snore."

"I don't snore."

"You do indeed."

She yawned. "That's only because I'm on drugs. Marty said I could…"

Once the morphine was eliminated, Jesse felt human again. The pain still held her, but her mind was clear. She tossed and turned, cranking the bed up to sitting, back to reclining, down to flat so she could sit cross-legged and see out the window. She watched the first snowflakes swirling around the light posts, whirling in miniature tornados to the ground. It was the golden hour just before sunset in the late New York afternoon. She itched to be outside in the pristine snow. She itched to be anywhere but in this hospital bed. At least they finally were letting her wear her own pajamas.

"Hello, Jesse."

Turning, she saw Ben Wyndham peeking around a huge

bouquet of pink roses nestled in a crystal vase.

"Hi, Ben. I hear you came to visit a couple of times and I rudely ignored you."

The man's smile collapsed into a frown.

"My God, Jesse. You almost died." She warmed at his sincere concern.

"But I'm fine now…getting better anyway. Are you here to help me escape?"

Her gaze shifted to the door as a nurse entered. "I heard that, Miss Graham. Nobody's going to break you out of here yet. We still have needles to stick into you and various other forms of torture to apply." She grinned as she wrapped a blood pressure cuff around her arm. "We want you to get your money's worth. How are you, Mr. Wyndham?" She nodded at him as she pumped up the cuff.

Jesse winced as the device tightened around her arm. Any discomfort seemed magnified as her body struggled to heal from the beating it had taken in the tunnel collapse. She bit her lower lip, fighting the urge to whimper. That's when she caught Ben watching her closely.

He glanced at the nurse's name badge. "I'm fine, thank you, Sharon. I think having her blood pressure taken is uncomfortable for Jesse. Is it necessary?"

She flashed him a dazzling smile. "Everything we do is necessary." She released the cuff, and Jesse inhaled deeply. "Miss Graham has been an exemplary patient…but not a patient one." She winked at her. "For some reason, she can't wait to leave us."

"Because you keep torturing me."

"I'll bring your medication soon, hon," the nurse said as she opened the door, nodding to Ben. "Mr. Wyndham."

"Jesse, what can I bring you to make you more comfortable?" He pulled up a chair to the bedside and sat down.

"Honestly, Ben, if I could just get out of here and go home, I would feel great."

Scanning the stitches along her face, he shook his head. "I don't think so. But you could be released to Wyndham Manor and have twenty-four hour nursing care."

Though she was tempted, Jesse knew the ramifications of that choice—moving in permanently. Given that alternative, the hospital was a better option.

"No, thank you. I'm fine here."

"But you just said…"

"Listen, we need to talk about this once and for all. I've made my view on being the heir to Wyndham estate very clear. I have no interest in it." She had his undivided attention, and she was feeling strong enough to take him on. Add the element of his sympathy, and this was the perfect time to pull out the secret weapon she and Al had worked out in the library. She hated using it as her defense since it usually went against her belief in equality, but she was about to put those old laws to good use for once.

"Surely, there is a provision in a document drawn up in the 1800s to exclude a female child from being the heir. Women couldn't own property at that time, could they? So it would automatically pass on the first male child."

She wanted to add "Aha!"

"I don't understand." He shook his head. "Actually, there is no provision restricting a daughter from inheriting—it just never happened until you were born. Nothing in the contract forbids that, so legally, you are the heir."

She slapped the mattress. "But I don't want it, Ben. And, honestly, I don't understand your push for this. You've raised Al—your own son—to inherit and step into your shoes. Why are you so determined to crown me as the heir? I show up from nowhere—hell, you hardly knew I was alive—and now you prance me around like some prized Thoroughbred at the Kentucky Derby. Explain this to me."

Ben shifted in his chair and looked out the window. But he didn't speak.

Jesse sat forward, leaning into his vision. "We're going to discuss this. Now. Help me to understand why you are trying to force something on me that I don't want. Something that will spoil the future for your own son. It doesn't make sense."

"Jesse…"

The nurse, Sharon, came back in with a tray bearing a water pitcher, glass, and small paper cup that signaled it was time for her pain medication. Jesse flopped back, moaning with the movement. Pouring a glass of water, Sharon handed it to her with the paper cup. Jesse tossed back the pills and took a long drink.

Sharon cranked the bed up to reclining, plumped the pillows and helped her lie back. Pulling the sheet and blanket over her and tucking in the sides, she said, "You need to take it easy. Don't overdo it. Your body needs rest so you can heal."

"I know. Thanks."

Sharon narrowed her eyes at Ben before she bustled out of the room.

"I think we need to have this conversation later, Jesse." He rose from the chair.

She sat up. "I think we have to have it now, Ben."

Relenting, he slumped back down. Then, sitting forward, he placed his forearms on his knees and folded his hands. He breathed deeply and began.

"I told you about the day your father, my brother Albert, died, but I didn't tell you about our conversation that morning. Helen's body had been found the night before, and he was inconsolable—and tremendously worried about you. He made me swear that I would support him in making sure you would be raised as you should be, as the heir to the Wyndham fortune. He was like a wild man, pacing back and forth. He stopped and grabbed me by the shoulders. 'Promise me, Ben. Promise me!' I made that vow to him.

Ben dropped his face into his hands. Jesse waited, the muffled sounds from the corridor a backdrop to their silence.

"I didn't know that would be our last conversation. We got news later that morning that Bert had been killed in a car accident." He wiped his hand along his face, staring at the floor. "Some speculated that it was intentional, that he committed suicide because he was so distraught over Helen's death, but I don't believe that." He finally looked at her. "Because of you. He would never have left you." He shrugged. "And he would never have put another driver in danger. But don't you see? I promised him.

"Father was furious that I'd made that promise and refused to take you into our home, though I insisted that's where you belonged. Mother believed so, too, but she never was strong enough to stand up to him. Nor was I, until that moment. My promise to my brother was sacred—even more so after his death." He dropped his face into his hands again.

Jesse looked out at the snow, falling heavier now, a curtain of white blocking the scene outside, flakes chasing each other madly on their race to the ground. She tried to picture what it must have been like for Ben as a young man defying his powerful father. Once he'd taken that stance, it surely grew within him, a part of his being. He could never back down from it.

She began to understand.

"While you were with Jim and Eileen, I visited and kept them up to date on the progress I was making to instate you into the family. My reports were always more optimistic than reality. When I visited, I could see the strain between them. I wasn't surprised when Eileen left, though we were all surprised that she took you with her. As I've told you, Jim and I hired detectives but couldn't track you down.

"As the years progressed and there was no word of you, we gave up hope. I'd married and had a son. My father was still alive and insisted that we name him Albert so he could carry on as the Wyndham heir."

"And then I showed up," Jesse said.

Ben sighed. "Yes. I didn't handle our first meeting well, but I was so shocked. I did a lot of soul searching in the following days, but the point is, I promised my brother. And now you're here, and I intend to keep my promise."

"But what if it's not what *I* want?" she asked.

Ben frowned. "How could you not?"

Jesse sighed and pulled the sheet up. She shrugged her shoulders.

"When I moved here, I was running away from a life of comfort, even luxury. It symbolized people who hurt me because they valued wealth over love. To me, money canceled out genuine love. I now know that's not true. I think I was mistaking wealth for a lack of meaning, a lack of having to fight for what you want in life so that you appreciate what you earn, not just have it handed to you. No easy passes. It's not about the money—I want a life of gratitude for what I have. That's why I want to live simply, surrounded by people I love."

Ben shook his head.

"You belong at Wyndham Manor. You are the heir, and it's your rightful place. You'll recuperate there, and when you're up to it, you'll become involved with estate matters, sit on the board, and learn the business."

Her head throbbed. While she had insisted on curbing the pain medication against the doctor's recommendation, that might have been premature. Her limbs ached, and the stitches pulled at her skin. The fluorescent lights assailed her eyes, and the constant hum only amplified her headache.

Enough.

"You keep telling me what I *will* do. I *will* move into Wyndham Manor. I *will* be more involved in running the estate. I *will* recover there instead of in the hospital. You're just like your father—pushy and powerful. But I don't have to dance to your tune." Her blood pressure rose with her voice. "Your brother—my father—is dead. Your promise is dead, too, Ben! I can't survive to salve your guilty conscience, so give it up. You can take the Wyndham estate and shove it up your—"

Sharon rushed in. "What is it Jesse? Are you all right?"

Jesse sank back against the pillows.

"I think visiting hours are over, Mr. Wyndham." Sharon's voice was firm.

Ben stood, crossing his arms. "I have been nothing but kind to you, Jesse. You are an ungrateful little brat."

Sharon grabbed his arm and led him to the door. "This is the last thing she needs right now," she said as she shoved him out the door.

Jesse lay back, closing her eyes. She heard Sharon return, felt the nurse hold her wrist and take her pulse.

"Are you okay?" Sharon asked.

She nodded, wincing. Even that movement sent spikes of pain through her head.

"I'm going to get you something."

Jesse didn't protest.

Soon, she was dreaming of chasing Ben Wyndham with a pitchfork while riding on the back of a Thoroughbred. She smiled.

CHAPTER TWENTY-FIVE

Jesse rested her head in her hands and closed her eyes after her last class left, their voices echoing down the hall. Her first day back had been more difficult than she'd anticipated. Although her injuries were healing, her body ached with exhaustion. Hearing footsteps, she looked up. Becky stood in front of her desk. The girl's face was sunken, black circles hollowed out her eyes. Her uniform hung on her frame, evidence of her lack of appetite.

Dear God, please help this child.

"You wanted to see me, Miss Graham?"

"Yes. Have a seat, Becky. Remember that bead necklace you showed me?"

Becky nodded.

"Do you remember the exact spot where you found it?"

She nodded again. It was as if speaking required too much energy. But it was critical to finalize the promise Jesse had made to the Weeping Woman; she practically pulsed with the urgency.

"Can you take me there?"

"Now?" Becky asked, her eyes wide.

"Yes. We still have an hour or so of daylight. It's not that far, is it?"

"Nooo...."

"Becky, I think this will help us to stop the hauntings."

The girl trembled.

"I think the location of the necklace is also the location of the grave. Once we find it, we can find the child and bury him properly. That's what the Weeping Woman longs for. Are you up to it?"

Becky slowly nodded.

Jesse stood, swaying a bit. *But am I?*

In the woods, the feeble sunlight strained to reach through the branches. The light dusting of snow squeaked beneath their boots as they made their way along the path through the trees. Neither had the strength to talk. Jesse's lungs throbbed with every breath of damp, chilly air. She knew they were following the route to the cabin, and, for a while, the way was easy with a well-worn path. Becky turned off, following a narrow track hidden beneath the snow. A light wind blew through the trees, raising a hollow wail. Pulling up her coat collar, Jesse burrowed into the wool to keep warm. She estimated they had at least an hour before sunset—plenty of time to locate the burial mound.

They broke into the clearing where the cabin stood, gray and desolate. Becky walked to the left, circling the structure, and entered the woods beyond. A little way into the trees, she stopped and pointed to a rise just ahead of them.

"That's where I found it," she said.

It was uniform in shape, about nine feet across. How was she going to determine where the child's remains were?

"Do you remember the exact spot?" she asked.

Becky walked to the nearest edge, indicating a large boulder. "Right by this rock."

That was a start. As Jesse bent to examine the ground, she heard Becky shriek behind her. *The ghost.* Turning, Jesse was shocked to see two men brandishing guns; one of them had grabbed Becky. She couldn't breathe. She couldn't move.

"Miss Graham, help me," Becky's plaintive cry stirred her to action. Adrenaline shot through Jesse; she jumped up. She had to get to Becky. Guns or not—she ran toward them.

They raised their guns. She stopped.

"Please. Please don't hurt her." Her voice quavered; her hands shook as she held them out, imploring.

The second man grabbed Jesse's arm, wrestled it behind her, and pulled her toward the woods in the opposite direction of the school. Her arms, barely healed from the tunnel collapse, screamed with pain.

"I don't know about killing another nun, Mitch," said the man holding Jesse.

"I told you before, Roy—the other one wasn't a nun! She was one of those marshals dressed up like a nun. You done the right thing, tossing her down the stairs. This one ain't no nun either," Mitch said.

"This is going to be more fun than we thought," Roy said. Jesse jerked her head away from his putrid breath.

"Just hold tight to that one. She has a temper," Mitch said.

How does he know anything about me?

Mitch smiled, though his eyes showed no humor. As if reading her mind, he said, "That's right, we been watching you since the night we threw that dummy in the road. The girls put it together for their little parties, but we wanted Newhart to find it and know that his kid was in danger. Then you interfered. We followed you home—we been watching you ever since.

"Later, you found the kid we were going to murder, thinking we had this one." He squeezed Becky closer. The girl tried to move away, but his grasp was too strong.

Please, hold still, Becky.

"This one got lucky that night. These damn girls all look alike to me. We staged it like an accident—like their little parties got out of hand. But Newhart would know exactly what we meant. He'll pay big time for flapping his mouth."

Jesse thrashed against her captor, and Mitch pointed his gun toward Becky.

"You cooperate, bitch, or the girl is dead."

She froze. Her brain stopped working except for an incessant humming. Everything sounded hollow, everything looked ashen, like an old, faded photo. Trees took on ominous forms, thrusting out their hideous branches like grasping arms. Thin sunlight cast brooding shadows across the glittering snow. The wind picked up its mournful howling.

She shivered—the icy blast.

Now the wind gusted, the tops of the trees swaying furiously. The keening grew and echoed around them as snow whipped up from the ground. Stronger and stronger, the wind tossed fallen branches and twigs in a funnel that centered on them. Just below the raging noise, Jesse heard chanting and the constant beat of a drum; for once she was happy to hear it. Roy gripped her tighter, dragging her along an invisible path. She could hear Becky whimpering behind her. *No!* Their best chance was to stay near the mound. She pretended to slip and fall. Roy pulled her arm, wrenching it tighter.

"Keep up, or I'll shoot you right here." His foul breath invaded her nose.

She looked back at Becky. The girl's face was ashen. She caught Jesse's glance, and her eyes pleaded with her. Jesse's heart broke. In an effort to free Becky from one danger, she had delivered her into another deadly one. These were the men Arnie had told her about, the men who had killed Becky's mother, the men who had killed Valerie and Sister Catherine, and who now intended to kill them. She couldn't let that happen.

The wind continued to whip around them. Roy yanked her forward along the path. Jesse heard a loud *crack!* as a large branch from a pine in front of them broke and careened down, striking the man's shoulder, knocking Jesse out of his grasp. The branch bounced, pinning him beneath it. He cursed as the gun flew out of his hand. She lunged for the weapon.

"Get this offa me," Roy yelled as he grappled to move the enormous branch.

Grasping the gun, Jesse pointed it at him from where she sat.

"No. Don't. Please." His upper arms trapped, he held his hands out before him in a pleading gesture.

"Stop!" Mitch roared.

Becky's screams bounced off the trees around them. Would that tree hold this guy? She couldn't be sure, but she needed to check on Becky. She cut her gaze to her right quickly, trying to keep control of the situation.

Mitch had his gun pointed at Becky's temple. "Give me that gun or I'll shoot her where she stands."

Jesse wavered, then stood. Her only experience with a gun had been Helen's old six-shooter. Joe had taught her how to handle it. This gun was heftier, and she didn't know if the safety was on or not. She dared not try to shoot him; he was holding Becky too closely.

"Bring it here," he yelled above the wind, holding out his hand.

Leaning into the wind, she approached him. She held the gun out, gripping the barrel, the handle toward him. She held her other hand in the air.

Trees were bending in the gusts that blew around them, snow whipped their faces, blinding them. Mitch twisted to the left, wiping his face with the hand that held his gun. If Jesse could move fast enough, she might be able to break his grip on Becky. She braced herself, slanting into the ferocity as she neared him. The crack of a gunshot blast rang through the air. Instinctively, she crouched down and reached for Becky. The girl was immobile, her terrified eyes wide. Had Becky been shot? Mitch's face twisted with rage, his mouth drawn down as he cursed. His eyes glazed and he slumped, tumbling, trapping Becky beneath him.

Straightening, Jesse reversed the gun and pointed it at Mitch's head. He didn't move, his dead eyes staring across the forest floor. She looked up at the sound of a branch snapping and saw two men creeping out of the trees toward them, guns drawn.

Oh dear God, it just keeps getting worse.

"Jesse, are you okay?"

Scott.

Her knees gave out, and she slid to the ground. She watched as he holstered his gun while the other man kept his trained on Roy.

She turned her face up to sky, noting the quiet air. The wind had ceased.

Scott knelt to pull the dead man off Becky, and the girl scrambled into Jesse's arms, shaking violently. Jesse placed her gun on the ground as she held her.

Scott put his arm around Jesse's shoulder. "You're safe now. Both of you are safe."

"We need to get her warm."

He slipped out of his coat and wrapped it around Becky. Scooping up the girl, he held out his free hand to Jesse. "Can you walk?"

"Yes, I'm fine."

Shielding Becky from the sight of Mitch's dead body, he led her toward the cabin. "Call in some help to clean up out here," he instructed the other agent.

The man nodded, reaching for his walkie-talkie. A loud click was followed by static as he turned toward the woods to make the call.

"How did you know?" she asked.

"We have our ways." Scott winked at her.

She stumbled.

"You okay?" he asked, stopping to steady her.

He carried Becky as if she weighed two pounds, her frail body disappearing into Scott's coat. She probably wasn't heavy. Her cheekbones pushed sharply against her skin, her eyes large and dark with fear. She clutched at Scott's collar.

"We're all right now, Becky." Jesse's voice was soft.

The girl nodded.

At that moment, Jesse heard a guttural yell. Turning, she saw Roy wielding part of the branch that had trapped him. He had managed to ease out from beneath it and now swung it toward the marshal's head. The marshal collapsed. Roy turned toward them, lurching forward.

The gun! It glinted on the snow just a few feet away where she'd set it down. Could she get there before him? She dashed forward, seizing it first. Icy cold and heavy, the gun almost slipped, but she clutched it with both hands. Grabbing her, Roy wrested the gun from her hand, jamming the barrel into her ribs.

"Miss Graham!" Becky's screech was like nails on a chalkboard. Jesse shuddered. She had to keep fighting—for Becky. For herself. Glancing in her direction, she saw Scott hustle the girl to a nearby tree and set her behind it, out of harm's way. He ran forward, but before he could reach Jesse, she caught sight of a flash of movement to her left. Joe leapt forward, startling Roy enough to give her time to twist out of his grip. As she staggered back, Roy raised the pistol at Joe and fired.

He doubled over.

She heard herself shriek as she ran toward Roy, fury fueling her movements. Turning, he now trained the gun on her as she ran headlong into that tiny black barrel. Any second she'd hear the report, feel the bullet puncture her flesh. But before she gave in to death, this man would pay, too. He would not win.

But the shot never came. In fact, life surged through her as she watched with startling clarity as Joe surged forward, tackling Roy. The gun slid across the snow to rest at Jesse's feet. Picking it up, she pointed it at the brawling men. Freezing cold, the gun stung in her grip and bobbled before she grasped it in both shaking hands. The men were wrestling. She couldn't take the chance of shooting Joe. Arms stretched forward, she followed their movements. Her finger pressed against the trigger. She wanted to shoot—she just wasn't sure. Jerking his foot up, Roy kicked at Joe, propelling him backward. Jesse fired. Roy yelled in pain and grabbed his shoulder. Joe jumped on him, locking him in a hold until Scott reached the pair and jammed his Glock into the man's temple.

"I think you're done here," he growled. Grabbing the handcuffs from his belt, he snapped them on the thug's wrists.

He gave Joe a hand up, and Jesse ran into Joe's arms.

"You're a lucky man, Riley, even though you almost just got killed," he said, grinning at them.

Joe nodded.

A rustling in the trees made them all turn. Scott drew his gun, and Jesse aimed hers. She gaped as Marty and another marshal emerged with Trevor Underwood between them, handcuffed.

"We found him in a van on the road just beyond these woods. He jumped out, yelling about us not having the victims. You should have seen his face when he realized who we were," Marty said.

Trevor scowled at Scott.

"So we finally have the mastermind. We've been waiting to catch you for a while now, Underwood. Thanks for making it so easy."

The other agent had come to and was slowly rising. While Scott checked on him, Jesse went to Becky, who was shaking with fear and cold.

"We have to get her back to the school."

Joe nodded. She saw the blood oozing through his shirt-sleeve.

"My God, Joe, we need to get *you* back there."

As Scott and the other marshal led the handcuffed men away, Scott paused to pick up Becky again.

"We're really safe now, I promise," he said.

She nodded and huddled deeper into his coat.

Joe grasped his injured arm, and Jesse placed her arm around his waist as they followed, their soft footfalls sounding on the still air. Without the fury of the Weeping Woman, the woods were silent and peaceful.

She saved us. She was protecting us.

"Thank you," she whispered to the trees, their branches etched against the darkening sky. "I vow I will keep my promise." A breeze touched her face, and she smiled.

CHAPTER TWENTY-SIX

Joe's face was white against the crisp linen pillowcase. While he'd claimed he'd only suffered a flesh wound, his pallor said otherwise. The nun tending him gathered up a clump of bloody cloths, nodding to Jesse as she left the room.

Tiptoeing to the bed, Jesse tried to stem her shaking. Joe could have been killed. The seriousness of the encounter slammed into her at that moment, and she stumbled to the chair beside the bed. As she sat, Joe turned his head, opening his eyes. A lazy smile crossed his face.

"Why, hello there, Just Jesse."

Her throat clutched as she fought back a sob. She took his hand, fighting back the tears that stung her eyes. Taking a deep breath, she fought to compose herself.

"Hey there, cowboy." She blinked back the tears, but a stubborn one trickled down her cheek. She swallowed the lump in her throat.

"I'm okay. Really, I am." He smiled at her.

Could he be any sexier?

"How are you feeling? You were hurt more than you let on."

He raised his arm, trying to flex it. He winced.

"No, I'm fine. Just lost a little blood."

His gaze held hers. She could stay here all day, just looking at him. She scanned his face, shoulders, his injury. She loved how the reddish-gold hair felt so soft as she rubbed her hand along his arm. Reaching the bandage, she edged across it gingerly, as if her touch could speed the healing. If love could do that, based on how full her heart felt at that moment, he would be instantly cured. *Dear God, thank you for protecting him.*

He covered her hand with his. "I'm more worried about you."

"How did you know where I was?"

"I went to your classroom to tell you we'd sealed up the tunnels. You weren't there, but there were papers on your desk and the light was still on, so it looked like you were coming back. When I glanced out the window, I saw you and Becky disappearing into the woods. So I followed your trail for a while, but lost it deeper in the woods. I heard voices…and a gunshot. I bolted in that direction and that's when I found you."

"Joe, you could have been…"

"But I wasn't."

He pressed his fingers to her lips. They were rough against her mouth; she cherished the feel of them. Reaching up, she grasped his hand, keeping it there. She closed her eyes, savoring his strength. His other hand reached behind her head, pulling her toward him. Opening her eyes, she saw the desire in his. Slowly, she bent to him brushing her lips against his. He pulled her in, deepening the kiss. His tongue traced her mouth then gently probed between her lips. She moaned. Oh, God, how she wanted him.

"I love you, Joe."

"I love you, too, Just Jesse. I always have."

Hearing him groan, she sat up, catching a grimace on his face.

"You need to rest."

"I'm feeling amazingly refreshed. What do you say we leave the convent and continue this healing process at your place?" Though his mouth hitched up in a half-grin, his hazel eyes were soft with desire. He pulled her to him again, kissing her, softly at first but then with the passion of a man who believed he'd lost everything. Jesse ran her hands through his hair, answering his passion with her own.

"Please tell me you're finished with ghosts and danger," he said.

"I sure hope so."

"Life with me will be pretty dull compared to what you've lived through lately," Joe said, smiling into her eyes.

She ran her hand along his face, tracing his brow, his cheekbone, his lips. "I've been telling ghosts to go to the light. Life with you will be heaven on earth, Joe."

As Jesse and Joe entered the parlor, Sister Therese and Scott were ensconced in deep discussion. Scott rose when they entered.

"How are you doing, Joe?"

"I'm fine, thanks, Scott." He offered his hand. "Thank you."

Scott shook it. "Thank *you*."

The two men looked at each other for a moment, then Joe resumed his place beside Jesse.

"We've found the place where those two had set up a stakeout," Scott said. "They were recruited by Trevor Underwood, who was behind the murder of Mrs. Newhart. He wants his lawyer. But we've found enough evidence to convict them all on attempted kidnapping and, potentially, murder. The two henchmen made the mistake of keeping notes of the plan and a record of their surveillance of Arnie and Becky."

"Will that be enough to convict them?" Jesse asked.

"More than enough. As it turns out, Mitch was the truck driver who killed Arnie's wife. There's plenty of evidence."

"What will happen to Arnie and Becky now?"

"They'll return to New York City so he can testify in the case in the nuclear power suit. We will still protect them, but I think the danger is over."

"Thanks for everything, Scott," Jesse said. She hugged him.

"My pleasure. And I *am* being truthful now." He winked at her.

"So all your flirting was just a cover-up so you could keep an eye on me, huh?"

He winced.

"I have to confess it started out that way. As you figured out, we had to do a background check before you could be hired. Based on what we found, it was obvious you were not only curious but determined to uncover secrets, although we thought our procedures were "Jesse-proof.""

Joe snorted.

Scott shot him a half-smile.

"We thought if I 'dated' you, I could keep you under control."

Joe snorted again.

"Exactly. We didn't know Underwood and his men were around until you found the dummy. Talk about timing. If that had happened sooner, you wouldn't be a faculty member at St. Bart's. You're too nosy."

Sister Therese held up her hand. "Now hold on, Scott—"

"Even though Sister Therese wanted you here from the get-go." He grinned at the nun. "You were a threat to our security procedures. And we didn't know you bring ghosts with you everywhere you go.

"But back to your original question: yes, at first I was just keeping an eye on you." He glanced at Joe then shrugged. "But you got to me after a while. It wasn't just my job any more. I truly began to care about you, Jesse." He gave a sheepish grin. "Even when you called me 'Joe' at the dance."

Joe's eyes popped, and his mouth twitched up.

Jesse covered her face, the heat confirming she was scarlet. "Sorry about that." Her voice sounded muffled through her fingers. She peeked at Joe. They all laughed.

"It was obvious you were in love with each other. But I gave it my best shot." Scott shrugged.

Joe put his arm around her. This time, she snuggled against him. His face was drawn and pale.

"Thanks again, Scott. I'm going to take Joe home, get him in bed." She gasped. "What I mean is, put him to bed. Make him rest. Get some sleep."

"I liked the way you put it the first time, Just Jesse."

CHAPTER TWENTY-SEVEN

Jesse balanced her teacup and bowl of soup on a tray as she maneuvered between the student tables toward the faculty lounge. She caught sight of a man entering the cafeteria door, and her heart thumped in her chest. She was skittish these days, and any change in routine shook her for a moment. But she recognized Howard Rutherford, and while the man was gruff, he wasn't dangerous. Trying to avoid him, she turned down an aisle in the other direction.

"Miss Graham," he called out.

"Crap," she whispered. She turned to face him.

"Hello, Mr. Rutherford." She braced for whatever onslaught he had in mind.

"Miss Graham, I would like to speak with you. I want Adrianna to be there, too."

What had she done to displease him this time?

"All right." She spotted his daughter eating lunch at a table with Madeline and Eleanor.

Adrianna spied them before they reached her table, and her eyes widened in surprise. She stood.

"Hello, Father."

Her eyes never left her father's face. Jesse was reminded of a puppy when its master came home. Her heart went out to the girl.

"Hello, Adrianna. Come with us, please."

The hope in Adrianna's eyes dimmed. When she caught Jesse's gaze, she masked her hope with indifference.

Jesse led them to her classroom. Mr. Rutherford closed the door.

"Adrianna, Sister Therese apprised me of your involvement in Miss Graham's nearly fatal accident. I am shocked and dismayed that you would do such a thing. Apologize to Miss Graham at once."

Adrianna maintained her expression of apathy as she turned to Jesse.

"I'm sorry, Miss Graham."

"Adrianna, that was not sincere. Say it again." His voice was stern.

"I'm sorry, Miss Graham." She might as well have been reciting the phone book.

"Adrianna—"

"Mr. Rutherford, insisting that Adrianna be sincere will not make it so." She placed her hands on the girl's shoulders, forcing her to meet her gaze. "Adrianna, I don't think you intended for things to get so out of hand. I think you wanted to play a trick, but I don't think you wanted me to get hurt. Am I right?"

Adrianna's eyes misted. She nodded.

"I am so sorry, Miss Graham." Her voice broke.

"I know you are. It's been a difficult year for us here at St. Bart's."

"I don't know how I can ever make this up to you, Miss Graham," Mr. Rutherford said.

"I do," she answered. She looked him in the eye. "You can take Adrianna on a trip for Christmas break. Take some time off from work and spend it with your daughter."

"What?" he blustered.

"Your daughter needs you. She doesn't need everything you can buy her. She needs *you*. If you sincerely want to make this up to me, start spending time with Adrianna. Get to know her. She can be a sweet girl."

She winked at her student. Adrianna's eyes were wide. Her face lit up with a smile Jesse had never seen before; her eyes sparkled with shared humor. *I knew there was a kind heart in her somewhere. It may take time, but she'll find it.* Jesse felt a rush of satisfaction.

Howard Rutherford's glower melted into a half smile.

"I see. Yes. All right." He took Adrianna's hand. "Yes. I will."

"I'll hold you to it, Mr. Rutherford."

"I have no doubt, Miss Graham."

Joe, Arnie, and Marty thrust their shovels into the ground, gently shook the contents, then dumped the dirt to the side in small piles. They had been working for an hour, and the thin sunlight offered little warmth in the gray November afternoon. Fortunately, the ground hadn't frozen yet, so it still yielded to their shovels. With each shovelful, Jesse's hopes waned.

"*Bella*, this may be a wild goose chase," Marty said softly.

Jesse ran her fingers through her thick hair. Was this a wild goose chase? Sure, this is where Becky found the bracelet, but it could have been unearthed years ago and moved from anywhere on the property. They could dig for days—weeks—and never find the child.

"No. We'll find the grave," Joe said, ramming his shovel into the dirt.

"We have to find it. Becky is weakening every day from the onslaught of this ghost," Arnie said, never pausing in his work. "We have to find it."

"We will." Marty resumed his effort.

Wind whistled through the high tree branches, and the occasional cawing of crows split the cold air. Jesse knelt beside one of the piles of freshly dug dirt, straining it through her fingers. The dirt was damp and cold; her hands were becoming numb.

"I think I've found something," Joe called.

The others ceased working and gathered around him. He held his shovel parallel to the ground, sifting the soil across his hand. As it filtered through, he grasped at something and closed his fist around it. As he eased open his hand, a tiny bone lay white against his dirt-streaked palm.

Jesse's stomach flipped. She swallowed. Deep within her mind, she heard mournful chanting. Swaying, she grabbed for something to steady herself. Joe clutched her arm. The chanting increased in volume as the dizziness worsened. She closed her eyes.

"Jesse, are you all right? Can you hear me?" Joe's frantic voice seemed to come from down a tunnel.

She turned her head in his direction to hear him better, but the drum and chanting grew louder.

Boom-boom-boom-boom. The drum sounded slowly—a death song. She crumpled under the weight of the sorrow.

"This is it. This is the child." Her own voice sounded disembodied.

A howling gust raged through the trees, blowing her hair into her face. Breathing became difficult—it was as though she were buried. Her chest heaved as she gasped, unable to open her eyes. Blackness surrounded her, and she sank to the ground. The wind picked up, its ferocity increasing, and she felt the woman beside her. All she could hear was the roar of the wind, terrifying and ominous.

Then—calm. She opened her eyes.

The Weeping Woman stood before her, shimmering in the shadows. Dressed in a deerskin tunic, skirt and leggings, she stood with her hands out, imploring. The tears on her face mirrored the tears on Jesse's cheeks. The woman nodded slowly before fading away.

Finally, Jesse inhaled deeply, the cold air burning her

lungs. Off to the side, three strapping men stood speechless in the pale sun. Her knees hurt from the stones digging into them. She rose.

"We've found it. Now we have to recover the rest of…we have to bury the child in the proper direction."

If they had been careful before, they were meticulous now, scooping small amounts of dirt at a time, sifting through each shovelful. It didn't take long before Arnie called for the others to stop.

"I've found the child." His eyes were full of sorrow.

Jutting through the soil were the bones of a tiny body cradled in a deerskin blanket. Surrounding the bones were a rattle, another bead necklace, and a miniature drum. The tiny form seemed curled up in sleep, one hand tucked beneath the skull.

"We have to change the baby's position. His head must point to the east," Jesse rasped. Her breath was still labored, her throat dry.

Joe and Marty gently lifted the blanket, trying not to disturb the bones. Painstakingly, they inched the skeleton up from the grave, edging around it until the skull was at the eastern side of the opening. Slowly, they lowered the child back into the ground.

Marty shifted from foot to foot. "Ah, should we say a prayer or something?"

They stood in silence for a moment. Jesse cleared her throat.

"In my research, I read about Sagoyewatha, also known as Red Jacket. He spoke to the U.S. Senate in the early 1800s. One line from his speech was so beautiful that I memorized it. His words might fit this occasion." She stepped to the side of the grave and folded her hands. "As we are going to part, we will come and take you by the hand, and hope the Great Spirit will protect you on your journey, and return you safe to your friends." She stood in silence, overwhelmed by the sacred moment.

Joe wrapped his arm around her shoulder. "Perfect."

Wonderland snowflakes swirled around her as Jesse approached the grand entrance to Wyndham Manor. Her breath hung in a white puff on the cold air, but the stillness of the night was magical. It would have been perfect if Joe were with her, but once again, he had voiced his reluctance when she'd invited him to the Wyndham Christmas party.

"We've had this discussion before," he'd said. "Plus, my crew is working overtime to finish the work in the dormitory to have it ready when classes resume at the end of the Christmas holiday. I need to be there to make sure there's no delay."

He had respected her boundaries as she worked through her acceptance of her love for him, but she was struggling to accept his rejection of who she was. She'd thought a lot about what Ben had told her about her father. All her life she had wondered what it would have been like to have a parent who truly loved her. Albert had. His last wish was that she be established as the Wyndham heir, that she be cared for and afforded a comfortable, safe, loving life. Didn't she owe him something? Appreciation? Acceptance? There had to be a way to honor his wish and honor her own desires.

There was!

She felt lighter as she bounced up the stairs to the entry. She stopped. For the first time in her life, she felt like she knew who she was and where she belonged, and she accepted it—on her terms. This would complicate things with Joe, but they would have to work through it. She hoped nothing would stand in the way of their life together.

I guess we'll see if love conquers all.

Gerald greeted her at the door.

"Good evening, Miss Graham."

"Good evening, Gerald. The snowy night is absolutely beautiful, isn't it?"

"Indeed, madam."

She couldn't help herself. Just once she would love to get him to crack a genuine smile.

"Hey, Gerald, what do you call Santa's helpers?"

Gerald raised one eyebrow. "Elves?"

"Subordinate clauses."

His face remained stoic.

Jesse hid her smile behind her hand, clearing her throat. "It's an English teacher joke."

"Indeed."

He took her coat and indicated the living room. "This way." He paused before opening the double doors and winked at her. Was that a twinkle in his eyes?

He ceremoniously swept open the doors, announcing, "Miss Graham."

In the few seconds it took for them to react, Jesse surveyed the room. Ben's wife, Monica, sat on the sofa, Al, beside her. Ben, dressed in a tuxedo, stood with his elbow propped on the fireplace mantle, balancing a wineglass. Bart Wyndham, his wife, and several other guests occupied the other sofa and various side chairs. It looked like a scene from *The Thin Man*. As if on cue, Al rose, Monica turned and smiled slightly, and Ben straightened.

"Hello, Jesse." Ben placed his glass on the mantle, welcoming her into the room. "What can I get you to drink?" He didn't add his usual, "I'm so glad you're here," or give her a peck on the cheek. She couldn't blame him.

"Hello, everyone." She smiled, nodding to the group. "Riesling, of course. Thank you, Ben."

He nodded.

It might be colder in here than outside.

Al kissed her cheek, whispering, "Heard about your discussion." He winked at her.

At least I've got one ally.

There was to be an intimate dinner before the remaining guests appeared for the evening's festivities. For now, Jesse would have to gut it out with the small group where she couldn't hide. Conversation resumed, and as soon as she had a chance, she caught Ben, taking him aside.

"Could I have a minute please?"

He nodded curtly and led her to his study. He didn't indicate a chair but remained standing, arms folded.

Jesse considered her words.

"First, I'd like to apologize. What I said in the hospital was uncalled for," she began.

Ben sighed, dropping his arms.

"Have a seat, Jesse. I owe you an apology, too."

Opening a door on the credenza, he reached for the Johnnie Walker Blue. Pouring two generous drinks, he handed one to her and sat in the leather chair across from hers.

She took a sip of the scotch. "Mmm. This night is getting better already."

He gave her a half smile. "You were right. I was being pushy like my father. I just…"

"I get it, Ben. Your promise to my father was sacred. You were trying to do what was right for him—and for me. Little did you know you would run into a stubborn, Irish redhead."

"Just like Helen. It was one of the things Albert loved about her."

She sighed. "I've been doing a lot of soul-searching. Initially, I wanted absolutely nothing to do with the Wyndham family, Wyndham estate, or Wyndham wealth. But I've come to care about you and Al, even Monica, though I don't know her well. My father wanted me to be a part of this—he wanted it so badly that he made you take a vow. A vow you desperately tried to fulfill. Despite my misgivings, this is my heritage; you are my family. And, I have to admit, I'm quite proud to be a part of it."

Ben sat forward, his face glowing.

"Don't get your hopes too high, Ben. I still don't want to be designated as the heir. I would like to be included in family events, and I would like to continue working at St. Bartholomew's."

"But a Wyndham shouldn't—"

Jesse held up her hand. "I want to help girls realize their potential instead of encountering roadblocks to their dreams. I'm willing to head up any charity or organization for women that Wyndham money supports. But I have no interest in, no talent for, and no grooming to be in charge." She gave him a wicked smile. "You don't want to see me run this place into the ground, do you?"

He tossed back the rest of his drink, and his eyes sparkled. "You drive a hard bargain—just like a Wyndham." He stuck out his hand. "I accept your terms."

Jesse laughed and shook his hand. She tossed back the rest of her scotch.

Returning to the living room, Jesse caught Al's eye and winked. From the hallway, she heard the doorbell and saw Monica shrug at Ben. Al approached, handing her a glass of wine.

"You look like the cat that swallowed the canary," he whispered.

"A big one." She clinked her glass against his. "No more worries about…"

"Mr. Joseph Riley," Gerald announced, clearly annoyed at this uninvited guest.

Her eyes grew large.

Wearing a perfectly tailored tuxedo, his red hair tamed and glistening in the soft light, Joe looked more handsome than ever. He smiled across the room at her, and her heart melted.

Al nudged her. "Go greet our guest."

She had to hold herself back from running to him. His smile broadened as she neared. Reaching him, she looped her arm through his.

"Sorry I'm late, Just Jesse," he said.

"You're right on time, Cowboy. I have to admit though, I'm surprised to see you."

"I've done…" Joe began.

"Dinner is served," Gerald announced from the entrance to the dining room. He slid the paneled doors apart to reveal a table covered in brilliantly white linen with tall candelabra stationed along the center. Crystal sparkled in the candlelight, and the silver place settings gleamed. A huge bouquet of calla lilies and roses reigned in the middle.

Jesse caught her breath at the beauty. Before she could follow the others in, Joe held her elbow, keeping her back. The others meandered their way into the dining room, Ben directing them to their seats.

"Why?" she asked Joe. "What made you come tonight?"

"I've done a lot of thinking. You know how I feel about these gatherings—they make me nervous and bring out my judgmental side." He eyed the group still milling around in the dining room. "They're not bad people, I know that. But I know something else even more. I love you. No matter who you are or what your heritage, I love you. I will do whatever it takes to be with you. If that means hanging around with people from the other side of the tracks, so be it. I'll suffer."

They laughed. He took her hands.

"I'll do my best to support you as the Wyndham heir. Mostly, I'll try not to embarrass you." He smiled tenderly.

Did my heart just flutter? My heart just fluttered! She squeezed his hands, fighting the urge to jump into his arms. "You don't have to worry, Joe. I've relinquished the title."

He furrowed his brow. "What do you mean?"

"Ben and I had a good discussion tonight, after I apologized for telling him to shove his estate up his ass." She snorted, then covered her nose. "See? I'm perfectly capable of embarrassing myself. Anyway, he finally accepted the fact that I have no desire to inherit all the wealth and responsibility of this place." Her gaze traveled over the crown molding, the enormous fireplace and the heirloom furniture. Despite the magnificence of the manor, nothing was as beautiful to her as the love she saw in Joe's eyes. "When I suggested I might run the place into the ground, he came around to my way of thinking. But I did accept being a part of the family—a contributing member. I don't intend to live here, but I will take part in some of their foundations and charities. Can you live with that?"

Joe wrapped her in his arms and kissed her forehead. "I can live with that."

He kissed her.

"Does that mean you'll marry me, Just Jesse?"

"It means exactly that."

"A-hem," Al's voice interrupted. "Whenever you two are finished in there, we'll have them serve the first course."

Jesse smiled at him. "We're finished here." She whispered to Joe, "Actually, we're just beginning…"

He kissed her again, offered her his arm, and escorted her into dinner.

THE CAVANAUGH HOUSE

This house held secrets. Secrets that wafted through rotting window sashes on the winter wind. Secrets that spiders wove into webs anchored between the ceiling and walls. Secrets that scuttled on the feet of cockroaches across stained kitchen linoleum and scurried into its cracks. Secrets that peered from holes in the baseboard from glinting mouse eyes. This house held the secrets close to its bosom where they had slept for decades. No one had disturbed these secrets in all the years the house sat decaying from neglect. There was no reason to, and there was no desire.

-ONE-

June 1968

This might be the biggest mistake I've made yet, thought Jesse Graham.

She climbed out of her three-year-old yellow 1965 Volkswagen Beetle and waded through tall grass and weeds that scratched at her sandal-clad feet. Looming before her, the two-story house—her house—hovered, insinuating more height than it could actually claim. Wrapped in chipped and peeling greenish-yellow paint, the house looked weary, and the once-red front door had faded to a dull russet. The roof sagged, and the tiny porch appeared to be giving up the fight to support the small roof above it. She stared at the house, and the windows stared back, blank. Above the front door, two windows mirrored her dismay as the wood trim above them bowed down. In her twenty-eight years, she had never seen a sadder looking house.

"Oh my God, what have I done?" she breathed.

She closed her green eyes, as startlingly brilliant as her mother's. She suspected they were all she had inherited from the aloof, career-focused woman, for she could see no other similarity. Once again the fear that she had been the cause of her parents' divorce in her early childhood crept into her mind: did her father leave because of her? Jesse always supposed that her father had wanted a boy, and when she arrived, his disappointment caused him to flee. She shook her head.

"That's nonsense. People don't run away because of the gender of their baby," she said aloud.

She combed her fingers through her thick auburn hair, a gesture she made when concentrating or trying to work through a difficulty. So much sorrow had entered her life recently both on a personal level and a national level with the assassination of Robert Kennedy two weeks earlier and Martin Luther King just months before that. Too much sorrow, and now she faced the consequences of her recent break-up with her fiancé, Robert.

She scanned the yard, which deepened her apprehension. Overgrown bushes hugged the house as if begging it to remain and the lawn had conceded the fight with weeds years before. Now crabgrass, nutsedge and dandelions grew knee-high, hiding even a path to the door. Age-old maple and oak trees dotted the property, providing shade from the June sun, their leaves motionless in the early summer air. The few houses on this road weren't adjacent as they would be in the town, but they were close enough to view this forlorn yard that perched at the dead end of the street. Anything she did would be an improvement.

Jesse's shoulders shook as she began to laugh, silently at first, then shaking with mirth. At first she feared she might be descending into hysteria, but she didn't feel out of control. In fact, she felt very much in control knowing that if she didn't laugh, she would cry. What had she expected? Valet service and a mint on her pillow? The house had been abandoned for over twenty-five years—weeds were going to grow, paint was going to chip. But they were *her* weeds and *her* chipped paint; no one was going to tell her what to do about them. And no one was going to take them away.

Circling the house, she was pleased to see that the windows, with the exception of one that was cracked, were intact, albeit the originals from when the house was built circa 1920. They would not keep summer heat and winter cold at bay.

"No, they're not 'bay' windows," she laughed, then groaned. "Geez, I even make lame jokes when I'm alone."

The house was wider than it was deep, although an addition at the back accommodated a kitchen. Two outbuildings stood farther back on the property, one an outhouse, the other a small carriage house.

"Oh, Lord, I hope there's indoor plumbing."

Plumbing! Not yet; she hadn't contacted the local utility companies to have water or gas and electricity turned on in the house. She checked her watch, relieved to see that it was just 1:30 p.m. She still had time to make it into town and take care of that.

Returning to her car, she rustled through her purse in search of the keys her mother had given her. Her fingers found the horseshoe-shaped key ring, smooth brass worn down by years of use holding three keys: a standard Yale lock key, a smaller brass key and a skeleton key. She headed for the front door and tested the first of three steps leading up to the porch. Feeling confident that they would hold her, she climbed them and faced the door. Her body tingled as if ants crawled beneath her skin; what would she find in there? This was the first step to her new-found independence. No one was coming to her aid if her plans failed. The house was a tumbled-down mess, but wasn't she as well? She had burned many bridges in Rochester, and the bridge with her mother was smoldering. Her father had been out of the picture for years, and she was an only child. Her dear friend Maggie was her sole support system.

Whatever existed on the other side of the door was now a part of her existence, too. This abandoned and rejected house was all she had. And she was all this house had. *We're in this together.* Straightening her shoulders, she took a deep breath and selected the key. She was surprised that the Yale key worked so easily in the old lock. Her heart pounded as she turned the doorknob and entered the house.

It took a moment for Jesse's eyes to adjust to the dim interior, for the windows were thick with grime, and the trees filtered out most of the sunlight. The centrally located door opened into a small foyer, a room on either side. Straight ahead was a staircase, and beside it, a hall led to the kitchen. Musty air invaded her nostrils, dust turned everything a dull pale gray, and she felt ancient, powdery motes settle upon her like a second skin. Lacy cobwebs stretched from the high corners to the brass light fixtures hanging in the middle of the ceilings. She heard scurrying at the far end of the hall and resisted the urge to run outside.

To her right was the dining room with a door on the far wall that led back to the kitchen. Turning left, she entered the living room, sparsely furnished with drop cloths draped over the pieces. A chair sat perpendicular to a sofa with a round coffee table in front. A floor lamp hung its head in the space between the sofa and chair, and nestled in a far corner was an oak secretary with a drop-down desk. Drooping at the windows were barkcloth drapes that once had boasted white gardenias on a rose background, but now hung in faded tatters, eaten away by dry rot.

Jesse turned slowly, surveying the room.

"Wow," she said. "Wow, wow, wow."

Her thoughts traveled to Robert's apartment with its white leather furniture, glass and chrome accent tables, and carpeting so thick it was like walking on moss. It was as though she was on a "Rat Pack" set when she was there; everything was sleek and modern, tasteful and expensive. She had lived in that world for the past two years. And like its furnishings, that world had turned out to be less ideal than it appeared. A world more than just miles away from this dilapidated house.

Mustering her courage, she pulled the fabric off the sofa. She shrieked as a flurry of grey shapes scattered in all directions—one straight toward her. She panicked as paws scurried across her sandaled foot. Mice! Goosebumps prickled her skin and adrenalin shot though her body. Heart pounding, she ran out the front door, off the porch and bolted to her car. Her knees gave out and she collapsed, trembling.

"Are you okay?"

Grabbing the door handle, she pulled herself up and looked around for the voice's owner.

"I'm over here," he said.

She looked toward the road and saw a blue pickup truck at the end of the driveway. Leaning out the driver's-side window was a man about her age, with tousled red hair. Humor lit up his mouth and softened his strong jawline and rugged face.

"Are you okay?" he repeated as he climbed out of his truck and started toward her.

Jesse brushed herself off and ran her fingers through her hair.

"Oh, yes, I'm fine," she said.

She saw his hazel eyes twinkle with amusement.

"I can see that. In a hurry to get somewhere? I noticed your quick exit."

She looked at her watch and gasped. It was after 2 p.m. If she were going to get any utilities started, she needed to get to town.

"I need to get my utilities started."

Oh, that sounded intelligent. She was a little off balance, and not just because of the mice encounter; this man's gaze was warm and unsettling. He chuckled.

"Well, I would never want to keep a woman from that."

"What I mean is…"

He held out his hand.

"Joe Riley."

She shook his hand and smiled.

"Jesse Graham."

"Nice to meet you, Jessica," he said.

"Not Jessica, just Jesse. The nickname for Jessica is J-E-S-S-I-E. I'm J-E-S-S-E. Pronounced the same, spelled differently."

"Oh, like Jesse James," he said.

"Yeah, I've never heard that one before," she tossed back.

"Sorry. Wow—I'm making a great first impression," Joe said as he scanned the property, avoiding her eyes. "So you bought the old Cavanaugh House, 'Just Jesse.'" It was a statement more than a question. His eyes studied the place, traveling over the roofline, down to the foundation and back to the outbuildings. "Mighty brave."

"I didn't buy it; I inherited it from my Aunt Helen."

He raised his eyebrows and nodded but didn't say anything.

"I just met the current residents—all one million of them, I think—when I pulled the drop cloth off the sofa. The mice took me by surprise. I panicked and ran."

He laughed and looked back at the house.

"If there were a million, I'd probably do the same."

"Okay, maybe a thousand. At least a couple hundred." Jesse laughed, feeling at ease with him. "I think a call to an exterminator is also in order. I'd better head into town and get things started."

"Can I help?" His face was earnest, his smile genuine.

"No, thank you. I can handle things myself," she said.

"Well, you can't stay here tonight with a million mice living in there. You'd be welcome to stay at my place."

She lifted her chin and looked at him sideways. "Right. Your place."

"No, no, no. You don't understand. I live with my mother less than a mile from here." His face was the color of summer tomatoes. "It's all legit. Mom would be a proper chaperone, and we have a spare room. I'm sorry. I didn't mean to imply…"

Jesse was touched by his sincerity. He was falling all over his words.

"No offense taken. And that is a sweet offer. It's just that… well…I need to take care of things myself. It's important to me."

"Oh, got it." He took a step back and looked around the yard. "Well, then, I'd best be leaving."

She saw his discomfort and rethought her words.

"No, Joe, it was very kind of you to offer, and truly, I take no offense. I'm just at a place where I need to depend on myself right now." She smiled at him, and he nodded and turned to leave.

"Wait, there is something you could help with."

He turned back to her.

"I do need a place to stay, but I have a friend in town who may have room for me. May I use your phone to call her?"

"Sure, follow me." He hopped into his truck as she locked the house and then backed her Beetle out to follow him. Looking back at the house, she was filled with ambivalence. On the one hand the house scared her, on the other, she already felt like she belonged there.

As she drove, Jesse remembered the day she found out about her house. On her twenty-first birthday her mother had presented her with a large manila envelope.

"You will probably want to sell this as soon as possible. Oh, and happy birthday," Eileen Graham said as she tossed the envelope to her daughter.

Opening the envelope, she sensed her mother's green eyes on her. She pulled out a sheaf of papers and leafed through them. Her Aunt Helen's will, the deed for the house, and the mortgage forms created a thick stack that intimidated her. Something else was in the envelope; she tilted it and a set of keys slid into her hand. She looked at her mother who shrugged, lit a cigarette and then examined her manicured nails. Breathing smoke as she talked, she gestured at the papers.

"For some reason, my sister wanted you to have the house. There was nothing I could do about it."

Jesse wondered at her last statement, but dismissed it as she looked through the documents.

"I own it free and clear. Aunt Helen has a trust that will pay the taxes," she said.

Her mother stubbed out her cigarette and left the room.

Jesse had never sold the house and, according to her mother, it had stood vacant for all twenty-eight years of her life. She'd had no idea what she would find when she arrived, but it would be hers and the house would be away...far away.

ACKNOWLEDGMENTS

Once again I have so many people to thank in the creation of this book. First of all, of course, my beloved husband, Rich, who patiently listened to my ideas, endured my agony of revision, and celebrated the triumph of clicking on "publish." He also brought to life the Weeping Woman on the cover. Thank you for your love, affirmation, and patience.

Thanks to my daughter and fellow author, Kate Bode, who listened to and supported me during our "Mondays with Mom" lunches. Her insights strengthened my story and invigorated my characters. Thanks to H.J. Smith, who read my manuscript almost as many times as I did and offered her incredible editing skills. A big hug and many thanks to my nephew and awesome jazz drummer, Charles Ruggiero, who spent a Saturday morning helping me wordsmith how the drum should sound. Thanks to Janet Martyn, whose advice led me to ruthlessly cut backstory, and to my beta readers: Stephanie Bisby, Diane Flannery, Luana Russell, Maris Soule, Diana Stout, and Sarah Yoder, who were like midwives during my process of revision. Thanks to Julie Sturgeon, who waved her magic wand over my manuscript and turned mice into footmen. I will be forever grateful for her insights and ability to help me wrangle this story.

Finally, thanks to my muse, Boris, who, during this crazy time, knew when to inspire and when to retire. He is my Divine Attendant Spirit, and many times I have read what he has inspired me to write, hearing it as if for the first time. Thank you, Boris, for helping me give life these characters and their story.

ALSO BY
ELIZABETH MEYETTE

The Cavanaugh House
Love's Destiny
Love's Spirit

ABOUT THE AUTHOR

Author, blogger, poet, and believer in dreams coming true, Elizabeth Meyette has journeyed through a career in education to a career in writing. To coin a friend's phrase, she's not retired, she's "refired" and loves her career as a writer. Her first two novels, *Love's Destiny* and *Love's Spirit* are historical romances set during the Revolutionary War in America. Her third and fourth novels, *The Cavanaugh House* and *Buried Secrets* are mysteries set in 1968 in the Finger Lakes region of upstate New York.

Elizabeth and her husband, Rich, enjoy living in Michigan surrounded by the beauty of the Great Lakes. They made an agreement that she cannot cook on writing days after he had endured burnt broccoli and overcooked chicken. Fortunately, Richard is an excellent cook.

She credits her muse, Boris, for keeping the stories coming. When Elizabeth is not working on a novel or poetry, she is busy keeping up with her blog, Meyette's Musings.

Find Elizabeth her Amazon Author Page: Elizabeth Meyette
or
Amazon Author page : http://tinyurl.com/zu8f6r3
Website: www.elizabethmeyette.com.
Blog: www.elizabethmeyette.blogspot.com.
Goodreads: http://tinyurl.com/hnfekf3
Facebook page: www.facebook.com/elizabethfmeyette
Twitter: www.twitter.com/efmeyette
Pinterest: www.pinterest.com/bettymeyette

Made in the USA
Middletown, DE
30 March 2018